THE MUSIC BOX ENIGMA

THE MUSIC
BOX ENIGMA

R. N. Morris

This first world edition published 2020
in Great Britain and the USA by
SEVERN HOUSE PUBLISHERS LTD of
Eardley House, 4 Uxbridge Street, London W8 7SY.
Trade paperback edition first published
in Great Britain and the USA 2021 by
SEVERN HOUSE PUBLISHERS LTD.

British Library Cataloguing in Publication Data
A CIP catalogue record for this title is available from the British Library.

ISBN-13: 978-0-7278-8955-3 (cased)
ISBN-13: 978-1-78029-709-5 (trade paper)
ISBN-13: 978-1-4483-0430-1 (e-book)

All Severn House titles are printed on acid-free paper.

Severn House Publishers support the Forest Stewardship Council™ [FSC™],
the leading international forest certification organisation.
All our titles that are printed on FSC certified paper carry the FSC logo.

Typeset by Palimpsest Book Production Ltd.,
Falkirk, Stirlingshire, Scotland.
Printed and bound in Great Britain by
TJ International, Padstow, Cornwall.

For Rachel

The Hampstead Voices' Christmas Concert 1914
In aid of Belgian Refugees
6.00 p.m., Thursday, 24 December
The Great Hall
University College School, Frognal

Choirmaster .... Sir Aidan Fonthill
With Special Guests .... Dame Elsie Tatton, Soprano
.... Émile Boland, Violin
.... Ekaterina Volkova & Andrei Kuznetsov,
Principal Dancers, Ballets Modernes
Orchestra .... The Hampstead Camerata
At the Piano, Organ and Harpsichord .... Donald Metcalfe

PROGRAMME
'Adeste Fideles'
'Joy to the World'
'We Wish You a Merry Christmas'*
'The Shepherds' Farewell to the Holy Family' from L'Enfance du Christ by
Berlioz
'For Unto Us a Child is Born' from Handel's Messiah
'Benedictus' from Oratorio de Noel by Saint-Saëns ...... Soprano, Dame
Elsie Tatton
'Hark the Herald Angels Sing'*
'Winter', from the Four Seasons by Antonio Vivaldi .....Violin, Émile Boland

INTERVAL

Excerpts from *The Nutcracker Suite* by Tchaikovsky .... Danced by Andrei
Kuznetsov and Ekaterina Volkova
'O, Little Town of Bethlehem'*
'In the Bleak Midwinter'
'Silent Night'*
'I Saw Three Ships a Sailing'
'Deck the Halls'*
'A Christmas Greeting' by
Sir Edward Elgar .... Soprano, Dame Elsie Tatton
.... Violin, Émile Boland
Encore:
'The Twelve Days of Christmas'

* The audience is invited to join the choir in singing those carols marked with an
asterisk.

PRELUDE

Saturday, 19 December, 1914

'Is he . . .?' Paul Seddon's gaze veered wildly between the screaming woman and the motionless figure sitting upright at the piano. The question did not need finishing, still less answering. The object sticking out of a bloody wound in the man's ear left little doubt. That object was both incongruous and apt. It was even peculiarly satisfying. Paul was conscious of thinking that he was not as shocked as he ought to have been, neither at the scene that confronted him, nor his own somewhat detached reaction to it.

It was all very unexpected. That was certainly true. But there was an air of unreality to it that left him strangely numb.

Perhaps he was in shock after all.

At last the screaming stopped. Lady Emma nodded energetically. 'Don't touch him. He's been murdered. *Aidan has been murdered!*'

'Murdered?' It was of course stupid of him to question this self-evident fact. If Sir Aidan was dead, as it seemed he was, the presence of a weapon (however incongruous, apt or satisfying) protruding from the side of his head led inevitably to the conclusion that he had been murdered. Unless he had driven it into his brain himself, which was unlikely.

Lady Emma nodded insistently. 'We ought to send for the police.'

'Of course. But are you absolutely sure he's dead?' He made as if to approach the piano.

'Oh, yes.' She spoke sharply. 'We must seal the room. No one must come in until the police have been. The police will know what to do.'

'Your hand.'

'What about it?'

'There's blood on it.' The same blood, he would hazard, that was pooled around the dead man's ear.

'Blood?' Lady Emma glanced in disgust at the hand with which she had been pointing at her husband. She slowly retracted the index finger. 'I felt for a pulse . . . on his neck. That must be how it got there.' She held the hand out as if it was not part of her but some dead animal she wanted rid of.

Paul noticed that the blood was not limited to the tip of her index finger, or even just that finger and the one next to it, as would be the case if she had been feeling for a pulse. It was all over her hand. In fact, it was all over both hands.

'Do you have a handkerchief?' She was calm, but her gaze was imploring and strangely commanding. Seddon did not hesitate to comply.

'I'll call the police. There must be a phone in the office. I think you should come outside. I'll get Metcalfe to guard the door.'

'Metcalfe?' She shook her head. 'There's no need to involve him. Or anyone. I shall watch the door.'

He had only said Metcalfe because he knew he was nearby. On reflection he was probably not the best choice. 'Are you sure?'

'Quite sure.' Her voice was decisive, her expression sealed off, unapproachable.

'We will have to . . . tell people,' he suggested tentatively.

'The police first. And then . . . tell Cavendish. He will know what to do.'

'Very well. Will you be all right for a moment?'

'All right?' Her face clouded as if she did not quite understand the question. 'Oh, yes,' she said. 'I shall be all right.' She distractedly handed back his handkerchief, which was now smeared with blood. Paul frowned uneasily as he wondered what to do with it.

Eventually, reluctantly, he pushed it down into his trouser pocket.

FIRST MOVEMENT

ONE

Two days earlier. Thursday, 17 December, 1914

'Splendid. Yes. Very good, Cavendish.'

Sir Aidan Fonthill, seated at the Danemann grand piano in the room he liked to call his studio, held a fresh proof of the concert programme at various distances from his nose to try to bring it into focus. He did possess a pair of reading glasses but didn't like to wear them, not in front of other people, especially not those who were younger than him. Most particularly, not in front of young ladies. But also not in front of younger men, such as Cavendish.

In truth, he did not know for sure that Cavendish was younger than him, but suspected he was. Cavendish was one of those chaps who seemed to have been born middle-aged. Bit of a stuffed shirt, truth be told. A stickler, you might say. Sir Aidan supposed it went with the territory. Accountant. Clever with numbers, but dull. No imagination. The balding head didn't help. Sir Aidan thought proudly of his own full head of sand-coloured hair. He sported a foppish fringe that had to be repeatedly swept from his eyes. He eschewed facial hair too, believing a clean-shaven face suited the varsity look he was trying to cultivate. It was his little weakness that he could not pass a mirror without looking into it. Not as gratifying an activity as it once had been, he had to admit, but it was generally enough to reassure him that he still had 'it'.

Sir Aidan rose from the piano and transferred to his desk, on the grounds that it had more light being situated beneath the window. In truth there was not much light to be had anywhere today. Sir Aidan glanced up to take in the view of the garden. It was not looking its best at the moment. The wind and rain had given the stark wintry plants a battering. He placed the programme down on the green leather-topped desk and twiddled distractedly with a signet ring on the little finger of his left hand. The signet itself was of a trefoil or shamrock, a reference to his family's Irish origins. It was a habit he had, this obsessive turning of the ring, whenever he was preoccupied.

A lot of the younger chaps had signed up, which was dashed inconvenient as it left the tenors and basses severely depleted. But one could hardly blame them. The call to arms was hard to resist. So perhaps Cavendish wasn't as young as all that. Or perhaps he was a coward. You would have thought he would have been glad to get away from that wife of his. Of course, she was always very pleasant to Sir Aidan, even if it was in that dreadful, simpering way she had. He winced a little at the thought of her and gave Cavendish a quick, pitying look. By all accounts, she made Cavendish's life hell.

But the man had a decent enough voice, and so Sir Aidan was grateful for whatever it was that kept him out of the army.

He liked to think that, had he been a younger man, he would have applied for a commission himself. But it remained a hypothetical question. He was honest enough to acknowledge that he was relieved, rather than frustrated, that it need never be put to the test. He felt that he had work to do, important work, which was best done in a civilian capacity.

He read the front of the programme and nodded approvingly.

'And how are ticket sales going, do we know?'

Cavendish's answer was to clear his throat, a curiously despondent sound, similar to the sound of the rain hurtling into the windowpanes. He stood by the fire, on the other side of the piano, half-hidden by it, warming the filthy weather out of his trouser legs.

Tea had been brought. On a silver tray – another mirror for Sir Aidan's opportunistic vanity, to go with the large one hanging over the mantelpiece.

'We are virtually sold out.' Cavendish's tone was inexplicably morose.

Sir Aidan put the programme to one side and looked round at the treasurer from his green leather-topped desk. 'Splendid.'

Cavendish grimaced. 'Is it?'

'Of course it is! Why would it not be? We want to sell as many tickets as possible, do we not? To raise as much money as possible for . . .' Sir Aidan consulted the programme again. 'For the refugees.'

'Yes, but . . . at the last rehearsal . . .'

'What?'

Sir Aidan wished Cavendish would stop pulling those faces. 'Are you quite all right, Cavendish? You look like you're suffering from indigestion.'

'We sounded awful,' said Cavendish bluntly. 'It doesn't help that we're missing so many of our best singers. There are all the men we have lost. And Miss Seddon, of course. The sopranos are certainly feeling her absence.'

Now Sir Aidan was the one to grimace. 'There's still work to do. I grant you that. But it will all come together. It always does.'

'It certainly is a shame about Miss Seddon, though.'

Sir Aidan's expression settled into a frown. What the devil was Cavendish getting at, bringing up Anna like that? He let it go, however. The fellow's impertinence did not merit a response.

Cavendish pressed on in his insistent, carping drone, 'The next rehearsal will be with the orchestra and the professionals. I don't think we're ready, do you?'

'I can always call for extra rehearsals if we need it. It would help if people would learn the music, you know.'

But Cavendish was not reassured. 'I fear this time we may have bitten off too much.'

'Nonsense.' Sir Aidan picked up the programme again and opened it. 'There's nothing here that any half-decent choir shouldn't be able to sing with their eyes closed.'

'There will be paying members of the public coming along to this. The press may well be there. We don't want to embarrass ourselves.'

'We won't, Cavendish!' Sir Aidan insisted forcefully. 'Good grief, you're such an old woman. If anyone should be worried, it ought to be me. It's my reputation on the line. I am the one who has pulled strings to ensure the participation of our distinguished guest performers. I have also managed to secure the attendance of a certain very important personage.'

'He's coming, is he? Churchill?'

'The First Lord of the Admiralty has expressed that intention to me, yes.'

'Ah, an intention.'

'Winnie won't let me down.'

'Winnie now, is it?'

'We were at school together.'

'So you said. I expect a lot of other boys were too.'

'What do you mean by that?'

'Are you sure he remembers you?'

'He remembers me.'

Cavendish shook his head woefully. Really, it was hardly surprising that his wife treated him so roughly. He would have brought out the harridan in the saintliest of women. The man was a wet blanket.

'You have nothing to worry about,' insisted Sir Aidan. 'He will be there.'

'That's just what I *am* worried about. It's making the choir nervous, the thought of performing in front of such a prominent individual. We are not at our best under such circumstances.'

'On the contrary, I am confident that the presence of such notables will inspire the choir to new heights of excellence. I certainly hope so, for I am also expecting the presence of another celebrity in the audience. One whom I understand to have the most exacting musical standards.'

'Who?' Cavendish asked warily.

'Sir Edward Elgar.'

Cavendish's eyes bulged. 'You do know we're performing one of his pieces?'

'Naturally. That's why I put it in the programme. To entice him. A local choir singing his Christmas Greeting in a Christmas concert? He won't be able to resist.'

Cavendish shook his head. 'This won't end well.'

'Don't be such a doom-monger, Cavendish. Mark my words, this concert will put us on the map. I see it leading to all manner of invitations and opportunities.'

'For you?'

'For the choir. Festivals, even the Proms – who can say?'

'Are we ready for that?'

Sir Aidan ignored the question. 'And in the meantime, we will be supporting a very worthy cause. How much have we raised already, by the way?'

'I don't have the figures with me.'

'Roughly. Off the top of your head. You must have some idea.'

'I think we are close to two hundred.'

'Seats?'

'Pounds.'

Sir Aidan nodded approvingly. 'Excellent, excellent!'

'The residents of Hampstead have been most generous. Many have paid in excess of the ticket price. There are some expenses that must be met out of this, of course. The hire of the harpsichord, for example. And there are the new Performing Right Society fees to be paid. But we are fortunate in that our principal artists have agreed to appear pro bono.'

'But this is excellent news, Cavendish. It calls for a celebration, do you not think? Would you care for a brandy and soda?'

Cavendish seemed to recoil from the suggestion. A mistrustful, worried look entered his eyes. He muttered a weak demurral.

Sir Aidan rose from his desk with a spring in his step. He crossed to a glass-fronted cabinet displaying a collection of crystal decanters, containing various levels of subtly different dark-hued liqueurs. This was the thing to do with Cavendish, loosen him up a little, flatter him with attention, make him feel important. Fix him a drink, in other words.

Sir Aidan held out a satisfyingly weighty cut-glass tumbler, filled with effervescent amber liquid. He breathed in its intoxicating whiff as he surrendered it. 'I may incur some expenses in relation to the concert myself.' He was careful not to look at the treasurer as he said this.

Cavendish's dubious expression sharpened into out-and-out suspicion. 'What expenses?'

'Small, small expenses. I wouldn't want to trouble you with the details. You already have so much on your plate. Perhaps the easiest thing would be for you to pre-sign one or two cheques for me . . .' Seeing the look of horror on the treasurer's face, Sir Aidan quickly changed the subject. 'How is Ursula?'

He went back to the cabinet for his own drink, raising his glass with what he hoped was a broad, easy smile. In fact, he found that it took considerable effort to pull it off. And he still could not look his treasurer in the eye.

That dark tone was still in the treasurer's voice. 'Why do you ask?'

There was something eating Cavendish, that much was clear. Sir Aidan had no wish to get to the bottom of it. Something to do with his wife, no doubt. They must have had another argument. He made a nonchalant gesture with one hand. 'Good old Ursula. She really is a brick.' What he hoped to achieve by these bland observations, he really had no idea.

He felt the man's gaze boring into him, to the point that he could not ignore it any longer. He glanced up, startled by the glare of animosity that was directed at him.

Sir Aidan frowned and gave a brief, bewildered shake of the head, before dipping his eyes to focus on his suddenly very interesting drink.

TWO

The coals in the grate cracked and settled, heating the room to a toasty warmth. The fire gave off more than warmth, however; it gave off contentment, which the sleeping tabby curled up on the hearthrug inhaled with every gentle snore.

Two children sat at an undersized nursery table, absorbed in the activity of turning sheets of paper into artefacts of their imaginations. A young woman squatted on a chair that was much too small for her, encouraging them with her benign and smiling presence.

'Here, Daphne, let me help you with that.' Hattie Greene reached across the table towards the sheet of pink paper that four-year-old Daphne was at that moment grappling with.

'I can do it,' Daphne insisted.

But it was a difficult fold, along the length of the foolscap-sized sheet, which appeared gigantic and unruly in Daphne's dear little hands.

Hattie carefully suppressed her own instinct for perfection, remembering that it was a different kind of perfection she was aiming for – the perfection of a happy, confident girl, who would one day grow up to be an accomplished woman. No, she must smile and nod and utter approving sounds and even whole words of encouragement, without going so far as to lie, of course. She must let Daphne know how pleased she was with her for making the attempt.

'That's very good!' And actually, it wasn't too bad, though by no means the perfect alignment of edges that was necessary for the next stage in the construction of a Chinese lantern.

'No, it's not,' said John, with a brief, contemptuous glance down at his sister's handiwork. He effected all the hauteur of the senior sibling, although it was only two years that separated them. 'It's no good. When you cut the slits, they will be all skew-whiff.'

A more fragile personality than Daphne might have been reduced to tears by such forthright criticism. But the fact was she could see nothing wrong with the loosely folded paper in her hand. As far as she was concerned, she had achieved exactly what she had set out to achieve. Which was, quite simply, to sit next to Hattie Greene and play with paper.

'Don't be unkind, John. Daphne's doing very well.'

John sat up and appraised Daphne's work again, this time with deeper consideration, indicated by a conscious furrowing of his brow. At length, he stuck out his lips and gave a deliberate shrug, followed by a heavy sigh: John was bored and he wanted them to know it. He had long finished making his lantern, which was, of course, a perfect example of such artefacts. It stood on the table in front of him as an advertisement of his superior skill.

Hattie could read the signs, and if she wasn't careful, John's boredom would turn into something nastier. He would continue goading his sister until he provoked a quarrel.

If they could get to jam sandwiches and cocoa without tears, it would be a miracle. The trick with John was to distract him. 'I say, John, dear, why don't you find a book to read while Daphne finishes her lantern.'

'Will you read to us?' said John, brightening, and Daphne also smiled to herself at the prospect.

'Perhaps I will, if you find something that everyone will like.'

John jumped up from his seat and crossed to the bookshelves. He cast Hattie Greene a sly, sidelong glance. He knew exactly which book to pick.

Hattie gave a little smile too, for she was fairly sure which one he had in mind.

And, sure enough, he came back clutching to his chest the splendid illustrated edition of *The Wind in the Willows*, which he had been given as a present the previous Christmas.

It was wonderful and strange, the spell the book held over his young imagination. He was particularly fascinated by the illustrations, which, in truth, Hattie found rather disturbing. John's favourite was a colour plate depicting Mr Toad in a garishly lit corner of Toad Hall, his shadow cast sharply against the wall. Indeed, he had opened the book to that page now.

In Hattie's view, the illustration had a slightly nightmarish quality, quite unlike a picture in a children's book. For one thing, the animal was shown naked, as a real toad in the wild would be, of course, but this toad was standing upright, in a most un-toadlike way, gesticulating with his webbed fingers. The characters in the story behaved in an all too recognizably human way, but by emphasizing their animal natures in his paintings, the illustrator seemed to be hinting at something feral within the human heart. This was not a story about animals who behaved like humans, but humans who were revealed to be animals.

Miss Greene preferred the clothed and homely creatures who populated Beatrix Potter's books.

John ran his finger along the line of the toad's mouth, as if he was willing it to open and speak to him.

Hattie smiled indulgently. 'Now, where did we get to?' she said, moving her seat so that she could look over John's shoulder at the book.

Just then, the wind hurled a ragged volley of winter against the panes. It was a vast, weary sound. A gasp of frustration and despair. Although she was not in fact cold, Hattie gave a momentary shudder.

'Just a moment.' She sprang up from her tiny perch with the lithe decisiveness of a cat (though the tabby on the hearthrug showed no sign of stirring) and crossed to the window.

Hattie stood for a moment, gazing into the glassy blackness. She saw her face reflected back at her, pale and tremulous, floating like the face of a ghost.

There was something out there that she wanted to keep at bay. Something huge and hostile and unimaginable that threatened the calm peace of the nursery that she worked so hard to create. It was impossible to think of reading the story while she sensed it looming.

She strained to hear it. The boom of war. Men shooting precision-engineered projectiles into other men. But it was on the other side of the darkness. Even so, she knew it was there.

Hattie herself had a brother and several cousins and one very dear friend, who would soon be joining in that terrible endeavour. They were safe for the moment, bored silly in various training camps dotted around the country, and that consoled her.

The letters that she received from them were determinedly droll and arch, as if drollery and archness could protect them from the onslaught to come. It pulled at her heart to read how impatient they were for action. Their greatest fear, it seemed, was that they might miss out. The war would be over before it had even begun. Their glib self-effacing witticisms drew laughing sobs and had her shaking her head, half in admiration, half in anguish.

Only that special friend, James Delaware, dared to speak to her with anything she recognized as honesty. He alone confessed that he was afraid, but that it was the thought of her – taking care of her precious little charges – that gave him courage.

Drawn by an eruption of giggles, Hattie redirected her attention to the children. She was startled to see their father standing in the doorway of the nursery. How long had he been there watching her? There was something about his unguarded look, when she first caught sight of it, that she did not like. Something that reminded her, more than a little, of the leering Mr Toad.

Sir Aidan bowed a condescending greeting as he stepped into the room, closing the door quietly behind him.

'Good afternoon, Miss Greene.'

'Papa!' cried Daphne, noticing her father for the first time. 'Look what I made!'

'You haven't *made* anything, Daphne,' said John. 'You've sort of folded a piece of paper.'

Sir Aidan exchanged an indulgent look with Hattie, which left her feeling oddly compromised.

'Well, I must say,' declared Sir Aidan, his avid gaze lingering on her still, 'it is very gratifying to find everyone so industriously employed today.'

'We're making Chinese lanterns,' said John.

'Are you? Are you indeed? That's jolly clever of you, I must say. And Miss Greene has taught you how to do this, has she?'

'Hattie Greene,' said Daphne, for no very good reason.

'Hattie Greene. Yes. Indeed. Hattie Greene.'

Hattie bowed her head and felt herself, foolishly, blush. What was it about his repetition of her name that so unsettled her? It was almost as if he were casting a spell. As if the presence of her name on his lips gave him some claim over her.

Well, he was her employer and so she supposed he did have some claim over her. He was perfectly entitled to come to the nursery, her place of work, and satisfy himself that she was doing her job in a manner that met with his approval.

'You children must be very good for Hattie Greene, you know. You are very lucky to have such a . . .' Sir Aidan trailed off. Hattie could not resist looking at him. And she saw that he was gratified by her curiosity. 'Delightful . . . yes, such a delightful . . . such a delightfully pretty young nanny to look after you. Oh, Hattie Greene, you would not believe some of the frightful old horrors we have had before you . . .'

She wanted to tell him that she did not think it was right to talk so disrespectfully of her predecessors in front of the children. But it was not her place, surely, to do so?

'Isn't that right, children?'

She didn't like the way he drew the children in either, making them complicit in his nastiness.

'Remember Miss Hardcastle? What an old battleaxe she was!'

Perhaps not understanding what he meant by battleaxe, or perhaps sensing Hattie's unease, Daphne and John did not respond, except to frown uncertainly.

'Sir, please, I . . .' Hattie raised her eyebrows pleadingly towards the children.

Sir Aidan, if he understood the meaning of her gesture, refused to acknowledge it, except with a sly ratcheting up of his grin. 'She was no fun. Not like Hattie Greene, was she, children?'

And he looked her up and down approvingly.

'Do you sing, Hattie Greene?'

'Sing, sir?'

'Yes, sing. You look like you have a fine pair of lungs.'

'I don't know what you mean, sir?'

'You're young, healthy. You keep yourself in good shape. Anyone can see that. Haven't I heard you singing to the children? I'm sure I have.'

Sir Aidan walked over to the old upright piano that stood against one wall. An album of nursery songs was open on the music stand. The fingers of his right hand effortlessly picked out the melody of 'Mary Had a Little Lamb', while with his left he improvised an elaborate arpeggio accompaniment. He winced at the fractured notes produced. 'Must get this old box tuned.'

'We do, sir. We do sing. The children like to sing.'

'Will you sing something for me now?' Sir Aidan had found a dead key, a high F natural, and was repeatedly hammering it.

'Now, sir?'

'I would very much like it. And I'm sure the children would like it too. Wouldn't you, children?'

But the children's response was not unanimous. While Daphne was enthusiastic, and was even now giving her own lisping rendition of the song her father had just played, John was suddenly abashed. He watched his father with a wary scowl.

'Come over here, my dear Hattie Greene, and let me look at you.'

It was endearing when the children called her by her full name. But somehow, Sir Aidan's adoption of their habit struck a false note. She found it increasingly sinister.

Hattie told herself that she was being a fool and approached the piano.

'What would you like to sing for me?'

'I could sing one of the songs from that book?'

'A nursery rhyme? No, no, no. That will not do. I was hoping for something more romantic. Something passionate. Something that shows me a little of the fire that burns within you. There is a fire burning within you, is there not, Hattie Greene?'

'I am sure I don't . . .'

'I am sure I do. How about "I Can't Tell Why I Love You But I Do"? Do you know that one?'

'I d-do . . .'

'Splendid.' Sir Aidan sat at the piano stool and briskly vamped the introductory chords, giving Hattie the nod at her cue to come in.

Hattie swallowed down her apprehension and began to sing, in a small, tentative voice: 'On a summer's day in the month of May—'

Sir Aidan broke off playing. 'No, no, no! That won't do at all.'

He sprang up from his seat and looked her up and down appraisingly. 'Stand up straight, Hattie Greene.'

He came up to her and stood behind her, placing one hand against the small of her back as he gently eased her shoulders back with the other hand. 'Shoulders back, chest out. Nothing to be ashamed of there, Hattie Greene.' He came round the front of her now and looked down approvingly at her breasts. He touched her chin and tilted her head up, as if he were moving the parts of an artist's mannequin. 'That's better, so much better. You're very beautiful, you know, Hattie Greene. That's why we do all love you so. Isn't that right, children?'

But John and Daphne said nothing, simply watched in open-mouthed stupefaction at their father's handling of Hattie Greene.

'Stand with your legs slightly apart and your toes angled outwards.'

Hattie adjusted her posture. All she wanted was for the ordeal to be over. She thought that if she did as he said he would leave her alone. But it was not to be.

'Almost. Let me help you.'

Sir Aidan dropped to his knees and took hold of one of her feet, twisting it into the desired angle. 'I do like your shoes, Hattie Greene.' And he stroked the left shoe once to show how much he liked it, finishing by cradling her ankle in his hand. She yanked her foot out of his grip. He gave a throaty laugh. 'Spirited! I like that. Let it show in your performance. I want to hear something of that passion coming through. But this won't do, you know. You've lost your position.' Sir Aidan took hold of the recalcitrant foot once more and returned it, with rather more firmness than before, to the required spot.

He breathed in deeply through his nose, which happened to be inches from Hattie's crotch. 'Ahh!' And with a wistful gaze, he tore himself away from the contemplation of that part of her body and resumed his seat at the piano.

'Let's try that once more, shall we? This time, with heartfelt emotion, please. You are in love, remember. Is that so hard to imagine, Hattie Greene? You have abandoned yourself to a passion that you do not understand, perhaps one that you do not even welcome, but one which you absolutely cannot deny.'

She closed her eyes and sang the song through with a full-voiced emotion. But it was not the passion that Sir Aidan had asked for. It was anger.

At the end of her performance he held his hands over the keys of the clunking, discordant piano and listened to the tremulous dying of the last chord as if it was the most beautiful sound in the world.

'I knew you had it in you,' he said at last. 'I just had to find a way to get it out.'

THREE

He was in there.

She didn't need to press her ear to the nursery door to know. Who else would it be? The baritone rumble of his voice was unmistakable. She felt it in the pit of her stomach. But whereas once that vibration would have stimulated a warm tingle of excitement, now it was like the twanging of an over-tightened violin string. It provoked the entirely unpleasant sensation that something was about to snap.

Not that Lady Emma Fonthill was spying on her husband. It was not a question of that.

Well, perhaps it was. But she had her reasons.

He had to be protected from himself. She had given him too much latitude as it was. He'd made a fool of himself over the Seddon girl. Hadn't he learnt his lesson by now?

She heard a few thin chords strummed out on the nursery piano. Despite the horrid tone produced, she recognized his touch: firm, deft, assertive. Under normal circumstances, he wouldn't have gone anywhere near the old, out-of-tune piano, not for musical purposes at any rate. Why would he when he had the Danemann in his study? But his purposes here were not musical.

She ought to burst in on them now and put an end to this embarrassing courtship display before the damage was done. But something kept her on this side of the door. Was it a lingering illusion that she might be wrong?

Surely, she thought, he would not be so stupid, so crass, as to *carry on* in front of the children? She didn't know whether she loathed him more for his behaviour or because he forced her to think in such vulgar clichés.

Certainly Emma was under no illusions about his feelings for her. Oh, he might still declare his undying love, repeatedly, frequently, his face set into a caricature of anguished contrition after each fresh peccadillo was discovered. He might even go down on bended knee to impress on her his sincerity, although the effect of such a performance was precisely the opposite of what he intended.

She saw a blurred shape reflected in the glossy white paint of the door. It was her face, but with all the features obliterated, as if erased by a frustrated artist. She stared mutely at this wan image, barely recognizable as human.

However, she didn't need a perfect mirror to know that her face no longer held the youthful freshness that had once attracted him, that still attracted him in others.

Emma was eighteen years her husband's junior, but that clearly cut no ice with him. Even if she was younger than him, she would always be older than she had been. That seemed to count as some kind of betrayal in his eyes, as if she were growing older only to spite him.

The galling thing was she considered herself to have kept her looks, and her figure, to a degree that did her credit. Yes, she had put on a little weight after the children, and those extra pounds had proven stubbornly resistant to her efforts to shake them off. To compensate, she had learnt to disguise that comfortable spreading about the waist and hips by a judicious employment of couture. At the same time, she persisted with her occasional fasting and a punishing regime of physical jerks every morning.

She was doing everything she could to keep her part of the bargain; the least he could do was to refrain from committing his indiscretions right in front of her.

But no. It seemed that was too much to ask.

It was so unfair! Why should the balance of power always be with him?

He was getting older too, wasn't he? His jowls had begun to sag. His hairline was in retreat, even though he sought to conceal the fact by growing a long foppish fringe. The loop his tailor's tape measure made around his waist was increasing with each passing year. But somehow none of that seemed to count. In fact, it made it all the more important that he should see himself reflected in the (preferably adoring) gaze of the latest young thing to cross his path.

The piano started up again, and this time a reedy woman's voice began to sing. Emma recognized the song, 'I Can't Tell Why I Love You But I Do'. His choice, she did not doubt.

Miss Greene had a not unpleasant soprano voice, if a little weak and faltering, and girlish. Emma sensed a tension there, as if the girl were singing under duress. Or perhaps the tremble in Miss Greene's voice was excitement not fear? She would not be the first young fool to be flattered by the attentions of a distinguished older man.

Almost as soon as the singing had begun, it broke off. As did the piano accompaniment. She heard the scrape of furniture, then footsteps, followed by Aidan's familiar rumble, *sotto voce*.

Emma could not make out his words. She recognized the tone, however: intimate, wheedling, insistent. She strained to hear how the girl responded, listening for any signs of encouragement she might give, whether flighty giggle or throaty purr. But to her credit, as far as Emma could tell, Miss Greene remained steadfastly silent.

Not that that would discourage him, of course. He would even take a slap across the face as a come-on.

Emma stepped back decisively from the door, so that the reflection in the paintwork vanished altogether.

It would not be possible to get rid of Miss Greene so easily. The children adored her. Besides, terminating Miss Greene's employment would not solve anything. There would always be someone else. She could not isolate her husband from every pretty young member of the female sex.

The singing started up again. If she was not mistaken, Miss Greene's voice sounded firmer than it had before, almost defiant. Was that his doing? No doubt he would take credit for it.

The song was sung through to the end. The girl had carried it off creditably. So much so that Emma almost felt like applauding. Although, of course, her applause would be sarcastic. She would not be applauding Miss Greene's performance, but her husband's. She would be telling him that she was on to him.

But she kept her fists clenched by her side.

It was too much. He had gone too far this time. The children had to be protected.

Of course, it would be unpleasant. She hated scenes.

But he had driven her to this.

She put her hand on the door handle and felt it turn before she was able to grip it. Someone was coming out.

He answered the fierce accusation in her eyes with a dignified silence, tilting his head upwards defiantly.

Emma felt a quivering rage work its way through her body. It climaxed in a violent tensing of her lips that almost robbed her of speech. She felt also that somehow he had already got the better of her. Nevertheless, she did not back down. 'What were you doing in there?' She spoke in an urgent, angry whisper.

Aidan stepped forward, forcing her to back away as he closed the door behind him. He was reinforcing the impression that she was in the wrong, and that the children were to be protected from her. 'Am I not allowed to pay a visit to my own children as they are engaged in their adorable nursery pastimes? You should try it some time, Emma. I believe it would improve your disposition enormously to have your maternal inclinations re-stimulated.'

'You did not go to see the children. I heard singing.'

'Ah, yes. I took the opportunity to audition Miss Greene for the choir. You know we're short of voices.'

'We're short of men. The soprano sections are adequately filled.'

'Oh, no, my dear. Have you forgotten that we never replaced Anna Seddon . . .?'

'How dare you mention that name to me.'

'Well, whatever may or may not be said against Miss Seddon, she was a stalwart of the first sops. And we have sorely felt her loss.'

'In that matter, you have no one to blame but yourself.'

'I hardly think that's fair, my darling. It is always a complicated business apportioning blame. Was it not you who insisted on her leaving the choir?'

The quivering rage returned, if indeed it had ever gone away. Now she felt it in her trembling jaw. 'This has to *stop*!' She forced the words out through her clashing teeth, the final word exploding in a screech that she instantly regretted. She had wanted to stay calm. For the children's sake as much as for her own.

'I don't know what you're talking about.'

'Do you think she welcomes your advances? Do you think any of them do?'

'I don't have time for this.'

'You don't have time for what? For me?'

'This is ridiculous. You're making a fool of yourself, Emma.'

'I am not the fool in this marriage.'

'Oh dear. This is . . . embarrassing. Let us at least move away from the nursery if you will not keep your voice down.'

'You went there! In front of the children! Do you have no sense of propriety?'

'You are making this out to be something that it is not! Nothing transpired. Nothing of the nature you are insinuating.'

'Let us ask Miss Greene. Let us see what she thinks transpired.'

'No, no, no. I cannot allow that. That is preposterous. Have you lost your senses? We do not involve the staff in our marital arrangements.'

'You went in there! You involved her!'

'I went to see the children.'

'Liar! And by the way, there are no *arrangements* in our marriage. What arrangements do you think we have?'

'Oh, come on, Emma.'

There was something so insufferably dismissive in that *come on, Emma*. So much assumed in it. She could not help herself. Her right hand whipped out to strike him across the cheek.

The blow forced his head to one side, his ridiculously overgrown fringe bouncing and flopping like the wing of a startled bird. He took a moment to brush it out of his eyes. 'Feel better now?' His face was flushed, though whether with emotion or the impact of her slap, she could not say.

'Get her out here.'

'I cannot permit that.'

'Then I will take it that you are unwilling to allow her to speak because you are afraid she will contradict you.'

'No, it's just . . . one simply doesn't . . . Good God, Emma, what has got into you?'

'I am going to stop your money.'

'What?'

'Until you start showing me the respect I am due as your wife.'

'Of course I *respect* you!' The emphasis he gave the word could only be insulting. 'Besides, I have my own money.'

'No, you don't. There's nothing left.'

'You don't know that. You have no idea.'

'Very well. In that case, it won't hurt you if you have no more of mine.'

'But this is silly. It's so unnecessary. There is nothing between myself and Miss Greene. I tell you, nothing transpired.'

'Then what objection can you have to my asking her?'

'You dear old thing . . .' He made to lay a hand on her shoulder. She flinched away from his touch. 'I merely wish to save you from further embarrassment.' He dropped his voice to a whisper, his eyes flashing side to side as if on the lookout for eavesdroppers. 'You know how servants talk. This has gone too far already. Let us draw a veil over this whole unfortunate episode.'

'Oh, you would like that, wouldn't you?'

'Let us put it behind us and move on. We have the concert to prepare for, after all. Or have you forgotten that?'

'I couldn't give a damn about your precious concert.'

A flash of alarm showed in his eyes. He resumed in a more conciliatory tone: 'I admit I was wrong to bring up Miss Seddon in the way that I did. Your judgement was quite correct on that matter. We could not permit her to remain in the choir, no matter how excellent a musician she is.' His voice had taken on a sanctimonious tone.

This was how he did it. How he defeated her. Not by cruelty, or even brutality, not by blatant lies or unreasonable demands, just by eliding the truth, omitting it, belittling it. Which was to belittle her.

She felt her rage dissipate. It left her unspeakably weary. 'I only want you to be honest, Aidan.'

This seemed to strike him as an astonishing idea. His eyebrows rose as if they would take flight. What good would honesty do them? he seemed to be asking.

'You speak about her, about that girl, as if you had nothing to do with what happened to her.'

Aidan glanced behind him at the closed nursery door. Then he fixed her with a steady gaze and repeated, 'I don't know what you're talking about.' There was a steely quality to the words now, which made them sound like a warning.

FOUR

The baby was crying. His noise filled the small flat, along with the permanent dankness of his laundered nappies as they hung to dry on the clothes horse.

Anna was sitting in the kitchen, staring blankly at the wall. The door was closed but it did not seem to mute the sound at all.

When she grew tired of looking at the wall, she would look down at her hands. They were bright red, the skin cracked and broken from eczema.

How had she got such hands?

She would chop them off at the wrist and throw them in the dustbin. Or perhaps she should wrap them up in brown paper and string and send them to *him*.

But how could she tie the ends without fingers?

She did not like to look at the baby when he was crying. She had done so once and his face was so tightly clenched into a tiny knot of rage that it had frightened her.

She became aware of another noise that was strangely in time with the waves of the baby's crying. Was it the neighbours pounding on the wall again?

Or could it be? Had *he* come at last?

Her heart rippled, as if a hand had got hold of it and was kneading it. It was a hand with long cold fingers.

She had looked forward to this moment for so long. Fantasized about it. Each time she played the scene in her imagination it came out differently.

In one scenario, she was obdurate and unforgiving, steeling her heart to his entreaties. In another, she wept her own bitter tears and threw just recriminations in his face. In yet another, she welcomed him with open arms. Her tears were tears of joy – she never doubted him, her love never wavered.

In this scenario, she closed her eyes as he kissed away her tears and fell swooning into his arms.

But then she had to remind herself of her anger, focus on it, nurture it. Or rather, stir it and prod it, like the glowing coals of a dying fire, until it flamed again. Her anger would chase out the chill of her dread.

No, she could not forgive him, at least not so easily.

The way she imagined the denouement of this little playlet was like one of those scenes depicted in a moralistic painting, perhaps by Holman Hunt. It might have been called 'The Corruptor Penitent' or some such. His head would be bowed, too ashamed to meet her eye. She would be shown holding the baby, of course, her gaze fiery and unforgiving. One arm might even be extended as she pointed for him to go back whence he came. The artist would not shrink from showing the state of her hand, stripped raw by the unfamiliar contact with washing soda. Around them would be clothes horses (artistic licence multiplying the number) hung with wet baby clothes and nappies.

The whole history of their relationship would be told in the configuration of objects and human figures.

Only after she had sent him away, only after she had been the one to reject *him*, only after he had come crawling back to her on his hands and knees a second time. Only when she had ruined *him* and had the chance to rescue *him*.

Only then would she even consider having him back.

The banging was still going on, intermittently. The baby seemed to be screaming even louder to compete.

She would have to face him.

*   *   *

'At last.'

For a moment, she did not recognize the man standing there before her. She had so expected it to be *him* that her brain could not process the image that was presented to it, even though he was her own brother.

'Oh, it's you.'

Paul stomped past her unceremoniously into the flat. His shoulders were hunched into an aggressive posture. He looked like a man who had come to 'have things out'. The subject of a Punch cartoon, rather than a Pre-Raphaelite painting. 'Who the Devil did you think it was?'

Paul was ten years her senior, but he had always behaved towards her as if a whole generation separated them, more like her father than older brother. At thirty-five he was prematurely balding, for which he sought to compensate by growing an immense black beard. Anna rarely saw him without a disapproving – or at least querulous – scowl upon his face.

She followed him into the main room of the flat, mumbling 'Never mind' at his back.

Paul settled himself with an air of entitlement on the small, artificial leather sofa that provided the only seating in the room.

He took over her flat like this whenever he came. She supposed he had a right to do so, as he was paying the rent. But did he need to make her feel her dependence on him so keenly?

Paul was something in banking, having been inducted into the same bank where their father had held a senior position. He understood about money and finance and investments. She assumed he was successful, at the very least comfortably off. He never gave her any reason to think otherwise. He was also a bachelor, with simple habits, and a small household in Highgate. He bicycled everywhere, as the clip around one trouser leg hinted.

His only indulgence, as far as Anna was aware, was his pipe, which he took out now and fussed over, stuffing the bowl with tobacco.

Their parents were both dead. Mother from a sudden illness that had turned out to be liver cancer, Father – well, they did not like to talk about the circumstances of their father's death.

Paul, being the elder child and male, had naturally inherited the lion's share of the estate, apart from a small private income left to Anna, which she came into on her majority.

'I was knocking for ages, you know.'

'I thought you were the neighbours. Banging on the walls.'

'Poor blighters! What must they think? You ought to be careful, Anna. I wouldn't be surprised if they had you evicted.'

'They couldn't do that!'

'It's the moral aspect as much as anything. This was a respectable mansion block before . . . well, I don't need to say it, do I.' Paul's constitutionally sour face crimped into an expression of exceptional peevishness. 'You have to stop it making that din. It only draws attention to your situation. It will turn them against you, if they're not already. What's wrong with it, anyway?'

'What?'

'The baby! It sounds like it's going to choke.'

'It always sounds like that when it cries. And it's always crying. It's a baby. That's what they do.'

'It doesn't sound right to me.'

'It's fine.'

'I don't know how you can hear yourself think.'

'You get used to it.'

'Aren't you going to see what's the matter with it? Maybe it's sick. Or hungry. Or needs its nappy changing. It certainly smells like it.'

'What's the use? As soon as I change the nappy it fills it up again. I can't make it stop. It just keeps on doing it.'

Paul's mouth dropped open in an expression of incredulity. 'Good God, Anna. He's your son. I mean, it's one thing me calling it *it* . . . but you're its mother.'

She was aware of her hands itching. She willed herself not to scratch them, not only because that would make them worse, but also because she did not wish to draw attention to their condition. It would only provoke further criticism from Paul. But the effort of holding herself back caused her whole body to twitch.

Her brother stared at her in appalled disbelief. 'What's wrong with you?'

She didn't answer, except to scratch the back of her right hand with the nails of her left.

He had no sympathy, only disgust. 'Look at the state of your hands!'

'I can't help it! It's all the washing I have to do.'

'Aren't there women who take in washing?'

'I can't afford that!'

'Well, don't look at me. I cannot be expected to sacrifice more than I have already. Really, Anna, I have to say it. You have brought this on yourself, you know.'

There it was. She gave a bitter laugh.

'What's so funny?'

'Do you think that I impregnated myself? Or that this is the result of . . . what do they call it in biology? Aphids do it.'

'What are you talking about?'

'Parthenogenesis. Isn't that the word?'

'What's that got to do with anything?'

'Well, how do you imagine I got pregnant?'

'Of course I know how you got pregnant. As for the bounder responsible, you have not thus far revealed his name, so we have never been able to get any satisfaction from him.'

'Satisfaction! Do you mean to challenge him to a duel?'

'You are being wilfully obtuse. You know that I meant recompense. I think I have a right to expect the fellow to contribute something. I'll give you one thing, Anna. You were ahead of the game with this having a baby out of wedlock business. It's quite the fashion now, so I believe. Girls are falling pregnant everywhere these days, courtesy of their soldier sweethearts. You don't even have that excuse, do you? Your beau clearly knocked you up long before war broke out.'

'Do you have to use such a vulgar expression?'

'It is a vulgar act.' Paul wrinkled his nose distastefully.

Anna felt a vindictive urge to prick her brother's pompous hypocrisy. 'You would not believe it if I told you who the father was.'

'Do you mean to say it is someone I know?'

'Oh, yes. You know him very well!' Anna realized that this tremendous secret gave her power. It was thrilling to dangle the knowledge she had withheld from her brother – from everyone – in front of him.

The baby's crying had entered a new phase. It had lost its force, become mechanical, as if he was only going through the motions now. He seemed to have given up hope that anyone would come and was crying only to keep himself company. It was an inexpressibly sad sound.

Brother and sister looked at each other in awed despair.

'Who is it? Who is the father?'

'Can you not guess?'

Paul's face was set in an angry frown. 'Don't play games with me, Anna. If you mean to tell me, tell me.'

Anna could not help smiling. He was hopeless – clueless, in fact. Just like a man, he had no idea what was going on right under his nose. For Paul was also in the Hampstead Voices. He was a tenor, and like her he had one of the better voices in the choir. Both of them were often selected for solos. She remembered Aidan nervously joking that he hoped Paul was not thinking of enlisting as he couldn't afford to lose one of his stars. Paul had assured him that that was hardly likely. At thirty-five, he was above the upper age limit for enlistment. And besides, he believed he would serve his country better at the bank than at the Front.

The siblings had inherited their musicality from their mother, who had also sung with the Hampstead Voices before her illness. Indeed, it was to honour her memory that they had both joined.

So Paul had been in as good a position as anyone to notice the affair. Perhaps, though, as her brother, he had been excluded from much of the gossip that had circulated. However, Anna saw it as typical of his male self-absorption, exacerbated by his longstanding lack of interest in his little sister.

'How is the rehearsal for the Christmas concert going?' She made her tone light and casual.

He waved a hand impatiently. 'Don't try and change the subject.'

Anna grinned. Really, he was so stupid. 'Who says I'm changing the subject?' Something of her usual anger flared in the question.

Paul's expression clouded in confusion. 'Oh, I know you think it was unfair, the way you were asked to leave.'

'I wasn't asked to leave. I was forced out.'

'But what you must remember, Anna, is that you have brought this upon yourself.'

'So you have said!'

'You can hardly blame Sir Aidan . . .'

'Ha!'

'In fact, I believe that Sir Aidan was very much inclined to allow you to stay. Once you had had the baby, of course, and suitable arrangements had been made. A return to the choir in a year or so was not out of the question, if only you had behaved reasonably. It was quite naturally expected that you would give the child up for adoption. Why you have persisted in this perverse course of action is beyond anyone's understanding. And it is to no one's benefit, least of all yours, judging by the state of your hands and this flat. It was, I think, Lady Fonthill who insisted on your removal. She was no doubt guided by the moral example it would set to the other female voices. The younger women in particular, I mean.'

'Ha!'

'Stop saying ha!'

'Ha!'

'Oh, you really are insufferable!'

'Ha!'

'You're such a child.'

A wave of unexpected emotion came over Anna. She was cast back to being six years old again, forever dismissed by her big brother, so remote, aloof and superior.

She felt hot tears trickle down her face. A jagged arpeggio of sobs broke from her throat. It was a shocking sound. It even seemed to have silenced the baby's crying.

A look of horror came over Paul. He shrank back into the sofa, repulsed by her display of emotion.

'I'm so alone. I have no one.'

Paul's face flushed bright red. 'What good does this do? Come on now.' He averted his gaze to stare in fascination at his own boots.

Anna dabbed at her eyes with the cuff of her dress. She was aching for someone to hold her. Out of the corner of her eye, she saw Paul's arm jerk out towards her as if he had sensed her need and was on the verge of acting on it. But his hand went towards his face where he vigorously rubbed a sudden itch on his nose.

'I will give the baby up. As you said, it is the best thing. The best thing for the baby.'

'If that is what you wish.' Paul's tone was suddenly constrained.

'I do appreciate everything you have done for me.'

Paul waved his hand dismissively.

'And I know I have brought this on myself, as you keep on telling me.'

Paul's gaze shifted from his boots to a threadbare patch in the carpet.

'This is not how I thought it would be, you know.'

'No. I dare say it isn't.'

'He . . . he led me to believe . . . that he would leave his wife.'

'He is a married man?'

'Yes. He is a married man!'

'Good God, Anna!'

'Can you not, for one moment, refrain from judging me?'

'I merely wish to point out to you how it must appear!'

'I am well aware how it must appear. How it must appear is the least of my concerns.'

'Evidently. Otherwise you would not have got yourself in this mess!'

'Have you never fallen in love, Paul?'

The colour in her brother's face deepened. 'Oh, let's not muddy the waters!'

'It's all very well for you. For you *men*. You can sow your wild oats and not worry about the consequences!'

'I . . .'

'Oh, I'm not judging you. Whatever you do, I don't judge you. Perhaps you visit prostitutes? I don't know. I don't care.'

Paul's eyes widened in outrage. 'I never thought I would hear . . . language like that from my sister. If mother and father were alive now . . .'

'Well, they're not, are they? It's just you and me. And . . .' Anna turned her head in the direction of the bedroom where her son was now sleeping in his cot. 'I just honestly, honestly want you to be happy, Paul. And I don't think you are. I think you're miserably unhappy. And I'm sorry. I'm sorry if it's my fault. If it's because of me. Because of this. Because of the baby. Because of the shame of the baby. Because of the burden we are on you. But I honestly don't think it is. Because I think you were unhappy before this, Paul. I think you were angry before this. I think this just gives you something to point your anger at.'

She had not known she was going to say all this. Still less had she known how he would respond to it. She certainly had not expected the massive sigh that he heaved up from somewhere deep within him.

She took it as encouragement to go on. 'I think you're angry and upset and grieving. And you can't allow yourself to be happy. And you mustn't allow anyone else to be happy. Least of all me. But don't worry. There's no chance of that. If it's any consolation, I would say I'm almost certainly as miserably unhappy as you are. So that's good, isn't it?'

Paul shook his head pensively. 'If I ever get my hands on the cad who has done this to you . . .'

Anna glared with alarm at her brother. Of course, he didn't mean it. He was speechifying. His words sounded like something he'd read in a novel.

Her voice came out as a sibilant whisper: 'It's Aidan. The father. It's Aidan.'

His face expressed more than simple shock. He was bewildered by her revelation. '*Sir* Aidan?' As if the title was all that was needed to disprove the allegation.

She nodded and watched his eyes skitter wildly. He seemed to be casting about for the last scraps of meaning as they vanished from the world.

FIVE

Friday, 18 December, 1914

The parcel was left on the doorstep.

The doorbell was rung, but by the time Marie opened it, there was no sign of anyone. In fact, at first she thought she was the victim of a game of Knock, Knock, Ginger. She was about to slam the door in the face of a squally gust when some instinct impelled her to look down.

It was a cube of approximately five inches by five inches by five inches, wrapped in brown paper that was becoming rapidly sodden in the driving rain. Marie clicked her tongue against her teeth in disapproval. Really, this was not like Mr Beevor, their regular postman, who would always ensure parcels and packages were delivered into someone's hands. But she noticed as she stooped to retrieve the parcel that it did not bear any postage stamps of any kind, and so had not been delivered by the Royal Mail. Mr Beevor was not at fault, after all.

The only writing on the parcel was SIR AIDAN FONTHILL. There was no address, which suggested that it had been delivered in person by the sender. Which, when you thought about it, made the whole thing all the more strange.

The mail was normally delivered to its recipients on a silver tray kept on the table in the hall. Somehow the practice had arisen that

Marie would take Lady Emma her correspondence and Mr Callaghan would take Sir Aidan his. This strict regime of a female servant for the mistress and a male for the master was insisted on by Lady Emma for reasons Marie could only guess at. She gathered that the previous girl had been something of a looker. Evidently, she had caught Sir Aidan's eye. Evidently too, Lady Emma had been highly displeased by this eye-catching business.

By all accounts, there had been quite a to-do. The girl had left suddenly. Under something of a cloud, although the gossip was that not only was she provided with a favourable reference, but also a financial inducement. The rumoured amount varied from ten shillings to a hundred pounds. What the true figure was, if indeed there was a settlement, Marie did not know. What she did know was that henceforth no female servant, whether a looker or not, was to be trusted alone in a room with Sir Aidan.

Marie set down the parcel on the tray. She straightened her pinafore in front of the big mirror that hung on the wall by the front door, ideally placed for the lady of the house to give one last appraising glance at herself before going out for the night. Although, from what Marie had observed of Sir Aidan, she suspected he was as likely to be the one checking his appearance.

She pursed her lips critically at her own reflection. Marie did not like mirrors. She was occasionally obliged to look into them because her position required her to be well-presented at all times. Whenever she did so, she avoided focusing too closely on what was above the neckline. It was not that she was ever shocked by the red wine birthmark that stained half her face. Of course not. She could have drawn, and coloured in, a perfect map of it from memory.

Even without her birthmark, she knew that she did not have what it took to catch Sir Aidan's eye. She was a dumpy wee thing, sure enough. And without the birthmark hers would have been a very ordinary face.

Marie doubted that Sir Aidan very much regretted being deprived of the opportunity of seducing *her*. As for any of the other female servants, well, there was no accounting for taste, she supposed. That said, the children's nanny was a pretty young thing, but a nanny could not properly be counted as a *servant*, and Marie did not suppose that Sir Aidan would be so foolish as to try anything on with the girl who was charged to look after his children.

She lifted her gaze to confront at last the burgundy sprawl around which her thoughts so often shaped themselves. One hand came up, the fingertips tentatively exploring the surface of her skin where it appeared to be stained. She half-expected the flesh there to glow with a fiery heat, as if its dark colour was caused by a flood of hot blood.

It did not, of course, but perhaps it did make her more sensitive. She often imagined herself inside other people's skins. And whenever she saw another slighted, she felt their wrongs almost as keenly as her own.

Sometimes she could not help thinking that she had been hired solely on account of her disfigurement. And so, perhaps, she ought to be grateful to it. It had landed her a good situation. The pay was generous enough for her to send a shilling home each month, and even now and then set aside something for herself.

That said, as good as her position was, she knew herself to be friendless here.

Marie met her own gaze without self-pity. The clenched lump she felt in her chest was the grip of loneliness on her heart. She accepted it without complaint.

Whenever it came upon her, as it did now, she would lose herself in thoughts of home. She would try to picture Ma and Da's dear faces, anxious and careworn with love, the quick and easy smiles of her younger sisters, Edie and Maggie and Bridie. That way Bridie, the youngest, had of rolling her top lip in with her bottom lip, a shy, nervous, lovable tic.

She would try to remember some of the things they said. Their quick wits and ready cheek. And the weight and warmth of them against her body.

The longer she spent away from them, the fainter their laughter echoed in her mind. The harder she had to concentrate to summon them.

And so, she did not hear the door to his study open, nor his footsteps in the hall.

In fact, the first that she knew of his presence was his laughter.

'Admiring yourself in the mirror! Goodness me. I've seen it all now.'

It wasn't his words so much that stung. After all, she might have given voice to a similar sentiment herself if she had suspected for one moment that it was vanity that prompted her to stand before this or any mirror. No, what drew a blush as dark as her birthmark to the rest of her face was the angle of his smile, which was precisely calibrated to express his contempt.

SIX

Fonthill watched the maid (what was her name now . . . he never could remember the ugly ones) as she scuttled away out of sight. They all seemed to come out of the woodwork and disappear back into it. Like so many black beetles. He imagined that this one, with the blotchy stain all over her face, was some kind of exotic species. He had no idea how many maids they employed. He left all that to Emma. To him they were mostly interchangeable, apart from Deirdre. Deirdre had been different. Deirdre had been irreplaceable.

Indispensable, you might say.

But Emma had dispensed with her. Emma had sent her packing.

Fonthill let out a short sigh of regret. Then shrugged. It was perhaps for the best. These diversions had a habit of turning into entanglements if allowed to drag on beyond their course.

But there were more pressing matters at hand. Once again, he had mislaid his reading glasses. He hated having to wear the things, which was probably why he had a habit of carelessly discarding them about the house. Unfortunately, he could not read scores without them. This made it particularly difficult when conducting. He was forced to choose between being able to see the score or the faces of the choir.

His hunt took him into the drawing room at the front of the house. The room was dominated by the twin portrait of himself and Emma by Augustus John which hung over the fireplace.

It had been made on the occasion of their engagement more than ten years ago. It had been Emma's idea, both to have the portrait done in the first place and to commission John to do it. At the time, Fonthill had been aware of a vague reluctance on his own part, which he had not been able to articulate even to himself, except to raise objections to the choice of artist.

Of course, Emma had taken his resistance the wrong way.

'Why do you not want to do it?' she had demanded. 'Is it because you're ashamed to be in the same picture as me?'

Naturally, he had laughed at such a preposterous suggestion, and wisely kept to himself the idea that it prompted: that perhaps it would be better if they had two separate portraits done, which they could hang side by side as a pair.

'Is it because you don't, in your heart, want to marry me?' she had persisted.

The question had shocked him. And he had protested at its injustice. Of course he wanted to marry her. He wouldn't have gone to the trouble of asking her if he hadn't.

'Sometimes I think you don't even love me, Aidan.'

Oh, how typical of a woman! To turn an argument over something quite specific (a painting) into a generalized discussion of . . . of, well, of *that*. To drag love into it, in other words.

There had been tears, of course. And so, he had been forced to concede. There would be a picture. It would be of the two of them together. And it would be painted by that insufferable Welshman.

Ah, but he should have seen the whole business as a sign of the trouble that lay ahead. For one thing, Emma was not as mollified as he felt she ought to have been by his concession. The atmosphere in the sittings was inexplicably prickly. It did not help that Emma comported herself in such an undignified way. As fawning as she was towards the famous 'genius', she was proportionately frosty towards her own fiancé. Naturally, at the first opportunity, Fonthill had discreetly warned her that she was making a fool of herself. He reminded her too that John was the son of a solicitor, and as such was owed no deference from them.

But she had not the grace, or the sense, to heed his well-intentioned words. She had laughed in his face! And roundly insisted that Augustus John was the true aristocrat – an aristocrat of art, whatever that meant. Fonthill had hoped that he had as much reverence for the artistic path as the next man, but societal standards had to be maintained. It was at that point that John had returned to the studio from whatever business had called him away.

Fonthill and Emma had fallen into an immediate sulky silence. By his conceited smirk and ironically cheery manner, John let the lovers know that he had detected the friction between them. Perhaps he had even been listening at the door. Fonthill wouldn't have put it past him. He had proceeded to be excessively charming to Emma and excessively condescending to Fonthill. The nerve of the fellow!

It went without saying that he hated the resultant painting, as his instincts had told him he would.

First, there was the crude lading on of paint. Oh, no doubt there was some flashy skill involved, but why could these modern artists not paint with any finesse? After all, one would not expect a concert violinist to stand up and play like a gypsy fiddler.

As for the portrait of himself, Fonthill could not deny that it bore more than a passing resemblance to the man he had been ten or so years ago. Even so, he did not recognize himself. It both *was* him and was *not* him.

The artist succeeded in converting Fonthill's natural pride in his own powers into an empty swagger. The tilt of his head, the swelling of his chest, the firm line of his mouth, even the unwavering gaze of his eyes, became indications of imposture rather the deserved confidence of a born leader. The picture had the effect of making him feel more than a little ridiculous.

The couple were shown with Fonthill standing behind the wing-back armchair upon which Emma was seated. It was almost as if one had to look over her to notice him. And whereas John's representation of Fonthill bordered on merciless caricature, his portrait of Emma was, to Fonthill's eye, exceedingly flattering. He made her seem both wiser and more beautiful than she actually was, while seeming to present her truth.

From the outset, of course, Emma had expressed the utmost satisfaction in the painting. The more so because she knew he hated it.

Well, let her have it. Let her mock him with it before their friends and passing strangers alike.

If that was how she chose to punish him, then he could handle it.

But this latest threat. Well, suffice it to say that he did not like the sound of that one bit.

It was dashed awkward, there was no question, the way Emma had caught him coming out of the nursery like that. He would have to be more careful from now on, that was all there was to it. If he behaved himself with the nanny, then there was every chance that the whole thing would blow over and they could get back to normal.

Of course, the essential problem was the institution of marriage itself, which simply did not reflect the reality of the relationship between the sexes. It was patently unreasonable to expect a man like him – a man of huge appetites and unbounded energy, a man in whom the *élan vital* surged and pulsed – to be bound by the absurd restrictions of monogamy. Was it not the case that marriage was in essence a legal and, if we ever dared to be honest about it, a financial arrangement, into which love had no business intruding? Indeed, the very idea of romantic love could be said to be a late invention. To be fair, in many ways, it was an invention he approved of. He clearly had nothing against love per se. But the mistake many people made – and he included his wife among them – was to believe in its unchanging permanence. As well as its exclusivity.

There was no term to love. It might last an instant or a lifetime.

And, he maintained, it was perfectly possible to fall in love with many people at the same time.

If love was a force that existed, independent of individuality, between the male and the female sex (he would leave aside those perversions of it that he had witnessed at school) as a universal principle, therefore it followed that it could exist between any given woman and any given man at any time, provided the attraction was strong enough. Human constructions such as matrimony and morality could have no sway over it.

One of his former lovers, Lady Amelia Saville, had once accused him of being a greedy boy. He had not argued with her on that point, although he had taken issue when she had said that she did not believe he had ever truly loved anyone except himself.

She had made the observation that for him love was a mask that he put on to attain his object, which was purely the biological act.

'That said,' she had added, 'it is a mask that suits you.'

She also intimated that it did him credit that he at least felt it necessary to don the mask. It was a courtesy on his part, a compliment paid to the woman in question. 'Without it, you see, it's all so sordid.'

Over the years, he had thought about what she had said and decided that there was probably something in it.

Except, more and more, he was growing impatient with the mask. Wouldn't it be better, he thought, if men and women could be honest about their sexual natures and needs? He knew that women were as capable of enjoying sex as men. In fact, from some of the female climaxes he had been present at, he rather suspected that Teiresias had it right when he maintained that women experienced by far the greater pleasure in the sexual act. And Teiresias should know, having lived both as a man and a woman.

Of course, most women did not have the courage for such honesty. They played an elaborate game with themselves, pretending to a virtue that did no one any favours.

The older he got, the less time he had for such games.

Less time too for his wife's attempts to curtail the natural expression of his life force. For if she was not prepared herself – as she was increasingly not – to fulfil her duty as the primary recipient of his sexual exuberance, what right did she have to close down his opportunities for seeking outlet elsewhere?

Emma looked down at him from the portrait. Although it had been fixed a decade ago, her expression seemed extraordinarily attuned to the current moment in their relationship. Haughty and mocking, but worst of all, triumphant. As if she had him right where she wanted him.

A scowl tensed across Fonthill's face as he turned his back on the painting. A gritty clatter drew his eye towards the window. The weather had turned brittle, the wind hurling bullets of ice against the panes. Glass rattled against frame in complaint. Fonthill felt the shiver of a wheedling draft.

It was not a day to be out in, he thought complacently, at the same time as his attention drifted to the figure of a man loitering on the other side of the street. A hailstorm had settled in, darkening the morning and smudging the view out of the window into a grey blur. But as far as Fonthill could tell, the figure appeared to be a man in a belted raincoat with the collar turned up against the elements and a flat cap on his head. And he appeared to be looking directly at the house.

SEVEN

'Metcalfe?'

'Masters.'

A squall of wind took hold of the shop awning under which the two men were sheltering and snapped it through itself, then whipped it back and forth with an angry clatter. Pellets of ice hurtled into Masters' face. He closed his eyes against the onslaught, then bowed his head before being driven back into the shop doorway. Metcalfe was right behind him. The two men were now squeezed together like sardines – except they were like two sardines in an otherwise empty tin. Metcalfe had a habit of standing far too close to a chap. It wouldn't have been so bad if – well, not to put too fine a point on it, if he didn't smell.

Roderick Masters inched away from his unwelcome companion. But what small space he managed to create Metcalfe soon invaded.

Masters shook his head in irritation. 'What are you doing here, Metcalfe?'

'What are you doing here?'

'You can't just repeat the bally question. I asked first.'

'I got wet.'

Masters could feel the dampness soaking through his clothes. He took off his cap and shook the excess water from it. 'Yes. Me too. Wet through.'

'Have you been to see Sir Aidan Fonthill?'

'Sir Aidan what? No. What makes you say that?'

'He lives near here. Fonthill House, 63 Netherhall Gardens, Hampstead. It's that street there.' Metcalfe's arm shot out at right angles to his body. 'Do you know who else lives on Netherhall Gardens? Sir Edward Elgar. He lives in Severn House, 42 Netherhall Gardens, Hampstead.'

'What of it?'

Confusion clouded Metcalfe's features, though he continued to hold his arm out in front of him.

Masters went on: 'I loathe and detest Elgar. His music is intellectually bankrupt. It lacks authenticity. And originality. It is sentimental twaddle, straining for effect. It panders to the worst nationalistic instincts of the Englishman. It is nostalgic and vulgar and showy. It strives too consciously to please the ear.'

At last, shakily, as if in shock, Metcalfe lowered his arm. 'Sir Aidan Fonthill has chosen one of his songs to be performed at our Christmas concert.' Metcalfe began to hum the melody to 'A Christmas Greeting', his falsetto voice carrying the first soprano part. 'I have the music here.' He held up a slim brown leather music portfolio, which he was carrying in his other hand.

Masters looked away. 'Sir Aidan Fonthill is a fool and a philistine.'

'Do you say that because he has refused to include your new composition in the programme?'

'That has got nothing to do with it. There are other composers besides myself and Elgar, you know. Where is the Schoenberg in his programme?'

'Schoenberg? He's Austrian.'

'What of it? Music knows no boundaries!'

'I do not think Sir Aidan would consent to have an Austrian composer in the programme. Winston Churchill will be in the audience. Winston Churchill is a member of the government. We are at war with Austria. And Germany.'

'Very well, Stravinsky then. The Russians are on our side, I believe.'

'It is a Christmas concert. I did not know that Stravinsky has written Christmas music. Has Stravinsky written Christmas music?'

'That is precisely the attitude that is stultifying this country's cultural life. I am surprised at you, Metcalfe. Why must only Christmas music be performed at a Christmas concert?'

'That's what the audience expects.'

'Then we must educate them.'

'They do not want to be educated. They want to be entertained.'

'And there you have put your finger on the very crux of the problem!'

Metcalfe's startled expression gradually relaxed into one of thoughtful reflection.

The two men stood without speaking for some time, cowed by the stamina as well as the ferocity of the downpour.

'Will you be coming to the concert?' asked Metcalfe at last.

Masters let out a contemptuous snort. 'You've got to be joking.'

'I shall be playing.'

'I know you will.'

The two men had been contemporaries at the Royal College of Music, and before that were students together at Haberdashers'. Despite these connections, they had never been friends. At RCM, Masters studied composition under Parry, while Metcalfe had studied the piano. For as long as Masters could remember, Metcalfe had been a precociously talented pianist. His obsessive dedication to his chosen instrument was either a refuge from the difficulty of human interactions or the cause of his social inadequacy. At any rate, he had always stood out as something of an oddball. As soon as they had arrived at the college, Masters had sought to distance himself from him. And yet, like the proverbial bad penny, Metcalfe had the habit of always turning up.

Masters screwed his face into a frown. 'Anyhow, how do you know about the piece I gave to Fonthill? Did he show it to you?'

'No. He left it in the Great Hall at UCS. That's where we rehearse. I don't think he wanted it any more. It was on the floor.'

'On the floor!'

'I picked it up.'

'Oh. I see. You did, did you?'

'Yes. He had dropped it on the floor.'

'Dropped it?'

'Yes. "Rubbish," he said. And then he dropped it.'

'Rubbish? Is that what he said?'

'Yes, rubbish.'

'I'll give him bloody rubbish!'

'I picked it up.'

'So you said.'

'It had your name on it. Roderick Masters.'

'I know what my bally name is.'

'It said "Mistletoe". Words by Walter de la Mare. Setting by Roderick Masters. That's how I knew it was yours.'

'Did you play it?'

'I played it.'

Masters waited for the other man to deliver some kind of verdict on the piece. When none was forthcoming, he said, 'Well, I would very much like it back, if you've finished with it.'

'It's interesting.'

'What?'

'Your piece. It's interesting.'

'You liked it?'

'I said it was interesting.' Metcalfe hummed a line from the setting, now singing in his natural voice, a high tenor.

'You remembered it!'

'Of course. I remember every piece of music that I play.'

Masters felt a twinge of disappointment. Metcalfe's memory of his work was indiscriminate, and therefore meaningless.

'It's interesting,' repeated Metcalfe.

'Yes, you said that.'

'It's interesting, because it does not resolve. The ear wants it to resolve but it does not.'

'That's deliberate. I wanted to express a feeling of longing – of unrequited yearning.'

'It's a minor sixth. There. At the end.' Metcalfe sang the interval.

'Yes, I know.'

'There are many strange intervals in it. It sounds as though it was written by someone who does not understand the principles of Western music.'

'I would prefer to say that it is written by someone who is challenging the principles of Western music.'

'It is not in any definite key.'

'That is deliberate too. It is to express the eerie, supernatural quality of de la Mare's poem.'

'You forgot to put the bars in.'

'No. There are no bars. No time signature. I wanted it to be somehow outside time, you see. In keeping with the mood of the poem.'

'And you wanted Sir Aidan Fonthill to include this in the Christmas concert he is organizing in order to raise funds for Belgian refugees?'

'Why not?'

'It's very difficult to sing.'

'It's perfectly possible to sing. You yourself just sang an excerpt from it.'

'Yes, but I am an accomplished musician. The Hampstead Voices are all rank amateurs. It is beyond them.'

'But it's not rubbish, is it? He said it was rubbish. It isn't that.'

'No. It's . . . interesting.'

'I take that as a great compliment, coming from you.'

Masters felt himself scrutinized by his companion for an uncomfortable minute.

'Why should you care what I think?' The question was asked flatly, without self-pity. It seemed that Metcalfe was genuinely interested to know the answer.

Masters could not help but feel embarrassed. 'Naturally, I value your opinion, old chap.'

'Do you? You have never sought my opinion. On anything. You have never shown the slightest interest in my opinion.'

'Well . . . we haven't really ever . . .'

'You have never shown the slightest interest in me.'

'I . . . don't think that's fair . . . I have always admired you as a musician. I have followed your . . . progress with interest. From a distance, admittedly.'

'All the time that we were at the Royal College of Music, you never once spoke to me.'

'I don't think that's true . . . Is it?'

'Yes.'

'Well, I could equally say that you never spoke to me!'

'I did. I tried to. But you ignored me.'

'I don't think . . . I mustn't have . . .'

'You were with your friends. It was in the refectory. I said, "Hello, Masters." You looked straight past me. As if I wasn't there. And then you said something to your friends. And all of them laughed at me. You laughed at me too.'

'No! My dear fellow, no! You must have got the wrong end of the stick there. I assure you, we weren't laughing at you. We couldn't have been. It's just that I didn't see you, I'm sure. If I had, I would have . . . I would have . . . well, I would have invited you to join us.'

'You cut me so many times that in the end I stopped saying "Hello, Masters" because it was obvious that you did not want to be my friend.'

Masters' face was drenched from the melting hail. But a wrench of emotion streamed warmth into the icy moisture. 'I'm sorry.'

He felt Metcalfe's gaze scour his face. Whatever the other man was looking for from him, he seemed to find. He gave a small nod of satisfaction at last.

EIGHT

Sir Aidan laid the score to Elgar's 'A Christmas Greeting' open on his desk.

His horn-rimmed reading glasses, retrieved from the table in the drawing room, pinched his nostrils. With the tip of his forefinger, he pushed them back on to the bridge of his nose, screwing his face into an unfocused squint. The fact was he was not used to wearing spectacles and so always struggled to find the best position for them. Emma would say that it was time for a new prescription. She seemed to take delight in his physical degradation. Quite naturally, Fonthill abhorred visiting the optometrist as much as he did any member of the medical profession. Whatever they pronounced, it was always some variation on the inevitable refrain. 'You are getting older!' The prognosis was always mortality.

The glasses gradually slipped back down his nose under their own weight. By carefully adjusting the angle of his head, and its distance from the score, he was able to bring the sheets of music into focus.

Pencil in hand, he scanned the first few bars. He could hear the notes of the opening violin duet play in his head. It had an immediate calming effect on his emotional state, which had been disturbed by the sight of the stranger outside the house.

Working on a score was a peculiar mixture of the visual and the aural. He heard the music in his imagination, where it had a ghostly quality, which he strained to latch on to. But he was reliant on the printed notation to conjure up the elusive effect.

Given the deficiencies of his eyesight, and the pressures he would be under on the night – one of his violinists was a world-renowned virtuoso, and the soprano solo would be taken by an operatic prima donna – Fonthill had resolved to memorize all the pieces so that he would not be reliant on the score when conducting.

It was not just a question of memorizing the notes. He had to pay attention to the sections in the music that required particular care to achieve their effects. Take the refrain of 'Friends', first encountered at F. It was one of the most effective moments of the song, where the sopranos hang on an ethereal suspended chord. The vocal lines of the music are marked *p* at that point, while the violins and piano play *pp*, following the *diminuendo* indicated in the preceding bar. It is a moment of great delicacy and, paradoxically, power too. But so much can go wrong. Especially with a choir of amateurs. He must take control of the timing. There is no *rallentando* indicated in the score, but in his judgement it could safely be assumed, picking up the tempo again at G. There were certain members of the choir who found it unaccountably difficult to cope with variations of tempo. They would be looking for him at that point to guide them. All well and good. That was what he was there for. Except that some of them had a tendency to panic. And when they concentrated too hard on timing issues, their pitch went all over the shop.

In fairness, such shortcomings could most often be laid at the door of the basses. And thankfully this song did not require basses, or any male parts at all.

It had been his original idea to assign the two soprano parts to soloists, with the soprano sections of the choir coming in for the chorus. Dame Elsie would of course take the first part. Anna was to have sung the second. It would have been a wonderful opportunity for her – his gift to her. But that was not to be. And so, he had divided the parts so that Dame Elsie sang sop one and all the choir sopranos sang the second part together, splitting into sop ones and sop twos for the refrain.

It was really very simple. And yet it seemed to provoke no end of confusion among the choir members. There was much raising of eyebrows, shaking of heads, furrowing of brows – all the many little ways those who are commanded have at their disposal to question the decisions of those who command.

They would all come round in the end, of course. They always did. So why on earth they insisted on going through this period of resistance baffled him.

There had been a time when he could count on Emma's support, but he had lost that a long time ago. Fortunately, there had been a series of loyal devotees to take her place, the latest of which had been Anna.

Perhaps that was why he was interested in recruiting Miss Greene to the choir. Her voice was good, surprisingly so. She had potential. Of course, she was not in Anna's league, and probably never would be. But she was mouldable, he felt. She lacked confidence, which meant that he could build her up and then reap the benefits of her dependence. The challenge for now was to find a way to progress matters, at the same time as seeming to back off. The important thing was not to provoke Emma further.

He needed to get back in his wife's good books somehow. Naturally, it made life easier if they were on good terms. But it was more than that. Fonthill experienced a momentary tightening in his chest. A small surge of panic took away the air from his lungs as he thought back to the figure he had caught sight of through the drawing-room window. He might need Emma's assistance sooner rather than later.

There was a knock at the door. Fonthill almost jumped out of his skin. But there was nothing to be afraid of. He recognized it as the gentle, professionally discreet rap of Callaghan, his butler.

'Come in.'

Callaghan carried before him the silver tray reserved for the post. It bore a single item. A small square package. 'This came for you, sir.'

'Thank you, Callaghan. Just put it there, will you.' Fonthill indicated a space at the edge of his desk. The butler negotiated his way around the piano to do as he was bid. Fonthill eyed the parcel distractedly. 'Is that the only post today?'

'The post hasn't been yet, sir. This must have been delivered by hand.'

Fonthill sat up. The parcel had his full attention now. He felt his heart pounding in his chest. There was no doubt – the appearance of the mysterious man watching the house had put him on edge. It gave everything a sinister cast. For some insane reason, he imagined the package containing a still-beating heart.

'If that will be all, sir?'

Fonthill looked up at the bland, imperturbable face of his butler. Callaghan's expression concealed his emotions as effectively as the brown paper and string concealed the contents of the parcel. It was the first time Fonthill had ever really looked at Callaghan – as a man, as a human being in his own right, rather than as a semi-invisible lackey who had no thoughts or desires of his own and existed only to fulfil the wishes of others. Fonthill felt a stab of grief. For reasons he could not quite admit to himself, he suddenly felt lonelier than he ever had in his life.

His gaze latched on to Callaghan's features as if he were latching on to the only familiar and safe place in a hostile world. The carefully trimmed moustache, the equally unruly eyebrows (a strangely touching blindspot given the man's otherwise impeccable grooming); the filigree pattern of broken veins on his cheeks that looked as if they had been painted in by a skilled artist with a superfine brush; the salt and pepper hair, the thickness of which must have been a source of pride to Callaghan; and more than anything those eyes, which Fonthill noticed for the first time were a startling green.

Part of his grief was the awareness that he had taken Callaghan too much for granted. He had treated him like a dog, in the best sense of that expression: presuming his unconditional loyalty and devotion even. Suddenly he felt he owed Callaghan – what? An explanation? An apology? A word of gratitude or kindness? Something.

'How long have you been with us, Callaghan?'

'It will be eleven years next March, sir.'

'Eleven years! Good heavens. You must like it here then?'

Callaghan gave a small bow but said nothing. It was not exactly the ringing endorsement Fonthill had been fishing for.

'I . . . certainly . . . hope . . . that is the case. That you are . . . satisfied . . . more than satisfied . . . *happy* . . .' Good grief! What a word to say to one's butler! He must be out of his mind! '. . . in your position here.'

A tremor of confusion animated those impressively bristling eyebrows. They had the appearance of two caterpillars trying to make a break for it.

'It is satisfactory, yes, sir.'

Although he sensed his butler's discomfiture, Fonthill found that his need to keep him there with him was greater than the desire to spare him any further embarrassment.

'Good. I wanted you to know that we have valued your service over the years. Your discretion, in particular, is something that I personally have appreciated. And perhaps I have not expressed my appreciation as much as I might.'

A second bow, deeper than the first. The man's whole body was tensed to turn on the balls of his feet and bolt from the room. But Fonthill would not release him yet.

'I wonder, did you see who delivered this?'

'No, sir. I am afraid I did not. Marie took delivery of it.'

'Marie? The one with the . . .?'

'Yes, sir. I believe she found it on the doorstep after someone had rung the bell. She did not see who left it there.'

Fonthill took this in. 'Have you seen any strangers coming to the house recently? Perhaps to the tradesmen's entrance?'

'Strangers, sir?'

'I saw a man earlier.'

'A man?'

'Yes. I couldn't see him distinctly but . . . I had the impression he was watching the house.'

Those untameable brows came together in consternation. 'Would you like me to call the police, sir?'

'No. That won't be necessary.'

'Very well, sir. If there is nothing else . . .'

'There is nothing else. You may go.'

But the haste with which the man fled the room was wounding.

Fonthill turned his attention to the parcel. He could not say why it unsettled him so much. It seemed to squat on his desk, defying him, inexplicably malevolent. Daring him to open it. Why should he not?

In all likelihood, it was nothing to do with the mysterious figure he had seen.

It was probably an early Christmas present from someone. But from whom? Anna, perhaps. That would explain why she had run off without being seen.

He knew that it had not ended well with Anna. To say she had taken it badly was an understatement. She had said things which no doubt now she regretted. He had not imagined so much anger and bitterness could be contained in such a petite and delicately boned creature. But then her voice was a revelation, too. And where had she learnt to swear like that?

Perhaps this was a peace offering. Her way of saying all is forgiven. Of apologizing even.

At last he found the courage to pick it up. It was heavier than he expected. If it was a present from Anna, its satisfying heft suggested something flatteringly substantial. A bronze or marble bust, perhaps. Might she even have commissioned a bust of him? No, no. That would be expecting too much. A statuette of Orpheus perhaps? Had she not said that he was her Orpheus? Of course, the myth of Orpheus and Eurydice did not end entirely happily, at least as far as Eurydice was concerned. But at the time he had taken it for the compliment it was no doubt intended to be.

At the very least it might be a paperweight. He imagined a highly polished lump of some semi-precious stone – he would not want her to spend too much of her resources on the gift. Something in obsidian or jet. That seemed somehow the kind of thing Anna might give him at this particular moment in time.

He felt a pang of guilt. He had not got anything for her. But there was still time to rectify that, which was perhaps why she had delivered the present early, to make sure of a reciprocal gift. Ah, but that wouldn't be easy to accomplish, given his present financial embarrassment.

He looked at the handwriting on the outside of the parcel. But did not recognize it as Anna's. She had written to him, letters which were now safely burnt. The little fool. How could she be so stupid as to consign their affair to writing? But he had read them quickly and had not given much conscious attention to her hand. He remembered it was vaguely what you would expect it to be, somehow feminine and pretty, even if some of the sentiments she had given expression to were not. On balance, he rather thought this was not her writing. But he could not be sure.

Of course, there was only one way to find out what the parcel contained and who it was from.

He took his paperknife to the tautened string and cut it with a resonant pop.

He peeled away the brown paper, revealing a varnished wooden box, made from some dark wood, mahogany most likely. The top was inlaid with a marquetry design representing a lyre. And so, yes, there was an allusion to Orpheus in the gift. Although there was no card, the reference was a strong indication that it was from Anna.

There was a small keyhole in the front. He lifted the box out of its wrapping to see if there was a key lying beneath it. There was not. He soon discovered that the lid was not locked, however. And when he raised it, he discovered the key there. The interior of the box was far shallower than the exterior suggested, just as its weight was greater than he would have expected from a simple wooden box of that dimension. There was obviously a concealed mechanism.

He put the key in the keyhole, closed the lid and began to wind. Each crank of the clockwork lightened his mood.

When the spring was fully wound he put the music box back on the desk and opened the lid again. The key in the front of the box began to rotate back on itself. A mechanical tinkling began.

Although his expectations had not been high, the sound the machine emitted grated on his senses unbearably. Ground out in staccato metallic plinks, a single ten-note sequence was repeated over and over again, but the notes were so devoid of resonance they were virtually toneless.

It could not be called a tune. It had no melodic coherence, did not even seem to be in a recognizable key. It went nowhere. Made no musical sense. It seemed to have been composed by a lunatic, with the sole purpose of putting any listener's nerves on edge. It was an assault on Fonthill's ears, an insult to his sensibility.

No, he couldn't accept that this infernal object was from Anna. And it was not just his vanity that refused to believe it. It just didn't make sense. Why would she go to the trouble, let alone the expense, of sending him this calculated expression of her hatred?

But if it wasn't from her, who was it from?

Fonthill closed the lid. The key in the front stopped turning. The jarring noise was silenced.

He turned the box over. Scratched into the unvarnished underside were four German words:

EHRE VERLOREN, ALLES VERLOREN

Fonthill felt a chill go through him, like the first shiver of a long sickness. The music box fell from his trembling hands, clattering on to its side on his desk. The lid popped open. And the soulless grinding out of noise struck up again, each thin note a pin pricked into his deflating hope.

NINE

'I understand.' Charles Cavendish could not bear to look at his wife as he said the words, which perhaps undermined the sincerity of his claim. Or perhaps his embarrassment came from the fact that he understood too well, better than she could have imagined. Certainly, he was embarrassed.

He found it easier to focus his attention on the blue willow pattern teapot that sat between them on the kitchen table. The tea set had been a wedding present from Ursula's parents. A reminder of happier times? He did not think so. He was not sure there had ever been happier times. And if he was honest, he had never liked the china. It was more her parents' taste than theirs. At times, it gave him great satisfaction to imagine smashing it. All seventeen pieces of it.

'How can you?'

The undisguised bitterness in her voice did at last draw his gaze, if only for a fleeting instant. He was both relieved and disappointed to see that she could not look at him either. She was looking out of the window, almost with longing at the filthy weather as it swirled through the sky. As if she would rather be out there in that than in here with him.

Her face was flushed and glistening from the heat of her emotions. He could not in all honesty say that Ursula was a beautiful woman, but there was something fierce and defiant about her looks, something profoundly unapologetic, that fascinated. That fierceness was concentrated in her eyes, which were dark and glowering beneath heavy brows that often met in a frown, though never of confusion – of anything but. Of dissatisfaction, impatience, frustration, anger, or as now, contempt.

It would not be true to say that Ursula did not care what people thought of her. It was rather that she believed she had a right to be thought highly of.

It was a point of view that made her easy to admire but difficult to love.

It struck Cavendish as almost comically English that they were having this conversation while waiting for a pot of tea to brew. For all the tense emotion of the moment, for all Ursula's bitterness and misery, there was the milk jug, there was the sugar bowl with its tiny silver-plated tongs for lifting out the sugar cubes, there were the waiting cups and saucers. They must drink tea. Whatever else happened, they must drink tea.

They were three storeys up in a mansion block in Hampstead. This was their home. But Cavendish felt curiously cast adrift, as if the violence of the wind outside was about to rip the room they were in from the fabric of the rest of the building and hurl them into the void.

He knew that his marriage to Ursula was not perfect. But it was all he had.

The fault was undoubtedly his. He fell short in some way. She found him lacking and she was right to. He was dull. Unimaginative. Weak. Cowardly.

If he had been married to Charles Cavendish he would have been unhappy.

And so, he braced himself for the onslaught of her complaints, while all the time fantasising about smashing that damn tea service.

'How can you understand? You have no idea!'

'No, of course not. I didn't mean to suggest that I . . .'

'She's here! In the building! Our building. Our home. With that . . . bastard!'

'Ursula, really! Is it really necessary . . .?'

'It is a bastard child! I am merely using the word in its correct, literal sense. She is unmarried. An unmarried mother. The child therefore is a bastard.'

'Yes, but I really think . . . she has to live somewhere. *They* have to live somewhere.'

'Why here?'

'Would you have her cast out on the street?' Charles let his glance flit to the storm-lashed window, as if to underline his point.

'I don't care! Why should I care where she goes?'

'But to get up a petition? I . . . I . . . I . . . Isn't that rather harsh?'

'This is a decent, respectable block. Or at least it was until she moved in here.'

'But what about the child? The child is innocent in all this.'

'If she does not go, then we must go. I will not live in the same building as that harlot.'

Cavendish picked up the teapot and felt the weight of it. The handle of the pot felt precarious. He imagined it snapping off, the pot smashing against the wooden surface, the hot tea spilling everywhere, dripping off the edges of the table and scalding his lap. He would welcome the physical pain as a relief from the intractable misery of his emotions.

But there was something instantly comforting about the trickle and gush of the tea into the cup. It made it seem possible that there would be a solution, that they would find a way through. If only they could all just sit down and have a cup of tea together.

Ursula was not a heartless woman. He knew that. She did not really want Anna Seddon cast out on the street. Not just before Christmas. Not when there was practically a storm raging outside. Not at any time. In any weather.

It's just that she was hurting. And the only way she knew to process her hurt was to inflict a greater one on someone else.

There were things he needed to say to his wife, but it was not a conversation that he wanted to have. Not now, not ever. It was a conversation that, once begun, could take them to a very dangerous place. It might easily destroy everything. But perhaps everything needed destroying.

Charles Cavendish sighed deeply. 'Sit down, Ursula. Come, drink your tea.'

She glared at him in outrage, as if he had just struck her. But she did as he had bade.

'It seems to me that this is not about Anna.'

Her fierce eyes bulged at the mention of that name. Not merely at the mention of it, but at the provoking sympathy in his voice as he said it.

But he pressed on. He had begun the conversation now. He had no choice but to see it through. 'It seems to me that this is about him.'

'Him?'

'Sir Aidan. Fonthill.' He added the surname as an afterthought, as if to distinguish between multiple Sir Aidans of their acquaintance.

'What about him?'

He sensed that somehow the balance had tipped in his favour. There was a tremor in her voice, trepidation – fear, even. He thought about standing up to push home his advantage. But he had no wish to make this more difficult for her than it was already.

'I know that you're in love with him.'

'What?'

'I understand. Practically all the women are.'

'Don't be ridiculous.' But the flinch of her head away from him told him that he had hit home.

'Apart from Emma, and that's only because she knows him better than the rest of you.'

Ursula pursed her lips in distaste at the mention of Fonthill's wife.

'Would it make you happy if you had his baby?' He had not meant to ask such a question, so directly. And the boldness of it almost took his breath away. Almost had him laughing out loud. It was something he had thought, but never meant to voice.

'Are you suggesting that Sir Aidan is the father of that bastard?'

That was not the response he had expected; he considered it a diversionary tactic on Ursula's part. 'Who else could it be?'

'Who can say?'

This was getting away from the point. Cavendish laded three sugar cubes with determined energy into his tea. He pressed on. 'Perhaps not have his baby. But become his mistress. Would that make you happy?'

'What has got into you, Charles?'

'I am just trying to find some way forward for us. I am just trying to discover what it is that you want. What would make you happy, as I so evidently do not.'

He had her attention now. She watched him closely, her mouth gaping. 'You sound like you are about to make some kind of a proposal.'

Cavendish stirred his tea thoughtfully. 'It's not for me to propose anything. For one thing, I do not know what has occurred between you and Sir Aidan. For all I know, your present unhappiness may be the result of his already having rejected you.'

'Why do you say that? He has not rejected me!'

'So you *are* lovers?'

'No.'

'But that is what you want?'

'Are you sure you want me to answer that question, Charles?'

Cavendish raised his teacup to his lips. The drink was satisfyingly strong and sweet. 'It depends what the answer might be.' He gave a disarming smile. 'I have been thinking, Ursula. The war, and everything, rather focuses one's mind. I am not too old to sign up. Or rather, apply for a commission. They might have me. I am not the most splendid physical specimen, I know that. But they might overlook my obvious shortcomings if things get any more sticky over there. A word in the right ear might do the trick. If there was nothing for me here, no one who wanted me to stay, then I should think it would be a good thing to do, all things considered.'

'I don't want you to go off and get yourself killed, if that's what you mean.'

'Oh, don't you worry, I don't intend to get myself killed, either. I'm pretty sure I could get myself a cushy billet, what with my accountancy qualifications and all. The army needs bean counters, I dare say, as much as it needs frontline soldiers. I've pretty much made up my mind to do it, if I'm honest.'

'Then I don't see why it is necessary to have this distasteful conversation.'

'Because I want to know how things stand between us. I wouldn't want to entertain any false expectations. Especially if anything should happen.' He left that thought ominously vague. 'And after it's all over, it would be good to know if I have anything to come back to.' At that he risked a glance at her over the top of his teacup and added: 'Or not.'

'This is all rather unexpected, Charles.'

'And there's one other thing too.'

Ursula cocked her head.

'If I should take myself off and leave you to . . . to do whatever you want. With him. You must promise me one thing.'

'What?'

'That you will leave that poor girl alone. That you will not petition for her to be evicted. You do realize, don't you, that it is the height of hypocrisy when the thing you want most of all is to be his mistress?'

Cavendish drained his cup and replaced it in its saucer with meticulous care, as if the blue willow china tea set was his most treasured possession in the world.

TEN

Fonthill left the box on his desk and hurried back into the drawing room.

The man was still there. Standing opposite the house, his collar still turned up against the weather, flat cap pulled down tightly on his head.

This time, he didn't even bother to withdraw when he saw Sir Aidan watching him through the window. He was daring Fonthill to acknowledge his presence.

Fonthill felt his face burn with shame. By now he had no doubt who was keeping vigil on his house. If he was honest, he had known it from the moment he had first seen him. But he had dreaded this man's reappearance in his life for so long that his mind had obliterated the memory of their first encounter, just as earlier the sudden hailstorm had obliterated his form.

He thought back to the night in question. It had started off innocuously enough. That is to say, when he had left the house he had not been aware of any intention on his part to go down the path that had led to his present difficulties. Perhaps there had been a vague and nagging sense of resentment against Emma, which is always a dangerous mood to start the evening in. But at the time he had simply wished to put distance between himself and his wife.

The business with Anna had come to a head, and so Fonthill had taken himself off to his club. The place was a refuge – a bolt hole – when things got too sticky on the outside. It did him good not to see a female face for a while. It was like a respite from himself, from his nature, his appetites. To compensate, he always tended to indulge what might be described as his other vices, though they were mild enough. Before the war, he could always count on the club to provide a slap-up dinner. Admittedly, the fare had become somewhat more frugal in recent weeks, testing the chef's initiative and the members' forbearance, but the cellar was well stocked with enough French, and even German, wine to hold out for some time yet.

And the company was invariably convivial. One always bumped into someone. That evening there had been quite a party. Old 'Soapy' Soames had been there, together with the incorrigible Symington and the mercurial Lucas, and some fellow called Parker or Porter or Potter or some such, who apparently had been at Sandhurst with Winnie. He must have been a new member, or someone's guest, because Fonthill didn't remember seeing him before. Lucas had a quite appalling story to tell about him, which he imparted in a confidential undertone, tapping the side of his nose at the finish. Fonthill paid no attention to it at all, as Lucas had a reputation as an outrageous peddler of scurrilous lies. Quite understandably, Winnie himself was *not* there, what with the war and everything. There were a few others, whose names eluded him now, and whose faces had blurred into anonymity.

The other chaps had persisted in a rather tiresome joke, which he seemed to remember had started with Lucas. As Fonthill had been at Harrow at the same time as Churchill, Lucas thought it was amusing to get Fonthill and the Parker/Porter/Potter chap mixed up. It was part of his joke that he claimed they were virtual doppel-gängers, which of course they were not.

After God knows how many brandy and sodas, and several bottles of Château Pomys 1890 (a good year, as it happened), together with a snort or two of 'Doc' Symington's pick-me-up, he had felt capable of anything. At a certain developed stage of the proceedings someone – he could not for the life of him remember who – had gleefully and inanely pronounced, 'The night is young!' The phrase had appealed to him inordinately. He declared himself to be very much in favour of the night and all young things. Someone else, he suspected it was Lucas, had suggested they move on. The fellow was strangely sensitive to subtle shifts in atmosphere and mood, and unerringly knew when it was time to vacate one location for somewhere more conducive to whatever was afoot.

And so, capes and hats had been called for. They had bundled noisily out of the club, picking up a few extra roisterers along the way. Taxis had been hailed. Directions given. And off they had hurtled, into a night which, though young, was undeniably dark. Fonthill had no idea where he had been taken, except that it was to a nondescript room in a nondescript house on a nondescript street, where there were tables, and men seated at those tables for the purpose of playing cards for money. Gambling, in other words. For high stakes, too, judging by the seriousness of the participants' demeanours.

It was all oddly exhilarating, and irresistible.

'You know where we are, don't you?' Lucas had whispered. 'This house used to belong to a murderer, a very nasty murderer, or so they say. It was here where he used to commit his grisly crimes.'

'Here?' Fonthill had looked around open-mouthed.

'Right here was where he used to drain the blood from his victims.' Lucas's eyes had widened with excitement as he had murmured his thrilling confidences.

Somehow the knowledge of the crimes that had been committed there made the whole thing even more intoxicating.

When he crossed the threshold to that room, he felt himself stepping into a place of danger and risk. And he could feel Emma's disapproval dogging him, which of course made him all the more eager to throw himself into whatever excitements the evening offered.

Yes, it was all very well with hindsight saying that he should have known better. He remembered only too well the way things had ended the last time he had been tempted to woo Lady Luck. (He felt a second flush of shame at the memory of that, his hands tightening on the sharp-edged object in their grip.) But that had been at roulette. A game of chance. This was different. All he had to do was keep his wits about him. To watch the cards and read the faces of his opponents.

Besides, he had had the conviction – the absurd conviction, he now acknowledged – that lightning does not strike twice. In other words, the very fact that he had lost so catastrophically at the casino in Baden-Baden all those years ago meant he could not possibly lose now.

And he had been carried along by the momentum of the evening. Despite the fact that the game was taking place in a decidedly unglamorous room, its nondescript walls exuded a kind of allure.

The room seemed to favour him. The flicker of its gas lights was like the flirtatious glance of a pretty girl. It fortified him. Somehow, from somewhere, he picked up the idea that he couldn't lose.

And there was something about the way the other players were looking at him. They seemed to acknowledge his superiority. He believed he could see the defeat in their eyes as soon as he walked in.

Everyone accepted that tonight was his night. He was 'the one'. Everything would go his way.

He felt it. They knew it.

Lucas, it was all Lucas' fault. Lucas shouldn't have raised his hopes with his confidential asides. How it was possible to make ten thousand a year as a professional gambler. If he hadn't then proceeded to reel off the names of a whole host of chaps who managed to do so. Quite ordinary chaps possessing no special qualities, or skills. The least likely professional gamblers, in short.

If it hadn't been for Lucas, the fatal idea would never have taken hold of him: *Well, if they can do it, so can I.*

At first the game had gone his way. Which had added to his already exalted sense of invulnerability. The compliments of his opponents lulled him. Not to put too fine a point on it, it was clear that everyone was in awe of him.

They were meek and humbled, humiliated even. Some people even threatened to leave the game if things carried on the way they were going.

But of course, things did not carry on the way they were going.

The table had turned on him.

And before long, the solemn mood that he had first picked up on turned gleeful. They scented blood. Their awe evaporated, if it had ever been there at all.

IOUs were signed. Lucas – the damnable fiend – had vouched for him, up to a point that is. He would not, of course, stand as guarantor for his debts. But he had assured the room that Sir Aidan Fonthill was good for a long line of credit. Didn't he have a rich wife, after all?

Fonthill had laughed nervously at that but had been obliged to go along with it because he needed to win. And to be able to win, he needed to play.

If he couldn't play, he couldn't win back his losses. And then go on to win the fortune that the room had promised him. Though, to be honest, it had lost whatever allure he had once imagined it to possess. It now looked positively sinister.

The energy from the stimulants he had taken earlier in the evening suddenly deserted him. His palms grew moist. The cards slipped and slid in his fingers. At one point he even dropped his hand on the table, to much predictable hilarity among his opponents.

The cards slipped through his mind too. The numbers confused him. He mixed up suits. He forgot the most basic rules of the game – even what game they were playing.

Soon he could feel the beads of sweat trickling down his face, so that he was obliged to mop his brow with a handkerchief that grew quickly sodden. He pushed his fringe back out of his eyes and rolled his shoulders.

'Are you all right, old chap?' Of course, it was Lucas, feigning concern but secretly delighted.

Like all the other players, he had grown fangs and talons. Or so Fonthill suspected – he could no longer look any of them in the face to confirm this impression.

At some point he had noticed the unpleasant smell in the room and realized soon after that he was the source of it. It was his fear.

One by one the others dropped out. Soapy, Symington, the Parker-Porter-Potter fellow, and all the nameless blurred faces, pocketing their winnings or cutting their losses before it was too late. Even Lucas eventually cashed in his final hand, leaving only Fonthill to face a man who was the most unprepossessing of them all, a man whom Fonthill had hardly noticed at first, but who had emerged over the course of the night to be his veritable nemesis.

A man with the bulbous eyes of a frog, and a wide, loose mouth from which, at any moment, Fonthill had expected to see a long reptilian tongue whip out and snap a fly from the air. And a common, cockney accent, with a vulgar turn of phrase and a habit of sniffing noisily, so violently that it caused his eyes to pop out even more than usual. It ought to have been a tell, but neither Fonthill nor any of the others could work out what it told them, as he seemed to engage in it indiscriminately.

At last, the end had come. The pop-eyed cockney had sniffed and pulled his winnings – so many scribbled IOUs – towards him for the last time. Fonthill's whole body had turned to ice. He had simply no idea how much his losses amounted to. How much he would have to go cap in hand to Emma for.

He remembered how his hand had trembled involuntarily on the baize surface of the table.

And how the man's eyes had stood out even more as he fixed Fonthill with a steady gaze, the very blandness of his expression more chilling than any histrionic demonstration of power.

'You good for this.' A statement, not a question. A slow blink offered no relief from the oppressive sense that time had stopped.

'You'll have to give me some time, of course.'

The man's eyes had stayed on him, growing even more bulbous if that was possible, as the most violent sniff yet drew half of his face up. 'I don't have to give you nothin'. You have to give me . . .' Somehow the man kept his eyes on Fonthill while managing to tally up the various notes. 'Five hundred and sixty-two pounds, thirteen shillings and six pence. I tell you what, I'll let you off the six pence.'

'That's very generous of you.' Fonthill had felt his jaw tremble as he had spat out the sarcastic riposte.

Lucas had leaned in to whisper something in Fonthill's ear. He hadn't caught the words exactly, but he got the drift. It was a warning. *Steady on, old chap!* perhaps. Or, *I say, don't you know who that is?*

Fonthill knew the man's name all right. He had written enough promissory notes to him in the course of the evening.

T.G. Benson, Esq. was the name he had been directed to make the notes out to.

It had seemed an ordinary enough name. The sort of name a clerk might have. Or a shopkeeper. Or a minor official in the civil service.

It was only in the cab on the way back to the club that Lucas had filled him in.

'Tiggie Benson. Not the kind of chap you want to be in debt to, if I'm honest.'

Fonthill didn't like the sound of that *Tiggie*. It had a sinister ring to it. He distrusted its faux chumminess, and its dissonant air of playground nostalgia. What kind of man holds on to such a name? 'What do you mean?'

'Far be it from me to spread rumours.'

'Come on, man. Out with it.'

'Well, it is said that he is something of a rotter.'

'What kind of a rotter?'

'A rather professional and well-organized rotter. The kind of rotter who would not think twice about causing trouble for a chap who owed him upwards of five hundred pounds. Quite a tidy sum, old thing.' This was added in an infuriatingly censorious tone, as if Lucas hadn't been the one goading him on to take ever greater risks to recover his losses.

'What kind of trouble?'

'Oh, you mustn't pay any attention to rumours. I shouldn't have said anything. I have myself always found him a perfectly charming cove. But then, I have never been in debt to him.'

'Is he some kind of . . . criminal?'

'Good heavens! You ought to be more careful what you say, dear thing. You can't go around calling Tiggie Benson a criminal. That's slander. Tiggie Benson don't take too kindly to slander. I believe the last fellow who slandered Tiggie Benson came to a very sticky end. Found floating face down in the Thames with his throat cut, he was, if memory serves.'

'Isn't *that* slander?'

'Shouldn't think so.'

The cab disgorged them outside the club on St James's Street. They got out groggily, the early morning air shocking them into a buzzing wakefulness.

Fonthill had felt suddenly sick, for all sorts of reasons.

'Buck up, old chum.' Lucas again. The man was a human gadfly. 'It's not like you have anything to worry about. Emma will straighten you out. Damned smart move that, marrying into money.'

'It's not quite that simple. Emma and I . . .'

'What's this? You haven't been biting the hand that feeds, have you? Oh, that's why you're staying at the club! Of course! Tut, tut. Naughty boy.'

'It's not funny, Lucas. I can't pay this Benson fellow and I can't go to Emma for the money. I say, I don't suppose you could . . .'

'That's not the way it works, dear heart. Frightfully sorry and all that.'

'Perhaps if everyone . . .'

'A whip-round? No, no. That's not the done thing at all. A gentleman has to settle his own gambling debts, you know. Or get his wife to. Don't you worry. It will all look better in the morning, after a good night's sleep.'

'I'll pay you all back. You know I will. I just need time to sort things out with Emma.'

'Perhaps you should join the Methodists and become a missionary in the Congo. I doubt very much Tiggie Benson would follow you out there.'

Lucas had been right about one thing. In the morning, it had all looked very different. In fact, the whole thing had felt like a bad dream and Fonthill had decided the easiest thing to do would be put it out of his mind. In the meantime, he would do what he could to get back in Emma's good books.

Despite his best efforts, he had not been entirely successful in the latter objective; the former, though, he had achieved almost too easily. Until now.

Until Tiggie Benson himself stood outside his house, his ugly face resolutely set for confrontation.

ELEVEN

He'd given the fucker long enough.

You must be gettin' soft in yer old age, Tiggie, he had said to himself.

Nah. No chance of that. It was just, he knew the longer you left it to call in a debt, the more power you had over the debtor when you finally went knocking on their door. Because one thing Tiggie Benson would bet his shirt on was that Sir Aidan La-di-da Fonthill had not forgotten. No more than he, Tiggie, had.

It was a seed of fear planted in the fucker's brain. It would have grown to quite a tree by now. Spreading its roots and stretching its branches, cutting off the sunlight of hope, taking all the goodness out of the soil.

Or summink.

Tiggie was not much of a one for gardening. But he did know about fear. He knew how to scare the shit out of a cunt like Fonthill.

It was easy.

You just had to wait.

Mind you, this weather was giving him the right royal hump. Relentless, it was.

But it was something to stand like a statue in it. And the harder it was to do it, the more afraid Fonthill would be. And the more afraid Fonthill was, the better for Tiggie.

Still, his ears were getting cold. Something other than rain was dripping from the end of his nose. If he ended up catching pneumonia on account of this cunt, then he would make the fucker pay twice over.

So maybe it was time.

And if the fucker wouldn't come to the Tiggie, the Tiggie would go to the fucker.

Or summink.

Tiggie wasn't much of a one for sayings.

He had just made his mind up to make his move when the door to Fonthill's house opened and the fucker himself poked his head out.

It was funny. It had been several months now since the game, but Tiggie knew it was the man he was looking for immediately, even across the street, even with the hard, icy rain between them.

Fonthill's face was pinched and anxious. Afraid, Tiggie acknowledged with a glow of satisfaction. Shit-scared, he might even say. All the better.

Fonthill beckoned to him hurriedly.

Naturally, Tiggie took his time crossing the road.

'What the hell are you doing?'

'Ain't you going to invite me in? It's not very nice out here.' Though it was somewhat drier standing under the stone canopy jutting out above Sir Aidan's front door than it had been out in the street. And Tiggie was under no illusions that Fonthill would let him across the threshold. Still, he enjoyed pushing the toff's buttons. He pointedly peered over Fonthill's shoulder, taking in the well-appointed interior with a larcenous gaze.

'Whatever you've got to say to me, you can say here.'

'You know what I've got to say. You owe me seven hundred quid.'

'Seven hundred! It was more like five hundred.'

'It was five hundred and sixty-two pounds, thirteen shillings. I let you off the six pence, if you remember.'

'Exactly.'

'Yeah, well, you're forgetting about interest, aincha.'

'Nobody said anything about interest.'

'Nobody said anyfin' abah you keepin' me waitin' all this time.'

'Yes, well, I'm sorry about that, but as I explained at the time . . .'

'You got my money? You pay me now, we'll call it six hundred.'

'I don't have it. Of course I don't have it.'

'Wha' about your missus? She in? Shall I have a word with 'er indoors about it?'

'No! Now look here. You leave my wife out of this.'

'No, no, no. It don' work like that. It don' work wiv you tellin' me do this, don' do that. You owe me, my friend. That means until you pay me, I own you.'

'I'll get you your money. You have my word as a gentleman.'

Oh, Gawd! That was funny. Tiggie thought he'd never stop laughing at that. But suddenly he did. Suddenly it wasn't funny at all. 'Your word as a fuckin' gen'lman ain' worth fuck all to me, chummy. Your word as a fuckin' gen'lman? Wha' the fuck am I gonna do with tha'? You've got to be fuckin' jokin' aincha?'

Fonthill glanced nervously back over his shoulder, where it was all warm and cosy. Tiggie followed his line of sight, and heard children's laughter, feet drumming rapidly across floorboards upstairs.

'Got kiddies, 'ave yer? Li'l 'uns?'

Fonthill's eyes widened in alarm. It was a look Tiggie recognized and thrived on.

The happy sounds continued, and in fact grew louder. A door slammed somewhere. There was an excited cackle. Thunderous pounding. A moment later, Tiggie's question was answered when a boy appeared at the bottom of the stairs, propelled by the force of his hilarity. The boy looked up and met Tiggie's eye. A look of wonder came over the boy's face.

Tiggie raised his hand and waved.

Fonthill turned again. 'Go back upstairs, John.'

But John could not tear his eyes away from Tiggie.

'Now!' snapped Fonthill.

At last the boy turned and threw himself back upstairs as if his life depended on it.

'In the East End, where I come from, I 'earda 'ard-up mothers selling their li'l 'uns for cash. You know 'ow it is, too many mouths to feed an' all that. You'd be surprised what some toffs like you would pay for a scrawny underfed nipper from Whitechapel. Or maybe you wun'.' Tiggie gave Fonthill a hard stare. 'I dare say I could get you a decent price for one of yours.'

Fonthill made to shut the door in his face, but Tiggie was too quick for him, jamming his boot in the way. Tiggie leant forward to whisper through the gap. 'One way or another, you'll pay.'

'I-I'll get the money. I promise.'

'You will, will ya? Now why do I find that hard to believe? See, if you could get the money, I think you woulda got it me already. Doanchoo?'

The silence that came in response was more eloquent than any words.

'Now listen. Listen. I din' come 'ere just to give you grief. I don' wan' one of your children, tho' if you was prepared to part wiv one of 'em – girl or boy, don' matter – well, we migh' come to some arrangement.' Tiggie felt the pressure on his foot increase as Fonthill leant harder in on the door. ''Old up, 'old up! I know you prob'ly don' wanna. So I ain' even gonna ask. Not for now. We'll call that security, like wiv a bank. You know wha' I'm talkin' abah'? If I need to, I can always call it in. But for now, we won' even talk abah' it. Forget I mentioned it. Instead, I got a differen' proposal. Your *word* as a gen'lman ain't much use to me, I tell you that much. But if you take this door off my right foot, I'll tell you wha' is.'

There was a moment where Tiggie could almost hear the cogs in the fucker's brain turning. Then slowly the door eased open and he was free to move his foot again.

SECOND MOVEMENT

TWELVE

Saturday, 19 December, 1914

As he chained up his bike, Paul Seddon looked through the railings at the front of University College School and saw a man in dark glasses looking straight at him. The man didn't look away politely, as most people would when they realized they had been caught staring at someone.

Then Paul noticed that the man was holding a white stick in one hand.

Paul crossed the quad and went up to the stranger. The man had a full red beard, a respectable rival to Paul's own black one.

'May I help you?'

The blind man looked straight past him, as if at some point above his right shoulder. He said nothing but raised one hand, in which he held a battered satchel. He seemed to believe that this was all the explanation of his presence that he needed to give.

'Have you come to tune the piano?' For some reason Paul believed this was what the man meant him to understand. He took it that the satchel contained whatever tools he needed. 'But we're about to have a rehearsal. I don't think now's the best time, I'm afraid. Who booked you? I think there must have been some mix-up.'

'Sir Aidan Fonthill.' There was something unusual about the way the man spoke. He did not seem to be answering Paul's question so much as making a pronouncement.

'Oh, Sir Aidan. I see. That's strange. He doesn't usually handle this sort of thing. It's normally Cavendish, our treasurer. I think, really, you're going to have to come back some other time. Perhaps after the rehearsal.'

'I'll come back.' The man lurched straight towards him, tapping the ground in front of him with his stick. Paul was forced to jump to one side to avoid being hit. 'Do tell Sir Aidan I was here.'

'Who shall I say?'

But the man did not answer, except to hum a strange and broken melody.

Paul watched him tap his way across the quad. It was quite extraordinary the speed at which these blind chaps could move sometimes.

A moment or two after the fellow had disappeared through the school gate, Charles and Ursula Cavendish came in.

Cavendish's face was set in a distracted frown. His wife had the startled expression of someone who had just been given some unexpected news and could not decide whether it was welcome or not.

Cavendish greeted Paul with a wordless nod.

'I say, Cavendish, did you see the piano tuner?'

'What piano tuner?'

'Blind chap, with a stick. You must have seen him as you came in.'

Cavendish shook his head. 'I don't remember. Besides, I didn't organize any piano tuner. Not for today at least.'

'No. Sir Aidan arranged it, but I told him now was not a good time. He's going to come back later.'

'What the devil is Fonthill doing arranging piano tuners?'

Paul shrugged. Cavendish's anger seemed out of proportion to Fonthill's supposed offence. It was all the more remarkable because Cavendish was usually such an easy-going fellow.

'I shall have to have a word with him about that. I need to talk to him about another matter anyhow.' Cavendish gave his wife a dark look. She drew her head up defiantly.

Good heavens! Not Ursula as well! thought Paul. He held the door open for them to go in.

THIRTEEN

Ursula stood at the threshold of the Great Hall as Charles hurried in ahead of her, impatient, bustling with an energy she had not suspected he possessed, like a cork popping from a bottle of fizz. If only he had shown some of that before today, before he had already lost her, there might have been hope for them.

They were the first to arrive, it seemed, apart from Donald Metcalfe, who was already seated at the harpsichord, obviously eager to get his hands on the novel instrument. His fingers raced over the keys with that firm but effortless precision that almost always took her breath away. To say that Donald was a cold fish was an understatement. As far as Ursula could tell, it was not that he kept his emotions bottled in, simply that he did not have any. So how he was capable of producing such soul-wrenching music was a mystery to her. Were there hidden depths to him? Somehow she doubted it. Was he even aware of the effect his playing could have on others? She doubted that too.

The oak-panelled grandeur of the hall was saved from an oppressive gloom by a magnificent vaulted ceiling, inset with three large windows on either side and one at the back of the hall. An expansive light streamed in from the window behind her. Three impressive chandeliers were hung from the arches that divided the ceiling. Facing her were the pipes of the organ, arranged like the teeth of a great monster, and the organ loft. The stage below was set with banked seating for the choir. In front of the stage a space was left for the orchestra with a small podium where Sir Aidan would stand to conduct. Metcalfe's piano and harpsichord were off to one side.

The hall itself was filled with wooden seats arranged on either side of an aisle. She watched her husband stride away from her with brisk, purposeful steps. It struck her, curiously, as an ironic reversal of her wedding day, when she had walked down another aisle with a slow, measured tread towards Charles.

She heard the door swing open and was aware of someone shifting restlessly behind her, but she felt no inclination to get out of the way.

'Excuse me, Ursula.' The sound of Paul Seddon's voice stirred angry emotions, not so much on his own account – Ursula supposed she had nothing against the man – but because of his association with *that woman*. Ursula pretended not to have heard him, standing her ground so that he was forced to step round her. He gave her a look between pity and irritation as he bumped past her, buffeting her like a weathervane in the wind.

She felt the rage rise up.

Pity! How dare he pity her!

Ahead of her, Seddon bent over to take the bicycle clip from around his right ankle, presenting her with a sight that was either a considered insult or an invitation to a clownish act of subversion. If she had been able to move, it would have been to run forward and kick him in the backside. It was perhaps better for all of them that she felt herself frozen to the spot.

For as long as she could remember, Ursula had felt on the cusp of something. It was a dreadful feeling. It left her nerves frayed. Butterflies had taken up residence in the pit of her stomach. Her skin tingled as if it had been whipped with feathers. When she was not grinding her teeth, she was clenching her fingers or flexing certain internal muscles in preparation for some great feat of courage.

She wanted to scream or weep or howl with bitter, sarcastic laughter.

And yet it was not wholly a dreadful feeling.

This sense that nothing had been settled, that her life was up for grabs, contained within it a vast reserve of hope.

For now that Charles had taken the initiative to move things on, something had been set in motion. Things had been said which couldn't be unsaid and could only be followed through. Through to the end.

She heard her husband bark out a brusque greeting to Donald in a voice she could not recognize as having anything to do with her. Donald did not break off his playing to answer. Charles's voice reverberated in the vaulted ceiling, as if it were a demand he were making of the empty hall rather than the pianist. 'Is he here?'

It came to Ursula that what hope fears more than anything is resolution. There can be no room for hope when everything is settled.

She heard the door open behind her once more, followed by a burst of chatter as a group of singers came in together.

It was the push she needed to carry her forward.

FOURTEEN

Paul Seddon looked up at the plaster mouldings of the ceiling. All around him he could hear the clatter of chairs and music stands being distributed and arranged, the chatter of friends excitedly greeting one another and all the melodious hubbub of musicians getting ready to play.

Sir Aidan clapped his hands together to be heard over the din. 'If we could all find our places as quickly as possible . . .'

Paul's gaze settled appreciatively on one of the chandeliers. He couldn't help noticing that it was positioned almost exactly over Sir Aidan's podium. *If that dropped on him, he wouldn't stand a chance.* He allowed himself a small, secret smile.

'Come on now!'

Paul could tell that Fonthill was in a bad mood. And so, it was unfortunate that the choir was particularly excitable.

It was without doubt thrilling to see the members of the orchestra take out their instruments and run through their warming-up exercises: a few quick trills on the trumpets, a louche glissando or two from the trombones, the strings effortlessly conjuring forth those swooping arpeggios, the ominous rumble of percussion.

The presence of the celebrated guests added to the general excitement. When, earlier, the striking couple in furs had strode in, their heads held high as they looked for the adoration that they evidently considered their due, the room had been momentarily silenced. The realization that these were the dancers from the Russian ballet company quickly spread, and the volume of noise soon exceeded what it had been before their entry. The man wore a silk turban pinned in place by a huge diamond brooch, his ankle-length coat of many pelts slung loosely over his shoulders. The woman wore a red bycocket hat decorated with an enormous drooping feather. She possessed a delicate but austere beauty. She was as unsmiling as her partner, as if they had both been placed under a fairy spell that would turn them into toads if they registered pleasure of any kind. Sir Aidan had not yet arrived and it had been left to Charles Cavendish to greet them. It was quite possible that they took this as a slight. The disdainful angle at which they held their heads suggested that they were prepared to take everything as a slight.

Fonthill had arrived uncharacteristically late to the rehearsal and was mobbed by a series of people with demands on him as soon as he got through the door. Inevitably, that only worsened his mood, to the point that he had been rather rude to one of the musicians, a man with glistening, watchful eyes set deep in their sockets. His chin was buried in an oversized tartan scarf and his nose was pinched and red around the nostrils. There was something fine and sensitive about his features, so that even if he had not been carrying a battered violin case, you might have suspected him of being a musician. As he approached Fonthill, one hand held out to be shaken, he turned his head sharply and sneezed. 'No, no, no,' Fonthill protested in horror. 'Whatever you have, I don't want it.'

The man's eyes glared fiercely from the depths of their sockets, his rejected hand frozen in midair as Fonthill was led out of the hall by Charles Cavendish.

Outrage showed too in the suddenly bulbous eyes of the two Russian dancers, unceremoniously abandoned by Cavendish. They had the most wonderfully expressive faces, Paul decided. They danced as much with their eyes and lips and eyebrows as with the rest of their bodies. Every pout was a performance, every minute shift in posture, an expression of a profound emotional truth.

Soon after, Dame Elsie had arrived. Paul recognized her, having seen her sing La Traviata at Covent Garden, a role for which she was not physically well suited. Ah, but that voice! The voice made up for everything. All he had had to do was close his eyes and he could believe.

With Fonthill and Cavendish still missing, Paul had taken it upon himself to welcome the noted prima donna.

'Dame Elsie, what a great honour it is—'

'Sir Aidan?'

'I'm afraid Sir Aidan is busy at the moment.'

Unimpressed by this information, Dame Elsie tilted her head back disdainfully. 'Well, let's get on with it, then. Where do you want me?'

'Perhaps if you would care to take a seat for now. I'm sure I could arrange for a cup of tea—'

'Tea? No, no, no. I don't drink tea. It dries the throat.'

'I'm terribly sorry. Perhaps a glass of water then?'

'Why do you insist on forcing liquids on me? Do I appear particularly desiccated to you?'

'No, no, not at all. I shall tell Sir Aidan that you're here.'

'Do.'

And with that he was dismissed.

Seddon couldn't help smiling to himself as he hurried away to look for Fonthill. No doubt she was a prickly customer, but he rather enjoyed that about her, and indeed would have been disappointed if she had been anything else.

There was a practice room near the hall which Sir Aidan often used as his unofficial office. The door to it was slightly ajar and he could hear voices within. He glanced back quickly over his shoulder. It wouldn't do to be caught eavesdropping, and yet some puckish spirit inspired him to lean in, his ear close to the door.

The two men's voices overlapped but it seemed that Cavendish was dominating the exchange. 'The question is, what do you intend to do about it?'

'Nothing. Of course.'

'You won't talk to her?'

'Why should I?'

'To set her straight.'

'Well, as she's got herself all twisted around, I hardly think it's my job to straighten her out. You tell her. You're her husband.'

'She won't take it from me.'

'That's hardly my fault, old man. Is this why you won't . . .' But just at that moment, one of them scraped a chair across the floor so that Paul couldn't make out whatever it was that Cavendish wouldn't do.

People were still arriving. It was probably time he knocked once and went in. The interval between the knock and the entry was so short that the two men were frozen in the last moment of their argument, both their faces indignant at the intrusion as they turned towards him. The room was littered with bits and pieces of musical detritus, some of them broken, like the aftermath of a fight between music stands and orchestral instruments. Seeing Paul, Fonthill averted his eyes with a flinch of embarrassment. Cavendish's expression was impatient and resentful.

'Dame Elsie is here, Sir Aidan.'

Fonthill nodded tersely and bustled out.

Paul's questioning glance was met with a dismissive shake of the head from the treasurer. Paul turned and chased the choirmaster back into the Great Hall.

They had not gone far when one of the basses, a professional singer whom Sir Aidan occasionally called in to make up the dwindling numbers, stepped out to buttonhole Fonthill as he hurried towards the stage.

'Not now, Farthing!' Fonthill kept his head down and put his hand on the other man's shoulder to push him out of the way.

But Farthing held his ground, his feet planted firmly apart, his chest thrust out. 'I want my money.'

'Speak to Cavendish. He's the treasurer.'

'I did. Apparently, I am expected to perform pro gratis.'

'Yes! It's a benefit concert. That is generally how it is with benefit concerts.'

'Those were not the terms upon which I was engaged.'

'Nonsense! We didn't agree any terms.'

'No, no, no. That won't do. That won't do at all. I assumed, naturally, that I was engaged on the usual terms. If it wasn't the usual terms, you had an obligation to make that clear, which you did not.'

'Take this up with Cavendish. I don't have time for it now.'

'If the choir won't pay me, you must pay me yourself out of your own pocket.'

Paul Seddon cut in. 'Perhaps we can settle this later. For now, let's just get on with the rehearsal, shall we?'

'No fee, no me.' Farthing was clearly pleased with his little jingle. He jutted his chin out proudly.

Fonthill shook his head disparagingly.

'Dame Elsie, Sir Aidan,' reminded Paul gently. He felt himself blush at his habitual deference. Despite all that he knew about Fonthill, he could not help himself, it seemed.

Farthing's brows came together in a petulant frown. 'Ah, I see, the famous Dame Elsie Tatton awaits. More important than me, is she?'

'Yes!' cried Paul and Fonthill in unison.

'And what's more,' added Fonthill, 'she's performing without a fee.'

'That's as may be. Perhaps she can afford to give up her time for nothing. I, however, am a struggling musician. If I don't get paid, I don't eat.'

'You don't look exactly starving, Farthing.' Paul regretted the comment as soon as he made it. Not least because he hated being cast in the role of Fonthill's defender. And, also, it was an asinine thing to say.

Fonthill chuckled. 'Ha! That's true!' He dispensed a look of appreciation and complicity that once, not so long ago, Paul would have lapped up, but now it goaded him to oppose his former hero.

'Although perhaps Mr Farthing does have a point.'

Disappointment showed in the choirmaster's face. 'You think I should give this Shylock what he wants?'

Farthing took objection to the reference. 'I'm not a bloody Jew!'

'Stop acting like one then.' To Seddon, Fonthill added, 'Perhaps if you feel so strongly about it, *you* should pay him.' With that, he sidestepped Farthing and hurtled on towards where Dame Elsie was impatiently pacing the floor at the back of the hall.

Farthing turned his attention to Paul. 'So?'

'What?'

'Will *you* pay me?'

'No!'

'Right, I'm off.'

Paul held up a restraining hand. 'Look, I'll see what can be done. I'll talk to Mr Cavendish. Find out what's happened to your money. Please, for now, let's just get through this rehearsal and we'll sort it out afterwards.' Paul knew how weak the basses were without Farthing to boost them.

'Usual terms are I get paid upfront. In cash.'

'Yes, yes, I understand that. But there has obviously been a mix-up.'

'Mix-up? There's no mix-up. I know what's going on here. This is deliberate. You lot are hoping I'll cave in. You're exploiting my generous nature.'

Paul bowed his head sharply to hide the smirk he was not able to suppress.

'I see you laughing at me. It's all very well for you Hampstead types.'

'I live in Highgate, actually.' Paul knew very well that he was splitting hairs.

'You're still a bloody Hampstead type as far as I'm concerned.'

'Please, can you just take your place? I'm sure Sir Aidan will want to make a start soon.'

'He's the worst of the lot, if you ask me. It's all very well for him, with his fancy house and his rich wife. Well, just you listen to me, if he thinks he can cheat me out of what's mine, he's got another think coming. *Sir* Aidan Fonthill, indeed. I thought knights were supposed to be men of honour. He doesn't know the meaning of the word. Shameful it is, the way he carries on.'

Paul narrowed his brows. 'What do you mean?'

'Oh, come on. We all know what he gets up to. You tell him from me, if he doesn't want his affairs getting into the newspapers, he'd better make sure I get what's due to me.'

'I don't see why I should get dragged into this.'

'She's your sister, isn't she? The mother of his lovechild.'

Paul found he did not have the will to deny it. Nor the inclination. 'How did you know?'

'Anna told me.'

'She told *you*?' Paul could not keep the wounded tone from his voice.

'Of course. Anna and I are good friends.'

Paul doubted that. 'It hardly seems the action of a friend to use something shared in confidence as the lever for blackmail.'

'It's not blackmail. I'm only trying to get what I am owed.'

'Anna would not want the intimate details of her life to find their way into a newspaper.'

'Then it is in all our interests that I get my money.' Farthing's face was flushed and glistened with an overheated *patina*. He gave off an odour of stress.

Paul felt queasy as he looked into his eyes. He had the sense that the world was crumbling around him. If he stepped outside the school there would be nothing left, only ruins and chaos. And the source of the power that was destroying everything was located behind the eyes of this squalid, shameless, grasping man.

Farthing must have read Paul's gaze as a challenge. He drew himself up, bristling. 'This will be the last time he tries to get one over on me.'

It had sounded like a threat. And Paul had felt curiously elated to hear it.

Paul lowered his gaze from the ceiling and turned to look at Fonthill, like a hunter bringing a target into his sights.

'Thank you, ladies and gentlemen. Thank you very much. That will do.'

Fonthill turned to face the front pew where the Russian dancers were seated next to Dame Elsie. He gave a steep bow. Evidently he had succeeded in soothing the ruffled feathers of the eminent personages: Dame Elsie dipped her head condescendingly, managing even a magnanimous smile; the two Russians remained unsmiling, but they appeared at least gratified.

'Please extend the traditional Hampstead Voices welcome to the prima ballerina assoluta and the premier danseur noble of the great Ballets Modernes of St Petersburg, whose bold yet graceful movements have taken the citadel of ballet by storm, opening the eyes of the world to new and startling possibilities of an art form many had considered passé. I give you Ekaterina Volkova and Andrei Kuznetsov.' The dancers, whose English was not as good as their French, pricked up their ears at that 'passé'. But they were soon mollified by the applause of the choir and orchestra. 'You have opened our eyes, you really have,' continued Fonthill. Perhaps his gaze was rather too expressive of this sentiment as it lingered appreciatively on Ekaterina Volkova. It did not go unnoticed by her partner, who breathed sharply through magnificent nostrils, like a stallion snorting at restraint. *Was he more than simply her dance partner?* Paul wondered. If so, judging by the seething gaze he was fixing on Fonthill, the choirmaster was skating on thin ice. But Fonthill pressed on. 'Let me tell you, I have had the great privilege of seeing Mademoiselle Volkova dance the part of Salome in Paris, in a costume which, if I may say so, left very little to the imagination! Gentlemen, believe me, it was quite revealing of her extraordinary . . . talents!' There was nervous laughter from the men of the choir and some scandalized noises from the women. Certainly, Kuznetsov did not appreciate Fonthill's observations. 'Ah, dear me, I see that I may have offended Monsieur Kuznetsov. Forgive me, sir, I had assumed that like most of your fellow male ballet dancers you would be blind to such attractions.' Kuznetsov's scowl became dangerous. Fonthill hurriedly tried to dig himself out of the hole he had excavated. 'Being married as you all are to your art!' He was sweating now, Paul observed with a smile. 'At any rate, I thank you both sincerely, and heartily, for your participation in our little concert.' He bowed slightly as if he believed this to have made amends for what he had said. It was by no means certain from the Russian's expression that it had.

'And what can one say about our other guest?' Fonthill's smile was strained and nervous now. 'She is without doubt a huge presence—' Fatally, he broke off, closing his eyes as he regretted his choice of words. There was some tittering from the stage. Sir Aidan raised his voice over the disturbance, frowning in confusion. 'Her immeasurable talent has graced the boards of La Scala, Covent Garden and the Met in New York. And now she joins us here in the University College School, Hampstead, where we are honoured to be her chorus for a very special performance. Ladies and gentlemen, please, again, show your appreciation for Dame Elsie Tatton.'

Dame Elsie acknowledged the applause with a sour expression. Paul had to admit, it wasn't like Fonthill. He was usually in his element when dealing with celebrities. Charming, confident, never putting a foot wrong.

Not this time, however. Something must have thrown him off his stride.

Paul watched as he mopped the sweat from his brow. 'I believe we are still awaiting the arrival of Émile Boland, but perhaps we should press on? We do have a lot to get through.'

'Non!' The man was sitting in the front row of the audience seating, unseen by Sir Aidan, who had his back to him. He had a battered violin case in one hand, a bowler hat on his head, a bristling handlebar moustache, a glowering brow, a red nose, and his chin swaddled in a large scarf. He stood up with a terse nod. 'Je suis Boland.'

Paul watched Fonthill closely. He could see the gears whirring behind the man's eyes as confusion gave way to recognition, recognition to panic, and a mechanical grimace of a smile was cranked into place.

FIFTEEN

Emma had never seen Aidan so flustered. He was having trouble looking between his music and the singers. He lost his place more than once.

She saw the Russian dancers roll their eyes. This was obviously not what they were used to.

The orchestra was more or less ignoring his baton, and she had to say they sounded all the better for it. But unfortunately, orchestra and choir were rarely in time with each other.

There was an unpleasant spat with a trombonist, who was engaging in some obviously facetious banter with his neighbour. They were rehearsing the Elgar at the time, the accompaniment to which was scored for two violins and piano, and so did not call for the full orchestra. The brass section therefore sat idle, and this particular musician had evidently grown bored with Aidan's frequent stopping and starting. The prospect of Elgar himself being in the audience had clearly put the wind up him and he was desperate to bring off the delicate effect of the refrain. It was proving more difficult than he might have hoped and Aidan had already reduced Gladys Caldwell to tears by singling her out for criticism.

Aidan stood for a moment peering over the top of his spectacle lenses, waiting for the trombonist's joke to play itself out. The musician in question, realizing that he was the object of his conductor's attention, first raised his eyebrows in mock contrition, and then gave a sarcastic grin.

'Thank you. Yes, you, sir. This kind of behaviour may be acceptable in the tap room of the Flask, but I tell you I will not tolerate it in my orchestra. I expect my musicians to behave with discipline and decorum at all times, even when they are not required to participate in a particular piece. It makes it very difficult for those who are trying to rehearse if they must do so against this background of chatter and mockery. No doubt you think you are better than a choir of amateurs. But let me tell you, I have been listening to you. Yes, you. I have heard a number of decidedly off notes coming from your direction. I have ears, you know. Slurred speech is deplorable enough, but slurred playing is beyond the pale. I expect, no, I demand that my musicians be sober and proficient when they present themselves to perform in a concert for which they are receiving professional remuneration.'

There was a booming heckle from the basses. 'So *he's* getting paid, is he?'

Aidan was on the verge of losing control completely. It did not help when Émile Boland, who had consented to play the first violin part, chipped in. 'Perhaps it is you who are drunk.'

'I beg your pardon?'

Boland waved his bow around erratically. 'You cannot keep time. That is what you are supposed to do, I think? You are the conductor, no? But it is not consistent. You are too slow, you are too fast. You are too fast, you are too slow.' Boland shook his head disparagingly. 'And I think it is not wise for a conductor to insult the members of the orchestra whom he wishes to play for him. No?'

Bows were tapped against music stands, laps slapped, and even feet stamped in approval of this opinion.

Aidan's mouth gaped hopelessly. He looked lost, stricken, betrayed. He had always placed great store in the approval of those he considered his 'fellow musicians'. Despite a slightly condescending view of the status of professional players, there was no doubt that he valued their opinion and considered them his peers in music, if not in other matters. But now it was as if the veil had been drawn back. He glimpsed for the first time the contempt in which these men and women had always held him.

No, not even now did Emma allow herself to feel sorry for him. Not even when he flashed her a quick imploring glance. It was an instinctive moment. His habit to look to her for support and validation when things got especially sticky. Behind it was his assumption that, no matter what he did, no matter how badly he treated her, she would always acknowledge his precedence in music. He could count on her to affirm his talent. And if not her, then who? In that look was revealed the microscopic nucleus of self-doubt that he was normally so adept at concealing, from himself as much as from anyone.

This time she gave him nothing back. She kept her face stony and unresponsive, staring straight at him, but not meeting his gaze any more than a statue might. And then she turned from him, feeling a tiny spasm kink up the corner of her mouth.

SIXTEEN

B y the time it came to rehearsing the dancers, Sir Aidan found that his baton was shaking so violently that he was obliged to lay it down for a moment to flex his fingers.

When he picked it up again to tap the top of his rostrum it was as much to call himself to order as the musicians.

As it happened, the orchestra was sufficiently familiar with the music to be able to play it without direction from him. They were instead taking their cues from the leader, who was directing things with exaggerated head movements and eyebrow animations. Normally, he would have taken this as a slight, which would have piqued him into a show of dominance. But now he just wanted to get through the rehearsal without any further mishaps. He was aware that he might have made a few small faux pas himself. But the choir was proving particularly intractable today. And the almost mutinous attitude of the musicians had not helped.

It had been agreed that they would perform three excerpts from *The Nutcracker Suite*: 'March', 'Dance of the Sugar Plum Fairy' and 'Russian Dance'. The first would be danced as a Pas de Deux; the second was of course a solo by la Volkova; and the third was choreographed to bring Kuznetsov's talents to the fore.

The trombonist with whom he had been obliged to have words pointedly played the opening notes of the march with meticulous precision and conspicuous disregard of his conductor. His demeanour was gloatingly self-important. But Sir Aidan was wise enough, and magnanimous enough, to let it go. He had achieved the desired result. The fellow was at least concentrating now.

The dancers, of course, needed no help from him, which was just as well as he had his back to them. This meant that he could not see their steps, and so missed out on their interpretations. But he could see the expressions of delight in the faces of the choir members.

Once or twice he was tempted to cast a quick glance back over his shoulder. The evening might not be an entire disaster after all. The couple were not yet in full costume but had changed into rehearsal leotards and tights. Even that was enough to invest them with a kind of dramatic glamour. They had transcended being human to become characters in a magical story.

It was captivating to watch them, so much so that he naturally became distracted from what he should have been doing. He lost his place in the music and found that he was simply waving his hands ineffectually in time with the music, which he was making no effort to conduct.

Even so, when the choir burst into enthusiastic applause at the end of the first dance he had no compunction about accepting his share in the credit. He even bowed to acknowledge it.

There was an air of excited anticipation among the choir as Ekaterina Volkova took her opening position for the 'Dance of the Sugar Plum Fairy'. Sir Aidan waited for a nod from her and then turned to find Metcalfe, who ought to have been seated at the celeste by now, ready to play the distinctive part. But the bloody fool was standing helplessly next to the percussionist, with an expectant look directed towards his conductor.

'What is it, Metcalfe?'

'We don't have a celeste.'

'What?'

'We don't have a celeste.'

'I heard what you said. My interjection was provoked by incredulity rather than inaudibility. What do you mean, we don't have one? We absolutely must have one.'

'Well, we don't.'

'Cavendish?' Sir Aidan looked for his treasurer among the basses. Cavendish shook his head in the most provoking manner.

'Don't just shake your head at me! Where is the celeste?'

'No one said anything about a celeste.'

'I should not think it was necessary! We are performing the "Dance of the Sugar Plum Fairy". Any fool knows that we need a celeste!' Sir Aidan held up his hands in a gesture of despair and turned on his pianist. 'Don't stand there like a malodorous imbecile, Metcalfe, even if that's what you are. Play the part on the piano for now. Come on, come on. We've wasted enough time as it is.'

Metcalfe remained rooted to the spot for a moment longer. His gaze, inscrutable as ever, was fixed on Sir Aidan even when he started moving back to the piano. It was unnerving, but Sir Aidan was used to it. Metcalfe always played up a little when he chaffed him.

This time, Sir Aidan did not even look at the orchestra. One hand marked time with loose, sketchy gestures, while he watched the ballerina's dance closely. Viewed from behind, her body was lithe and slender, taut with a sinuous muscularity. He noted with approval, however, that it curved in places with a gentle femininity. She was not at all scrawny, as some of these dancers could be. He thought in passing that the leotard was the most marvellous of garments, and that a woman's body was the most marvellous of objects. The combination of the two was as sublime as any piece of music. As a connoisseur of female beauty, which he considered himself to be, he recognized this moment as one of rare privilege.

The racing of his heart played havoc with his timekeeping. A giddy excitement expanded inside him.

At last the dance came to an end. This time there were whistles and cheers at the end of the piece. Surprisingly for Sir Aidan, he noted that they seemed to grow in warmth when Metcalfe turned his head towards the choir. The conceited ass even bowed his head in acknowledgement! *How extraordinary!* Could he really believe that this enthusiastic appreciation was for him? Had he not just seen the glorious display of feminine grace and beauty that had taken Sir Aidan's breath away? Knowing Metcalfe, probably not.

Now it was time for Kuznetsov to step forward. It was natural that Sir Aidan's interest in the male dancer should be less than in his partner, but his glance was so cursory and dismissive that it could have been taken as insulting. He caught the fierce glare in the other man's eye. These Russians were a touchy lot, by the looks of it.

He held his baton up and waited for the orchestra to settle. 'Thank you. Next we have the Trepak, the Russian Dance. Now it's not just our wonderful dancers who have to be on their toes for this! We all have to be. Myself included. The tempo as you know is given as *Prestissimo. Molto Vivace, Prestissimo.* Which for me is this.' He marked the brisk two four beat with several swooping arcs of his baton. 'I have no doubt at all that you will be able to keep up with that. But I just wanted to give you fair warning that this is going to be . . . very very fast! And thrilling. And wonderful. So . . .' He turned briefly to receive a sullen nod from Kuznetsov.

He held both hands up as if he were holding the orchestra back. His heart was racing with excitement and terror. The dance was played at a fearsome pace. And whenever he had practised it, his forearm had tired before he was halfway through. He even had dreams where he was conducting the piece and his arm became as heavy as lead, or the muscles locked in a painful cramp – either way it was suddenly incapable of any movement at all. Even worse, uncontrollable spasms wracked his arm. In one particularly horrible variation of the dream, the arm detached itself from his shoulder and fell lifeless from his sleeve. How could he have forgotten that he had a false arm? And how could he have been so stupid as to take on the 'Russian Dance' with such a disability! At least he should have had the sense to fasten the prosthetic securely.

He shuddered away the memories of his nightmares.

No.

This was a moment to make his own. A moment, even, to enjoy. It was a moment of power, his power. He would not be cowed by the music. Or by the Russian dancer's glare. Or by the mutinous murmurings of the players. It was a moment of silence that held within it all the pent-up tumult of the glorious, blistering noise that he was about to unleash. For that was what it felt like, an unleashing.

He held himself up tall and breathed deeply through his nostrils, his arms poised and quivering.

Then, with a sudden lurch of energy, he threw himself into the path of the oncoming troika as it galloped full pelt over the ice and snow.

He was caught up and swept along.

His body was thrown this way and that. He kept his right arm swaying frantically, beating time as if he were beating off attackers, thrusting and parrying against the onslaught of music like his life depended on it. As he had feared, his arm grew weary, and sooner than he might have hoped.

But somehow he kept it together and kept it going. He surrendered himself entirely to his instincts. There wasn't time for conscious thought or intervention. He had to pull himself up into the driving seat of the troika and take hold of the reins.

He noticed that more and more of the musicians were looking to him. Perhaps this had started sceptically, as they allowed themselves a quick glance to enjoy his incompetence, no doubt expecting to see his arms flailing uselessly. But his instincts seemed to be coming through for him. He felt buoyed up, exhilarated. He had stopped being afraid of the tempo and was relishing it.

By the time they reached the rousing *fff prestissimo* at the end, his sense was that the orchestra regarded him with a new respect.

Of course, in reality, it was over almost as soon as it had begun. And all these impressions of the performance came and went as quickly as the notes themselves.

He let his arms hang limply by his side and bowed his head. 'We'll break for lunch now,' he finally managed to get out, his voice trembling with emotion.

SEVENTEEN

'Have you seen this?' Peter Farthing thrust the programme out aggressively.

Paul looked down and scanned the page. 'What of it?'

'Am I or am I not to sing the Saint-Saëns "Benedictus" with Dame Elsie Tatton?'

'I have no idea. Are you?'

'Yes, I am. Obviously. I would not ask the question in that way if I wasn't. It was clearly a rhetorical question.'

Paul generally had little time for rhetorical questions. He supposed they had a place in political speeches, or courtroom summations, or advertising copy, but in ordinary conversation they were simply tiresome. 'And so? Your point?'

'My point is that only she is credited on the programme, despite the fact that everyone knows it is a duet between soprano and baritone. So who is to sing the baritone part? A ghost?'

Another rhetorical question, no doubt. 'Look, I'm very sorry, but this is nothing to do with me. I don't know where you got the idea that it was. You should speak to Cavendish about it. Or Sir Aidan,' he added as a mischievous afterthought.

'Oh, don't you worry, I shall.'

Farthing threw the programme away in disgust. He then went out of his way to knock Paul with his shoulder as he jostled past. He affected the forward-leaning, head-down walk that communicates 'storming out'.

Paul consulted his pocket watch. An hour had been allotted for lunch, giving people enough time to wander into Hampstead village and back if they wished to. But it was now getting on for an hour and a half since they had broken off, and there was still no sign of Fonthill. Had he taken himself off for a rest after the rigours of the 'Russian Dance' and inadvertently fallen asleep somewhere?

Paul spotted Cavendish in the audience seats. He was sitting next to his wife, both unspeaking, their bodies turned away from one another, frozen in a tableau vivant that might have been entitled 'Loathing'.

Paul casually slipped into the seat next to the treasurer. 'Where is he?'

No sooner had he sat down than Ursula took herself off.

Cavendish blinked at him as if a spell had been broken. 'Who?'

'Sir Aidan, of course. Who else?'

'How should I know.'

'Just thought you might. The natives are getting restless, you know.' It was true. The first quizzical grumblings of some of the more old-womanish choir members (of either sex) had amplified into an unruly din. True to type, the brass players and percussionist had gone off to the pub. Dame Elsie was pacing about operatically. Émile Boland was long gone, as were the Russian dancers, but their part in the rehearsal was at an end anyhow. 'We ought to start again soon or I fear we may have an out and out mutiny on our hands.'

To which Cavendish replied, rather unexpectedly, 'I'm leaving Ursula.'

'Oh.'

'Or she's leaving me. I'm not quite certain which. At any rate, we're leaving each other.'

'I'm . . . sorry.'

'I'm not.'

'What brought it on?'

'She's in love with *him.*'

'Yes, I'd rather gathered that.'

'He's not interested, of course.'

'Well, that's something.'

'It's not enough.'

'No. I can see that.' Paul winced sympathetically. 'Well, if you're . . . not sorry. Then you're . . . *happy*? Perhaps?'

'I'm not that either.'

'No. Sorry. Stupid thing to say.'

'We'll do the concert, then go our separate ways. I have decided to apply for a commission.'

'Oh. I see.' Paul felt a pang of conscience. If even Cavendish was thinking of answering the call to the colours then perhaps he should too?

Paul felt himself blush and did his best to change the subject. 'By the way, I just bumped into that Farthing fellow. Quite literally, as it happens. He seems none too pleased about not getting top billing on the programme, or some such. Positively murderous, he was.' But he could see that Cavendish was not interested. In fact, the other man frowned at him as if he had been speaking in a foreign language.

The two men sat next to each other in silence for a few minutes longer.

'Well, I suppose someone ought to go and look for his nibs, if only to save him from the wrath of the Farthing. Shall it be me? Not that I have any particular desire to protect him. But, well, you know. One can hardly condone violence.'

Cavendish looked at Paul uncertainly as if he could not quite place his face. It was a disconcerting sensation, which Paul was anxious to flee.

He looked around for Lady Emma. Perhaps she would know where Fonthill was? Although, given what he now knew about the state of their marriage, would she care? As it happened, there was no sign of her.

There was no sign either of Donald Metcalfe, which was odd because usually the accompanist did not go far from the piano during breaks. It was his habit to sit on the piano stool, eating the potted beef sandwiches that his mother made for him or drinking tea from a Thermos flask.

Paul left the Great Hall by the main entrance. In the corridor, he found Metcalfe in conversation with a young man whom he did not recognize.

'Pardon me, but have you seen Sir Aidan? We really ought to be getting on.'

The unknown young man bolted off with his head down. It struck Paul as a little rude at first, but then he remembered that he had been the one to interrupt the two men's conversation.

'Yes, I have seen Sir Aidan,' replied Metcalfe, his voice strangely mechanical, as if he were giving a prepared answer or speaking from a script.

'Where?'

'In the Great Hall.'

'Oh? He's not there now. When did you see him there?'

'It was a minute off half past twelve.'

'What? Oh, yes, of course. *I* saw him then. We *all* saw him then. I meant, have you seen him since then?'

'No,' said Metcalfe flatly.

Paul studied Metcalfe for a moment. Sometimes it was difficult to tell whether the fellow was being deliberately difficult or simply did not understand how to interact with other people. Either way, the result was the same. He was a decidedly tricky person to warm to.

At that moment, a soft, rhythmic tapping drew Paul's attention. He glanced up to see the back of the blind man he had encountered outside. The man was making his way along the corridor, away from the practice room where Cavendish and Fonthill had been arguing earlier.

At virtually the same moment, there was a piercing scream, which seemed to come from that very room.

Paul looked quizzically at Metcalfe, whose expression did not change.

Paul felt himself frozen to the spot for what seemed like an age but was almost certainly no longer than one or two seconds. He was torn between giving chase and answering the cry which was still going on. The two events – this man's appearance now and the ungodly sound – were somehow connected, he felt certain. Both repelled him in equal measure.

It was hard to ignore the scream, though. The longer it went on, the more compelling it was. He had to admit it was quite a feat of voice production. It rose in pitch to reach a firm, resonant note that might even have been a top C. This was held for an impressively long time before swooping down in a steep glissando to what sounded like the G below.

He moved tentatively towards the source of that sound, at the same time reaching out an arm ineffectually towards the blind man. 'I say, you there! Hold on a moment, will you.'

The blind man picked up his white stick and began moving with surprising speed. In fact, it was hard to discount the idea that he was running away.

But that scream could not be ignored any more.

Paul thrust open the door.

Lady Emma Fonthill stood in the centre of the room. She turned towards Paul as he came in, her eyes fixed on him with a fierce glower. Her mouth was open in a shape that appeared almost premeditated. The extraordinarily musical scream continued to come out of it. How could she keep it up for so long?

She held one arm extended in the direction of an upright piano. It was disconcerting to notice that the hand at the end of that arm was covered in blood.

Someone, a man – good God, was it really, could it be . . . Sir Aidan? – was seated at the piano, motionless, his back to the room. The lid of the piano was closed, his hands resting upon it. His head was bent forward at an acute angle, his face hidden from Paul. Blood was streaming from one ear, from which also, oddly, there protruded the U-shaped end of what appeared to be a tuning fork.

THIRD MOVEMENT

EIGHTEEN

Detective Chief Inspector Silas Quinn returned the telephone earpiece to its base and looked across his desk at the man who was standing before him. Detective Sergeant Inchball held himself slightly stooped beneath the sharply sloping ceiling. When it had been decided by the powers that be – most notably, Lieutenant-Colonel Kell of MO5 (g) section – that the Special Crimes Department should be reinstated with essentially double the manpower, no provision was made for finding them a larger office. Admittedly, this doubling of resource only meant an increase from two officers serving under Quinn to four. But the room in the attic of New Scotland Yard which was SCD headquarters had already been cramped when there had just been the three of them in it – Quinn, Inchball and DS Macadam. Now there were five men crammed in like sardines around three desks. It was impossible to move around without having to climb over a colleague, or to get him to pull his chair in so tightly that the edge of the desk dug into his abdomen. Tempers were often frayed.

Being policemen, they were not on the whole small men. And Inchball was the biggest of the lot. His imposing physique was useful for certain kinds of interrogation techniques. Quinn did not generally value evidence extracted by physical violence, but he recognized that the threat of force sometimes had the effect of focusing a suspect's mind and encouraging cooperation. A fair number of the villains they had to deal with were bullies, and so he had no compunction about treating them to a taste of their own medicine.

The stoop that Inchball was forced to adopt gave him a hangdog expression, which was curiously appropriate to the bombshell he had just dropped, right at the moment that Quinn's telephone had rung.

'We'll talk about this later,' Quinn said now.

Inchball's brows came together in a deep frown. He shook his head in frustration. The sergeant had never been good at hiding his emotions. 'There's nothing to talk about, guv. I've made up my mind. That's all there is to it.'

Quinn glanced across quickly at DI Leversedge, who was pretending to be engrossed in reading through a case file, but it was obvious that he had been listening attentively to the conversation between Quinn and Inchball. Quinn suspected that Inchball's unhappiness was due to the addition of an extra layer of command above him. The original team had worked as a tight unit, the skills of each individual officer complementing his fellows'. Inchball had brought brute force and energy. But more than that, he had a directness of approach that often cut through confusing complications. His impatience could be a liability, but Quinn had learnt not to underestimate the man's detecting instincts. To dismiss him as the hired muscle was a mistake – and one which DI Leversedge had been quick to make. The thing was that although Quinn had clearly been the commanding officer, he had both trusted and respected his men. Often it had felt as though they were three equals working together in a common endeavour. If he could at all help it, he would rarely fall back on simply pulling rank. He preferred to win their cooperation because they understood and agreed with his directions. And besides, their contributions often played a part in shaping his strategy, Macadam, the autodidact, with his fund of idiosyncratic knowledge and Inchball with his bluntness and instinct. And Quinn, of course, with whatever it was he brought to the team. Although they were at times hard-pressed and overstretched, they had achieved a certain balance, which the addition of the new members threatened to throw out of kilter. DC Willoughby wasn't so much of a problem, being as he was the junior party, subordinate to everyone. That said, he had succeeded in putting Macadam's nose out of joint by driving the department's vehicle, the Ford Model T that had until now been Macadam's sole prerogative, as well as his pride and joy. Unfortunately, Macadam's recent injury, a gunshot wound sustained in the line of duty, meant that he was not as quick at responding to the command to 'bring the car round' as young Willoughby was. Sometimes Quinn even directly charged Willoughby with driving, having got into the habit during Macadam's period of convalescence.

But surely none of this was grounds for the decision that Inchball had just announced?

Quinn could not help giving voice to his sentiments. 'I cannot allow it.'

'There's nothing you can do about it.'

Quinn sensed Leversedge bristle on his behalf at Inchball's insubordinate tone.

'I'm a free man. And I answer to my own conscience, nobody else's.'

'I simply don't see why you would wish to do this.'

'We're at war!'

'Yes. And you would serve your country better by remaining in your post as a police officer.'

Inchball shook his head. 'You don't see the way they look at me.'

'Who?'

'People.'

'And how are they looking at you?'

'Like I'm a coward! Am I a coward?'

'No, of course not.'

'One bitch even gave me one of those bloody white feathers! The nerve.'

Quinn had a vague memory of Inchball mentioning this once before. 'But that was months ago. You haven't been fretting over it all this time?'

'I don't fret. If I don't like something, I do something about it. And I'm doing something about it now.'

Quinn shook his head impatiently. He really didn't have time to go into this now, but neither did he want to lose his sergeant. 'There's no need for that. Just wear the war service badge. Then people will know you're doing your duty.'

'I do wear it. But people still think you're a shirker.'

'Look, all I ask is you wait. That call . . . we have a new case. A murder. I need you with me on this, Inchball.'

'I've made my decision. I'm leaving the force. I'm going to join the Military Police.'

'Just so that you can wear khaki?'

'Well, what's wrong with that?'

'Because . . . don't you see? That is more of an act of cowardice than staying here.'

Quinn could see immediately that he had blundered. Inchball's face darkened in fury. 'So you *do* think I'm a coward?'

'No!' But Quinn found himself shouting at Inchball's back as he pushed his way through the obstacles formed by his colleagues. 'Wait!'

Inchball hesitated at the door, head bowed, fists clenched. Quinn could see that he was trembling with rage. The whole room waited on what he would do next.

He turned slowly to face Quinn. 'If that's what you think of me, then you'll be better off without me.'

Quinn winced his eyes shut as Inchball took the final few steps of his storming out. 'Bloody fool,' he said. What the men watching him did not know was that he was addressing that remark to himself, not Inchball.

After a moment, he scratched an imaginary itch in his left eyebrow and sighed. 'Willoughby, bring the Ford round, will you.'

He caught Macadam's eye just as Willoughby rushed from the room. His remaining sergeant's expression was hurt rather than angry. Quinn gave a small shake of his head, which was somewhere between discouraging and apologetic.

'What's the case, sir?' The eagerness that Leversedge injected into the question seemed a little overdone.

'There's been a murder,' said Quinn. After a moment, he added: 'In Hampstead.'

Leversedge nodded briskly, as if this were exactly what he had been expecting. And Macadam, Quinn sensed, seemed to revive at the announcement. There was something about investigating a murder that could compensate a man for any disappointment.

NINETEEN

On reflection, it was perhaps not such a good idea for Macadam to occupy the front passenger seat of the Model T next to Willoughby.

'Come on, boy, you can get past that.'

'Put your foot down!'

'What are you waiting for?'

'You could get a bus through there.'

'Sound your horn! Sound your horn!'

This was the only one of Macadam's instructions that Willoughby did not need any encouragement in. His hand was never far from the rubber bulb of the car's horn. In fact, Quinn suspected he was using it as means to drown out Macadam's constant exclamations. These were accompanied by much shaking of the head and angry gesticulation. Perhaps his tactic was to make Willoughby so uncomfortable that he no longer wished to volunteer as the driver. It was possible his intention was even darker: to throw the young copper off his stride and force him into a mistake, or even an accident.

Eventually, Quinn was obliged to lean forward and put a restraining hand on Macadam's shoulder. Macadam turned round sharply, glaring in surprise at Quinn's slow shake of the head.

Quinn was aware of Leversedge looking at him but did not give him the satisfaction of meeting his gaze. If Leversedge had something to say, let him say it. At last he did speak, though it was not to do with Macadam's behaviour. 'So . . . who is the victim?'

Quinn sighed heavily. 'A gentleman by the name of Sir Aidan Fonthill.' He glanced briefly at Leversedge, who was nodding as if the name meant something to him. 'Do you know him?'

'No. But he sounds important. Some kind of bigwig, I imagine? Something to do with the war effort?'

Quinn hesitated a beat before giving his answer. 'Not as far as I know.'

'Then why are we being brought in?'

'Probably because the local boys are short on manpower. We're helping them out.'

'Out of their depth?'

Quinn was wary of Leversedge's testing question. 'I didn't say that.'

Leversedge narrowed his eyes as he tried to calculate what was behind Quinn's stonewalling. 'You didn't need to.'

Quinn looked down at his upturned bowler on his lap, as if he would find what to say to Leversedge inside it. 'We are simply required to go there and do our job. Examine the scene for evidence and talk to people.'

'Making sure they haven't missed anything, you mean?'

'We just do our job, that's all.'

'But why SCD? What's *special* about this murder? The victim?'

'I suppose that's one of the things we shall find out.'

Quinn turned his hat over so that the bowler's perfect dome was uppermost. It was somehow a discouraging gesture. It had the effect of closing down the conversation.

They travelled the rest of the way in silence, apart from the frequent horn blasts from Willoughby. He seemed determined to show himself proficient in this most important of driving skills.

The afternoon was darkening rapidly by the time they reached the leafy, well-to-do avenue of Frognal.

An icy drizzle pierced the gloom. It held within itself the threat of something more substantial: a storm of hail, or snow, that it would be more than willing to unleash if they did not turn back now.

They were met at the school gate by an older man in an ill-fitting special constable's uniform. He had a sensitive, rather melancholy expression, exaggerated by a drooping moustache. However, his gaze was probing and direct, with an edge of challenge to it, as if he might be quick to take offence or already had. His demeanour was a strange combination of distinguished and chippy.

Quinn approached with a terse nod. 'DCI Quinn of the Special Crimes Department, Scotland Yard. Who's the officer in charge here?'

'Inspector Pool.' The special constable spoke with an educated voice. Some local dignitary doing his bit for the war effort, Quinn decided. There was something about the way he announced the OIC's name that left them in no doubt as to his opinion of Pool, who might be his superior in rank but whom he considered in no way his equal in any other respect. *The man's a fool* seemed to hang in the air.

'Where is he?'

'He's inside.'

'Take us to him.'

The elderly special constable seemed to hesitate. A pained expression winced across his face. 'What rank did you say you are?'

'Chief inspector.'

'Yes, that's what I thought. Very well.'

The special constable locked the school gate behind them with meticulous care, then led the way across the quad towards the school building, which was lit up like a Christmas tree. A cluster of regular bobbies sheltered beneath the grandiose entrance, watching sullenly as the party of detectives approached.

'Oi, Elgar, who's watching the gate?' one of the regulars snarled from the corner of his mouth.

'You needn't worry about that. I locked it.'

'Wasn't you told not to budge from there?'

'Yes, but I was also ordered by this gentleman, who is a chief inspector, of Scotland Yard, no less, to leave my post. A chief inspector outranks an inspector, I believe. And when one is given two contra-dictory commands, one is obliged to obey that of the most senior officer.' Special Constable Elgar turned to Quinn with a probing look. 'Is that not so?'

'You may leave us here, if you wish. One of these officers can take us to Inspector Pool.'

Elgar sighed heavily. He treated Quinn to a complex look. 'Whatever I do is wrong.' The remark was not aimed at anyone in particular and seemed not so much a comment on his experience in the Special Constabulary as a complaint about his life in general. He shook his head lugubriously and turned away.

'Bloody amateurs,' muttered the uniform who had challenged the special constable. 'I mean, who does he think he is?'

'Inspector Pool?' Quinn reminded him.

The man tore himself away from his companions to lead the way inside.

Quinn sensed Macadam fidgeting away excitedly beside him. Eventually, his sergeant could contain himself no longer and tapped him on the shoulder. 'Elgar. Didn't he say the chap's name was Elgar?'

'What of it?'

'You don't think it could be . . . Sir Edward Elgar?'

'The composer?'

'I do seem to remember reading something in the papers about his joining the Special Constabulary in Hampstead. And it did look like Elgar, don't you think?'

'I really couldn't say.' Quinn sensed that he was not responding with sufficient enthusiasm. 'But you're probably right. It's an unusual name.'

More uniformed police milled purposely about in the school corridor. They regarded Quinn and his team with a wary curiosity, breaking off from making cynical asides to follow them with their eyes.

The copper led them round several corners to a closed door,

outside which another constable was stationed. There was a small window in the door, which had been covered up by a sheet of newspaper from within. 'He's in there.'

The officer guarding the door drew himself up, bristling.

'It's all right,' said the other. 'They're from the Yard.' He turned to Quinn. 'This is where it happened. Naturally, we ain't taking any chances. The guv'nor said not to let anyone in.'

Quinn pushed open the door without knocking, just as an explosion of flash powder froze the room in a glare of brilliance. The photographer was hunched over a Brownie camera mounted on a tripod and directed towards the dead man at the piano.

Two plainclothes detectives looked up from a hushed conference. Quinn felt himself appraised, every detail of his appearance weighed and assessed, from his favoured herringbone ulster to the bowler on his head.

One of the men dwarfed his companion, and in fact everyone in the room. He was a clear six foot seven, with a build that would have stood him in good stead as a prop forward. He stepped forward with his right hand outstretched. 'DCI Quinn, is it?' He had a deep, booming voice to match his imposing physique.

Quinn's hand was engulfed in the other man's and shaken.

'We were told to expect you. I'm Pool. This is Sergeant Kennedy.'

The smaller man contented himself with a nod of acknowledgement and a sniff that gave little away.

Quinn introduced his own men. He was eager to get down to business. 'Who found him?'

'The wife, or should I say widow, of the deceased. Lady Emma Fonthill. She has also identified the body. Sir Aidan Fonthill, of 63 Netherhall Gardens, Hampstead. She raised the alarm and one,' Inspector Pool broke off to consult his notebook, 'Paul Seddon found her here.'

'Cause of death?'

'Well, the medical examiner is yet to make his report, of course. But I should say it's something to do with that thing sticking out of his left ear.'

Quinn glanced over to the corpse as another flash went off. 'What is that?'

'It appears to be a tuning fork, but we won't know for sure until the ME has extracted it.'

'Any prints on it?'

'We haven't dusted it yet, but again, we will as soon as the ME has finished.' Pool allowed a touch of impatience to enter his voice. 'I'm sure you have your own way of doing things in the Special Crimes Department, but we go by the book in CID.'

Quinn looked around the room briefly, taking in the clutter. 'What's his connection with the school?'

'He is choirmaster of a local amateur choir.' Pool consulted his notebook. 'The Hampstead Voices. The choir hires the school hall for rehearsals and concerts. There was a rehearsal going on here today when this happened.'

'Someone must have seen something?'

'There were a lot of people on the premises at the time. Choir members. Musicians. A couple of dancers. But they were all in the Great Hall.'

'All? Someone wasn't.' Quinn allowed that observation to settle. 'Do you have an approximate time of death? I know the medical examiner hasn't made his pronouncement yet. But have you been able to construct a timeline?'

'The choir broke for lunch at twelve thirty. That was the last time Sir Aidan was seen alive. It was around two o'clock when Lady Emma raised the alarm.'

'Where was Lady Emma for the whole of that time?'

'She went for a walk. Into Hampstead.'

'She wasn't with her husband?'

'He likes to be left alone when the choir is rehearsing. So that he can gather his thoughts.'

'Who told you that? Him?' Quinn pointed at the corpse.

'No, Lady Emma.'

'Ah, Lady Emma, yes.'

Pool and Kennedy exchanged an alarmed glance. 'I would invite you to examine the fatal trauma, sir.' Inspector Pool gestured over to the body.

Quinn felt his heart quicken. At the same time, his mouth filled with saliva, as if he was about to be sick. He swallowed back the impulse and waited for the nausea to pass.

He had confronted death in many forms, all of them violent. He had seen young men drained of blood; female victims of strangulation and ritual murder; one body mauled by a bear, another charred in a bomb blast; he had even been forced to examine the mutilated bodies of children.

Why should this particular body provoke such a reaction now? Was it something to do with the war? he wondered. With so many young men heading off to the Front to kill and be killed on behalf of their country, did it make the act of civilian murder – whoever the victim was – seem all the more unnecessary and, yes, obscene?

'You will be able to see for yourself that the brute force required to insert the murder weapon into the victim's ear to such a depth as to cause death is well beyond the capacity of a lady. This implement, if it is what it appears to be, is, I believe, blunt at its other end.'

'I once moved a fully laden wardrobe in my sleep,' said Macadam. 'In the morning, when I was awake, I was unable to restore it to its original position.'

'The mind,' added Quinn, 'is an extraordinary thing.' He bent down to follow the promptings of his subconscious mind. He focused his attention on the wound. And then it came to him, the most salient detail of the crime. He experienced a lightening of his spirit. All his self-doubt and self-disgust evaporated. This was what he was meant to do. He was good at it.

The blood. Or rather, lack of it. The simple fact was there was not as much blood as there ought to have been. What blood there was ran in a narrow streak down the back of the victim's neck. The curious thing about this streak was that one side of it appeared sharply defined, almost as if a line had been drawn and coloured up to.

Quinn frowned, stood up and took a step back to weigh up the configuration of the body as a whole. The dead man was sitting upright at the piano. His hands lay on top of the lid of the instrument. Quinn noticed that there was blood on one of the hands – the right.

'He was not expecting this.' There was more he could have said, but for now that would do.

'What is SCD's interest in this case?' DS Kennedy had a high, aggrieved voice that sounded as though he had laryngitis.

'We just go where we're told,' said DI Leversedge. He could not resist, however, flashing a resentful look in Quinn's direction.

Quinn nodded in agreement. 'We're here to help.' With that he took out a magnifying glass from the inside pocket of his ulster and began to scan along the surface of the piano. His attention became focused on one particular area of the front of the instrument. He tracked down rapidly, settling at last on the piano lid. A long brass hinge ran the length of it, and it was a section of this that seemed to interest Quinn especially.

'Macadam, do you see this?'

He handed his magnifying glass to his sergeant, who bent down to examine the hinge himself. 'Yes, I see it.'

'What is it?' asked Leversedge impatiently.

Quinn took out a pair of tweezers, which he handed to Macadam. 'Can you get it?'

After a moment, Macadam held up the tweezers with a single hair pincered in their pointed grip. Quinn took the tweezers carefully from his sergeant and held the hair next to the dead man's head.

'It's not his,' observed Leversedge.

It was true. The hair in the tweezers was significantly redder than Sir Aidan's.

'You see how the surface of the piano is quite dusty, like everything else in this room? And yet here . . .' Quinn indicated the area of the piano that had first caught his attention.

'It's clean,' observed Leversedge.

'It has been cleaned,' corrected Quinn. 'Wiped clean. Polished, you might say. And see, here, how the clean sweep continues down to this point here . . .'

'Where the hair was,' finished Macadam.

'Exactly.'

'Whose hair is it?' asked Constable Willoughby.

Quinn turned to the young policeman. 'That's a very good question. Whose do you think?'

'The murderer's?'

Quinn gave a non-committal eyebrow ripple.

Inspector Pool pushed his considerable bulk forward and held out a giant hand for the magnifying glass. 'May I look?' His tone was belligerent, despite the formal politeness of his request. The piano seemed to shrink as he bent down to scrutinize its surface. He stood up to his full imposing height and thrust the magnifying glass back at Quinn. 'What does it mean?'

'It means things are not as they seem.'

Pool looked at the dead man at the piano and nodded his head briskly. Whether he was agreeing with Quinn or confirming some private thought that had just occurred to him was not clear.

TWENTY

There was no mistaking it. A baby was crying.

Quinn frowned and looked to Inspector Pool for an explanation. The other detective heaved his shoulders in a massive shrug.

And then that sound was joined by one even more extraordinary. One that immediately had the hairs on the back of Quinn's neck standing on end.

It was barely human, so raw was the suffering it expressed. A woman's voice, he would hazard, raised in anger, anguish, or some other heightened emotion: an extended shriek of denial, the sound a spirit makes when it is turned through itself. It was strangely impressive. Quinn had the sense that he was not the only one of those hardened coppers who desperately wanted it to stop.

At last the cry gave way to a demand: 'Let me see him!'

Another female voice, calmer, but still fierce in its resolution answered, 'No!'

'You can't stop me!'

'Oh, yes, I can.'

It was difficult to tell for sure, but there now seemed to be the sounds of a scuffle coming from the corridor. All the time, the baby kept up its crying.

Leversedge made a move towards the door, but Quinn held out a restraining hand.

'Get out of my way!'

'You're not going in there.'

'I have a right to see him!'

'It's for your own good, Anna.'

'What do you care about that? What do any of you care about that?'

There was some release now. Sobbing. A sense of collapse.

Quinn gave a decisive nod. It was as if a spell had been broken.

Out in the corridor, the baby's crying was irrefutably loud. It was an appalling sound, because it seemed to suggest that life begins with an inconsolable existential howl.

A young woman, presumably the baby's mother, was slumped

to the floor, her back against the wall. She was wearing a long, fawn-coloured overcoat trimmed with fur and a simple black hat.

Streaks of black cosmetic ran from her eyes. Her hair – how long had she laboured to get her hair just right? – was pulled out in unruly frizzes from under her hat, which sat askew on the crown of her head.

Bent over her was a slightly older woman, somewhere in her thirties, Quinn would have guessed. She straightened in some embarrassment at the sudden bursting out of all these men. There was something awkward, Quinn might even have said unnatural, in her manner. Her hands went towards the other woman, but not so far as to touch her. She was either putting on a show of comforting her friend (if 'friend' was the right term) or was genuinely conflicted.

It was not long before her gaze back at them settled into a commanding defiance.

'Ah, Lady Fonthill,' said Inspector Pool. Somehow it did not surprise Quinn to learn the identity of the woman. She had an intelligent, practical face, devoid of sentiment. 'This is Chief Inspector Quinn, who has come to help us discover your husband's murderer.'

'Can we not do something about that . . . noise?' wondered Quinn with a distracted grimace.

Lady Fonthill turned to the woman on the floor. 'Anna?'

But the younger woman's expression was glazed with grief. She was beyond reach. Lady Fonthill arched an eyebrow at Quinn, in which was expressed the precise impossibility of his request.

But Quinn was wilfully immune to such signals. 'Can't you . . .?' And when Lady Fonthill's face registered her horror at what he seemed to be suggesting, he added, 'Madam,' as if that would be enough to persuade her.

'I . . .?'

Quinn glanced quickly about at the male police surrounding him, as if to say, *Well, we obviously can't.*

'That child . . .' But Lady Fonthill closed her eyes and shuddered, unable to bring herself to finish what she had been about to say.

'Couldn't you . . . at least pick it up?'

'Do you have any idea what you are asking?'

Suddenly the woman on the floor began to laugh. It was the most extraordinarily bitter laughter. 'Yes, Inspector . . . Do you?' Anna smiled mockingly. Quinn did not understand the joke. But he sensed that it was at the other woman's expense.

Lady Fonthill sniffed distastefully.

At that moment there were hurried footsteps along the corridor and a man's voice cried out, 'Anna! What are you doing here?'

A tweedily dressed man of around thirty was rushing towards them. His face was darkened by a full black beard and an intense, angry expression.

Quinn cast a quick enquiring glance at Inspector Pool, who answered with a muttered aside: 'Paul Seddon. Anna Seddon's brother.'

'This is the fellow who . . .?'

Pool nodded.

'Good God, Anna! What on earth were you thinking? And to bring the baby here, too!' The balance of anger and concern in Seddon's voice tipped decisively towards the former.

And now a wholly unexpected thing happened. At least, to judge by the look of amazement on Anna Seddon's face, she had not expected it.

Paul Seddon went over to the pram and picked the baby up.

The move seemed to take the baby by surprise too. For a moment it was startled into silence before beginning a new phase of mewling. Seddon held the child to his chest and jogged it gently as he paced about. Before long, the only sounds coming from the baby were the gentle snores of exhausted sleep.

Paul Seddon carried the child over to its mother. 'Get up.' His voice softened into a whisper, though his words remained harsh. 'For once, think of someone other than yourself. This child needs you. He needs his mother.'

Her brother's words had some effect on her. She picked herself up off the floor, brushed herself down and took her son from Seddon.

As if to make amends for any previous neglect, she made a great show of cuddling the baby, humming a lullaby as she gently rocked him in her arms. From time to time she cast dark, brooding glances at Lady Fonthill.

Her singing was effortless, and something more than a mother's usual soothing murmurings. In fact, Quinn might have said there was too much performance in it. When a mother sings a lullaby, it is an intense, focused transmission of love and calm, meant for her child alone. Anna Seddon was singing for an audience.

At last, when she was sure that the baby was securely asleep, she laid him back in his pram. She looked up at her brother as she arranged the child's blankets. Her voice was low but firm as she spoke. 'Why should I not bring my son to see his father?'

Lady Fonthill glared as if she might be about to say something regrettable. In the end, she contented herself with an emphatic tut.

Paul Seddon took on the role of peacemaker. 'Can you not see how hurtful this is to Emma?'

'Hurtful?' Anna spoke in a harsh whisper, mindful of the sleeping baby but eager at the same time to get across the full force of her bitterness. 'I never meant to hurt anyone. Love . . .'

Lady Fonthill groaned. 'Oh, please! Don't bring that into it!'

'Ha! You see! Can you blame him for seeking love? Wherever he could find it.'

'He didn't love you, you little fool. He didn't love anyone. Apart from himself.'

'Not true. Not true. He loved me.'

'You think he loved you? Only this week I caught him making love to another woman. Our children's nanny.'

'No!'

'He pretended to audition her for the choir – as your replacement. But he wanted her to replace you in other ways too.'

For a moment, Quinn thought that Anna was about to strike Lady Fonthill. But her counterattack when it came was far more lethal than a mere slap. '*You* killed him!'

Anna's brother was quick to intercede on Lady Fonthill's behalf. 'Now, now, Anna. Be careful what you say – there are policemen here, you know. They might get the wrong end of the stick. They might even take you seriously!'

'I am serious!'

'No, no, no. Emma didn't kill Sir Aidan. It's quite impossible.'

The conversation having reached this interesting point, Quinn felt compelled to interject. 'Pardon me, sir, but how can you be so sure?'

'Because I saw his killer.'

'Good God!' This heartfelt cry came from Inspector Pool. 'Why didn't you say so before?'

'I did. I told your sergeant about the man I saw running away.'

'Running away?' said Quinn. 'So you didn't see his face?'

'Not then. But I did earlier. It was the blind piano tuner, except I don't think he was blind and I don't think he was a piano tuner. The same fellow collared me outside the school and gave me a message for Sir Aidan. Now that I think about it, I am convinced it was some kind of threat.'

'Why didn't you stop him?' demanded Leversedge.

'On what grounds? At that point, I didn't know Sir Aidan was dead.'

'You let him go,' said Quinn dejectedly.

'I could hear Lady Fonthill's cry for help. Naturally, I made it my priority to go to her aid.'

'Why do you suspect he wasn't blind?' wondered Quinn.

'He had a white stick, which he was tapping the ground with. When I spoke to him, he picked it up and ran off.'

'Can you describe this man?'

'He had a beard. A large red beard.'

'I don't like suspects with beards,' said Quinn darkly. 'And the larger the beard, the less I like them.'

'Why's that, guv?' wondered Willoughby.

'Beards are there to distract. If they are not actually false, they may be easily shaved off. Which would naturally change the appearance of the suspect entirely.'

The heavily bearded Paul Seddon shifted uncomfortably. 'So you think this piano tuner was the murderer?'

'If he exists, then certainly. Why else would he be bearded?'

Seddon's embarrassment exploded into outrage: 'What do you mean, *if he exists*?'

Quinn turned to Inspector Pool. 'Has anyone else mentioned this piano tuner in their statements?'

Pool deferred to his subordinate: 'Kennedy?'

'That chap Cavendish mentioned him.'

'That's right! Cavendish and Ursula saw him,' piped up Seddon, desperately hopeful.

'Ursula?' wondered Quinn.

'Ursula Cavendish. Charles's wife.'

Sergeant Kennedy consulted his notebook. 'Cavendish confirmed you told him about some geezer with a white stick. He says nothing about clappin' eyes on him hisself.'

Paul Seddon looked imploringly towards Lady Fonthill, but she turned away as if embarrassed to meet his eye.

'Why would I lie about such a thing?' Seddon must have wished he hadn't asked the question. The only possible answer was writ clearly in the faces of all the policemen.

'Come on, Anna, I'll get you home.' Seddon reached out a protective arm towards his sister.

'Not so quickly, if you don't mind,' said Quinn. 'I have a few questions for your sister.'

'What can she know? She's only just got here.'

A questioning look shot from Anna Seddon towards her brother. It appeared she was not used to him looking out for her in this way.

But there was something about Seddon's remark that bothered Quinn. 'Have you, Miss Seddon, only just got here? In which case, I wonder, how did you get past the constable at the gate?'

'I told him that I was Sir Aidan Fonthill's mistress and he simply must let me through.'

There was a shriek from Lady Fonthill.

Evidently in Special Constable Elgar's eyes, a mistress outranked both a detective inspector and a detective chief inspector. No doubt he ought to be reprimanded, but his lapse had proved useful to the enquiry. 'I see,' continued Quinn. 'And so, may I ask, *why* did you come here today, Miss Seddon?'

Anna considered a moment before answering quietly, 'I came to see Aidan.'

'Why?'

'He's never seen his son. I thought it was time he did.'

'The baby is Sir Aidan's?'

'Yes.'

Quinn glanced at Lady Fonthill. She did not offer any denial.

'I thought if he saw Tristan, he would relent.'

'Relent?'

'Acknowledge him.'

'Perhaps you hoped that he would leave his wife for you?'

Anna Seddon shook her head. 'I had no such expectation.'

'Then it was money you were after?' This was Leversedge.

'I didn't want anything from him,' insisted Anna. 'Except that he look at his son.'

Leversedge shook his head incredulously, his mouth twisted into a cynical leer.

'You had a right, I think, to expect some material support,' suggested Quinn gently.

Paul Seddon drew himself up self-righteously. 'I am perfectly capable of providing for my sister and my nephew. We neither expected nor needed any help from Sir Aidan.'

Anna Seddon's eyes opened wide in amazement at her brother's declaration. 'But you didn't know he was the father until yesterday. And before I told you who it was, you were all for getting some contribution from . . . whoever. I believe you used the word *bounder*.'

Seddon bowed his head in contrite embarrassment. 'I am sorry. I had no right to say what I said. I was in a foul mood. I didn't mean any of it.' He lifted his face and looked directly into his sister's eyes. 'Of course, I will take care of you. Of you both. You are my family. I will never turn my back on you. No matter what. We have each other. And even if that's all we have, it's enough.'

His words hinted at orphanhood. Quinn saw in Seddon's expression the unhappiness of a misunderstood man. The intensity of his avowal to his sister was inexplicably moving. He felt an unexpected wave of sympathy. And yet, he had to be careful that this did not blind him to the facts. Almost reluctantly, he honed in on the crucial detail. 'I just want to be clear about one thing. You only found out that Sir Aidan was the father of your sister's child yesterday?'

Seddon did not reply, except to turn his head away with a telling sharpness.

'And today he is dead?' Quinn narrowed his eyes as he considered the implications of his own question.

TWENTY-ONE

'Do you wish to see the Great Hall?'

Quinn answered Inspector Pool's question with a quizzical frown.

'It's where the choir was rehearsing before it happened. We're holding everyone there for now.'

'Naturally.'

'I have explained to them the importance of our taking statements while everything is fresh in their minds. Quite a few members of the choir are somewhat on the elderly side and their memories may grow more unreliable with the passage of time. Normally, I would release people once my men have taken statements from them, but when I found out that SCD was to be called in, I thought it better to hold on to as many people as we could in case you wanted to speak to them yourselves.'

Quinn gave a small bow.

'This way, if you will then,' said Pool. 'Unfortunately, some of the people who were here have already slipped away. We are dependent on people's goodwill, you see.'

'Do you know who we are missing?'

'Some members of the orchestra,' replied Pool. 'And those what you might call celebrities. Dame Elsie Tatton, for example. They all scarpered PDQ.'

Pool opened a door to release a rising clamour of discontent. Multiple overlapping conversations competed in a constantly increasing volume of noise. As the detectives entered, an expectant hush descended.

The uneasy calm lasted only a few seconds before an even louder din erupted. Quinn knew only one way to get the room's attention. He reached inside his ulster and removed his Webley service revolver, holding it above his head. A loud collective gasp gave way quickly to an enthralled silence.

'Thank you, ladies and gentlemen.' Quinn returned the revolver to its hidden holster. 'My name is Chief Inspector Quinn.'

There was a murmur of excitement. A thrilling whisper crackled along the seated rows: *Quickfire Quinn!*

Quinn walked slowly down the aisle dividing the auditorium seats, his boot tips clicking on the polished floor. The room was so quiet now you could hear a pin drop – or two hundred necks swivel. 'I have no doubt that you all wish to go home as soon as possible. Believe me, I don't want to detain you any longer than is necessary. I do apologize for the inconvenience, but as I am sure you are aware by now, a man has been murdered here today. The murderer may well be here among us.'

The response to this admittedly melodramatic pronouncement was a second gasp, gratifyingly louder than the first.

'It is possible – more than possible, *likely* – that some of you saw something today that could help us in our investigations, perhaps without even realizing it. That's why we must take statements from you all and why we cannot let you go until we have spoken to everyone. In some cases, you will be interviewed by more than one officer. This is nothing to be concerned about. It simply means we are anxious not to overlook a single detail that may prove crucial to the case. We, the police, see it as our duty to investigate this horrible crime with meticulous and methodical care. I believe we owe that to the deceased, and to all of you who knew him. To that end, I crave your cooperation for a while longer.'

Having reached the front of the hall, Quinn turned and nodded to Inspector Pool, who strode with long, easy steps to join him. 'What was the name of that chap Seddon spoke to about the piano tuner?'

'Cavendish. Charles Cavendish. He's the treasurer of the choir. An accountant by profession.'

'I shall talk to Mr Cavendish first. And isn't there a wife? Ursula, wasn't it?'

'You want them both together?'

He answered Pool's question with a quick nod. 'And could you find me a room. Somewhere without a corpse would be preferable.'

Quinn sat behind the teacher's desk in a classroom on the ground floor. On the wall was a large map of the world with the territories of the British Empire shown in pink.

The itch of chalk dust took him back to his own school days. He had been a hardworking student, bright enough, he supposed, but not especially brilliant. He could remember certain subjects being a struggle, mathematics in particular. But he had been eager to impress his teachers and live up to his father's expectations, and so he had never been willing to give up on a problem. At the root of his approach was the belief that there always was a solution, and that his teachers would not have set the problem if they did not expect him to be able to solve it. It struck him now that it was a surprisingly mature approach for a boy to take.

Was it to please his father, he wondered, that he had in particular applied himself to the scientific subjects? Certainly, for as long as he could remember he had wanted to follow in his father's footsteps and become a doctor. That was not to be, of course. Events had conspired against him, the most significant of them being his father's suicide when he was a medical student.

He looked across the desk at the couple seated in front of him. Ursula and Charles Cavendish held their bodies turned slightly away from one another. If he had not been told that Cavendish was an accountant, he would have guessed it. Ursula, it was clear, had been crying. That was understandable, given the circumstances, and did not necessarily imply any untoward relationship with the dead man. And yet, Quinn couldn't help wondering. Perhaps Anna Seddon wasn't the only female member of the choir whom Fonthill had seduced. If so, he noted, Ursula Cavendish was neither as young nor as pretty as Anna, which suggested that perhaps Fonthill had been rather indiscriminate in his affections.

It seemed odd that Charles Cavendish was making no effort to comfort his wife.

'Do you have children?' Quinn had not expected this would be his first question. But sometimes, as an investigator, it was as important to surprise one's self as it was the people one was interviewing.

'I beg your pardon?' Ursula Cavendish flushed deep red.

'What has that got to do with anything?' demanded her husband.

Quinn gestured around at the classroom. 'I was just thinking, it's a terrible place for a murder to happen. A school. Who can say what the effect on the children will be?'

'Is there any good place for a thing like this to happen?' Ursula's voice was indignant, her expression appalled.

It was a fair point, as Quinn conceded with a nod. 'What was your relationship with the deceased?'

'*Relationship?*' She clearly balked at the word.

Interestingly, it was her husband who answered for her. 'We are members of the choir. Sir Aidan was our choirmaster.'

'That is the only relationship you have with him?'

'I am the treasurer of the choir too. From time to time I have met with Sir Aidan to discuss choir business.'

'What do you mean, choir business? Did Sir Aidan take an interest in the choir's finances?'

'He was naturally interested to know how ticket sales were going.'

'And how were they going?'

'Well. The concert was practically sold out. There were, in addition, a number of donations made.'

'Sir Aidan must have been pleased.'

'Yes. He was most gratified. So far we have raised more or less two hundred pounds for the refugees, though what will happen now, I don't know.'

'More or less?'

'I do not have the exact figures in front of me.'

'That's a lot of money. Where is it kept?'

'The choir has its own bank account. Any cash I keep in a secure box at home until I have the opportunity to pay it into the account.'

'Did Sir Aidan have access to the account?'

Cavendish's eyes widened. 'Why do you ask that?'

The man's barely contained panic convinced Quinn that he was on to something. 'I'm merely trying to establish if the money could have provided a motive for Sir Aidan's murder.'

'No, he was not authorized to access the money. However . . .'

'Yes?'

'He asked me to make over some pre-signed cheques to him.'

'And did you?'

'No. I refused.'

'What did Sir Aidan want the money for?'

'I don't really know. He said something about incurring expenses.'

'Was it a normal request?'

'No. It was most extraordinary.'

'You have never made out blank cheques in his favour before?'

'Certainly not.'

'What expenses was he referring to, do you know?'

Cavendish shook his head blankly. 'I cannot say.'

Quinn squeezed his lips between his thumb and forefinger as he took this in. 'And you, Mrs Cavendish? How would you describe your relationship with Sir Aidan?'

She stared at him for a long moment before shaking her head with vehement force. Whether she was refusing to answer the question or denying that there was any relationship between them, Quinn could not be sure.

'Now, Mr Seddon says that he saw a blind piano tuner – or a man who was disguised as a blind piano tuner – and that he spoke to you about this man. Is that correct?'

'Yes, I do remember Seddon mentioning it. As I said to the other policeman, I thought it was odd because normally I am the one who books the piano tuner and I knew nothing about this. It's not our piano anyhow, so naturally I would not presume to have it tuned without the agreement of the school. The harpsichord is supplied by a rental company who take responsibility for the tuning of the instrument.'

'Are these the kind of expenses that Sir Aidan had in mind?'

'I don't know. Now that you mention it, I do remember Seddon saying that it was Sir Aidan who had organized the piano tuner. Or that's what the man told him.'

'Did you see this man?'

'No,' said Cavendish emphatically.

'How about you, Mrs Cavendish?'

Ursula Cavendish appeared to be half in a daze, staring in deep fascination at Quinn's face.

'My wife is in shock.'

'Yes.'

'She . . . we all . . . Sir Aidan . . . was a huge part of all our lives.'

'Naturally.' Quinn allowed a beat before asking: 'Did you know Sir Aidan was the father of Anna Seddon's baby?'

A strange noise, a kind of animal yelp, escaped from Ursula Cavendish's throat.

'Yes,' said Charles Cavendish simply.

'Did he have affairs with many of the women in the choir?' Quinn was watching Ursula closely. She closed her eyes and shuddered as the colour drained from her face.

'What kind of an investigation are you conducting here?' demanded Cavendish.

'A murder investigation.'

'I do not see why it is necessary to engage in scurrilous, and quite frankly offensive, speculation of this nature.'

'Did he have an affair with you, Mrs Cavendish?'

'How dare you!' cried Cavendish on his wife's behalf.

But Ursula Cavendish ignored her husband's objection and merely shook her head with that same curious half-dazed, half-fascinated automatism.

Perhaps it was unrealistic to expect her to admit to an affair in front of her husband. But Quinn somehow believed her and indeed read more into her response than simple denial.

'What an extraordinary man he must have been,' mused Quinn.

Quinn turned to look at Cavendish. His mouth was pinched tightly as he stared unhappily at a knot on the teak surface of the desk. 'It must have been difficult to bear, to see your wife in love with another man.'

Cavendish gave a barely perceptible shake of the head. 'You don't know anything about it.'

'You went to have it out with him. Lost your temper – and in a fit of jealousy . . .'

Ursula emerged from her daze enough to let out an incredulous, 'Ha!'

Quinn and Cavendish turned to her in astonishment.

'Charles? Jealous?' She produced a sound as dry and cold as falling stones. It took Quinn a moment to process it as laughter.

Charles Cavendish's face flooded pink as he wrinkled his brows. 'The honest truth is I did go to talk to Sir Aidan about Ursula. I told him that if the two of them were in love and wished to be together, I would not stand in their way. My only wish was for Ursula to be happy.'

Quinn felt his eyebrows shoot up at that. 'And what did he say?'

Ursula Cavendish seemed to stiffen in her seat. Quinn noticed her hands ball into tight fists and her jaw clench.

'He practically laughed in my face.'

Quinn winced on Cavendish's behalf.

'The whole thing was very unpleasant.'

'Why did you do it? I mean, it seems a rather odd thing to do, to go to a man and offer him your wife.'

'I don't see why we should not be able to settle these things in a civilized way. We're all adults, after all. I wanted things settled before . . . well, I have made the decision to fight, you see. And I wanted to make sure that Ursula would be all right.'

'You are an extraordinarily selfless man,' said Quinn. 'If we are to believe you.'

'Why shouldn't you believe me?'

Quinn left the question unanswered.

'I'd had enough,' said Cavendish simply. 'I couldn't stop her falling in love with him. No more than I could stop the world turning. And so, what *could* I do? According to the conventional way of doing things, they would have conducted a secret affair, which perhaps I would have discovered, or at least suspected. And I should have been expected to play the part of the wronged husband. Should I have got jealous? Should I have raged and stormed and wept and begged? What a waste of time and energy that would have been. It wore me out just thinking about it. How much more civilized it would be to talk it over like adults.'

'Still, not many men would react the way you did.'

'I'm not so sure. Mankind is evolving, I believe. I have read of certain experimental modes of living in Russia. Socialist communes, where all is held in common, and free love is practised. If a man and a woman wish to engage in sexual intercourse – regardless of whether they are married, either to one another or anyone else – then not merely is that condoned, it is positively encouraged. The frustration of the sexual urge is seen as a great evil.'

'It's all very well in Russia,' said Quinn. 'Between some hypothetical man and woman. But here in Hampstead, with your own wife and Sir Aidan Fonthill? That surely is a different proposition?'

'It shouldn't be. It is, in fact, the ultimate test of one's principles.'

'And after all that, after you had girded yourself up to make this fantastically selfless offer, he laughed in your face.' For Cavendish to have his serious principles ridiculed must have been provoking, to say the least. 'I wonder, did you tell Mrs Cavendish how he reacted?'

'Well, naturally, Ursula was interested to know the outcome of my conversation. Weren't you?'

Ursula did not respond, except to pucker her lips distastefully.

'It's regrettable that these details must come out,' Cavendish continued. 'But in the light of Sir Aidan's death, I feel that I have no choice but to be completely open with you. I had no motive to kill Sir Aidan. You must believe me.'

'What about you, Mrs Cavendish? Sir Aidan rejected you. That must have been humiliating. Especially as your husband was playing the role of matchmaker.'

'Aidan was a gentleman. What else could he say to Charles? Naturally he would deny his true feelings.'

'Why?'

'To avoid a scene, of course. There was nothing Aidan hated more than a scene.'

'He did enough to cause them,' commented Cavendish in a muttered aside.

Ursula Cavendish was warming to her theme. 'He probably thought that Charles was trying to trick him into some kind of confession, and then . . . who knows what might have happened? He might have turned violent.'

Quinn tapped seven times on the desk with the nail of his left middle finger while he tried to gather his thoughts. 'Can you think of anyone who might have wanted Sir Aidan dead?'

The estranged couple exchanged a meaning glance.

Then, at precisely the same moment, they each said a different name.

TWENTY-TWO

'What? Who? You first, Mr Cavendish.'

'Well, I don't like to point the finger. And it may have been nothing . . . but, *Peter Farthing*, that's who I would have said.'

'Peter Farthing?' Quinn made a note of the name.

'Yes.'

'And who is Peter Farthing?'

'A singer.'

'With the choir?'

'No. He is a professional singer whom Sir Aidan brings in from time to time to boost the basses. Also, he was due to sing a solo, or rather a duet with Dame Elsie.'

'Dame Elsie?'

'Dame Elsie Tatton.'

Quinn noted this name too and nodded for Cavendish to go on.

'Farthing had got it into his head that Sir Aidan was trying to cheat him out of his fee.'

'Was he?'

'Well, oh, I . . . there was some confusion over the fee, I will give you that. But Farthing is a prickly character, quick to take offence. And he had also got himself worked up over the programme notes for some reason.'

'What about the programme notes?'

'Oh, it was nothing, just Farthing's vanity. He was not credited for the duet I mentioned, whereas Dame Elsie was. He took great umbrage, as you might imagine he would if you knew him.'

'Do you have a copy of the programme?'

'I don't see that what it has to do with anything, but, yes, here you are.' Cavendish fished in his inner pocket to retrieve a folded sheet.

Quinn scanned the programme. 'Why was his name left off?'

'A simple oversight.'

'It wasn't a deliberate insult?'

'Of course not. In fact, I don't think we knew he would be the one singing with Dame Elsie at the time we had the programme printed. I rather think Farthing had not confirmed. He likes to keep Sir Aidan dangling. Either that or Sir Aidan was holding out the hope that he might get someone better. Or at least more pleasant. Farthing is a good enough musician but he does himself no favours with his attitude. An arrogant boor, he is. At any rate, he was in quite a fury over it. I believe Paul Seddon overheard him threaten to kill Sir Aidan.'

'Strange,' remarked Quinn. 'Seddon did not mention this just now when we spoke to him.'

Cavendish seemed to lose faith in himself. 'Oh, perhaps I was mistaken.'

'You yourself did not hear Farthing threaten Sir Aidan?'

'No, I'm afraid not.'

'So once again, we only have Mr Seddon's word to go on?'

'Possibly Seddon was not being wholly serious. It may have been a joke.'

'A joke? Rather an odd thing to joke about, is it not?'

'Yes, but . . . well, I don't know. You will have to talk to Farthing about it.'

'I shall, don't worry.' Quinn turned the pages of the programme in his hands as he studied its contents thoughtfully. 'One other question, if you don't mind. How did Farthing get hold of a copy of this?'

'I really can't say.'

'They had not been distributed to the performers?'

'No-o-o.'

'And so, someone must have given him a copy?'

'Must they?'

'How else would he have got hold of it?'

'He might have found one lying around.'

'Who organized the printing of the programme?'

'I did.'

'And who had the copies of the finished programmes?'

'I did.'

'And who else had you shared a programme with?'

'I'm not sure. Sir Aidan, certainly.'

'Anyone else?'

'Perhaps . . . I might have . . . I can't remember for sure.'

Quinn fixed Cavendish with a thoughtful gaze as he slowly closed the programme. 'May I keep this?'

Cavendish shrugged his acquiescence.

'Is it possible, Mr Cavendish, that you gave the programme to Farthing yourself?'

Quinn watched Cavendish squirm. 'I . . . well, what an extraordinary . . . Good heavens . . .'

'Perhaps you left it somewhere where you knew he would find it?'

Quinn did not press the treasurer for an answer. Instead he turned his attention to Ursula Cavendish. 'And you, Mrs Cavendish, who was it you thought of?'

'Donald Metcalfe.'

'Ah, well, no. Now, really, I don't think so,' protested Cavendish.

'Ursula, you really can't mean that! Not Donald, surely not. I know he's rather an odd cove but . . . no, no!'

'Who is Donald Metcalfe?' Again, Quinn made a note of the name.

Ursula Cavendish sat with her face pinched into a grim, self-righteous frown.

'He's our accompanist,' explained Cavendish. 'A very talented musician . . . He is something of a queer fish, I grant you.'

'Queer fish? Cold fish, more like.' Ursula shuddered in disgust. 'You should have seen the way he looked at Sir Aidan. You could see it in his eyes. Hatred, pure hatred. Such a horrid man.'

'But he plays like an angel!' objected Cavendish.

'Why did he hate Sir Aidan?' said Quinn.

Ursula let out a long sigh. 'To some extent, Aidan only had himself to blame.'

'Why do you say that?'

'Aidan could be quite . . . cruel. Or it could seem that way if you didn't understand what he was trying to accomplish.'

'What was he trying to accomplish?'

'Perfection. And yet his tools were very far from perfect. He often grew frustrated. And he would take out his frustrations on Metcalfe.'

'He was a bully,' said Cavendish bluntly.

But before he could expand on this, the piercing blast of a police whistle came to them from outside.

TWENTY-THREE

A resolute look passed between Inspector Pool and Sergeant Kennedy, a split second of hesitation before they threw themselves into a yelling rush towards the door.

At the same moment, Quinn sprang up from his seat. 'Inchball, Macadam!'

'Inchball's not here, sir,' Macadam winced as he corrected Quinn.

'I meant Willoughby. *Willoughby* and Macadam. Come with me.'

'What about me?' asked Leversedge.

'You stay here and finish taking their statements.' Quinn nodded towards the Cavendishes. 'And when you have done that, find Peter Farthing and Donald Metcalfe and have them wait here for my return.'

If Leversedge felt any slight in this, he was clever enough not to show it. He puffed himself up with a display of satisfied self-importance as if he would have it no other way.

Quinn followed the shouts out into the quad, where the sudden night was pierced by the crisscrossing beams of electric lanterns.

A huddle of bobbies was bent over something stirring on the ground near the main gate. The bobbing lights seemed to pick out the shape of a man.

'It's Constable Elgar!' came back the shout.

'Good God!' cried Macadam. 'That's a national disaster!'

The distinguished composer – if Macadam was right in his identification – was helped to his feet. His special constable's helmet had been knocked from his head, and his hair was in disarray. He drew himself up to his full height, and the full extent of his dignity. His hands trembled slightly as he took back his helmet, which one of the other bobbies had retrieved for him.

There was no shortage of police to shout questions at the victim.

'Who did this to you? Did you see?'

'I didn't get a good look at him. He came at me out of the dark.'

'Didn't you have your lantern switched on, man?'

'I thought to conserve the electricity.'

'Don't you know you get eight hours of charge out of these things?'

'That's not my experience.'

'Everyone! Switch your lanterns off!' Quinn's abrupt command provoked a chorus of confused grumbling, dispelled with a forceful, 'Now!'

The men stood silhouetted in the lights from the school.

'You should have been able to form some impression of his general size. For example, was he as big as DI Pool here, or as small as DS Kennedy?'

'Steady!' objected Kennedy.

'Somewhere in between,' said Elgar. 'In terms of his height. As for his build, I would say he was thinner than both these gentlemen.'

'A man of medium height and slight build then.' It was not much but it was something.

The police lanterns began to come back on again. The general feeling was that Quinn's experiment had not resulted in any significant information. Quinn himself had to admit that the world is full of scrawny men, middlingly tall.

The mood was one of impatience. 'Never mind that, which way did he go?'

'He went out on to Frognal and then ran away in that direction.' Constable Elgar pointed to the right, north towards Church Row.

Quinn had to hold out an arm to prevent Macadam from giving chase. 'Let Willoughby go.'

His sergeant pushed against the restraint, but Willoughby was already off, with a bunch of uniforms hard on his heels. The clack of their hobnails clattered along the road as they ran headlong into the darkness.

Macadam was not so practised at hiding disappointment as Leversedge. His body twitched unhappily as he looked anywhere but at his governor.

'It is not so long since you sustained a gunshot wound in the pursuit of another suspect.'

'I am fully recovered from that, sir.'

'Let Willoughby go. His legs are younger.'

'You think I am too old for active police work?'

'I thought I'd lost you once. I'm not ready to go through that again.'

Meanwhile the questioning of Constable Elgar continued, with Inspector Pool taking the lead. Whatever stock of sympathy might have been extended to him when the attack had been discovered was obviously spent. The tone was critical, to the point of hostile.

'How did he get past you?'

'I wasn't expecting violence. I had been led to believe they were musicians in there.'

'And one of them may well be a murderer! Did that not occur to you?'

'Naturally.'

'Wasn't the gate locked?'

'No. I was told to unlock it.'

'Yes, unlock it. By all means unlock it. But that doesn't mean you were to let every Tom, Dick and Harry come and go as they pleased. You were supposed to be guarding it, were you not?' This was not so much a question as an expression of the prevailing impatience.

Someone even said, 'Bloody amateurs.'

'What did he strike you with?' asked Quinn.

Elgar hesitated a moment before replying uncertainly, 'I'm not sure. His fist, I believe.'

That he should allow himself to be taken out by a mere fist provoked a chorus of disdainful snorts.

'And did you not think to cosh him with your truncheon?'

'I didn't have time to wield it. It was all over so quickly.'

There was much tutting and shaking of heads at this. Constable Elgar did not appear to be bearing up well under this barrage of criticism. He was breathing heavily through flared nostrils. His agitated moustache quivered at the apparent pursing of his concealed lips. His brows came together in a thunderous expression as he stared fixedly down at his helmet, which he was dusting off with the truncated cuff of a tunic that was too small for him. He looked as if he might explode with either rage or tears at any moment.

Sergeant Macadam did his best to stand up for the beleaguered special. 'Come now, it could have happened to any one of you fellows, you know. Why was Constable Elgar left alone on the gate? That's what I want to know. Given the circumstances, the fact that a violent criminal is at large, I would have thought it wiser to have had two officers positioned at such a strategic point. With firearms. That would have been sufficient to deter a sole assailant.'

'Are you criticizing my orders?' Pool loomed threateningly over Macadam.

Macadam flashed a look of appeal towards Quinn.

Quinn thought it wise to bring the discussion back to the matter in hand. 'Did he say anything, the man who assaulted you?'

'He said, "That's for Land of Hope and Glory."'

'Good heavens!' cried Macadam.

'What do you think he meant by that?' asked Quinn.

'I am used to the hostility of music critics, but it has not hitherto reached such violent proportions.'

'I was right! You are Sir Edward Elgar!'

Macadam's eager exclamation was met with a discouraging wince. 'While I am on duty with the Special Constabulary, I am simply Constable Elgar.'

'Are you aware that one of your compositions was to be performed in the concert the choir was rehearsing?' Quinn took out the programme that Cavendish had given him. '"A Christmas Greeting."'

'My music is performed all the time by any number of musical societies around the world.'

'Forgive me, you live in Hampstead, do you not? Presumably that is why you volunteered here?'

'Yes.'

'And so, this performance, by a local choir, would have come to your attention, would it not?'

'He may have written to me about it.'

'He?'

'That Fonthill fellow. The one who's dead.'

'Sir Aidan wrote to you?'

'People write to me all the time. I can't remember them all.'

'But you do remember that Sir Aidan wrote to you? About the concert?'

'I suppose so. Damned impertinence. As if I should willingly inflict upon myself the torment of hearing my music mangled by that talentless ass.'

'So you knew Sir Aidan?'

'He had tried to make himself known to me by various clumsy subterfuges. Such as the staging of this concert. It was all designed to procure my approval and further his own ambition.'

'I had understood that the concert was to raise money for the relief of Belgian refugees.'

'Is that so?'

'That's what it says on the programme. Have you heard of Dame Elsie Tatton?'

'Indeed I have.'

'In what context?'

'She is one of our finest sopranos.'

'And she was to sing in the concert?'

'Was she?'

'Sir Aidan did not mention her participation in his letter?'

'He might have.'

'Did he also mention that she would be singing a solo in "A Christmas Greeting"?'

'What if he did?'

'Did it not sway you? I mean, Dame Elsie was hardly likely to *mangle* it, was she?'

'Look, if she's prepared to jeopardize her reputation by taking part in this fiasco, then that is up to her. It's got nothing to do with me.'

'What about Émile Boland?'

'What about him?'

'Have you heard of him?'

'Yes.'

'Is *he* any good?'

'He is a great artist.'

'He was taking part too. And performing in "A Christmas Greeting".'

'Yes, yes, I am aware. And so, do you see how transparent this fellow was? How he sought to flatter and manipulate me into attending? That's what it was all about. That's why it was done. Well, let me tell you, I wasn't having it.'

'Do you still have the letter?'

'Alice deals with all that. Though I doubt she's kept it.'

'Alice?'

'My wife.'

'I see. I would be grateful if you could—'

Elgar impatiently cut Quinn off. 'I can't see that it has anything to do with anything.'

'You have been attacked here today, and it is possible the reason you were attacked was not because you were the special constable on duty guarding this gate but because you are Sir Edward Elgar, the composer. You may have been deliberately targeted, in other words. Which leaves open the possibility that there is some connection between the attack on you and the attack on Sir Aidan. Perhaps he was killed because he had included one of your works in the programme?'

Elgar gave a bitter laugh. 'Are you suggesting there is someone who hates my music so much that he would kill to stop it being performed?'

'In truth, I have known men kill for less.' Quinn looked past Elgar through the railings to the road beyond. He could hear the shouts of the police who had given chase, snatches of noise, distant, disembodied. It sounded like the inarticulate night was choking on its frustration.

TWENTY-FOUR

Willoughby had often had dreams in which he was running. Arms and legs pumping nineteen to the dozen, his chest bursting as it pulled ragged breaths out of the void. But for all this effort, he would make no progress. A muscular ache

would creep over his whole body and he would be running on the
spot as if some invisible force was holding him back, a thick rubber
band, for instance, or a strange thickening of the night which it was
impossible to part.

Sometimes his legs would seize up altogether. No matter how
hard he tried, he could not manage to put one foot in front of the
other.

They were horribly unpleasant and frustrating dreams, if only
because Willoughby did not see himself as one who would hold
back in any situation.

What made those dreams *nightmares*, he realized, what gave them
their particular and personal horror was not so much being unable
to escape some monster pursuing him but rather the sensation that
he was being prevented from rushing into the fray.

For, in reality, if there was a suspect to be pursued, as now,
Willoughby would always be first off the blocks, leading the pursuit.
His greatest fear, these dreams told him, was that he might be
thought a coward.

Willoughby did not believe that he was a coward. He would not
claim to be an especially brave man either. That was for others to
judge. He did not act out of bravado. He did what was necessary.
That was all. He was a copper. Sometimes it was necessary to chase
down danger.

If so, he would not hold back.

So here he was, now, running. It was not like those dreams at
all, he told himself. Except that something made him think of them.
Was it the dark? The way the dark created the impression that
he was running without getting anywhere.

Or the fear that when it came to it, he would betray himself, that
his legs would lock as in the dreams, and he would be shown to be
a coward after all.

He came to a divide in the road and slowed his pace, allowing
the shouts of the other police to catch up with him.

He pointed at the lane which went off to the left. 'One of you,
down there. The rest of you come with me.'

A few paces on and they reached another split. Willoughby took
the path off to the right, directing the others to go straight on, telling
them to separate in the same way when they came to the next junction.
He grasped the hopelessness of the pursuit at that moment. Any further
divisions and they would run out of men.

It was all down to luck now whether they caught the attacker or not. Given that the fellow had a start on them, he did not reckon much for their chances. He felt the tension go out of his body. With a mixture of relief and disappointment, he realized it was probably a wild goose chase. But then he was immediately wary again. It's just when you think the danger's gone that you're most vulnerable. He knew that.

And it was important to see the task through. And not simply to go through the motions either.

Who was it who had said to him? 'You have to make your own luck in this game.'

Ah, yes, he remembered. And then immediately wished that he hadn't. His old boss. DCI Coddington.

He would do better not to think of Coddington right now.

Which was worse? he wondered. To be a bent copper or a coward? Neither was good, of course.

The path he had taken brought him to a church which stood at the end of a broad, illuminated residential street with large houses and mansion blocks on either side. The lights of the main road were visible, four hundred yards or so away at the other end of the street.

If the attacker had come this way, would he have made it to the main road by now? Quite possibly. In which case he was beyond Willoughby's reach. But somehow Willoughby's sense was that he would not have gone that way. Although it appeared to be deserted, the street was open and well-lit. He would have felt exposed, conspicuous, when his instinct would have been to hide.

Probably not inside the church itself. He would have felt trapped in there. The building could be surrounded, the entrance blocked off. Willoughby realized he was trying to think like his new governor, Silas Quinn; that is to say, psychologically. Somehow the church presented too obvious a refuge. It seemed to be tempting him to enter, which was why he instinctively rejected it.

A low railing ran around the churchyard, giving Willoughby a clear view in. There were a few well-established trees there, behind which a man might easily hide. Or someone could be crouching down behind one of the gravestones.

Another reason not to go in. He would make himself vulnerable to attack. Was this cowardice? Or intelligence?

Sometimes it was hard to tell the difference.

Opposite the church was a graveyard separated by a lane. This presented a more likely hiding place, Willoughby decided. From here you could watch and wait until you saw your pursuers go inside the church, as they would if they allowed themselves to be drawn by the lure of the obvious, which most men – most policemen especially – would. Then you could make your getaway.

As he walked around the church, Willoughby's senses grew heightened again, his body once more tensed and wary. He strained to hear the subtle signals of another man's presence. A rustle of foliage pulled him up short. His body froze. The sound had come from above, from the branches of a large tree that overhung the churchyard perimeter. He looked up to see the two eyes of a cat watching him, diamond bright in the black night. He could make out something else up in the tree, another small animal that the cat seemed to be stalking. Perhaps fearing that the man would deprive it of its prey, the cat suddenly pounced. It caused the other creature to fall limply down on to Willoughby's upturned face.

He gave an instinctive cry of repulsion and clawed at his face to bat the thing away. Whatever it was, it was damp and loathsome and, yes, dead. It lay at his feet without moving.

He could see it there, shining in the dim glow of the street lighting. He toed it tentatively. It did not respond, except to roll inertly in the direction his boot pushed it.

Willoughby felt a little foolish and somehow strangely embarrassed, as if he were being watched or even tested. Of course, the cat was still in the tree looking down at him, no doubt disgruntled that it had lost its prey to its new enemy. The unpleasant sensation of being watched grew stronger. Willoughby turned his head in the direction of the graveyard and saw a dark human figure looming.

'Oi! You! Police! Hands up where I can see them.'

But the figure did not move. And never was going to move, Willoughby now realized. It was a memorial statue looking across at the church, contemplating eternity.

Willoughby let out a heavy sigh, feeling more foolish than ever. He stooped down and grasped the thing at his feet. It was too light to be a dead animal after all. There was nothing to it, only hair. He turned and held it up to the nearest streetlamp.

He could imagine the ribbing he would get over this. He appeared to have bravely captured a false beard.

Willoughby stood up tall, self-consciously so: that sense of a hidden watcher again.

He turned his head decisively, taking in all the possible routes by which the man he was pursuing could have got away from him.

The lane that he was standing on now ran in one direction back to Frognal. If the suspect had gone that way, it would bring him back towards the uniformed officers who had given chase with Willoughby. There was a chance he would go that way if he wasn't thinking straight. Or perhaps he might think he was being very clever, by doing what no one would expect him to do and doubling back on himself.

In the opposite direction, the lane turned into the street that gave on to the main road. As Willoughby had already calculated, if the man had gone that way, he would be away from him by now, though he might have been seen on his way. He could have picked up a cab, or ducked into a public house, or slunk off through one of Hampstead's many narrow alleyways.

There was a lane running up the side of the graveyard. He did not know the area, so he could not say where that led; perhaps nowhere. A second lane, a little further on, ran parallel to that. There was the chance the two lanes joined up at some point, so if he guessed correctly he might run into the suspect going in the opposite direction. But really, how could he prove that a man he met so far from the school was the same person who had assaulted the special constable? And why should he assume that the first person he encountered was the suspect?

Or he could have gone into the church. He had to admit that was always a possibility.

If you included the graveyard, that made six options and Willoughby was one man on his own. There was no way he could close down every possible escape route available.

He looked down at the hairpiece in his hand. Something settled inside him. Not quite despondency, more like resignation. It was time to cut his losses and take the clue he had found back to his governor. The possibility that it might be an important piece of evidence lightened his mood.

But first, maybe he ought to check out the church, after all. Sometimes it's a mistake to overlook the obvious.

He pocketed the false beard and drew out his service revolver. If the fugitive was in there and felt himself trapped, there was no saying what he might do to evade capture.

TWENTY-FIVE

Special Constable Elgar was led inside and sat down, while a cup of sweet tea was procured for him. He was given the once-over by the medical examiner, a certain Dr Emsley, who had by now arrived to confirm what they all knew: that Sir Aidan Fonthill was dead.

Long-limbed and lean, Dr Emsley was a brisk, energetic individual of about fifty, whose indelible cheerfulness was oddly inappropriate to the circumstances. He examined Elgar through a pair of tortoise-shell-rimmed half-moon glasses. He held up various fingers for the special constable to count and track before happily declaring his patient unharmed in all but dignity. Indeed, he seemed inclined to make light of the violence done to the eminent composer, as if it were a pleasant diversion from the main business of the day.

'Where did he hit you? I can find no bruise?'

'Hit me? I . . . well, suffice it to say, he knocked me about a bit.'

'He did, did he? What an absolute bounder.' And yet the doctor's sincerity could not be taken entirely at face value. 'It must have been more than just a bit to knock you off your feet like that. A big chap like you.'

Macadam was vocal in Elgar's defence. 'No doubt it was the shock of it that caused Sir Edward to lose his footing.'

'It's not so shocking as all that, is it, a policeman getting punched?'

'Well, it damned well ought to be,' was all Macadam could say to that.

The doctor bent down to examine Elgar's ears with his otoscope. 'Have you suffered on any other occasion from loss of balance or vertigo?'

'Yes.'

'Tinnitus?'

'Yes. I have been diagnosed with Ménière's disease. At times, it is intolerable. It makes it impossible to work.'

'Ah, Ménière's disease. That explains it. Why didn't you say?'

'It didn't come up.'

'I'm awfully sorry, old chap, but do you really think you can be a policeman with this condition?'

Elgar looked suddenly dejected. 'But if I don't do this . . .'

'What?'

'I'll have to . . .' Elgar's next word came out as a barely audible groan: 'Compose!' His eyes glazed over. His whole body slumped. He made a pitiable sight.

Dr Emsley drew Macadam and Quinn to one side, to confide his opinion out of Elgar's earshot. 'If you ask me, there's no evidence he was physically assaulted.'

'Are you doubting the word of a special constable and a gentleman?' Macadam objected.

'His pride has been wounded certainly. And so perhaps he exaggerated the severity of the incident in order to divert any censure that might be directed at him?'

'Censure?'

'For allowing this person to get past him.'

'Ah, so you do not doubt that there was *someone*?'

The doctor shrugged with infuriating ambivalence.

As they made their way back to the classroom, Macadam evidently still brooding over what the doctor had said, they were intercepted by Inspector Pool coming out of the Great Hall. 'People are getting restless. I'm not sure how much longer we can hold them. And once you lose the public's cooperation it becomes an uphill fight.'

Quinn nodded in agreement. 'Have your men finished taking statements from everyone?'

'Yes. We've got them all now. And contact addresses in case you want to follow up on anything.'

'Anything jump out?'

Pool blew out his cheeks. 'Well, it seems that there is no shortage of people willing to point the finger at someone else. And if you believe them all, no shortage of people with a grievance against Sir Aidan. Whether any of them amount to a strong enough motive for murder, I do not know.'

'For example?'

Pool consulted his notebook. 'He was heard to make disparaging remarks about the Russian dancer . . .' Pool made some indistinct nasal sounds which Quinn guessed was his attempt at the dancer's name. 'And also, apparently, he was observed looking at the female dancer in a rather lascivious way. You know what these foreigners are like. Jealous, ain't they.'

'What do the Russians have to say about it?'

'We haven't been able to talk to them. They were amongst the ones that had gone before we got here. Apparently, their part in the rehearsal was over. Which is convenient, shall we say.'

Quinn nodded automatically as his thoughts settled into place. 'If it was the Russian who killed Sir Aidan, for the reasons you have mentioned, then we have to accept that the attack on Constable Elgar is unconnected to the murder. Elgar made no mention of his attacker having a Russian accent, which he surely would have noticed.'

Pool frowned as he took in what Quinn was suggesting.

'Conversely,' continued Quinn, 'if Elgar's attacker was the murderer, then that rules out the Russian gentleman.'

Pool shook his head in disappointment. 'Bloody Elgar,' he said, as if he held the special constable responsible for the Russian's apparent escape from justice.

'What do you make of Seddon's story?' wondered Quinn. 'About this blind, bearded fellow he saw?'

'Fishy.'

'It would not be the first time a murderer has invented a mysterious stranger whom only he has seen, and of whom there is no trace.'

'My thoughts exactly.'

'Although it is not quite true we found no trace. We found a single red hair, don't forget.' Quinn felt suddenly weary. He pinched the bridge of his nose. 'There are two more men I wish to interview. I believe Inspector Leversedge should have them ready for me. Once I have taken their statements, I think we may be in a position to let everyone go.'

'What about Seddon?'

'Yes, Seddon too. I don't think we have enough yet to hold him. Nor do I think we will get anything more out of him today.'

'Shall we not at least take his prints? In case anything shows up on the weapon.'

'No. I don't want to make him jumpy. If anything, I would rather have him with his guard down. When it comes to it, you may thank him for his help and assure him that we are doing everything we can to find his mysterious blind piano tuner.' Quinn nodded to the door of the classroom. 'But first, if you could bear with me a little longer . . .'

*   *   *

Quinn knew immediately which of the men waiting was Farthing and which was Metcalfe.

Both were seated behind pupils' desks, but at opposite corners of the classroom. One of them had clearly sought to distance himself from the other.

Only one of the men turned round at Quinn's entrance – the one seated towards the back of the classroom, his face screwed up into an indignant scowl.

'About time! I can't afford to sit around here all day, you know. I've already given a statement. You have no right to keep me any longer.' Despite the petulance of what he was saying, his voice had a deep, resonant musicality to it. It was even pleasant to listen to, and part of Quinn wanted the man to carry on berating him.

This was surely Farthing, the truculent singer.

The other man, sitting in the front row of desks, was absorbed in the study of several sheets of musical manuscript. He did not look up, not even at the other's outburst. Quinn walked to the front to get a better look at him.

Eventually, Metcalfe – for it was surely him – glanced up blandly.

Farthing's rage was understandable. Today had been an emotion-ally charged day and he was clearly a man in whom the negative emotions predominated, and rage most of all. But possibly with him even love would manifest itself as rage. It did not mean, necessarily, that he was Sir Aidan's killer. Neither did it exonerate him.

Metcalfe's calm, on the other hand, was interesting – and more difficult to interpret.

Instinctively, Quinn felt that he would get more out of Farthing, and so he was inclined to start with him. The man's temper would work against him and he would reveal more than he meant to.

And there might be something to be gained from having Metcalfe stew in his juices a little longer. Perhaps he could be goaded out of his strange, impassive calm. Although Quinn doubted it.

And so, Quinn had Macadam take Metcalfe outside while he and Leversedge went to work on Farthing. Quinn asked the ques-tions; Leversedge loomed menacingly.

'Do you know anyone who might have wanted to kill Sir Aidan?'

'Why are you asking me?' Farthing bristled belligerently.

'We're asking everyone.'

Farthing was somewhat mollified. 'I really have no idea. But I wouldn't be surprised if there were some.'

'What do you mean?'

'Well, if you go around treating people like he did, you're bound to make a few enemies.'

'Would you count yourself as one of his enemies?'

'I didn't kill him, if that's what you're getting at.'

'Did you not threaten to kill him?'

'No, I did not.'

'You were heard making threatening remarks.'

'Who was it? Seddon? He's a bloody liar.'

'You had quarrelled with Sir Aidan? You don't deny that?'

'If I killed everyone I had a quarrel with . . .' Farthing left the thought unfinished, perhaps sensing that it was not helping his cause.

'What was this quarrel over?'

'The usual. Money.'

'You believed that Sir Aidan owed you money?'

'*Believed?*' shouted Farthing indignantly. 'There's no *believed* about it! I am a professional singer. I was contracted to perform in this damned concert of his. Therefore, I should have been paid for both rehearsal time and the performance itself.'

'Do you have the contract?'

'There was no *written* contract.' Farthing writhed with fury in his seat. 'He made sure of that. It was a verbal agreement. A *gentleman's* agreement. But that bastard was no gentleman.'

'My understanding was that it was to be a charitable concert. Doesn't that mean that everyone gave their time for free, in order to raise funds for the cause?'

'I'm not a bloody charity!'

'And so, you went to confront Sir Aidan about the money. There was an argument. You lost your temper. Saw red. We all know how it is. You took whatever was to hand. And lashed out. A freakish accident. You didn't mean to kill him. Just wanted to make him listen.'

Farthing stared at Quinn in disbelief. 'You don't seriously think I killed him?'

'You weren't thinking. It was manslaughter, not murder. Tell us what happened and I'll make sure you are charged with the lesser crime.'

'This is insane! You're insane.' Farthing looked desperately from Quinn to Leversedge. 'He's insane!'

Leversedge remained tactfully silent.

'I didn't do it!' insisted Farthing. 'Why would I? With Sir Aidan dead, the concert probably won't go ahead at all now, which means my chances of getting paid are next to zero. Much as I hated the man, I had nothing to gain from his death.'

It was a valid point, but only if Farthing had been in control of his actions. 'Rage takes over you, though, doesn't it? It makes you do things that are not in your own best interest.'

'No, no, no! It's not like that at all. Look, I admit I have a temper on me. I like to blow off steam. But that's the end of it. The ones you have to watch out for are the ones like that fellow Metcalfe. It's all hidden with him. All bottled up and beneath the surface. He had much more reason to hate Fonthill than me. But he never showed it. He's just the type to suddenly lose control and blow up.'

'Why do you say Metcalfe had reason to hate Sir Aidan?'

Farthing more or less repeated the allegations that Ursula Cavendish had raised, although she had been at pains to play down Fonthill's role as a bully. Farthing showed no such qualms.

Farthing's denials had the ring of truth to them. The man's temperament was such that his emotions were all out in the open. Whatever he felt, he expressed. To use the common phrase, he seemed to be a classic case of bark louder than bite.

Of course, one could never be sure. But Quinn would have put money on it that Farthing was not Sir Aidan's killer.

Metcalfe, though – Metcalfe was a different kettle of fish.

Quinn started the interrogation of Metcalfe with the same question. 'Do you know anyone who might have wanted to kill Sir Aidan?'

'Yes.'

'Who?'

'Me. I might have wanted to kill him.'

Quinn hadn't expected that. At least not so soon. 'And did you? Kill him.'

'No.'

'Of course, if you had killed him, the chances are that you would deny it.'

Metcalfe thought about this for some time. 'But that would mean lying to you.' It seemed that this was an inconceivable prospect.

'In my experience, murderers often do lie to policemen.'

'I don't lie.'

'Never?'

'Never.'

'That would make you a very unusual person.'

Metcalfe had nothing to say to this.

'Did you think about it? About killing him?'

'Yes.'

'Often?'

'Yes. Often. If I thought about killing him, I found that I no longer wanted to kill him.'

'When you thought about killing him, how did you imagine doing it?'

'Different ways. For example, I would think about stabbing him with a knife. Here.' Metcalfe rubbed himself to indicate his kidneys. 'Or I would think about cutting his head off with a sword.'

'A sword?'

'Yes.'

'Do you have a sword?'

'No.'

'Any other ways?'

'I would think about bringing a hammer down on his head. I would picture the crown of his head and imagine smashing down on it with a hammer.'

'Do you have a hammer?'

'Yes. I do have a hammer.'

'Any other ways?'

'I have thought about cutting him in half on a circular saw. The kind that is used to make planks of timber out of tree trunks.'

'Is that it?'

'I have thought about shooting him in the heart with a gun.'

'Do you have a gun?'

'No. I do not have a gun.'

'Is *that* it?'

'I have thought about pushing him in front of a bus.'

'Any other ways?'

'No.'

'How about a tuning fork? Do you have a tuning fork?'

'Yes. I do have a tuning fork.'

'Have you ever thought about killing him with a tuning fork?'

'How could I kill him with a tuning fork?'

Quinn let the question go. 'I hear that he was . . . not very nice to you? That he could be unkind.'

Metcalfe shrugged. 'Yes.'

'Was that why you wanted to kill him?'

Metcalfe looked at Quinn without betraying any emotion. When he gave his answer, his voice was level and calm. 'Yes.'

'But you didn't do it?'

'No. I didn't do it.'

'Why did you stay with the choir if Sir Aidan was so horrid to you?'

'I have played for the Hampstead Voices for eleven years, four months and two weeks. I did not want to change to a different choir.'

'A different choir would have had a different choirmaster,' suggested Quinn gently.

'Yes. That too.' Paradoxically, it seemed that Metcalfe was seeing this as a reason to stay, rather than to leave.

'One who did not torment you.'

Metcalfe's eyes widened, as if this possibility had never occurred to him before now. 'Sticks and stones may break my bones but names will never hurt me.'

'Can you honestly say that he did not hurt you?'

'I can honestly say he did not hurt me.'

'Other than yourself, can you think of anyone else who might have wanted to kill Sir Aidan?'

'Roderick Masters.'

'Who is Roderick Masters? Is he in the choir?'

'No. He is not in the choir. He is a composer. We were at the Royal College of Music together. He sent Sir Aidan a piece he had written. He wanted it to be included in the concert. But Sir Aidan did not like it. Sir Aidan thought it was rubbish. But it was not rubbish. Sir Aidan was wrong about that.'

'You saw it?'

'Yes. I saw it. And I played it. Masters had achieved some quite interesting effects.'

'And so, you think Roderick Masters killed him? Because Sir Aidan rejected his composition.'

'Roderick Masters was very angry. He hated Sir Aidan. He hated Sir Aidan almost as much as he hated Elgar.'

'Roderick Masters hated Elgar?'

'Yes.'

'Is Roderick Masters here now?'

'No. Roderick Masters is not here now.'

'What do you mean? Was he here earlier?'

'Yes. Roderick Masters was here earlier.'

'You saw him?'

'Yes.'

'And spoke to him?'

'Yes, I did. But only briefly. Paul Seddon interrupted our discussion and Roderick Masters ran away.'

'When was this?'

'In the lunch break. Shortly before the screaming started.'

'And that was the last you saw of this Masters chap?'

'Yes.'

'How do you know he hated Elgar?'

'Because he told me.'

'Did you know that Elgar is here at the school? He is a volunteer special constable. Someone attacked him, apparently. At least, someone shouted at him rather viciously.'

'What did they shout?'

'"That's for Land of Hope and Glory".'

'That sounds like Roderick Masters.'

'Do you know where we might find Roderick Masters?'

Metcalfe frowned as he considered the question. 'No,' he answered decisively.

Although the man was evidently no imbecile, there was clearly something odd about the way he processed information and communicated. Quinn decided to spell it out in the simplest terms. 'You've never been to his house? He didn't tell you where he lives?'

Again, Metcalfe thought carefully before answering. 'No.'

Quinn had the distinct impression that Metcalfe knew more than he was saying. There was something disconcerting about the steadiness of his gaze.

'Do you think Roderick Masters killed Sir Aidan?' Metcalfe asked bluntly.

But if Quinn had an opinion on that question, he was not prepared to divulge it yet, at least not to Donald Metcalfe.

TWENTY-SIX

Willoughby held the gun in his right hand, arm extended in front of him, steadied at the wrist by the grip of his other hand.

He moved slowly through the churchyard, pivoting left and right as he went, his senses alert for the slightest disturbance.

He saw now that there was a light on inside the church, a faint glow deep within, suggesting a candlelit vigil rather than a service.

Perhaps the vicar was inside on church business – Willoughby couldn't imagine what, but who else could it be? Members of the congregation decorating the church for Christmas perhaps? But wouldn't that be more easily done in the daylight?

He had heard that churches were traditionally kept open at all times, offering asylum to all. Despite his relative youth, Willoughby had had ample experience of the criminal side of human nature. He couldn't help thinking that this was asking for trouble.

If there was someone in there, it didn't necessarily follow it was the man he was looking for. The way he saw it, it still didn't make sense that the murderer would take refuge in a church. If you had just taken another life, surely the last place you would want to be was inside the house of God, with Jesus looking down at you from the cross? Unless you were a religious kind of person, that is. In which case, your conscience would no doubt be giving you a hard time. And you might have come to the church to pray for the courage to give yourself up.

Willoughby wondered therefore whether he really ought to be going into a church with his weapon drawn.

But if it was his man in there, even if he was a religious-minded killer, he was still a killer. And by the looks of it a killer who had also attacked coppers. A desperate man cornered, in other words. The fact that he was in a church was irrelevant. Except that if there was a firefight on holy ground, whatever the outcome, the papers would have a field day with it.

What would the guv'nor do?

Willoughby didn't need to think too hard over the answer. They didn't call him Quickfire Quinn for nothing.

Keeping his righthand grip tight, Willoughby drew the revolver close to his cheek, while reaching out towards the door with his left. Best to get in quick, he reckoned, giving whoever was in there as little time as possible to ready themselves or hide.

He clicked the latch, holding the gun out in front of him again as he slipped inside in the lee of the door. He found himself inside a small, dark porch and suppressed a glimmering claustrophobia. What if someone had been waiting for him in there with a cosh, or even worse, a gun of their own? He would be a dead man by now.

His heart was pounding as the small space filled with his panic. *Pull yourself together! You're not dead, are you? Bloody idiot.*

After a moment, he mentally added, *Pardon my French.* To enter a church with a gun drawn was one thing, but to start swearing? May God forgive him! Even if it was just inside his own head.

He waited for a moment for his eyes to adjust to the peculiar density of darkness in the vestibule, then turned slowly through 360 degrees, holding the gun out in front of him.

He sensed more than saw a door on each side, as well as the inner door leading to the church and the open door he had come through.

So if the man he was pursuing had come in here, there were three possible doors he could have gone through. If Willoughby chose the wrong one, he would leave the way open for the suspect to get away – or even worse, to take a shot at him, if the fellow had a gun of his own, that is.

He had to do something. But what?

The door facing him would be the first door the suspect would see, and therefore the most likely one for him to take. If he had come in here at all, it was a sign that he wasn't thinking straight. He was walking into a box that could be easily sealed by police. Panic would have been driving him. Panic and instinct.

That gave Willoughby the rational justification he needed.

He groped with his free hand and found the inner door to the church.

His mind continued to present him with justifications for his action: if he was right and the killer was a religious type, then it was certain that he would have gone into the nave. The whole point of coming here would have been to commune with God.

If that idea of the criminal was correct, then Willoughby's best hope of getting out of here without either shooting or being shot was to appeal to the man's conscience. He slipped his gun back into its holster.

Sorry, guv!

His best bet was to keep things calm.

The door creaked as he eased it open. He waited a moment, allowing the affronted hush of the church to settle.

'Is there anybody there?' His tremulous voice reverberated, as the natural sounding box of the church amplified his nervousness as well as his words.

Still as it was, quiet as it was, Willoughby's instinct was that there was someone there, someone who wanted to keep to the shadows. Not a vicar quietly praying to his God for inspiration for tomorrow's sermon. Or a parishioner hanging festive bunting.

He moved forward one step into the gloom. The grinding crunch of his boot against the stone floor echoed ominously. The unseen light source was at the front of the church, low down, casting a dim glow upwards. There was no smell of burning wax, so he guessed that it was a low-wattage electric lamp.

He had to admit there were too many hiding places in the church for his liking and it made him nervous. Jumpy. Bound to.

First there were the two rows of columns that ran the length of the nave. A man might easily conceal himself behind any one of those, on either side. Or he might be lying down beneath a pew, or crouching in the gallery, or lurking behind the altar screen. Even the pulpit.

Willoughby might stalk down the aisle like a cat in the long grass, but he couldn't help feeling like he was the one being hunted.

A strange excitement throbbed in his throat. 'I was just passing and I saw a light on.' The words came out in a hoarse whisper, as if he did not want to disturb the peace any more than he already had. 'I confess I haven't been in a church for a long time. My folks never did go in for all that God-bothering business so much. But you get to thinking, don't you? Especially what with Christmas just around the corner and all that. And with this war on. Sometimes I wish there was someone I could talk to, you know, like God. We had a teacher at our school, Mr Bamforth. RI master, he was. I remember he once said, "You can always talk to God. No matter how bad things get. God will always listen." That's what he said anyway. So, like I say, I was passing and I saw the light on, and I thought, well . . . I wonder if God will listen now. Is that why you came here? Got something you want to get off your chest? We all do things we regret, you know. You think you're in a tight corner. Everything looks hopeless. But then you talk it over and you realize it's not so bad as all that.'

'Who are you?' The voice came from above. It was deep and resonant and commanding. If not the actual voice of God, then certainly the voice of a toff. Willoughby looked up and scanned along the gallery. He could just about make out a dim shape lurking in the shadows at one end, near to the exit, as if he had been about to make his escape but had been detained by Willoughby's little speech.

Although he was nervous about revealing himself as a policeman, Willoughby intuitively felt the need to be honest from the outset. It was the only way to build trust, and if it came out in the future it could damage whatever relationship he might have established with the fellow, to say nothing of its effect on any legal case. 'My name is Willoughby. Detective Constable Willoughby, of the Special Crimes Department, Scotland Yard.'

There was a heavy groan from the gallery. Then a flash and the thunderous crack of a gun discharging.

The smell of his own blood was the last thing Willoughby knew.

TWENTY-SEVEN

The crowd in the Great Hall was growing increasingly restive, craving the comfort of their own homes more than the once reassuring proximity of bobbies, whom they were now growing to resent. The decision was made to let people go. The assembly broke up in chaos, with some confusion over whether a statement had been taken from everyone there. But once the tap had been opened and the flow begun, it was impossible to check it.

The detectives would have to hope that nothing significant had been missed, although Quinn knew that in a criminal investigation hope was not a factor to be relied on.

By an unfortunate coincidence, the victim's body was carried out on a stretcher at the same time as the rush to exit was underway. Dr Emsley and the ambulance men had covered the body in a blanket, or had done their best to. Several hours had now elapsed since the murder and rigor mortis had begun to set in. And so the tented shape presented by the stiffening body beneath the blanket – with forearms extended to play the piano and legs bent in the seated position – created a rather gruesome and upsetting effect, especially as it had been necessary to leave one arm protruding from the side of the blanket. If this admittedly imperfect measure had not been taken, the narrowness of the blanket would have created a gap through which the face of the deceased would have been visible.

Despite these considerations, the sight inspired a degree of horror in those who saw it. And in none more so than Donald Metcalfe, who stood frozen to the spot, his mouth gaping as he struggled to find words for the emotions stirred by the grotesque spectacle. In the end, he had to be satisfied with, 'No, no . . . it's not right.' Which was perhaps as fair a reaction to what he was seeing as any.

Dr Emsley, his demeanour rather more solemn than before, walked alongside the stretcher with his head bowed. Quinn jogged across the quad to intercept him.

'Doctor, anything you can tell me that might help my investigations?'

Emsley raised his eyebrows as if he were surprised by the question, although perhaps it was simply the slight air of desperation in Quinn's voice that he had not expected. 'You'll have my report on Monday.' Emsley gave a wide, wincing smile. 'But in the meantime, you may be interested to know this detail.'

Quinn nodded for the doctor to go on.

'I removed the fatal implement, which I naturally surrendered to one of your policemen.'

'The tuning fork?'

'It appeared to be a tuning fork, yes. However, the metal handle had been ground to a long, lethal point, reminiscent of the blade of a stiletto.'

It was Quinn's turn to raise his eyebrows.

The doctor bowed and went on his way, leaving Quinn to take in the implications of this new information.

Just then, one by one, the uniforms who had set out with Willoughby in pursuit of Special Constable Elgar's attacker began to return, each shaking their heads glumly to signal their failure.

Quinn counted them in and demanded, 'Where's DC Willoughby?' of the last man.

The copper blew out his cheeks and shrugged. 'We all split up.'

'Which way did *he* go?'

'Turned off down Church Row.'

'Did you not think to go look for him when the rest of you had drawn a blank?'

Another shrug. 'I thought he must have come back here.'

The fact that Willoughby had not returned yet could mean one of two things. He had had sight of Elgar's attacker and was still chasing him down. The second possibility was not something Quinn wished to consider. 'Macadam!'

'Sir!' The steely tension was audible in his sergeant's reply, hissed through gritted teeth.

'Leversedge!' All his doubts about the DI were put aside. He needed his men about him.

'I'm here!'

Quinn pointed at the shrugging policeman. 'Show us.'

To Pool: 'I need some men, as many as you can spare. With torches.'

Quinn drew out his revolver. Somehow there was the feeling that this was what everyone had been waiting for.

The darkness ran at them as much as they ran into it.

The pounding boots of the racing policemen, the half-panicked cries, male-scented aggression wafting on the night breeze, the bobbing beams of light – the night seemed to relish it all, as if it had an infinite appetite for danger and fear. The hoot of an owl perched in one of the spectral trees had a gleeful note to it. It was calling them on to something fateful.

The other two officers of the SCD had taken their cue from their governor: they had their guns drawn as they advanced. The Hampstead bobbies held truncheons in their right hands, torches in their left. The Hampstead CID had not thought to issue themselves revolvers, and so they brandished the small cudgels favoured by detectives.

Whether they were closing in on a helmet tipper or a murderer, they weren't prepared to take any chances.

They slowed to a trot at the entrance to St John-at-Hampstead. Quinn saw the door to the church was open, a dim rectangle of light indicating that the inner door was open too.

A terse nod was the only command he needed to give. Leversedge took charge of directing the details of the operation, communicating by means of precisely executed arm gestures. Macadam understood himself charged with taking a contingent off to sweep through the churchyard to secure the rear. They duckwalked noiselessly between the tilting gravestones, holding to an unspoken formation as if the knowledge of such manoeuvres was something they held in the marrow of their bones.

Leversedge led a second contingent in a shallow arc behind them, circling round to seal off the front and sides of the building.

Quinn alone walked upright, straight towards the open door.

Quinn alone picked up the scent of death in the cold, sanctified air.

Quinn alone found his constable.

The boy – Willoughby seemed especially boyish now – was lying face up in the aisle, eyes open in wonder, an unvoiced question on his lips. His bowler lay upturned beside him, hat doffed for death.

For there was no doubt that he was dead. No room for hope in that neat red circle in the centre of his forehead. It seemed incredible, outrageous, that such a small wound could undo a life. You could clean that spot with cotton wool and iodine, surely, and set him right on his feet again.

But the darkness that pooled around him, claiming him for its own, made savage mockery of that illusion.

TWENTY-EIGHT

It started in his hands. The cold.

The shivering cold.

The numb, shivering cold.

He couldn't feel his hands.

The Webley service revolver shivered from his grip and clattered to the floor, like an oath, a blasphemy, a desecration.

Then it spread. The numb, shivering cold spread through his bones, through his veins, through his nerves. He was nothing now but the numb, shivering cold.

And the cause of the numbness, the source of the cold was nothing but the realization that this was his fault.

He had sent this boy to his death.

If he had allowed Macadam to go, as he had wanted to, would Macadam be dead now, or would Macadam's experience have saved him?

'*I thought I'd lost you once. I'm not ready to go through that again,*' he'd said. And he had sent Willoughby instead. He had sacrificed Willoughby.

Willoughby's blood was on his hands. His cold, shivering hands. He stooped to retrieve his gun. He had to pull himself together – he owed it to Willoughby to pull himself together. And he couldn't do that without a gun in his hand.

'Here, in here.' His voice cracked.

The blood pounding in his ear beat a jarring counterpoint to the thud of approaching boots.

The world was out of step with itself. And nothing would ever be in step with anything again.

He couldn't make sense of it. He couldn't make sense of anything.

He had been so sure that the murderer was long gone, that the person who had knocked SC Elgar's helmet from his head was not the killer. That the two events were, in short, unconnected, except by proximity in time and place.

The thudding boots were slowed and stilled and silenced by the scene before them. The blood continued to pound in his ear.

'Good God.' It was Leversedge at his shoulder.

Perhaps it was simply shock that gave those two words their edge. Or was there something sharper in his tone? Something recriminatory?

Quinn raised his gun and made a sweeping scan of the church, as if he was casting about for something – or someone – to take a pot shot at.

'Guv? What shall we do?'

Quinn glanced distractedly towards Leversedge, a frown of irritation in place.

He doubted very much that the killer was still there, but that was what he had thought before, at the school. He had been wrong then and if he was wrong again, it would mean they were all sitting targets for whoever had killed Willoughby. And so, by rights, he should order them all to take cover.

Instead, Quinn stood with his arms outstretched, the revolver now hanging limply in his right hand.

He closed his eyes and waited, keeping his arms horizontal, like some kind of Christ inviting sacrifice.

Genuinely, in that moment, he wished that he had been the one shot and not Willoughby. And if he had believed in prayer, the prayer he would have offered was that God take him instead.

He heard Leversedge take charge – decisive words, clear instructions, a man dispatched to fetch the ME from the school, others dispersed about the church.

Then the heavy footsteps and the warning shouts of police about their duty, stomping up the stairs to the galleries, weaving between the pews, closing down the spaces of the church to squeeze out the presence of any gunman, should there be one there still.

And you had to let them know you were there, and you had to let them know who you were. *'Police!'* shouted at the top of your lungs, inviting them to take potshots at you, as Willoughby no doubt had, because if you didn't, heaven help you. The law obliged you to give them the opportunity to surrender, which meant the advantage was always with the criminals. Some would say that Quinn, at certain points in his career, had ridden roughshod over such legal niceties. That was his reputation, certainly. But it was one that he disputed. Decisions made in the heat of the moment. Decisions that could mean the difference between life and death. His life, the other man's death.

But the other man was supposed to be the villain, not one of his own.

He should have warned the boy. He should have given him fatherly words of advice. *Whatever you do, don't put yourself at risk. Don't go into an enclosed space where a gunman might be waiting. If you think you have him cornered, wait for support. Use your whistle if necessary. Better to run the risk he gets away than to put your own life in danger. And whatever you do, don't do this. Don't go and get yourself killed.*

He wanted so much to have said all this that he almost believed that he did.

'All clear, guv.' Leversedge's voice seemed to come to him through some intervening medium, as if the church had filled with a viscous jelly while his eyes were closed.

Quinn's arms came down slowly, a bird folding its wings. He felt the weight of the revolver like a magnet's pull.

'We found this upstairs.' There was something hopeful in Leversedge's voice that encouraged Quinn to open his eyes at last and turn towards it.

Leversedge was holding out a brown and somewhat age-worn leather satchel in one gloved hand and a white stick in the other.

'Looks like our *blind man* was here.' His emphasis underlined the scepticism they all felt about the piano tuner's apparent handicap. 'The bag's empty, by the way. In case you were wondering.'

'It was just a prop,' said Quinn, unsurprised. 'Part of the disguise. It might have held the weapon, but that's all.'

Leversedge nodded and lowered the bag.

It was a valuable find. Quinn knew that he ought to give Leversedge credit. But he found it curiously difficult to do so. Instead, his next observation came out almost as an objection: 'Constable Elgar said nothing about his assailant having a white stick. Or a bag.'

'It was dark. He didn't get a good look at the man.'

'Even so, he would have noticed a white stick. No, this is not the man who knocked Elgar's helmet off.' Quinn looked down at the dead detective. The wonder that he had discerned in his eyes before had settled into a look of mild surprise. 'Willoughby came looking for a prankster and found a murderer.'

Leversedge nodded and lowered the bag. 'Well, one thing we can say, it seems even less likely now that the murderer was one of those we had in the Great Hall. Whoever it was must have been hiding here already when poor old Willoughby stumbled in.' He looked down at Willoughby's body in silence for some time. 'Do you want me to tell his folks?' Leversedge's voice was strained. This was clearly one responsibility that he would not object to being relieved of.

Quinn holstered his gun and fixed Leversedge with a long stare. 'No. I'll do it.'

He filled his lungs with air and turned his back on the altar.

FOURTH MOVEMENT

TWENTY-NINE

He had Macadam drive him.

They were silent in the car. There was nothing to be said. Nothing that could be altered by words.

Macadam was focused on the shifting pool of road picked out by the beams of the car's headlights. It felt like something unspooling, the flickering image of a strangely monotonous moving picture show.

Quinn saw the tension in Macadam's shoulders, could sense his jaw clench and grind. He could take a guess at the other man's thoughts. It would be something to do with the arguments they had had over who should drive. He had finally got his way, he would ruefully, bitterly be thinking. And it would afford him no satisfaction.

Quinn knew his sergeant well enough to bet that he would forego driving ever again if it would bring his fallen comrade back. He could imagine Macadam growing to hate his once-beloved Model T, because each time he drove it would be a reminder that Willoughby was dead instead of him.

They had called in at the Yard on the way, to get the details of Willoughby's next of kin from his employment file. The file contained a copy of a letter of commendation from Willoughby's previous commanding officer. The words were warm. They spoke of the young man's courage and intelligence, of the invaluable contribution he made to the team, and the bright future he no doubt had ahead of him.

They might have provided some comfort to Willoughby's parents, if they had not been written by DCI Coddington.

Quinn had dropped the letter as if it were contaminated. It lay in the folder, a thin, tawdry thing, devalued and miserable, all the sadder because it must once have been a source of pride. Quinn closed the file on it.

He would find his own words to say to Mr and Mrs Willoughby.

Quinn felt the car's vibrations in his joints. The engine chugged and rattled unfeelingly, as if they were on an unremarkable journey into a perfectly ordinary darkness. They were going, in fact, to Deptford. But place names had lost their meaning now. There was just this part of the universal darkness – and *this* part, and *this* part – each an indistinguishable atom of chaos.

It was some time after eight when he knocked on the door of the terraced house, Macadam shivering uncontrollably at his side. The curtains were drawn, but a faint light showed. The street was quiet. The urgent hammering of the knocker must surely have told those inside the whole story.

A stirring inside. The slow, reluctant surfacing of dread. Footsteps circling. Muted voices, panic-edged.

Somewhere in the distance a drunk began to sing.

The door was opened by a girl aged about sixteen. She looked at them fearfully and pulled a woollen shawl tighter across her shoulders. A middle-aged woman, as comfortably round as a dumpling, materialized at her back.

A look of mild concern suddenly hardened into one of pinched grimness.

'Steve, fetch your pa.'

As she spoke, Quinn knew immediately where Willoughby got his quick, relentless intelligence from. She had taken in the situation immediately. There was no illusion in her eyes. They did not flinch from confronting that which had to be confronted. He sensed she had been bracing herself for this knock at the door for a long time.

A quick slither of boyhood slipped out between them and hotfooted it towards the drunken singing.

Quinn removed his bowler and clutched it in both hands in front of him. He sensed Macadam do the same.

'Mrs Willoughby, may we come in?' Quinn did her the honour of meeting her fierce gaze directly.

'You'd better had,' she said, and turned her back on them.

She led them into a stuffy, overheated parlour. Red coals glowed cosily, unfeelingly, on the hearth. The room was hung with home-made paper decorations. A Christmas tree stood in one corner, a box of decorations open beside it. Quinn was shocked by this reminder of the coming festivities.

She nodded for them to sit down, and in that nod was

acknowledgement of what they had come to say to her. She sat down too, primly, quickly, decisively, as if to say they had better get this over. 'It's Martin, isn't it?'

Her daughter stood watching at the door, her mouth a small circle of fear.

'I'm afraid so. I'm very sorry, Mrs Willoughby.' Quinn left it there. It was enough. Enough to say that and continue to meet her gaze. (No, he would not look away. He would not turn from her in her moment of grief.)

The cry in her throat, the flesh of her throat tensed and straining, a grating of flesh, a taut, high, trembling cry. Agony. Agony to hear. Agony given voice. Agony quivering in her throat, finding its voice, feeling its range.

The girl threw herself towards her mother, her own grief catching in her throat as if she were trying to cough it up.

And now another noise crashed into this, doors thrown open, the thunder of boots, all hard-edged and brutish, as Willoughby's father burst into the room.

Disarrayed by drink he might have been, but now something else had undone him utterly. His eyes stared wildly as he tried to take in the scene. A bedraggled moustache jumped and writhed as his mouth twitched with questions he could not bring himself to ask.

Quinn and Macadam rose to their feet, as if they had been caught out doing something they shouldn't have.

'Mr Willoughby?' Quinn tensed his lips together, as if he was determined to hold in the terrible news it was his duty to share. 'I'm Detective Chief Inspector Quinn, Martin's commanding officer. I'm afraid I have some bad news. Martin is dead. He was shot in the line of duty earlier today. We don't as yet know who killed him, but please be assured that we are doing everything in our power to apprehend his murderer. There will be an inquest, of course.'

The father stood stupefied, uncomprehending, as if he could not grasp it, not even after Quinn had spelled it out so bluntly. But no, that was unkind. It was simply that he could not take it in, or more likely refused to. Quinn suspected that, unlike his wife, he had not prepared himself for this moment at all.

The boy, dead? It was impossible. He had seen him only that morning, and he was as alive as any of them.

Such were the thoughts Quinn imagined rushing through the father's head.

Willoughby senior shook his head in vigorous denial. An unvoiced no, no, no, repeated and repeated and repeated.

His face darkened, incomprehension making way for rage. Rage, surely, against the men who had brought this hard word – *dead!* – to his door, and had smuggled it into his parlour and smeared it about, defacing the walls of the little house his wife kept so neat and tidy. It was a credit to her, really it was.

There was no place for such words in here.

He shook his head, still, silently gainsaying the news they had brought.

Any minute now, Quinn thought, he will start shouting.

The rage will be too much for him. And the drink, the drink will have him shouting.

But no. Instead he turned his face to the wall, so that they could not see what havoc was being played with it now. There was a groan, a deep, suffering groan, then the man's whole body seemed to quake. A vein bulged on his neck. His right arm tensed. Quinn watched in horror as he threw a punch. There was a sickening crack. The man's fist crashed through the flimsy lath and plaster partition. The smell of plaster dust. Forever, now, Quinn would think of it as the smell of grief.

Willoughby's father began to whimper, as he stood there with his broken knuckles half-buried in the wall.

It was strange to see them so isolated from one another in their pain. The mother, cleaving to her daughter for comfort. The father, lashing out at the very fabric of his ruined home, as if he would tear it down around them.

Quinn and Macadam exchanged a look and slipped away.

The boy Steve stood in the hall, outside the room, looking in, awestruck by his parents' emotions.

Quinn reached out as if he might tousle his hair. He stopped himself just in time, his hand hovering uselessly between them.

'Can you make your ma and pa a cup of tea, Steve?'

The boy nodded.

'Then do that, why not. Do that for them. Make it sweet, very sweet, if you have sugar. They've had a shock, a terrible shock.'

Quinn nodded, then bowed his head as he charged out into the waiting darkness.

In the distance, the drunken singing continued.

THIRTY

I t had been a long day, but Quinn was not ready for it to end yet. He was running on a kind of buzzing, empty energy that left him exhausted but incapable of even thinking about sleep.

He had Macadam take him back to the Yard, where he trudged heavily up to the attic room that housed the Special Crimes Department. He was surprised to see a light on there, and even more surprised to find DS Inchball at his desk.

Inchball looked up as Quinn came in, his expression more complicated than Quinn was used to seeing. A little shamefaced, contrite even, but still retaining enough bullishness that Quinn could be sure it was Inchball sitting in front of him.

Quinn turned his back on Inchball to hang up his bowler. He slowly extricated himself from his ulster before asking, 'What are you doing here?'

'I heard. About Willoughby.'

'Yes? And?'

'I knew you'd be back. So I waited for you.'

'I thought you were leaving us.'

'I haven't left yet.'

'No? I thought you had.' Quinn felt a sudden welling of anger.

'I'm here, ain't I?' was Inchball's quite reasonable defence.

At last, Quinn turned to face Inchball again. He acknowledged the truth of his sergeant's observation with a small spasm of his lips. It was as close to a smile as anyone could expect under the circumstances.

Inchball nodded sharply to acknowledge it. 'I reckoned you could do with some help.'

Quinn sighed. 'What do you know?'

'I know he was shot. In a church. In Hampstead.'

As Quinn filled Inchball in on the other details of the case, Macadam came into the room. He took his seat quietly. Quinn consulted his pocket watch with a frown. He had already told Macadam to go home after parking the Model T, but he could hardly blame him if he was feeling the same impulse to work, to do something, anything, to track down Willoughby's killer.

'So we're looking for a blind man with a beard?' summarized Inchball when Quinn had got to the end of his account.

'Except he's not really blind, and the beard is more than likely false.' Quinn heard the weariness in his own voice.

'Oh, that's just perfect! And he wasn't the feller who knocked the helmet off the special constable?'

'Not in my view, no. Special Constable Elgar's assailant is, I believe, a man called Roderick Masters. Although one witness has fingered Masters for Sir Aidan's murder, I do not believe he did it.' It was only now that he voiced it that Quinn realized his position on Masters. 'First there is the question of motive. The witness in question is Donald Metcalfe, the accompanist for the choir. A strange fellow. He claims that Masters killed Sir Aidan because he had rejected a piece of music Masters had composed. I suppose it's possible, but really? A young composer must have a considerable amount of rejection to contend with. Does he go around killing everyone who doesn't like his music? Macadam, you know more about these types than I do.'

'It's true. I used to play the piccolo in the Boys' Brigade marching band.'

This information was met with a scornful roll of the eyes from Inchball.

Quinn was more encouraging. 'And so?'

'Well, in my experience, musical types can be very sensitive. They are capable of bearing grudges. It's not impossible.'

Quinn nodded, but his expression was unconvinced. 'I don't know. There's something I can't quite put my finger on with Metcalfe. I suspect he isn't being entirely open with me.'

'Perhaps he's trying to frame Masters?' suggested Macadam.

'It's possible. Leaving aside motive, there's the question of opportunity. By his own account, Metcalfe admits that he was with Masters immediately before Paul Seddon discovered Sir Aidan's body. He says that Seddon saw them together, so we should be able to confirm that. The discovery of the white stick and the satchel in the church suggests to me that Paul Seddon was telling the truth about seeing a supposedly blind piano tuner fleeing the scene of the crime. This is our murderer, I believe. If we had not found these items, I would suspect Seddon. So, if we accept this theory, that Sir Aidan's murderer was someone disguised as a blind piano tuner, it can't be Masters. He simply would not have had time to disguise himself as a blind piano tuner, murder Sir Aidan and be seen by Paul Seddon in that disguise, only minutes after he had been seen undisguised.'

'We should talk to him, though,' suggested Inchball. A certain steeliness in his tone intimated he had a specific kind of *talking* in mind.

'And we need to find the piano tuner,' added Macadam redundantly. He looked purposefully towards the window where an inky blackness pressed against the panes. He fidgeted in his seat with a sprung restlessness, as if he wanted to be out there now, scouring the capital for the killer.

Quinn understood the sentiment and sympathized with it. 'We need to find out more about Fonthill's life. We'll look into every aspect of it, not just his work with this choir. Tomorrow I shall talk to Lady Fonthill again. There's something she isn't telling us, I'm sure. We know that Fonthill was unfaithful, apparently on multiple occasions. She doesn't have to have been the one who drove the weapon into his ear, but perhaps she knows who did, and is protecting him or her. It's not beyond the realms of possibility that she had a lover of her own.'

'She didn't seem the type to me, guv,' put in Macadam, morosely, as if he would prefer it if she was.

Quinn had to admit his own instincts chimed with Macadam's. But who was to say what a long-suffering wronged wife might be driven to do when she finally snaps?

'They have children, don't they?' continued Macadam. 'Whatever he was guilty of, do you really think a mother would do that to the father of her children?'

The door to the SCD burst open again. The three men turned to see DI Leversedge at the threshold of the room, his body set in a combative pose. His eyes were red as if he had been rubbing them. 'What's going on?'

'You too?' said Quinn.

The tension and fight suddenly went out of Leversedge's posture. His head hung forlornly as exhaustion came over him. He held up a buff-coloured folder. It seemed that his arm was barely strong enough to brandish it. 'I have the statements Pool's men took this afternoon. I thought you would want to look them over tomorrow. Wanted to get them on your desk so you would have them first thing.'

Quinn nodded his gratitude.

'Also, I have an address for that fellow Masters. It's not likely he's the killer but I thought you might like to talk to him all the same.'

'Yes.' Quinn frowned and cast a quizzical glance at his DI. He sensed his sergeants bristle with the same suspicion: had the man been listening at the door? Or was there a more innocent explanation? Perhaps he had simply come to the same conclusion independently. Still, it was impressive that he had an address already. It would save them a bit of time. 'That's useful,' conceded Quinn. 'How did you get it?'

'I found a sheet of music on the piano. It had Masters' name on it. Something he'd composed, by the looks of it. He'd also put his address on. It's in the file.'

Leversedge passed the file to Quinn, who gave the barest nod of acknowledgement.

Twin spots of colour came up on Leversedge's cheeks. 'How did Willoughby's folks take it?' He did not look at Quinn as he asked the question, as if this would minimize the impact of the answer.

'Not well,' said Quinn.

'It's a bad business.'

'Yes.'

'We have to get the bastard who did this.'

Quinn met Leversedge's gaze unhurriedly, as if preoccupied. 'Yes.' As if remembering himself, he opened the file and leafed through until he found the sheet of music Leversedge had mentioned. The first page was inscribed with the title, MISTLETOE. Beneath that was written, *Words by Walter de la Mare. Setting by Roderick Masters.* At the bottom of that title page was written, *All correspondence concerning the musical performance of this piece should be addressed to Roderick Masters, 7, Lynton Road, Crouch End.* 'Strange.'

'What is it, sir?' asked Macadam.

'Nothing. It's just . . . something doesn't quite add up.' Quinn shook his head as if to dispel a momentary daze. 'Inchball, you said you wanted to talk to Masters.' He read out the address for Inchball to note down.

Inchball gave a terse nod. 'Now?'

'Round up a couple of uniforms to go with you. And take a Black Maria. We want to make an impression. I don't mind if you have to drag him out of bed. Mind you, if he is the killer, the chances are he'll have done a bunk by now. Unless he's a very cool customer indeed. So, if you find him, put the fear of God into him. See how he responds to pressure.'

Inchball didn't need any further instruction. It was the kind of assignment that played to his strengths. He hurried out, grabbing his bowler from the stand on his way.

Quinn narrowed his eyes. He took a dim view of overgrown schoolboys knocking bobbies' helmets off, even if the bobby in question was only a volunteer special constable, and the attack had motives other than undermining the police.

'We should talk to the foreigners too,' said Leversedge darkly. 'And that Dame Elsie woman.'

'Very well,' said Quinn, 'if you think it's worth pursuing.' He made no attempt to keep the scepticism from his voice.

Leversedge felt the need to justify himself. 'I've read the statements. It comes up time and again. Fonthill insulted the Belgian, Boland, made unflattering remarks about Dame Elsie's weight and was rude about the Russian male dancer, practically accused him of being a nancy boy. Meanwhile he was lusting after the girl. He made numerous lascivious remarks.'

'Numerous?'

'Indeed. There are multiple witnesses to that. The consensus is the Russian chap is not a nancy boy after all but a hot-blooded male of the foreign type, passionately enamoured of his dancing partner, by all accounts. Unsurprisingly therefore, he waxed jealous and wrathful.'

'And then donned a false beard and pretended to be blind?' objected Macadam.

'Also, there's the question of the weapon,' said Quinn. 'The handle of the tuning fork had been sharpened to a point. Dr Emsley compared it to a stiletto blade. That indicates premeditation, not a crime of passion. Indeed, it almost suggests the work of a professional assassin.'

Leversedge conceded the justice of their objections with a splayed hand. 'I do not say I have all the ends tied up, but it is worth questioning the Russian, is it not? He strikes me as the type who would have access to such a weapon. Then there's the fact that he was one of the ones who disappeared sharpish before the local bobbies were on the scene. Oh, and on the subject of false beards, I can tell you that such an object was retrieved from DS Willoughby's pocket by the medical officer. He has not conducted any conclusive tests on it as yet, but he is of the opinion that it contains traces of a substance he believes to be blood.'

Quinn narrowed his eyes to take this in. 'Perhaps he was sprayed in the face as he thrust the weapon in.' There was a moment of silence as the other men reflected on this gruesome image. Quinn continued: 'A strange murderer, this, who scatters items of his disguise for the police to find.'

Leversedge was ready with an explanation. 'He's panicking. Wants to do a quick change into someone else and make his getaway.'

'Why go inside the church?'

'A sudden attack of religion?' Even Leversedge did not sound convinced by this hastily invented theory.

Quinn pursed his lips dubiously. 'Or perhaps he went to meet someone there. Which could mean . . .' Quinn did not complete his thought.

He did not need to. Macadam was there already. 'There were two of them in there when Willoughby went in.'

'Either one of which could have been Willoughby's killer,' supplied Leversedge.

Quinn crossed to his desk and sat down. He took out some blank postcards and a thick black pencil from his drawer. On the first, he wrote *Sir Aidan Fonthill*. He handed this across his desk to Leversedge, who pinned it in the centre of the largest wall of the attic office.

Each on a separate postcard, Quinn then wrote the following names: *Lady Emma Fonthill, Anna Seddon, Paul Seddon, Charles Cavendish, Ursula Cavendish, Roderick Masters, Donald Metcalfe, Peter Farthing*. The cards were handed to Leversedge, to be pinned in place around the first card.

'We need to map where each of these persons were at the time of Sir Aidan's murder. And by whom they were seen.'

Quinn then consulted the folded programme he had pocketed earlier and added further names for the wall: *Emile Boland, Dame Elsie Tatton*. He had to check the programme again to copy carefully: *Andrei Kuznetzov, Ekaterina Volkova*.

'The same goes for these.'

He laid two final cards on the desk in front of him. On the first he wrote: *Blind Piano Tuner? Who?*

On the next he simply drew a large question mark. He took his time carefully drawing the curve of the punctuation mark, thickening the line with meticulous shading.

He sat back to consider his handiwork, like an artist who has just completed the provisional sketch for a new composition.

He handed the *Blind Piano Tuner?* card to Leversedge without comment, leaving the other in the centre of his desk. He traced the question mark with the tip of his index finger, tapping once on the point at the bottom.

'This man is the key to it all,' he said.

He looked up abruptly with a new eagerness. The faces of the other men showed only doubt and confusion.

'Someone knows who he is. Someone knows what connects him to Sir Aidan.'

Finally, he relinquished the last card, watching in silence as Leversedge added it to the others.

THIRTY-ONE

The horse-drawn Black Maria clattered through the streets of North London, a dark missile piercing the night.

It was past midnight by the time it pulled up in the middle of a narrow, badly lit street in Crouch End with a restraining yell from the driver. The back doors sprang open, pouring out more darkness into that which surrounded it. This new darkness had shape and form and substance, as well as steel-tipped boots that clashed noisily with the cobbled surface. For it was made up of men. Men who had been coiled but were now sprung.

Men who had been pointed in the direction of a target.

Two of the men wore police uniforms and wielded truncheons. The third, in plain clothes, wearing a bowler hat and a dark suit, drew himself up in a posture of domination. He breathed in, filling his lungs with the night air.

Inchball gave a loud, dismissive snort. He had the measure of the neighbourhood, even in the dark. This was not a well-to-do street. Terraces of mean, little pattern-book houses, quickly built, occupied by manual workers and lowly paid clerks. Perhaps a few gentle folk who had fallen on hard times.

Most of the houses, including the suspect's, were already in darkness. That was the way Inchball wanted it. Everyone tucked up in bed, fast asleep. Or maybe they were getting down to their bedroom business. It was Saturday night, after all. The man of the house back from the boozer, expecting his missus to fulfil her conjugal duties. From what he knew of this fellow Masters, though, he doubted there was a missus. Some kind of musician, wasn't he? Probably batted for the other side. That was usually the way with these artistic types.

That would be interesting, if they caught him entertaining a friend. Something to hold over him. Could be useful.

Or more likely he was on his own. Crying into his sad, lonely pillow. Yanking his sad, lonely cock.

Inchball's smirk was concealed by the darkness. He raised his hand and grasped the cheap brass door knocker to bring it hammering down. 'Police! Open up!'

Somewhere down the street, a dog started barking.

Inchball kept up the pounding on the door, settling into a stubborn, belligerent rhythm.

At last a light went on, illuminating the two upstairs windows. A curtain twitched.

'Here we go,' muttered Inchball, to himself as much as to anyone. Although the occupants of the house were without doubt aware of his presence by now, he did not let up on the knocking. He was hammering away right up to the moment that the door was opened to the extent of its chain and a pair of ice-pale eyes peered out at him fearfully. The eyes were deep-set in a thin face, above a sharp beak of a nose. A high, domed forehead was fringed with tufts of silver hair. A mouth gaped anxiously beneath a white walrus moustache. An old man's face then.

'Roderick Masters?'

'No. I . . . I'm his father. What's this about?'

'Is your son in, Mr Masters?'

'Yes, of course. But he's in bed.'

Inchball showed his warrant card. 'I'd like a word with him, if you don't mind.'

The door closed as the chain was jangled free, then reopened.

Masters senior stood with his back against the wall to let the three policemen march through. The clamour of their boots was enough to wake anyone in the street still sleeping.

The narrow hall was lit by a single dim gaslight. Masters senior was wearing a long, striped nightgown, from the bottom of which protruded two bare, boney ankles and knobbly feet. He went to the bottom of the stairs and shouted up. 'Rod! There are some . . . policemen here to see you.'

They waited in silence until soft footsteps padded down the stairs. A man in his early thirties wearing pyjamas and a dressing gown appeared. He had the same thin, anxious face as his father. His hairline was beginning to go the same way too.

'Are you Roderick Masters?' Inchball demanded when Masters had joined them at the bottom of the stairs.

The young man looked apprehensively at his father. 'Y-yes. What is this about?'

Inchball nodded to the two uniforms. 'Get 'im!'

The men, although they were perhaps not the burliest examples of their type, were nonetheless imposing individuals, their helmets almost touching the ceiling of the cramped hallway. They rushed at Roderick Masters and wrestled him to the ground, twisting one arm up his back.

'Good heavens!' cried Masters' father. 'This is police brutality! My son is innocent!'

'Innocent, is he? We have a witness what says he is a murderer.'

The two uniforms hefted Roderick Masters to his feet. The young man was in tears.

Inchball sniffed the air. 'What's that smell?' he snarled in disgust.

Masters' face was red and streaked with wetness. Snot and blood trailed from where his nose had been driven into the hall rug. A damp patch spread out around his groin.

'He's pissed hisself,' observed Inchball with a derisive smirk.

Masters hung his head in shame.

The uniforms had the cuffs on by now and were shoving him towards the door.

'Don' you worry,' said Inchball to Masters senior with a wink. 'We'll take good care of him.'

Behind him, he heard the old man let out a high-pitched wail as he slumped to the floor.

THIRTY-TWO

Silas Quinn lived in a four-storey lodging house just off the Brompton Road, in a pleasant enough location close to Hyde Park and Exhibition Road. Once, he might have described it as a respectable house; certainly, that was how it had seemed when he had moved in. But the more he had learnt of his fellow lodgers, and, to be fair, the more they learnt of him, the less easy it had proven to maintain that appearance. Not that he, or they, were especially wicked people. Just that a certain messiness was inevitable in the lives of any group of men and women living in close proximity.

Quinn stood on the front step and turned the key in the lock. Something dark and immeasurable pressed at his back, hurrying him over the threshold.

He closed the door on it as quickly as he could without making a noise. Even so, he had the feeling that some of that darkness had slipped through. It was still there, dogging his steps, as he moved towards the stairs, his step as quiet and stealthy as a housebreaker's.

Knowing that he kept irregular hours, his landlady, Mrs Ibbott, had left the landing light on for him. It was one of the original gas lights – the house had both gas and electric lighting – and so Mrs Ibbott had been able to turn it down to a dim glow.

There was no secret any more about Quinn's occupation. For as long as he could, he had tried to maintain an air of convenient vagueness concerning who he was and what he did, hoping that none of his fellow lodgers would identify him as the notorious personality *Quickfire Quinn* whom they read about in their newspapers. Somehow, his modest habits and quiet demeanour had thrown everyone off the scent.

But then it had come out, and there had been nothing he could do about it. Mrs Ibbott and her daughter Mary had been the first to make the connection.

Besides Mrs Ibbott and Mary, there were only two original occupants of the house remaining, a retired army colonel called Berwick, and Mr Finch, a schoolmaster whom Quinn suspected of having socialist leanings. Old Berwick was becoming increasingly confused. Finch seemed to be giving Quinn a wide berth these days, which suited the detective. Everyone else who had known the truth about him was either dead or had moved out.

But he sensed that somehow the new occupants – three officers billeted there by the Ministry of Defence – all came fully primed with the knowledge of his identity. He suspected that Mrs Ibbott had confided it to them as she showed them their rooms, no doubt swearing them to secrecy. A more sinister explanation was possible, however – that one or more of the soldiers was a military intelligence officer, installed in the house to keep an eye on Quinn. Quinn knew that he had a tendency to imagine conspiracies and plots, a useful enough trait when investigating crimes but potentially damaging when he imagined them directed against himself.

By now the other occupants of the house should be asleep, or at least in their beds. Though for all Quinn knew, they were insomniacs staring at the fuzzy rectangles of their ceilings, projecting on to them their own anguished regrets, guilty secrets and humiliating memories.

If Quinn had to guess which of the men was the spy, he would have gone for the donnish, distracted-looking fellow who lived alone in the room previously occupied by the Hargreaves (and before that by Miss Dillard). Carstairs was his name. He spoke with a genteel Edinburgh accent, but only, so far as Quinn could tell, to say 'Good day' as they passed on their way in or out of the house.

Carstairs gave every impression of being the sort of chap who liked to keep himself to himself, showing no interest in anyone else's comings and goings. Which led Quinn to conclude that if there was a secret agent in their midst, here was the most likely candidate.

The other two fellows, Pringle and Epping, were of a common enough male type. Indeed, to some extent they were like older, less intellectual versions of the two young men who had occupied the same room before them, Appleby and Timberley. They shared the same facetious humour and the same facility for quick and easy banter (without the irritating habit of lapsing into Latin for their numerous private jokes); the same refusal, in short, to take anything too seriously, outwardly at least – events had proven both Appleby and Timberley ultimately capable of great seriousness. And they had shown their glib-witted cheeriness for what it was: a mask.

This was a period of transition, when the authorities were improvising solutions to cope with the huge influx of men into the armed forces. Current resources were stretched to breaking point, and the necessary provisions were not yet in place, if they had been thought of at all.

Quinn told himself, therefore, that there was little point forming any bonds of friendship with the new residents. In all honesty, he would not have done so even if their presence had been on a more permanent footing, but it was good to have the excuse. And Mrs Ibbott seemed less inclined than she once had been to try to get her guests together for social evenings in the parlour after dinner.

Mary too was less in evidence than she had once been. Quinn could not help thinking that it was largely to avoid him. She was no doubt embarrassed by the business with Hargreaves, and however grateful she was for the part Quinn had played in rescuing her, the sight of him was bound to be a reminder of a painful episode.

As he climbed the stairs, he felt his heart grow heavier with each tread. He willed himself to form the image of Willoughby's face in his mind, as if every moment that he did not hold it in front of him was a betrayal. But his imagination failed him. He squeezed his eyes shut and shook his head, in silent remonstration with a non-existent antagonist.

He reached the landing where Carstairs' room was. The sight of the door brought back difficult memories.

Once he had pressed his ear to that door, expecting to hear the sound of Miss Dillard's weeping. But instead he had heard a strange, unrhythmic thumping. Inconceivable that poor, sad, unloved Miss Dillard was 'entertaining' a 'gentleman friend' in her room, to employ two ridiculous euphemisms. But that was what it had sounded like, the banging of a couple going at it hell for leather. Alas, if only, but no. It had been the solitary convulsions of her body in its death throes.

He had always believed that by his ruthless pursuit of violent criminals, he protected weak and defenceless members of society like Miss Dillard from harm. That he took the danger that threatened everyone on himself and became a kind of avenging angel, striking terror into the hearts of those who would do evil. He faced them and he killed them. A necessary act of violence for the greater good.

But if that was true, why did so many who were innocent end up dead too?

Was he simply deluding himself? Or was it worse than that? Was he responsible?

No avenging angel, but an angel of death.

He killed the light that Mrs Ibbott had left for him, erasing the shape of the door he still thought of as Miss Dillard's despite the fact that he had carried her dying, thrashing body out of there himself.

At last he opened the door to his own room. His curtains were open, and some light came in through the window, the feathery glow of a gibbous moon.

He sat down heavily on his bed. The springs rattled complainingly as a violent shudder passed through his body.

The only concession he was willing to make to his own comfort was to unlace the boots that were now so heavy that he was unable to lift his feet from the floor. This unlacing took an eternity to be completed, a long eternity.

When it was done, he took off his bowler and dropped it carelessly on the floor.

He lay down on the bed, pulling his ulster around him, lifting his knees to curl himself around the emptiness.

His eyes were open. His mouth, open too. As if he were trying to emulate the look of muted wonder that he had seen on Willoughby's face.

And now he saw it at last, the darkness that had followed him into the house. And the darkness looked back at him, immeasurable still, and devoid of pity.

THIRTY-THREE

Inchball had the driver take them round the back streets of Hornsey, while he and the two uniforms worked on Masters in the back of the Black Maria. Nothing too rough. The threat of violence would be enough to crack this one. That and the darkness, and the fear of not knowing what might come out of it. He might fall over once or twice. Bang his head on the floor. That was hardly their fault was it. That's what happened when you resisted arrest.

'You know what we do to scumbags who kill coppers?'

'N-n-no. W-w-what?'

'Let's put it this way. Not a lot of them go to trial. You remember Cecil Edwards, that toerag what slit the throat of a bobby in Walthamstow? Found hanged in his cell, he was, by his own belt. Let's just say he might have had a little help. And let's just say it was Constable Wilson here what strung him up. He's done it before. He can do it again.'

'I tell you, I didn't do it. I didn't kill the policeman. I didn't know anything about it. I was nowhere near it?'

'Nowhere near it? So you deny you were at University College School in Hampstead earlier today, around one o'clock?'

'No, I was there. I admit, I was there.'

'So you admit you murdered Sir Aidan Fonthill?'

'No, that's not what I said.'

The Black Maria went over a deep pothole in the road. Somehow, Masters found himself on the floor, between the feet of the three policemen. Somehow, as they stumbled to help him in the dark, the odd boot or two may have made contact with his body.

When they had him back on the bench seat, Inchball tried a different tack. 'Now now, old chap, we might have got off on the wrong foot here. You can understand how we're upset, can't you? A policeman getting shot down in a church? It's not nice. We don't like it. We wanna find the bastard what done it. You can understand that.'

'It's not me. I swear.'

'I wanna believe you. I do. But you've got to give me something. I tell you what. Admit to the murder of Sir Aidan and we'll find someone else for Sergeant Willoughby.'

'What? No! I didn't do it. I didn't do it, I tell you. I didn't kill either of them. You have to let me go. I'm innocent.'

'Innocent, are you?'

'Yes!'

'But you wrote that music, din' you? What's it called now, Holly and the Arsehole?'

'You mean Mistletoe? It's called Mistletoe.'

'That's right. I knew it was something like that. The Mistletoe and the Arsehole.'

'There's no Arsehole!'

'Isn't there? Are you sure?'

'Yes.'

'So what? You sent it to Fonthill?'

'Yes . . . but I don't see . . .'

'Why d'you do that?'

'I don't know. I thought . . . I knew he was putting on a Christmas concert. I suppose I thought he might like to include it. It's a choral piece. He is the choirmaster of the Hampstead Voices, a fairly decent amateur choir. I thought it would be a good opportunity. For them. To include something a little more imaginative and modern in their programme.'

'He thought it was shite, though, din' he? A shocking piece of shite, he said. That's what I heard.'

'I don't know what he thought. He never acknowledged it.'

'That's rude, ain't it? Very rude, I'd call that. Very rude and disrespectful. To a proud young man like yourself. It must have rankled. Oh, how it must have rankled. Rankle, rankle, rankled. Ate away at you, did'n it? You couldn't let it lie. That's why you done him in, ain't it?'

'No! What do you mean? I didn't kill him.'

'Then, as you made your escape, you attacked the constable on duty at the school gate. Poor elderly volunteer constable. Struck him down then ran off. Whereupon you shot to death one of the officers sent to apprehend you. A young fella, younger than you. With a ma and pa of his own, and brothers and sisters too.'

'No! That wasn't me! I swear! I don't even have a gun. How could I shoot someone?'

'Listen, I'm gonna try and stop 'em, course I am. But what you need to know is, these two here, they don't take too kindly to one of their own getting murdered. Their blood's up, you understand.'

'Look, look. I confess. I confess. It was me who knocked Elgar's helmet off.'

'Special Constable Elgar to you.'

'No, no, to me he's *Elgar*. It wasn't because he was a policeman. It was because he was Elgar. It was just a stupid . . . stupid . . . prank. I don't even . . . My father adulates Elgar. He thinks he is the pinnacle of musical . . . genius. And everything I do is . . . rubbish.'

'Maybe it is.'

'Maybe it is. But do you see? I wasn't even attacking Elgar. I was attacking my father. When I found out there was to be a piece by Elgar in the programme, but mine had been rejected . . . Yes, I did . . . I was . . . angry. I knew my father would want to go to the concert. And yet if my piece had been included . . . well, I sincerely doubt he would have made the effort. But I didn't kill Sir Aidan and I didn't kill the policeman, honestly. You have to believe me. I even felt bad about Elgar. I didn't know he would collapse like that. I only meant to . . . I don't know . . . I don't know what I meant to do.'

'It's all very well you saying that, but can you prove you wasn't in the church when Willoughby was shot?'

Masters stirred tensely in the darkness, his body wracked by a sudden excitement. 'Yes! Yes, I can! I have an alibi! I really do have an alibi!' He began to sob with relief.

'What alibi?'

'After I left the school, I went to the pub. People saw me there. I must have looked like a madman! I was exhilarated, laughing and throwing my money around. I tipped the barmaid rather extravagantly.'

'Pub, you say?'

'Yes, I went to the Holly Bush. You know, the Holly Bush in Hampstead. I couldn't possibly have been in the church where the policeman was killed.'

Inchball received this information in silence, except to knock on the roof of the Black Maria sharply three times.

Soon after, the vehicle pulled up with a jolt.

The cuffs were taken off Masters. The back doors opened. And he was thrust out into a darkness colder, deeper, emptier than that from which he was expelled.

THIRTY-FOUR

Sunday, 20 December, 1914

The drab chill of a winter morning greeted Quinn as he left the house. His stomach rumbled. He was up too early for Mrs Ibbott's breakfast, which was anyway becoming an increasingly meagre repast as they progressed deeper into the war. But he often forgot to eat when he was at this stage of an investigation. Instead sustenance would come mainly from the mugs of strong, sweet tea that Macadam occasionally caused to appear. Inchball often joked that you could stand a spoon up in them.

The moon was large and low in the sky.

He wanted to get a head start on the day, to quell the creeping anxiety that dominated his mood. There was that sense he always had at the start of an investigation, the sense of much to do, without any clear idea of what it was he should be doing. A kind of impotence, in other words, combined with a restless and largely futile energy. The prospect of exhaustion was never far away.

He was still wearing the clothes he had slept in, or more accurately lain curled up and shivering in. From time to time, he had tried closing his eyes. And perhaps some of the times when he had done that he had fallen asleep. But if so, it was not a sleep that left him refreshed in any way.

The moon had shone through his window all night – he had not thought to draw the curtains – until eventually he had lurched from his bed like a drunk remembering he had somewhere to be. He had urinated long and heavily into the lavatory, his piss dark and smelling of gun smoke. Then rubbed his teeth and gums with a small amount of Calox tooth powder. The abrasiveness of the patented substance acted like a form of penance, a hair shirt for the mouth.

His head ached, his shoulders ached, his back ached, his joints were stiff and, yes, aching. The slightest movement set off a chain of twinges, like a series of fireworks arranged so that each ignited the next.

The dark, largely deserted streets of Kensington took on an unfamiliar aspect, as if he was walking through a strange quarter of a city he did not know, rather than his own neighbourhood.

It started to rain, a fine drizzle that he felt against his face, like the light touch of a blind man feeling his features.

As Quinn walked, he was aware of a leavening in the darkness. At the same time, the fine drizzle intensified into a more determined downpour. He was thankful for his crumpled ulster and bowler hat, off which the now heavy raindrops bounced. Other pedestrians hurried past him, their collars upturned and heads bent down, fleeting shapes forming in the murk. From time to time, he was forced to dodge the spikes of carelessly wielded umbrellas.

The day was coming up by stealth.

His bowler hat looked almost silver in his hand, the electric light reflecting off the tiny droplets that coated it. He gave his ulster a shake before hanging it up. A despondent puddle quickly darkened the floor at his feet.

He crossed the office, stooping slightly to avoid banging his head on the sloping ceiling. As he did so, he glanced briefly out of the window. Patches of blue were breaking through the clouds. *Typical. It waited till he got inside before bucking up.*

He had not been seated at his desk long when Inchball came in. He met Quinn's enquiring gaze with a terse shake of the head. 'Wasn't him.'

It took Quinn a moment to remember who Inchball was talking about. Ah, yes, Masters. Roderick Masters. Inchball had paid a visit on him last night. 'You're sure?'

'He's not our man. I did what you said. Leant on him.'

'And?'

'Pissed himself, din' 'e. Literally. Besides, he says he has an alibi for Willoughby's murder. Couldn't have been in the church because he was in the pub. I'll check it out, of course. But from the way he latched on to it, I'd lay good money it'll stand up.'

Quinn nodded. A loose end tied up, but no progress. 'What about the attack on the special constable?'

'Oh, that was him, all right.'

'Did you charge him?'

Inchball screwed his face up dismissively. 'I dealt with him, let's put it like that. Saved the courts the bother. I don't think he'll be knocking any more coppers' helmets off.'

The blaring ring of the telephone interrupted their conversation. Quinn stared questioningly at Inchball as if he believed his sergeant could tell him who was calling.

Inchball shrugged. Quinn reluctantly lifted the receiver off the switchhook and cut the catastrophic noise off.

'*Quinn. Admiralty. Now.*'

Quinn held the earpiece away from his ear but it was too late. The line had gone dead. The three fiercely barked words had already assaulted his eardrum. He was given no opportunity to demur.

He ignored Inchball's expectant gaze and returned the receiver to the candlestick stand on his desk without comment. The room seemed to buzz in the aftermath of the intrusion.

He had recognized the speaker as Lieutenant-Colonel Kell, the head of MO5 (g) and, since the outbreak of war, effectively Quinn's commanding officer. Sir Edward Henry, the commissioner of the Metropolitan Police Force, who had set up the Special Crimes Department in the first place, still exercised a watching brief over the department, and intervened occasionally to offer his advice. But it was ultimately to Kell that Quinn answered now, although usually via the mediation of one of Kell's subordinates. The fact that the call had come from the top man himself was not a good omen.

Quinn thought that he had been able to discern Kell's asthmatic wheeze between each word. If so, it was a sign of the man's agitation, which made the call even more inauspicious.

Quinn rose stiffly to his feet, then turned to confront the wall of postcards that he had written out the night before.

At the centre of the mosaic of names, Leversedge had pinned the card which bore only the large, neatly drawn question mark.

Quinn blinked away his exhaustion, swaying as the floor seemed to shift beneath him. The cards began to swirl before his eyes. The names he had written out so carefully blurred into a grey fog. The only card that remained legible was the one bearing the question mark. And now his tiredness played another trick on him: infinitely repeating double vision multiplied that one symbol into a restless throng of question marks.

He had to blink hard to still the spinning cards and bring the names back into focus, reaching out to touch the solidity of a desk to steady himself.

'You all right, guv?'

He drew himself up with a defiant sniff, not meeting Inchball's solicitous gaze. 'You'll chase up that alibi today?'

'I said I would, din' I?' was Inchball's prickly reply.

Quinn nodded decisively and crossed to the hatstand for his damp ulster. He experienced the sensation that he was still wearing his hat, which provoked a stab of panic, as he was sure he had taken it off just minutes ago. Hadn't it shone silver like the moon in his hand?

To his great relief, his hands confirmed his head was naked, while his bowler hung there on its hook in front of him.

He looked up as Macadam came into the room.

'What's happening, sir?' Macadam's posture tensed, as if he were readying himself for action.

'I have to speak to Kell. Wait for me here.' Quinn's glance darted towards the wall with the postcards pinned to it. It seemed that he was charging Macadam with the urgent task of not letting it out of his sight.

Macadam looked uncertainly at Inchball, who gave a bemused shrug, as if to say *Don't ask me*.

It was a short walk from Scotland Yard to the Admiralty building. The clouds had almost entirely cleared now, and the sky was a luminous, powdery blue. The pale disc of the moon was still in the sky, like the phantom of a dead sun.

Commander Irons, Kell's usual proxy, was waiting for Quinn in the lobby of the Horse Guards Parade entrance. Irons signalled to him with a brusque flick of the head and set off walking immediately.

Quinn had to run to catch him up, his heels echoing on the black and white tiled floor. 'What's this about, do you know? I have an investigation to lead. One of my officers was killed yesterday.'

'You think we don't know that?'

'Well, dragging me here to receive an ear-bashing from Kell is not helping my investigation, is it?'

'Who said you were going to have an ear-bashing from Kell?'

'Am I not?'

'Kell isn't the only one with an interest in this case.'

This was how they talked, these secret service Johnnies. In riddles that went round and round and communicated nothing apart from the fact that they knew something you didn't. Quinn was used to it. 'Who else then?'

'You'll find out. Soon enough.'

Typical.

Irons led him along blank white corridors, past innumerable closed doors. There was little decoration to relieve the monotony. The occasional portrait or bust of a presumably distinguished seafarer, seascapes with boats, some naval battle scenes.

At last Irons came to a halt in front of a door that had nothing to differentiate it from any of its fellows. He gave a sharp rap with his knuckles and went in without waiting for an answer, fixing Quinn with a warning glance as he held the door for him.

The room contained a long meeting table, at which Lieutenant-Colonel Kell was seated, smoking one of his pernicious medicinal cigarettes. Kell looked up, his expression drawn.

One other man, wearing the tunic of a senior naval officer, stood with his back to the room, his shoulders slightly slumped as he looked through the window over Horse Guards Parade. The man turned, revealing the gold braid on his cuffs, and stepped forward out of the cloud of pungent cigar smoke that surrounded him. Quinn recognized the First Lord of the Admiralty, Winston Churchill.

As he turned, Churchill seemed to transform himself, shedding the hint of gloom, of self-doubt even, that had apparently possessed him a moment before. He visibly drew himself up, as if to occupy some image of the man he believed himself to be. He set his mouth in a grim line of resolve, without which it might have been thought a weak mouth. He was clean-shaven with no facial hair to add distinction to his rather boyish features, or to hide behind, for that matter. He tilted his head upwards, with a look that appeared to have been practised in front of a mirror.

'This the fellow?' Churchill took several small puffs on the fag end of his cigar, before leaning forward to stub it out in a porcelain ashtray on the table.

Kell nodded morosely, as if he wished he was able to offer Churchill someone better, but sadly not. 'This is he. Detective Chief Inspector Quinn, of the Special Crimes Department.'

'Quickfire Quinn, they call you? That right?'

Quinn shook his head, not to contradict Churchill, but to signal his lack of enthusiasm for the ridiculous nickname. 'My work invariably brings me into contact with some very dangerous individuals. Men who would not hesitate to kill those who have been charged with their arrest. And so, it is sometimes necessary to take pre-emptive measures.'

'So you would prefer Pre-emptive Quinn? Doesn't quite have the same ring to it, does it?' Churchill's mouth curled in a mischievous smirk.

'I have never sought fame of any kind.'

'Fame, you call it? Notoriety, I call it. We don't want notorious policemen, Quinn. There are some cases where that is the very last thing we want. Where, on the contrary, what is called for is a certain discretion. What you might call sensitivity. Can you be sensitive, Quinn?'

'My main objective, always, is to get results.'

Churchill narrowed his eyes as he studied Quinn. 'Results are all very well, Quinn. As long as they are the right results.'

Quinn nodded. He had heard variants of this speech before. 'I take it you have called me here to talk about the Fonthill case? May I ask what your interest in it is?'

Churchill's eyes bulged as though Quinn had just been guilty of gross impertinence. 'My interest in it?'

Quinn held his ground. 'Yes, sir.'

'I was at Harrow with Sir Aidan. Or Byron, as we used to call him.'

'Byron? Was that because of his morals?'

'Morals? No. It came from Hellespont. You know, Fonthill . . . shortened to Font, rhymed with Hellespont. And so, Byron. Naturally. Nothing to do with his morals.'

'I don't quite follow.'

'Good grief, I thought you were supposed to be bright. Byron swam the Hellespont.'

'Yes, I knew that. I'm sorry. I had a bad night. I lost an officer, you know.'

Churchill looked Quinn up and down, not without sympathy. 'Yes. I can see that. You look, not to put too fine a point on it, like you've been dragged through a hedge backwards.'

'I'm sorry.'

Churchill waved his hand as if Quinn was to think nothing of it.

'So am I to understand that Sir Aidan was a friend of yours?'

'We were at school together, as I said. And I was due to attend this blasted concert he was arranging. God knows why I agreed to it, but I did.'

Quinn winced as a tremor of exhaustion passed through him. It was almost impossible to think over the creaking ache of his brain and the ringing in his ears. But something, dimly, was starting to come together. 'And so . . .'

'And so,' barked Kell from the table, 'you are to proceed carefully.'

Quinn frowned. He had thought he had understood what this was about, but now he was not so sure. 'Is there a connection? Do you think Fonthill's death has something to do with . . . you?'

Churchill turned his back on Quinn, to look out of the window again.

It was left to Kell to go some way to answering Quinn's question. 'Naturally, we don't know where your investigation will take you, Quinn. But I need not remind you that there is a war on.'

'No, you need not.'

'The office of First Lord of the Admiralty is central to the war effort.'

'Yes. And?'

'I think that's all I need to say for now. You will liaise with Commander Irons as usual.' Irons stirred at his post by the door. 'Anything sensitive that you discover in the course of your investigations you should communicate to him, and he will instruct you on how to proceed.'

'May I go?'

Kell did not look at Quinn as he nodded his curt dismissal. Instead, his gaze was focused on the medicinal cigarette between his fingers, as if he was wondering how on earth it had got there.

'What do you look like?'

Quinn knew the answer to this question. 'Like I've been dragged through a hedge backwards.'

Miss Latterly, seated at her typewriter outside Sir Edward Henry's office, was not impressed by the observation, not knowing that it had originated with the First Lord of the Admiralty. 'Did you sleep in that coat?' She screwed up her nose in distaste.

Quinn did not consider it a question that merited, or even expected, an answer. 'What are you doing in today? It is Sunday, you know.'

'There's a lot to do. Sir Edward needs me here. He is preparing a statement about—' She broke off tactfully and looked down at the paper in her typewriter.

'About Willoughby.'

Miss Latterly gave a tight little smile as she met his gaze again. 'I'm sorry.'

'It was my fault. I sent him off without . . . I should have warned him. I should have stopped him. I shouldn't have let him go.' Quinn thrashed one arm uselessly at the empty air.

'You mustn't blame yourself.'

'Who should I blame? Willoughby? He was a bloody fool.'

'No. The man who shot him. You should find him and . . .' Miss Latterly gave a barely perceptible nod. She did not need to say what he should do. She did not need to give any hint other than this slight movement of her head, so small that someone else might not have noticed it.

But he had seen it and he understood its meaning fully.

'Don't worry. I will.' He reciprocated with a firm and eloquent nod of his own.

THIRTY-FIVE

Paul Seddon knocked urgently on the door and waited.

He did not quite know what he was doing here, only that he had to see her. Admittedly, he felt a little guilty leaving Anna on her own with the baby, but they were both sleeping soundly when he had left. This had to be done. And he told himself it needn't take too long.

The door was opened by a maid with a red wine birthmark across half her face.

'Is Lady Fonthill at home?'

The maid nodded mutely, her expression fearful.

'Will you tell her that Paul Seddon is here? I wish to offer my condolences. We are . . . friends.' That word, dare he say it? All things considered, he believed he had the right.

The silent maid showed him into a drawing room and closed the door on him. He paced the room, looking around distractedly, overawed by his intentions more than his surroundings.

It was not too late to back out. He could slip away before she came, or he could simply keep to himself all the things he had it in mind to say.

He heard the door open. His heart quickened as he turned to face her.

Her expression was complex, wary, almost unwelcoming. It would take all his courage to go through with this.

'Paul? What are you doing here?'

'I just wanted to . . . see you.'

'See me?'

'To see how you're bearing up.'

'That's . . . very decent of you.'

'Also, I wanted to reassure you.'

Emma gave a guarded nod, encouraging him to go on, without committing herself.

'You have nothing to worry about. I destroyed it.'

'What are you talking about?'

'The handkerchief. With Aidan's blood on it. I burnt it for you.'

'I didn't ask you to do that.'

'No, but I thought . . . well, if the police knew how much blood there was on your hands . . . You needn't worry. I won't tell them.'

'I told you. I took his pulse.'

'There was a lot of blood, Emma. More blood than that.'

'That might have been your impression, but I can assure you . . .'

'It's all right. I understand. I know what a beast he was. Why you did it. You needn't worry. I won't say anything.'

'But you said yourself, it was that piano tuner person. You saw him.'

'Yes. Who was that? Someone who helped you do it? I hope it's someone you can trust, otherwise we're in trouble.'

'We?'

'Don't you see? I'm compromised too, now. I've destroyed evidence for you.'

'What do you want from me? Money, is it? For your sister and that child of hers?'

'Money? No, this isn't about money!'

Understanding dawned on her face, which did not result in the expression he might have hoped for. 'Oh, God . . . don't tell me . . .'

'I would do anything for you, Emma.'

'You don't know what you're saying. You don't know anything about it.'

'I know all I need to know. I know I . . .'

'Don't. Please, don't.'

'I understand. It's too soon. I just wanted you to know, you can count on me.'

A look of calculation came over Emma's face. 'I do appreciate . . . everything you've done for me. But it's not what you think. I can't explain now. Perhaps one day. Until then, you'll just have to trust me.'

'Of course.'

She rushed to cross the space that stood between them, taking his hands in hers, raising them to her mouth to kiss.

'Thank you, Paul.'

His heart felt like scattered feathers in the air.

THIRTY-SIX

DI Leversedge stood on the embankment and watched as the Model-T with the governor in the back was driven away by Macadam. He gave a small salute, which he may or may not have meant to be ironic, he couldn't decide. He didn't think so. Not ironic exactly. More sardonic; expressive, he hoped, of a shared cynicism. The grim cynicism of the professional police detective. A gesture of respect, perhaps, but one that asked for that respect to be reciprocated.

Leversedge accepted it was a lot of meaning to invest in a simple movement of the hand.

There was a sound like a gun discharging causing the car to swerve uncertainly. It was just the engine backfiring, but it had clearly been enough to throw Macadam off his stride. That was understandable. They were all jumpy, what with young Willoughby getting gunned down like that.

What would he have to do to prove his loyalty to Quinn? Obviously it would help if he could be the one to crack the Fonthill case and bring in Willoughby's killer. Yesterday he had felt sure that he was on to something with his theory about the Russian dancer. But now he was not so sure. Quinn's reaction had been discouraging.

Leversedge felt a kindling of resentment. No matter what he did, Quinn would never trust him. Nothing he could do would be good enough.

That was clear from the way he was being sidelined from the main investigation. What made it worse – and what made him hate Quinn even more – was that deep down he knew that he had brought all this on himself.

Naturally, they had to go through the list of suspects, eliminating those who had an alibi, or were otherwise in the clear, as Inchball had by all accounts done with that fellow Masters. But Inchball was a plodding brute, a foot soldier without ambition. He was even talking about leaving the force to join the army.

It wouldn't do for Leversedge to get caught in the same trap. That kind of methodical policing had its place, of course, same as house-to-house enquiries, and combing waste ground for clues. But Leversedge saw himself more as your brilliant detective, using deductive reasoning and a heightened understanding of human nature – dare he say *psychology*? – to make inspired leaps of the imagination to work out who the perpetrator was. Of course, he knew that there were dangers in this approach. One man's startling insights could be another's wild guesswork. And if you weren't careful it led to the kinds of shortcuts that his old boss Coddington had taken.

Coddington had been a great one for hunches. Never doubted his hunches. And if the evidence wasn't there to back them up, well, he'd make sure that it was, one way or another.

That wasn't Leversedge's way, never had been, though he was sure Quinn suspected him of shady practices. He found himself tarred with the same brush, through no fault of his own. Guilt by association, it was, and it wasn't fair.

The sensible thing would be to show him how he too could be the loyal foot soldier when required. Talk to the Russians and the Belgian and the opera singer, like he'd said he would. Maybe it would turn up something. Or maybe it would turn out to be a complete waste of time, and if so, who would that help?

He'd found out from Macadam and Inchball that Quinn had gone off to talk to Kell. He'd given nothing away when he'd come back, just ordered Macadam to get the car. But something had rattled him, Leversedge could see that.

Something to do with the case, too, he shouldn't wonder.

He knew Kell and his second in command, Irons, by sight. You could always tell when Kell entered the room from the pong of his medicinal cigarettes. And Irons could often be found propping up the saloon bar of the Red Lion at lunchtime, invariably drinking alone, downing a pint in resolute silence.

Leversedge consulted his pocket watch. Time he was heading over to the Ritz Hotel, where he had discovered from newspaper accounts that the Russians were staying.

If he played his cards right, there might be time to stop for a pint himself later on.

THIRTY-SEVEN

Quinn did his best not to look at the maid's birthmark as he asked to see Lady Fonthill. Before the maid had a chance to respond, another servant, a middle-aged man with salt and pepper hair and cheeks rouged by broken veins appeared behind her. 'Thank you, Marie, I'll deal with this.' The man's accent had a faint Irish lilt to it.

Quinn took out his warrant card. 'I am Detective Chief Inspector Quinn of the Special Crimes Department. These gentlemen are policemen too.'

Macadam was there on the doorstep beside Quinn. Also with them was Special Constable Elgar. This had been Macadam's idea. He had argued that Elgar's presence, given his celebrity, would act as a catalyst, helping to gain Lady Fonthill's trust and loosen her tongue. His musical expertise would come in handy too, or so Macadam theorized. Quinn was not sure how exactly, and suspected that Macadam only wanted the composer to be there so that he could spend more time in the company of one of his heroes. 'He has a great brain on him, you know,' Macadam had insisted. 'We should take advantage of it while we can.'

Quinn had been too exhausted to argue, and so they had called in at Hampstead Police Station to collect this invaluable brain. As it happened, Elgar was not on duty that morning, but Sergeant Kennedy was happy to provide them with his address. By a coincidence that Macadam insisted on seeing as fortuitous, it turned out that he lived on the same street as the Fonthills.

Elgar had been rather flustered by the arrival of the two detectives, protesting that he did not have his uniform and that he had work to do. At this, he looked rather sheepishly over his shoulder as a sharp female voice, presumably his wife's, had called out: 'Edward? Who is that? What are you doing?'

A moment later, the woman had appeared, an expression of stern disapproval on her face as she glowered slightly myopically at the strange men in conference with her husband.

'Who are these men?' she had demanded, her mouth set grimly.

'They are policemen. I have to go with them,' said Elgar, grabbing an overcoat and a rather dapper homburg from the hatstand by the front door. 'Duty calls, my dear.'

As he had closed the door behind them, Elgar had exhaled noisily in relief.

The Fonthills' Irish servant scowled furiously, as unimpressed by their credentials as Mrs Elgar had been. 'Her ladyship has already spoken to the police.'

'Yes. We wish to speak to her again.'

'She is with her children. The children are very upset.'

'Naturally. It is a terrible thing to lose your father,' said Quinn, his voice quavering with a wholly private emotion. After a beat, he added, 'So young. They *are* young, I think? I believe Lady Fonthill mentioned a nanny.'

'Yes, the children are very young. And they do have a nanny, Miss Greene.'

'Miss Greene, you say?' Quinn made a note of the name. 'According to Lady Fonthill, Sir Aidan had initiated an affair with Miss Greene.'

There was a gasp from Marie, who despite having been dismissed was still loitering in the hallway.

'What a damnable lie!' cried the butler. 'How dare you stand there on our doorstep and broadcast such terrible slanders!'

'Perhaps it would be better if we came in,' suggested Quinn, as if the main objection was the fact of his being on the doorstep. He looked up at the sky, which was sealed over with low cloud.

The manservant's jaw dropped in astonishment, all resistance disarmed by the detective's unconventional approach. Whether he meant to or not, he let them in.

'Just for the record, so that we have all the details straight, you are?'

'I?'

'Yes, you.'

'I am Callaghan.'

'Callaghan. I see. And this is?' Quinn indicated the maid with the stub of his pencil.

'This is Marie.'

'Hello, Marie.' Quinn tried very hard to smile reassuringly. From the way Marie jumped back in alarm, he was not convinced that he had pulled it off. 'Your surname, please.'

The maid blushed so deeply that her birthmark almost disappeared. She bowed her head and whispered something inaudibly in reply.

'I'm sorry. Could you speak up, please?'

She managed to find her voice, just, saying the two syllables of her name with a throbbing wonder as if it was the first word she had ever spoken: 'Driscoll.'

'Thank you. Miss Driscoll. I just need to ask you both a few questions, so that I can build up a picture of what happened here at the house prior to Sir Aidan's death.'

'I thought you wanted to talk to Lady Fonthill,' objected Callaghan.

'Oh, I will need to talk to everyone. Including Miss Greene. And possibly even the children.'

'The children? Man, have you no feelings? What do you hope to get from them? They are innocents in all of this.'

'In all of what, Mr Callaghan?'

'You come here with your dirty minds, digging things up. It's not fair, I tell you.'

'I'm just trying to understand what kind of a man Sir Aidan was. What kind of a husband he was. What kind of a father. What kind of an employer.'

'He was a good employer, if that's what you're asking,' said Callaghan, his head tilted defiantly, as if he expected to be called a liar over this.

'Miss Driscoll?'

The girl looked down and blushed again. She gave a helpless, wordless shrug that spoke volumes.

'There was no truth in what Lady Fonthill said then, about Sir Aidan and Miss Greene?'

Callaghan cut in quickly, as if to prevent Marie from saying anything. 'I don't know anything about that,' was his careful response.

'But you would not say that it was . . . out of the question, given Sir Aidan's . . . habits and . . . interests.'

'This is all just tittle-tattle,' exclaimed Callaghan disgustedly.

'And yet he was unfaithful to Lady Fonthill. We know, for instance, that he fathered a child with a woman called Anna Seddon.'

'I know nothing about that,' insisted Callaghan, his voice rising with desperation.

'We always start with a motive. Jealousy is a strong motive.'

'What are you suggesting? Have you come here, to this house, on this day, to a house in mourning, to make these vile accusations against a grieving widow, the mother of two beautiful children? The loving wife of their father?'

'Do you know of anyone else who might have wished Sir Aidan dead?'

'Oh, you are a man! You are quite a man!'

Quinn was not sure what Callaghan meant by this observation, but it seemed that the butler was struggling to contain a rage that threatened to explode in violence. 'Can you account for your own movements yesterday, say from twelve thirty p.m. onwards?'

'Me? You want me for it now, do you? Is it because I am Irish? Is that it? What? I have risen up against my master and slain him? Is this the bloody revolution come?'

'Is it?'

'You are a mockery of a man! Indeed, you are.'

'Now, now, if we can just keep it civil here,' said Macadam, stepping forward with a warning glare flashed in Quinn's direction.

Perhaps he had goaded Callaghan too much. But in so doing he had at least revealed the man's temper. Nevertheless, he was content to yield the interview to Macadam.

'We may have got off on the wrong foot here, Mr Callaghan,' continued Macadam, his tone conciliatory. 'DCI Quinn has been under considerable strain since yesterday's terrible events, as indeed have we all. You may have heard that as well as Sir Aidan, one of our own officers was killed.'

'Yes, I had heard that. A terrible business. Will you be accusing me of *that* now?'

'No, no, not at all. We would just like to know if you have seen or heard anything suspicious in the last few days. Anything out of the ordinary at all. Any strangers coming to the house? Did Sir Aidan seem anxious or out of sorts at all?'

Callaghan's head lifted minutely. His eyes narrowed. 'There was a man,' he said.

'A man?'

'I didn't see him. But Sir Aidan did. And it seemed to unsettle him, that it did.'

'Where did he see him?'

'He said he was out the front, watching the house.'

'Did he come to the house? Did he speak to Sir Aidan?'

'If he did, I did not admit him.'

'Marie, did you let in a strange man?'

The maid shook her head vehemently.

'When was this?' Macadam kept his tone admirably light and unhurried.

Quinn, on the contrary, felt himself tense with impatience. 'What did he look like, this man?'

'I told you, I didn't see him.' Callaghan's tone was hostile, wounded still by his earlier brush with Quinn.

'Did Sir Aidan not describe him to you?'

'Now why should he do that?'

Macadam winced. Quinn recognized that it was in frustration at his own intervention. He conceded his fault with a hesitant dip of the head.

'Can we get back to the question of when,' said Macadam patiently.

'Let me see. It would have been . . .' Callaghan jabbed a finger in the air, as if to pin down the day. 'Friday. That's it. It was the day that parcel arrived. You remember it, Marie. The mysterious parcel.'

Marie's head bobbed up and down energetically.

Quinn and Macadam looked at each other. Special Constable Elgar raised an eyebrow.

'What was so *mysterious* about this parcel?'

'It didn't come in the regular post. And it seemed to upset the master somewhat.'

'What was in the parcel?' demanded Quinn.

'I didn't see him open it,' replied Callaghan tetchily. The equanimity with which he answered Macadam's questions was not extended to those from Quinn. 'So I cannot say for certain. But there is an object has appeared in his studio that wasn't there before.'

'What is it?'

'It is a box.'

There were few things as conducive to mystery as a box. Despite his relative inexperience as a detective, Special Constable Elgar seemed to feel this instinctively. The eyebrow that had risen before was now hiked up another notch, as if it functioned as a gauge of astonishment.

*   *   *

Callaghan led them to a room at the rear of the house. Bookshelves lined two of the walls. There was a fireplace, at present unlit, so that the air had a sharp chill to it. A large gilt-framed mirror was suspended above the mantel, which made the room feel larger than it was. In one corner, a glass-fronted cabinet stood, containing various decanters and crystal glasses. A desk covered in green leather, with mahogany drawers, was crammed beneath a window that looked out on to a bleak, weather-blasted garden.

But the room was dominated by a single object: the black, highly polished grand piano that almost filled the remaining space.

Quinn tried to form an impression of the man whose room this was, beyond the obvious inferences. Musical, yes. But the imposing presence of the huge instrument suggested an insistence on his musicality to the expense of everything, and everyone, else. It smacked of ostentation. That was not to say that the piano was there purely for show. Or rather, the show was not for the outside world. The show was for Sir Aidan Fonthill himself, for him to bolster the idea and image of himself that he had constructed, that of a great musician.

It was here, in this room, that he had created the illusion of his identity.

Perhaps the word 'illusion' was too strong. But Quinn believed that most people's sense of their own identity was based on self-deception. Experience had shown him that this was especially so for two categories of humans: murderers and their victims. More often than people realized, the ultimate motive for murder was to prevent a truth emerging. Invariably, this truth was at its core to do with a version of self presented to the world. Equally, when someone ended up murdered, it often turned out that they were not the person those closest to them had believed them to be.

It also occurred to him that Sir Aidan's murder, given the choice of weapon and the location of the fatal wound, was a deliberate insult to his carefully constructed identity.

Over by the desk, Callaghan gestured to a small mahogany box, about the size of a tea caddy. 'Here it is.'

'Don't touch it.'

The butler appeared put out by Quinn's abrupt command.

'I'm sorry, but there may be prints on it that will enable us to identify its sender. Who has handled it so far, do you know?'

'As far as I know, only Sir Aidan.'

Quinn turned to Macadam enquiringly. Macadam held up his gloved hands in answer, then squeezed past to examine the box.

'Mahogany inlaid with marquetry formed from some lighter wood, perhaps ash. The design of a harp or lyre is depicted.' Macadam turned the object in his hands. 'I would estimate its weight to be three to four pounds. Perhaps a little more. There is a key projecting from one side. The underside is unvarnished and bears a crude inscription.' Macadam looked up significantly. 'In German.'

'German?' Quinn felt his heart quicken. Suddenly he understood Kell's interest; Churchill's too.

'I would say so, yes.'

'May I see that?' Elgar's softly spoken enquiry was strangely startling. It was the first thing he had said since they had left his house. And yet for all the self-effacing politeness of his voice, there was something steely and confident about this intervention.

Macadam held the bottom of the box up for Elgar to read.

'*Ehre verloren, alles verloren.*' His pronunciation was assured and persuasive.

'I am right? It is German?' said Macadam.

'Oh, yes,' confirmed Elgar. 'It is German.'

'What does it mean?' demanded Quinn.

'It means, "When honour is lost, all is lost."'

'When honour is lost, all is lost,' repeated Quinn.

'Yes.'

'Open it,' Quinn commanded Macadam.

Macadam lifted the lid, activating a single plink that was the last note of a dying melody.

'A music box,' observed Macadam.

'So it would seem,' agreed Quinn. 'Wind it up. Let's hear it play properly.'

Macadam closed the lid again and turned the key, ratcheting up the mechanism. When the spring was fully wound and the key would turn no more, he opened the box once more.

The tune that played, if *tune* was the appropriate word, was not one that Quinn recognized. It ground on relentlessly, repeating the same limited sequence of notes over and over, until at last, to everyone's relief, it stopped.

Elgar's expression was pained. It was clear that he considered the sound that had just been inflicted on him as an insult to his ears.

'What is that?' asked Quinn.

Elgar pulled a face and shrugged.

'You don't recognize the tune?'

'There is no tune. It's just a succession of random notes. May I?' Elgar gestured at the piano.

'Be our guest,' said Quinn.

Elgar seated himself at the piano, taking a moment to arrange the skirt of his overcoat, as if he were a concert pianist in a swallow-tailed coat. He lifted the lid and held his right hand over the keys for a moment while cocking his head, as if listening to a melody that only he could hear. At length, he nodded with satisfaction and picked out the same sequence of notes as the music box had produced.

The composer shook his head and gave a sigh of dissatisfaction. 'Musically, it makes no sense.'

'So why would anyone go to the trouble of constructing a music box that plays . . . *that*?' wondered Quinn.

Elgar played the sequence again, this time at double the speed, with a fluency that was impressive, despite the discordancy of the notes. He wrinkled his nose in disgust. 'Of course, it may be the work of some avantgarde composer of whose work I am bliss-fully ignorant. We live in an age when all manner of fraudulent trash is not only perpetrated but encouraged.'

'I cannot imagine that there would be much of a market for such items,' said Quinn.

'Nor I.'

Quinn completed his own thought. 'This must have been made to order, specifically for Sir Aidan. But why?'

Macadam repeated the words on the bottom of the box. 'When honour is lost, all is lost.'

'A warning? A reminder? A call to action?'

Elgar played the notes again, slowing them down and improvising a left-hand accompaniment to fill them out. It was an improvement perhaps on the notes by themselves, but still the odd phrase ended without resolution and carried with it no sense of shape or purpose. Elgar shook his head and smiled, ruefully, as if the notes were a puzzle whose solution had so far eluded him but which he was determined to crack.

'It must have meant something to Sir Aidan,' posited Quinn. He knew, as he said it, that it was by no means certain. But they had to start somewhere. That usually meant making assumptions, which may turn out to be valid or may not.

'Perhaps Lady Fonthill would know?' suggested Macadam, with a hopeful glance towards the butler.

Callaghan narrowed his eyes, as if he suspected some trick was being played on him. But in the end, it seemed he was as intrigued as the rest of them. He gave a small bow. 'If you will come this way.'

They left Elgar at the piano, picking away at the broken melody.

THIRTY-EIGHT

Leversedge took in the foyer of the Ritz Hotel with a sweeping glance. The place made him feel jumpy. He knew he didn't belong in this world. What was worse, he felt that everyone else there knew it too, from the liveried bellboys pushing around their arched luggage carts to the jewel-laden society ladies with their even more arched eyebrows.

The sense of resentment that had begun to smoulder earlier that morning flared into a hot flame. Not that he was one of those socialist types. Far from it. He was all for King and country. For Empire, too.

He had nothing against the rich, or the gentry. He was here on their account after all, looking into the murder of one of their own. The least they could do was not look down their noses at him. He had seen things they could not imagine and faced dangers that would have them shrieking in terror. On their account, all of it.

His eye was drawn to one woman in particular. She possessed a glacial beauty that provoked bitter anguish rather than desire. What was the point of desire? She was unattainable. He felt only a perverse desire to take her to one side and recount the details of Sir Aidan's murder. The peculiar weapon driven into his brain. The ruined ear. The blood running down his neck. Although he had not actually seen the blood flowing, of course, and in point of fact there was less blood than he might have expected. But still he would lay it on a bit, if necessary.

And he wouldn't stop there, with Sir Aidan. He would describe to her every mutilated corpse he had ever been obliged to confront. So that she fully understood the horror that existed in this world, through which she blithely flitted, cosseted in fur and satin, as yet untouched by grief and unmoved by the suffering of others.

The barbarians were not just at the gates. They were among us. That was what he needed to impress on her.

He did not know why he had fixated on this woman. Perhaps he was doing her an injustice. He had formed an impression of her based on her dress, her posture and her looks, ascribing to her a haughtiness that for all he knew she did not possess. He imagined the la-de-da lilt of her voice, her conversation laced with fashionable slang and automatic contempt. And yet she might have been the most charming of women. Certainly, judging from the silver fox stole draped around her shoulders, she was someone he ought to have respected, rather than fantasized about upsetting. So why did he take such pleasure in imagining that stole coming to snarling life and savaging her face?

He was not himself this morning. He could blame it on the death of young Willoughby. That had shaken them all. The real root of his discombobulation, therefore, the true cause of his resentment, was Quinn, for it was Quinn who had sent Willoughby to his death.

He also suspected that Quinn was holding things back from him, no doubt so that he could appear all the more brilliant when he stepped forward and presented his solution to the case.

The diamonds suspended from the woman's ears glinted with preternatural clarity.

Leversedge turned sharply round, allowing the doorman to hold the door open for him as he walked briskly out.

THIRTY-NINE

They were shown into a drawing room at the front of the house.

Quinn noticed immediately the rectangle of lighter coloured paintwork over the fireplace. He drew the butler's attention to it. 'What was there?'

'A painting. It was removed for cleaning. Lady Emma has it in mind to redecorate.'

'When was this done?'

'Yesterday.'

'Before or after Sir Aidan's death?'

'After, I believe.'

'On Lady Fonthill's instructions?'

'Yes.'

'How curious. I suppose grief manifests itself in many different ways.'

Callaghan made a move to go but Quinn detained him for a moment longer.

'What was the painting of, may I ask?'

'It was a portrait. A portrait of them both – Sir Aidan and Lady Emma, painted at the time of their betrothal, I believe.'

'And she asked for this to be taken down on the day of her husband's murder?'

The loyal Callaghan hurried from the room without providing an answer.

'What do you make of that, Mac?' asked Quinn.

'Well, we know it was not a happy marriage. A sham, perhaps, which she feels herself no longer obligated to maintain.'

'But would you not want to keep up appearances for a little longer? If only for the sake of the children? To show that you detested their father so deeply, so soon after his death – it must be rather hurtful to them, do you not think?'

Macadam looked around. 'Perhaps the little ones are not allowed in here?' The room presented a scene of immaculate tidiness that did not indicate the presence of children.

The door opened and Lady Emma came in.

She was wearing a black dress, showing that she was prepared to go this far at least in keeping to the conventions of mourning. That said, it was the kind of dress fashion editors described as 'chic'. Grief, he might have said, became her. Her face appeared strained and sombre, but there was strength in it too. There was no hint that she had been crying.

'How are they, the children?'

His question seemed to take her by surprise. She chose her words carefully. 'Confused. Frightened. Very sad.' Her bottom lip came out in sympathy, as if she was about to start crying. She did not.

'And you? How are you?'

'Confused. Frightened. Very shocked.'

'How old are they?'

'Daphne is four, John six.'

'They must have loved their father very much.'

Emma's look questioned what had led him to this conclusion. 'He was their father. They loved him. As all children love their fathers.'

'At that age though, the father is a hero. He can do no wrong.'

'Oh, Aidan was quite capable of doing wrong.'

'They are with the nanny now, Miss Greene?'

'Yes.'

'We would like to speak to her at some point.'

'Is that necessary?'

'You mentioned yourself, yesterday, that Sir Aidan had initiated an affair with Miss Greene.'

'I didn't say that. You are mistaken.'

'Forgive me. I am sure I heard you say as much to Anna Seddon.'

'He auditioned her for the choir. That is all.'

'You caught him making love to her. Those were your words, I believe.' Quinn glanced at Macadam, who nodded in confirmation.

Lady Emma's eyelids fluttered, as if they were the focus of an attempt to garner the strength that Quinn had seen signs of before. 'I – I was upset. Lashing out. I regret saying it now.' She opened her eyes fully and met his questioning gaze head-on.

She was lying. Of that, he was certain. The question was, why? Obviously, by minimizing Sir Aidan's fault, she was protecting his reputation. Preserving his image in the eyes of her children. But she was also protecting her own reputation and the myth of their marriage. More importantly, she was distracting attention from any possible motive she might have had for killing him.

Lady Emma must have sensed his scepticism. She made the decision to throw him something more. 'Hattie is far too sensible a girl to allow herself to be seduced by an ageing Lothario like Aidan.'

'But he did make advances towards her?'

She waved a hand dismissively. 'You might as well say, he breathed.'

But Quinn persisted. 'She might have found it difficult to resist. She might have feared that she would lose her position if she did not do what he wanted. It does happen, I believe.'

'I would not have permitted it to happen. I would have rather sent Aidan away. The children adore Hattie. I simply cannot imagine how we would manage without her.'

'She is indispensable?'

'Yes.'

'Unlike Sir Aidan.'

'What are you suggesting, Inspector?'

'He's a chief inspector, actually,' put in Macadam. Quinn waved a hand to let it go.

'Well, *Chief* Inspector then. What exactly are you suggesting? That I murdered my husband to protect my nanny from his unwanted advances? I suppose it is a slightly more plausible theory than that I did it simply out of jealousy. I think if you knew me at all you would know that I am not a jealous person. I could not have remained married to Aidan all this time if I was.'

'How long have you been married?'

'Ten years.'

'And when was the painting done? The one that you have had removed from above the mantelpiece?'

Something changed in Lady Fonthill's expression. The look of strain sharpened into something like wariness. 'You probably won't believe this, but the reason I took it down was out of respect to Aidan. He absolutely hated that painting. And I only insisted on it staying up there to torment him. Yesterday, after his death, I came back and looked at it and cried. I felt petty and ashamed. And yes, it seemed to be a lie. A terrible lie. I couldn't bear to look at it any more. So I took it down.'

'It was not to send it off to be cleaned then?'

'No.'

'Where is it now?'

'I destroyed it.'

'That seems . . . an extreme reaction.'

Lady Emma closed her eyes, with that same animated fluttering that had preceded her earlier lie. But this time she offered nothing, other than a look of stark defiance. *Say what you want*, she seemed to say, *I will not explain.* 'Was there anything else, Chief Inspector?'

'The music box that was delivered to Sir Aidan a few days ago . . . Do you know anything about it?'

'Music box?' Lady Emma's brows came together as she gave a little shrugging shake of the head.

'He didn't mention it to you?'

Her eyes darted away from his. 'No. I don't think so.'

Was this another lie? Quinn was beginning to suspect everything she said. 'Perhaps it was a gift from a lover? From Miss Seddon, for example?'

'If so, he certainly wouldn't tell me about it.' Lady Emma seemed pleased with her retort.

Quinn had to admit, it was a fair point.

'Your husband told Mr Callaghan that he had seen a man watching the house. According to Mr Callaghan, Sir Aidan was unsettled by this. Did you see this man, Lady Fonthill?'

'No. But Aidan did mention it to me. I believe it is the same man who came to the school disguised as a blind piano tuner.'

'What makes you say that?'

'Who else would it be?'

Quinn thought about this for a moment. Despite the assertive, almost belligerent way she asked the question, it by no means struck him as an inevitable conclusion to draw. What was interesting though was the force with which she insisted on it. He chose to leave the question unanswered. 'Did he give you a description of the man?'

'Only to say he looked . . . *sinister.*'

Despite Lady Fonthill's emphasis, the word did not ring true. It sounded too novelish. 'Did anyone else see this man?'

'Not that I am aware of.'

'That is unfortunate.'

Evidently there was something in Quinn's tone that Lady Fonthill did not like. 'Are you questioning my word?'

'Not at all. I have Mr Callaghan's word, too. So unless the two of you have cooked this up between you . . .'

'How strange. You seem to place more credence in the word of a butler than that of a lady!' Lady Emma was evidently more amused than offended by her own observation. 'What strange times we live in.'

'You misunderstand. I place equal credence in the testimony given to me by any individual, regardless of class. But when I have two independent statements confirming the same detail, I am more inclined to accept it as a fact.' Quinn gave the slightest of bows. 'Did you know that your husband asked Charles Cavendish to write blank cheques in his favour?'

A flush of emotion – anger? – flooded into Lady Emma's face. A word formed on her lips, a whisper of breath barely giving it voice. *Fool!* 'I trust Cavendish refused.'

'He did. Do you have any idea why your husband would want to take money from the choir?'

'No.'

'Were there no legitimate expenses that he might have incurred?'

'I suppose there might have been.'

'Were you aware of any money worries that he might have had?'

'My husband had no money of his own but I had a sufficient fortune to ensure that he had no anxieties on that front.'

'But there might have been a reason why he was reluctant to come to you? Perhaps someone was blackmailing him?'

'Yes. That must have been it.' Quinn was struck by the speed with which she accepted this explanation. She gave the impression of clutching at straws. 'The man who was watching the house, the same man who came to the school – he was blackmailing my husband. If only Aidan had said something. If only he had come to me.' This felt like her most egregious piece of playacting yet.

'Am I to understand that you would have given your husband the money he needed, even if it was to pay off a blackmailer?'

'Better that than embezzling funds from the choir, I think.'

'Do you really believe Sir Aidan was capable of such a crime?'

'Who knows what any of us is capable of?'

Quinn narrowed his eyes. Her comment was irrefutable but evasive. 'That might have been a motive for someone to kill him – to prevent such a scandal?'

'No, no – it was the blackmailer. I'm sure of it.'

The enthusiasm with which Lady Emma was promoting this theory puzzled Quinn. It simply did not make sense. If Sir Aidan was being blackmailed by the counterfeit piano tuner, it was hardly likely that the blackmailer would kill the victim from whom he hoped to extort money. If Sir Aidan had refused to pay, then the blackmailer would simply have exposed whatever shameful secret he was holding over him. That was the way blackmail worked.

It was conceivable that the supposed blackmailer had attempted to back up his threats with violence. Or perhaps the two men had quarrelled and some kind of struggle had ensued, resulting in Sir Aidan's death. But the scene in the music room was not consistent with a fight. And again, there was the question of the prepared weapon. Sir Aidan's death was not the result of a spontaneous outburst, but rather of premeditation.

There was something that needed unpicking here. But Lady Emma's insistence on blackmail being behind it all was distracting.

'Can you think of any grounds that this person might have had for blackmailing your husband?'

'I am surprised you need to ask that, Chief Inspector.'

'You mean his infidelities? But were they not common knowledge? He could have had no fear of them being exposed, because they were already out in the open. You certainly knew about them.'

'Yes, but the blackmailer didn't know that, did he?'

Quinn gave an involuntary wince. Like all amateur 'detectives', Lady Emma was piling supposition on supposition to create an exceedingly shaky theoretical edifice. It was pure hearsay that there had been a man watching the house. The only person who claimed to have seen him was dead. But even accepting that there had been such a man, there was no proof that this was the same individual who had later been seen at the school wearing false whiskers and carrying a white stick. And certainly no evidence that he had been attempting to blackmail Sir Aidan.

But Quinn did not attempt to argue her out of her position. There was little point. Besides, what he found most interesting was the eagerness with which she held to it.

'Was it someone in the choir, this blackmailer?'

'Oh, no. It wouldn't be one of our choir members!' Lady Emma seemed genuinely appalled by the suggestion.

'Then who?'

'Well, that's for you to discover, isn't it, Chief Inspector?'

'I would appreciate it if you could draw up a list of Sir Aidan's acquaintances.'

'Oh, it won't be someone *I* know, will it?'

'Perhaps not. Nevertheless, it will be helpful for us to have such a list. By talking to Sir Aidan's friends and acquaintances, a name may come up. As it is, we have nothing to go on. Other than mysterious personages whom no one can identify.'

'Very well. I shall see what I can do.'

Quinn nodded gratefully. 'It can't have been easy. Living with a man who was consistently unfaithful to you.'

The liveliness that had entered Lady Emma's expression while she had been speculating about a blackmailer suddenly drained from her features. Her lips were compressed into a thin line. 'I did not kill my husband, if that's what you're implying.'

'No. I wasn't. I simply meant there must have been times when it was difficult to be in the same house as him. You said earlier that you would have sent him away rather than lose Miss Greene. Have you ever had occasion to send him away before?'

'No. But there were times when Aidan understood that it would be wise for him to take himself off.'

'Where would he go?'

Lady Fonthill's expression flickered evasively. She settled at last on avoiding Quinn's gaze. 'I really don't know. That was his business, not mine.'

Once again, Quinn had the undeniable sense that she was lying. But why? That was the really interesting question. He could find out easily enough where her husband went; in fact, he already had a pretty good idea. But why Lady Fonthill was being so uncooperative, given that it was her husband's murder that they were investigating, that was a harder mystery to fathom.

'How did you and Sir Aidan meet?'

It was a simple question. But the micro-flare of amazement that it provoked was unmistakeable. She recovered quickly to give a burst of mocking laughter. 'How did we *meet*?' Her mouth twisted into a snarl of disgust. It seemed she considered this the most extraordinary question he could possibly ask her, though whether she thought it extraordinarily impertinent or extraordinarily stupid, he did not know. Clearly she did not think it was any of his business.

'Yes.'

She gave him a look containing equal parts pity and contempt. 'What possible interest can that be to you?'

'I am trying to understand your relationship with your husband. It would help to know a little about its origins.'

'Its origins, you say? Well, believe me, its origins have nothing to do with our meeting.' She must have noticed his confusion. 'What you have to understand, Chief Inspector, is that people like Aidan and I, we do not *meet* in the way that someone like you might meet a person. Nothing is allowed to happen by accident when it comes to such an important matter as arranging the union of a member of the aristocracy.' She snorted a bitter laugh, making it clear that her choice of word was laced with irony. 'Oh, don't worry, I'm not claiming such distinction for myself. I was not the member of the aristocracy, though I might be considered to be one now. I have married into that class, I suppose. And it was only by doing so that

I realized how much I despised it. My father was a successful industrialist. I was an only child. He left me a considerable fortune. That is how we *met*, Chief Inspector. Does that answer your question?'

'But you shared a common interest? In music?'

'Yes. That certainly helped in the beginning. It fooled me into believing that I loved him, and that he loved me, when in reality we simply shared a passion for something else. Something external to us both. It was a great distraction, you see, music.'

'A distraction? From what?'

'From the fact that he married me for my money and I married him because I was a fool. I didn't remain a fool, and that in a way was the great tragedy of our marriage.'

'Are you sorry that he's dead?'

She looked at him for a moment as if she didn't understand the question. Then remembering herself, answered, 'I'm not sorry that he's out of my life.'

For the first time in the interview, Quinn had the impression that she was being completely honest with him. And yet, at the same time, there was still something strangely evasive about the answer that he could not quite put his finger on.

FORTY

The Red Lion on Parliament Street was a favourite of many classes of people who had a role to play in the nation's life. Parliament was not in session at the moment; besides which, it was a Sunday, so there was not the usual throng of MPs and peers at the bar. Also absent were the political journalists who stuck closely to the coat tails of those illustrious beings, like pilot fish surrounding sharks.

And so the saloon was left to the men who laboured tirelessly on the public's behalf without recognition or gratitude, the Treasury officials and Admiralty mandarins, innocuous-looking individuals from all the various Whitehall departments, in particular the War Office, who dispensed the fates of millions at home and abroad in the flick of a pen nib and the fold of a paper docket. Who could begrudge them a pint or two of ale in the middle of the day, if it eased the crippling weight of responsibility that no doubt bore down on them, even if they managed to hide it so well? The laughter and conviviality that invariably prevailed in the pub was surely testament to their fortitude and resilience.

The Red Lion was close enough to Scotland Yard to have among its regular clientele a scattering of CID detectives, whose plain clothes protected them from censure. Willoughby had come here often with his former boss, DCI Coddington, who considered a spot of lunchtime 'lubrication' (as he put it) to be a necessary part of the investigatory method. 'Sherlock Holmes has his pipe. I have my dimple pot,' he had been known to say. Leversedge had never been sure that the habit led to any great clarity of thinking.

He rarely set foot in the place any more, not since transferring to SCD under the apparently abstemious Quinn. Now and then, he would meet one of his former colleagues to chew the fat. It didn't do any harm to keep up his contacts in CID. You never knew when you might need to pull in a favour.

It was on one of these occasions that Leversedge had first spotted Irons at the bar. He remembered looking at the man and thinking *I know you* without being able to put his finger on where he knew him from. Then, when he had turned his back on Irons, it came to him. This was the fellow who had lurked unannounced at the back of the room in various briefings. At the end of one of them, he'd seen him parleying confidentially with Quinn, and, despite their lowered voices, had managed to overhear enough to work out their relationship.

When Leversedge had looked back towards the bar to check whether he was right, he saw that the man was gone, the empty pot the only evidence that he had been there at all.

Even though that had been the first time Leversedge was consciously aware of noticing Irons in the Red Lion, he had the distinct impression that he had been there every time he had come in with Coddington. He was like one of those fixtures in a room that is so constant that you no longer see it.

What made it all the more impressive was that Commander Irons was quite a good-looking man: athletic build, chiselled features, compelling gaze. He was in fact just the sort of person you thought you would have noticed.

As soon as Leversedge entered the saloon, he saw that Irons was in his usual place. He kept his gaze fixed on his target as he hurried towards him. He knew from experience that if he let him out of his sight for a moment he was likely to disappear.

'Can I get you another to go in there?'

Commander Irons did not look up from his pint, which he was staring into as if it held a fascinating secret. 'Not unless you want to fall foul of the law.'

'Oh, yes. DORA.' Leversedge understood the reference to the Defence of the Realm Act. One of its less enforceable provisions was a ban on standing drinks for pals. 'I won't tell if you don't.'

'Ah, well, you see, Inspector Leversedge, the thing is, you never know who's watching.' Irons had still not looked at him, so it was especially unnerving to hear him use his name. Not only had Irons seen Leversedge, he knew who he was.

Leversedge could not help remarking on this. 'Well, at least that saves me the bother of introducing myself.'

Irons gave a loaded nod but otherwise remained tight-lipped, his face devoid of expression. The beer in his pot still held his attention.

'May I at least join you?'

'Join me in what?'

'Here at the bar.'

Irons pursed his lips. 'You may stand where you like.'

'Might I have a word with you while I stand here?'

'That's not how it works. If you have something to communicate to us, it must come through Quinn.'

'What if it is to do with Quinn?'

At last Irons looked up. Leversedge felt himself under scrutiny. It was an uncomfortable sensation. But at least he had the man's attention now.

FORTY-ONE

'Please sit down, Miss Greene.' Quinn held the door open and turned to the other woman in the room. 'Would you excuse us, Lady Fonthill?'

'Excuse you?'

'I wish to speak to Miss Greene alone for a few minutes.'

'You are ejecting me from my own drawing room!'

'If there is somewhere else you would rather we conduct the interview?'

Lady Fonthill was on her feet. 'No, no. Please don't trouble yourself on my account. I wanted to look in on the children anyway. If you need me, I shall be in the nursery.'

Quinn closed the door behind her, with a slow nod to Macadam who stood with his hands behind his back, looking for all the world as if he had no interest in the proceedings.

Hattie Greene looked up at Quinn nervously. It seemed to him that she was not much more than a child herself. She sat with her feet placed together primly, her hands clasped tightly to still their fidgeting, lips sucked in and tightly clamped.

A bundle of suppressed nerves, in other words.

Quinn did his best to smile and as usual could only hope the effect was reassuring. 'Thank you for agreeing to talk to me.'

One shoulder came up in a childlike shrug that struck Quinn as unspeakably poignant. 'Mr Callaghan said it was important.' Her voice was small, barely more than a whisper.

'I understand how frightening this must be for you.'

'It's the children I'm worried about.'

'Of course. How are they bearing up?'

The other shoulder now jerked up, as if yanked by an invisible wire. The movement initiated a wider spasm. This was more than a shrug. It was a silent howl of despair. 'They are asking a lot of questions. Naturally. I don't know what to say to them. It's so horrible. How do you explain something like this to children?' It appeared to be a genuine question. She gave Quinn a look of such exposed hopelessness that he couldn't take it any other way.

He wished he had an answer for her, but all he had was a question he knew she wouldn't like. He felt a heel asking it, especially now, because he knew that now it would have the greatest impact. 'How would you describe your relationship with Sir Aidan?'

Her look was one of sheer panic. 'What do you mean?'

'I understand that he made advances to you?'

'Who told you that?'

'Is it not true?'

'He came to the nursery and asked me to audition.'

'For the choir?'

'Yes.'

'Did he make you feel uncomfortable?'

Miss Greene furrowed her brows as if thinking deeply. 'I didn't want to do it. I'm not . . . I'm not a natural singer.'

She was choosing her words carefully. Quinn suspected that she was acting under the principle of *never speak ill of the dead*, which had no doubt been impressed on her by some older, wiser relative. He wondered how he could induce her to abandon it. 'And that's all there was to it?'

Now both shoulders rolled in a gesture that said more than any words could. She flashed him a look in which the whites of her eyes featured hugely, a revelatory as well as beseeching glance.

'Did you tell anyone about what had happened?'

Her face coloured with embarrassment at the thought of such a thing. 'Tell? Who would I tell?'

'I don't know. A friend, perhaps? A gentleman friend? Someone who might not take too kindly to your employer putting you in such an invidious position.'

'You think I told . . . someone who . . . who, who killed him!' The heat of emotion lent force to her voice. That first hesitation, however, told him that he was on to something.

'There *is* someone, though?'

'Jack wouldn't hurt anyone. *Couldn't.*' Miss Greene closed her eyes and shuddered. 'That's what's so terrible about this war.'

'He's in the army?'

Miss Greene's eyes were still closed as she nodded.

'Is he at the Front?'

At last she met Quinn's gaze. Her eyes glistened with tears. 'No, thank God. Well, not yet at least. He's at a training camp in Gravesend.'

'I understand. But we will have to check. Just to rule him out of our investigation. What's his name?'

'Jack. Private Jack Delaware.'

Quinn noted the name. 'Regiment?'

'He's with the Middlesex.'

'Thank you.'

'I didn't tell him. I didn't tell anyone,' she insisted, shaking her head in fierce denial.

'What about the children? Were the children present when he . . .'

'Yes.' Again the colour flooded into her cheeks.

'They saw everything?'

'Yes, but . . .'

'They didn't understand.'

'No. How could they have?'

'It must have been a very unpleasant experience.'

She rolled in her lips so that they disappeared from view. Her eyes flicked in all directions except at Quinn.

'How do you think it affected them?'

Her gaze steadied and at last dared to meet his. 'Children notice things, even if they don't fully understand them. It's as if they have emotional antennae.' She made a little mime of antennae with her hands. Then, remembering herself, clasped them together in her lap. 'Afterwards, John withdrew into himself. He became sulky. He is . . . well, little boys, you know, sometimes, they form attachments. He's very affectionate.'

'He's a little bit in love with you?' Quinn came close to adding, *I can understand that*.

'Don't mock him. His emotions are just as real to him as yours or mine are to us.'

'You think he was jealous of his father?'

'You're not accusing John now, surely?' She gave an incredulous, gasping laugh.

'Of course not. I'm just trying to understand.'

'He might have said something to someone. He might have told his mother. Is that who told you?'

Quinn gave a vague wince, which was all the answer she was going to get, then switched to another line of questioning. 'Did you see any strangers come to the house in the days before Sir Aidan's death?'

'No. *I* didn't.'

Quinn picked up on her emphasis. 'But someone did?'

There was a beat of tremulous silence before she answered. 'John. I thought at first that it was just . . . well, you know, that it was to do with what had happened. All part of acting up after his father's visit to the nursery. I thought he was making up stories. He has a vivid imagination. It didn't make any sense, you see, what he said.'

'What did he say?'

'He said he saw his father talking to Mr Toad. You know. Mr Toad of Toad Hall. From *The Wind in the Willows*.'

Quinn was aware of Macadam's agitation at the periphery of his vision. He turned to face it. 'Yes, Macadam?'

'What do you say we take the boy in, sir? Show him some mugshots.'

'Take him to the police station?' cried Miss Greene in alarm.

'To Scotland Yard,' said Macadam brightly. 'I dare say he would think that quite an adventure.'

Her expression brightened as she thought about it. But then suddenly clouded again. 'You would have to ask his mother.'

'What objection could she have, if it helped us catch her husband's murderer?' asked Macadam, evidently in all innocence.

But there was a possibility, Quinn thought, that his question contained its own answer.

Before they could act on Macadam's suggestion, the door to the drawing room was thrown open and a red-faced Special Constable Elgar burst in.

'Steady on, man,' cried Macadam. 'We don't want you fainting again.'

Elgar was waving a torn-off scrap of musical manuscript paper in his hand. He thrust it towards Quinn, who viewed it with suspicion but made no move to take it.

'I've got it! I've cracked the code!' It looked like Macadam's fears were about to be borne out: the great composer was short of breath and appeared unsteady on his pins.

But a gleam of excitement shone in his eyes.

FORTY-TWO

Commander Irons held his gaze for longer than was polite. Of course he did. That was how it was with these people. They were not polite. They used whatever dirty tricks they could to unsettle you. That gaze, for example, had the effect of making Leversedge feel like one of the suspects he interrogated. He felt every word he said was doubted, his motives questioned, his character disparaged.

Irons even kept his eyes on him as he downed the last half inch of his beer.

He smacked his lips in satisfaction, licking away the foam. 'Go on then. What have you got?'

Leversedge cast a nervous glance around and swallowed drily. He would have to choose his words carefully. 'Are you sure I can't . . .?' He gestured at Irons' empty glass.

Irons finally turned his gaze away and signalled to the barman. The pot was taken away and filled. Leversedge ordered a pint of bitter for himself and took a grateful draught from it. 'I know that this current investigation is of interest to you.'

Irons' expression gave nothing away.

'Naturally, you will want to be assured that it is being handled appropriately.'

Irons gave a loud gasp in appreciation of his beer. It was deliberate and disdainful.

But Leversedge ploughed on. 'I believe it will be useful to you to have someone inside Quinn's department reporting back to you on his conduct of the case. Given its importance and sensitivity.'

Still Irons maintained his impassive expression. Something twitched in one eyebrow, as if he was considering raising it. But it seemed that he thought better of the gesture.

Minimal as it was, Leversedge took it as a sign of encouragement. 'I'm willing to offer my services.'

Even this failed to provoke anything other than an aggressive sniff and a further swig of beer.

'There have already been a number of decisions that have caused me concern. To begin with, of course, there was the decision to send DC Willoughby to his death.' Leversedge waited for some response to this. None was forthcoming. 'Secondly, last night he directed one of his officers, Sergeant Inchball, to terrorize a witness. This man Inchball is well known for his brutal methods. It would not surprise me if his actions resulted in a complaint. At the very least, it draws attention to the department in a manner that I think you will agree is unhelpful.'

But there was no indication of agreement – or otherwise – from the intelligence officer.

'Finally, Quinn has had me pursuing an entirely fruitless line of enquiry, in what I believe is a deliberate attempt to sideline me from the investigation. *Why would he do that?* you may ask.'

But Irons showed no inclination to ask that or any other question.

'I do not say he is deliberately attempting to undermine his own investigation. Or at least I cannot prove that he is. Yet. However, you have to ask yourself, why would he send his most senior, most experienced, and dare I say it, ablest detective on what can only be described as a wild goose chase?'

Irons swilled a mouthful of beer around his teeth. It was an unpleasant but compelling sound.

Leversedge was forced to wait for it to finish before continuing. 'Don't get me wrong. I think Quinn is a great detective. I know his methods are unconventional, but he gets results. I'd be the first to admit that. That's why I was so keen to move over and work under him in SCD. To be honest with you, he was a bit of a hero of mine. But something doesn't feel right about this. It's not like him to drop the ball. He's not a fool. He's not incompetent. He's not lazy. There's something else going on here.'

The twitching eyebrow that had been limbering up earlier finally jumped up interrogatively. It felt like a breakthrough.

'I can't help thinking someone's got to him. Given the interest you chaps have in the case, which presupposes some kind of national interest, my fear is that the someone who has got to him could be an enemy agent.'

Irons slipped off his barstool and downed the remains of his pint standing. He placed the empty pot on the bar in front of him before tipping a terse nod in Leversedge's direction.

With that, he was gone.

FORTY-THREE

Quinn put a hand to Elgar's elbow and gently steered him back out of the room. Although he had little expectation of anything worthwhile arising from Elgar's outburst, he thought it wise to exercise a degree of caution. Whatever the special constable thought he had discovered, it was probably best not divulged in front of Miss Greene.

Macadam joined them in the hallway, closing the door to the drawing room behind him. Quinn looked warily up the stairs. Lady Fonthill had said she was going to see the children in the nursery, but he had no proof that she had in fact done so. She could easily be lurking on the upstairs landing. As far as he was concerned, her ladyship was by no means in the clear over her husband's death. And so, he put a finger to his lips and escorted the special constable back to Sir Aidan's studio.

When the door to that was closed behind them, he gave a nod of encouragement. 'Now then, Constable Elgar. What was it you wanted to say to me?'

Elgar once again held out the slip of paper for Quinn to take.

Quinn looked down at the lines of staves. On the first of them was written a sequence of musical notes. He was unable to make any sense of it. Music had never been his thing. Besides, it was typical of amateur detectives to be always looking for secret codes everywhere. He waved the paper dismissively. 'What is this?'

'It is a code. Of sorts. Don't you see?' Elgar hummed the snatch of discordant melody that the music box had produced, as if that was enough to persuade the policemen of his point. He then leant over the piano and picked out the same notes.

'May I?' asked Macadam.

'Ah, yes,' said Quinn, relinquishing the paper. 'I forgot, you used to play the piccolo.'

'Is this the treble clef?' asked Macadam.

Elgar looked up sharply. 'Of course.'

'You didn't mark it.'

'Well, I didn't need to. I knew.'

'No key? No time signature? No bars?'

Even Quinn thought Macadam was pushing his luck. After all, it was a bit rich for a former piccolo player in the Boys' Brigade to be criticizing the great Elgar on his standard of musical notation.

Elgar, however, seemed to take it in his stride. His tone was a little abrupt perhaps, and forcefully insistent. But it was clearly excitement, not irritation, that stirred him. 'Not necessary. This isn't music. As I said, this is a *code*. Although perhaps it would be more accurate to say cryptogram.' He came back over to stand next to Macadam as he studied the fragment of notation.

To Quinn's annoyance, Macadam seemed to be enjoying himself. 'Well, let me see. What you have is A, E flat, E flat. A, E flat, E flat. C, B. C, B.'

'Correct.'

'What does it mean?' Despite his scepticism, Quinn was intrigued. There was undoubtedly a pattern there.

'At first, I could make head nor tail of it. And then I remembered Bach.'

Quinn closed his eyes in exasperation. 'What about Bach?'

'Well, he would write his name musically. How could he do that, you may ask, given that there are only seven notes in the Western musical tradition? Those, as *you* will know,' here Constable Elgar addressed Macadam, 'are represented by the letters A to G. In short, there is no H. And so while he could write B-A-C easily enough, he could not add the final H. Except that in the German system of notation' – Elgar broke off for effect and was no doubt gratified by the interrogative bounce in Quinn's eyebrows – 'the letter B is used for B flat, whereas B natural is represented by the letter H. And vice versa. Letter representing note. Note representing letter. And so, Bach can be written by the notes B flat, A natural, C natural, B natural. You will see here, at the end of this phrase of ours, we have C natural and B natural repeated. Which, if I am not mistaken, spells C-H-C-H.'

'C-H-C-H? Where does that get us?'

Elgar held up a restraining hand, which only succeeded in infuriating Quinn further. 'What you have to remember is that even using German notation, the communicative possibilities are somewhat limited. It's not an effective code as such. It's more like a playful way of concealing hidden messages.'

'Playful? You think this is some kind of game? I'll remind you, one of my officers was murdered.'

A glint of steel shone in Elgar's eye. 'And what if this is the very thing that leads you to his murderer?'

'Hear him out, sir. You never know,' urged Macadam.

'Very well. Go on.'

Elgar nodded to acknowledge Quinn's concession. 'Such messages do not remain hidden to those who know what to look for.' Elgar gave a nonchalant wave of his hand, to signify that he was one such person. 'Now, to go back to the first part of our message . . . Using the same German system, A natural is simply A. However, E flat – well, if you think of how the Germans write the letter S in the Gothic script, it looks a little like the flat symbol, does it not? So E flat is Es, that is to say, the letter S. A natural, E flat, E flat spells Ass.'

Quinn's bafflement was profound. He gave voice to only one of many questions that perplexed him.

'Ass?'

'Yes. And if you repeat it, A natural, E flat, E flat twice spells Ass, Ass. Or rather, assass.'

'Assass?'

'Yes.'

'Which means?'

'Well, to put together the complete phrase, we have A-S-S, A-S-S, C-H, C-H. Or you might say, assass ch-ch. Remember, we cannot represent every letter in the alphabet. So we have to fill in the gaps ourselves. Assass could be short for assassin, perhaps. Or maybe assassinate. It could be a command. Assassinate ch-ch.'

Quinn felt his heart pound out a rhythm that seemed to match the broken tune of the musical code. 'Churchill.'

Macadam's eyes widened. 'Cor blimey, sir. You don't think . . .'

Quinn snatched the scrap of paper back from his sergeant. 'Churchill was due to attend the concert. He knew Sir Aidan. What we may have here is evidence of a plot to assassinate the First Lord of the Admiralty.'

FIFTH MOVEMENT

FORTY-FOUR

Monday, 21 December, 1914

Quinn was at his desk early again on Monday.

Elgar's apparent breakthrough seemed to take the case in a new direction. But despite his enthusiasm of the previous day, Quinn now found himself less than convinced that there was anything in it. He wondered if his resistance was down to the fact that someone else – an amateur, to boot – had made the discovery. Certainly, it niggled at him that a knowledge of music had been the key to unlocking the mystery. To put it bluntly, he wouldn't have had a hope in hell of cracking it, and he didn't like the feeling of being dependent on something he didn't wholly understand. On top of that, the solution that Elgar had proposed, ASSASS CHCH, was hardly conclusive.

That said, if correct, this was the first direct appearance of Churchill in the case. It was a further connection between Sir Aidan and the First Lord of the Admiralty, besides the fact that they had been at Harrow together.

What the music box was doing in Sir Aidan's possession and who had sent it to him were questions to which Quinn would dearly like to have known the answers.

As soon as Macadam got in, Quinn had him do a spot of background digging on Sir Aidan. It was the kind of work that Macadam thrived on. He would disappear to the library for hours on end, only emerging when he had exhausted whatever sources of information he had found. Invariably, it would turn up at least one nugget.

'Anything in particular you're looking for, sir?'

'When a man like Sir Aidan has a row with his wife, where does he go? To his club, would be my guess. So, you could start with a list of his clubs.'

'That's easy enough. Debrett's will have the answer. Although we could just ask Lady Fonthill, you know.'

'I'd rather keep her out of it, if it's all the same to you.' Quinn remembered the scene that had taken place shortly after their conference with Elgar yesterday. They had met Lady Fonthill in the nursery. She had not responded well to their efforts to question her son. Perhaps she was simply being protective. But obstructive was another word that had come to Quinn's mind.

'Whatever you say.' Macadam retrieved his bowler, which he had only just hung up. 'Oh, before I go, sir, I was thinking about that description. You know, the one the boy gave to his nanny. Mr Toad, didn't he call him? Remember? You know who that made me think of?'

'No, who?'

'When I was in CID, one of the villains Coddington had in his pocket – or was it the other way round? I never found out. Anyhow, this fella, he had the very face of a toad, he did. He was meant to be an informant, but I reckon he was running rings around Coddington and his cronies . . .'

With impeccable timing, it was now that DI Leversedge entered the office. He glared antagonistically at Macadam at this mention of Coddington's cronies – it wasn't so long ago that he might have been considered one of them.

'What are you saying?' demanded Leversedge.

'Go on, Macadam,' encouraged Quinn.

'Well, all I was saying is, you might want to include one Tiggie Benson's mugshot in the ones you show the boy. If I know anyone who looks like a toad, it's Benson.'

'What's going on?' asked Leversedge warily once Macadam was out of the room.

'The boy, John Fonthill, Sir Aidan's son, is coming in later to look at mugshots. Apparently he saw his father talking to a stranger. If there is a connection with this fellow Benson, it would be interesting. How did you get on yesterday?'

Leversedge gave an evasive shrug.

'What does that mean?'

'Waste of time.'

'Did you speak to the Russians?'

Leversedge hesitated a beat before replying, 'I didn't get anything useful out of them. A blind alley, I'd say.'

Quinn regarded Leversedge with a narrowed gaze. 'What about Boland? And Dame Elsie?'

'Err, couldn't track them down. I suspect they were out of town.' There was something strangely guarded about Leversedge's manner that piqued Quinn's suspicion.

'What makes you think that?'

'Just, well . . . they weren't at home. Let's put it that way. I'll get on the blower today. Save on the shoe leather. If you really think it's worth pursuing.'

'You were the one who was pushing this line of enquiry,' Quinn reminded him.

'Yes, yes. Just tying up loose ends really, isn't it? It sounds like you're on to something more promising with this lead from the boy. What time is he due here?'

Quinn consulted his pocket watch. 'We agreed eleven o'clock. Initially, his mother was dead set against it. She didn't want him upset any more than he was already. However, the boy was keen as mustard. When we explained that it might well lead to the arrest of her husband's murderer . . .'

'She changed her mind?'

'Strangely, no. She was even more opposed.'

'Interesting.'

'Yes.'

'So how did you persuade her?'

'The boy had a tantrum. She had to agree to it to calm him down.' Quinn pocketed the watch with a small wince. He had got the result he wanted, but the means of gaining it gave him no great satisfaction.

'Did you discover anything else that I ought to know?'

Quinn pursed his lips, indulging in a moment's hesitation before telling Leversedge about Elgar's potential discovery. He could not explain his reluctance to confide in Leversedge. But something about his DI's demeanour this morning had him put his guard up. Nevertheless, he brought Leversedge up to speed.

'What if he's wrong? What if it's just a broken music box? He could be finding patterns where there aren't any.'

Leversedge was no fool. His scepticism chimed with Quinn's own. And it was a useful antidote to Macadam's enthusiasm. Quinn rewarded him with a minimal nod.

Soon after, Inchball came in. Leversedge jumped on him

straightaway, briefing him to follow up on Dame Elsie and the Belgians for him. Inchball made clear his displeasure at being given Leversedge's donkey work to do with a roll of the eyes that was positively adolescent.

Quinn ought not to have indulged him. Especially as it might be seen by Leversedge as undermining his authority. However, it was unavoidable. 'Before you do that, I need you to do something for me.'

'Yes, guv?' Inchball's eagerness was in marked contrast with his response to Leversedge.

'Get on to the Middlesex Regiment in Gravesend. See if they can tell you the whereabouts at the time of Sir Aidan's murder of one of their men – Private Jack Delaware.'

'Will do.'

Quinn avoided Leversedge's disgruntled glare by affecting to be engrossed in the statements that the Hampstead police had taken on Saturday from the witnesses at the school.

It wasn't long before Inchball had a result. Quinn could tell by listening to one half of the telephone call – 'Yes, I see. Thank you. You've been very helpful' – that he had discovered something interesting. Inchball's jubilant nod as he hung up the receiver confirmed it.

'He's on leave. Has been since Friday.'

Quinn nodded appreciatively. So it was not true, as Miss Greene had insisted, that Delaware was with his regiment. 'They could have met, after all, Delaware and the nanny. She could have told him about Fonthill's attempted seduction.' Quinn would have the opportunity to press her on this apparent contradiction when she brought the boy in later. 'Did you get a home address for him?'

Inchball nodded. 'Do you want me to have a word with him?' He was already on his feet, halfway to the door, happy to escape the task that Leversedge had lined up for him.

Eleven o'clock came and went. By noon, there was still no sign of John Fonthill. Quinn could only assume that Lady Fonthill had gone back on her word.

He was about to put in a call to Inspector Pool at Hampstead to have him pick up the boy when the telephone in front of him blared into life. Quinn still hadn't quite got used to the presence of the infernal contraption on his desk. He loathed calling people on it because he knew how jarring its cry was. It seemed a callous act to inflict that on another human being.

Marginally worse was receiving a call. It always brought with it a sense of dread that was rarely relieved by picking up the receiver. 'Quinn?' He gave his name as an interrogative, as if his identity was in doubt.

'Pool here, from Hampstead CID.'

This was not the first time that Quinn had experienced this: no sooner had he thought of calling someone than that very person called him. It reinforced his fear and suspicion of the device, which he could not help but see as irredeemably sinister.

'Just had a call from Hackney police station.' Pool's voice as it came down the line was harsh and business-like. But there was an edge of something else there. It almost felt like panic. 'Someone broke into the mortuary there.'

'What of it?'

'Well, you know that's where they took Sir Aidan Fonthill's body?'

Quinn felt a sudden thrashing in his chest, like the frantic muscles of a trapped animal. He could barely hear what Pool was saying over it.

'The queerest thing . . . never known anything like it . . .'

The dread that always accompanied the ringing of the telephone crystallized into a specific premonition. 'It's gone,' said Quinn flatly. 'The body's gone.'

'How the devil did you know?'

Quinn held the receiver away from his ear while he tried to form an answer to Inspector Pool's question.

FORTY-FIVE

Macadam came back into the department just before one. He announced his arrival with a cheery whistle, a hangover from his piccolo playing days no doubt, which was curiously at odds with the mood in the room. It didn't take him long, however, to get his emotional bearings. 'What's happened?'

This time he didn't even bother to hang up his bowler.

'I need you to take me over to Hackney morgue,' said Quinn.

'I'm coming too,' insisted Leversedge, jumping to his feet.

'What if the boy turns up?' objected Quinn.

'I know what you're doing. You're trying to freeze me out.'

Quinn sighed. He didn't have time for a showdown with his DI right now. 'Very well. Come along if you must.'

It seemed an odd thing to say, and Quinn could barely admit it to himself, but Hackney Mortuary was one of his favourite places in London. From the outside, it didn't look like a mortuary at all, or any kind of public building. The exterior was well-maintained, cheery even, with tawny bricks and glossy red woodwork. It looked like someone's home, not a way station for the dead. The wide door in one side of the building hinted at something other than a domestic purpose, though few would have guessed it was for the passage of hearses through to the courtyard at the rear.

This homely building was located alongside the church of St-John-at-Hackney. Also nearby was the local police station. The proximity of these two buildings seemed somehow appropriate, representing as they did the forces of law and religion. They leant their influence, benignly, to their neighbour, and those who were brought there.

The setting, away from the main road, was tranquil, and would have been leafy in the summer. Now, the surrounding trees were stark, their stripped branches scratching the wintry sky.

Generally, it was a place where people spoke in hushed, respectful voices, although today, in the aftermath of the break-in, was a level of excitement in evidence that Quinn had not seen there before. A small crowd had gathered outside to enjoy the spectacle, rubbing their hands to keep them warm, or perhaps in glee, their day enlivened by the theft of a dead body. A local bobby did his best to keep them back. Quinn kept his eyes straight ahead, not wishing to engage the bystanders, whose air of giddy exultation did not sit well with him. He had the subliminal impression that there was someone there he knew, without doubt one of the newspapermen who habitually took delight in alternately lionizing and vilifying him.

Don't give them the satisfaction.

The three detectives from SCD were greeted by Inspector Pool, who looked as if he wished a hole would open up and swallow him. Given his size, it would have to be a big hole. DS Kennedy stomped around ineffectually, scowling and barking at the local uniforms, whom he seemed to hold personally responsible for what had happened.

'The burglary must have taken place last night or in the early hours of this morning.' If this was the extent of Pool's intelligence on the crime, then it did not amount to much.

Quinn raised an eyebrow. 'Burglary?' The word hardly did justice to the crime that had been committed.

Pool heaved his massive shoulders hopelessly. 'It's possible they made a mistake. They thought it was a private house and were expecting to find valuables.'

'And when they saw the corpses, changed their mind and decided to take one of those instead?' Leversedge made no attempt to keep the sarcasm from his voice.

Quinn crouched down to examine a heavy chain lying on the ground. The links were about a quarter of an inch in diameter. One of them was cleanly cut in two places. It must have taken a hefty pair of wire cutters to snip through it. 'It looks like a professional job. Whoever did it came with tools. Were any windows broken?'

'No. The locks were picked.'

Quinn hauled himself to his feet. 'Anything else taken, other than the body?'

Pool shook his head.

Quinn signalled he was ready to go inside with a nod. But an agitated shout from the crowd delayed him. 'It isn't right!'

There was something familiar about the voice. Quinn turned to scan the faces of those jostling forward to get a closer look. One man was pushing against the bobby, who was holding out his arms to keep him back. 'Mr Metcalfe?' said Quinn. 'What are you doing here?'

The policeman who was trying to restrain him cast a questioning glance back at Quinn.

'It's all right, let him through,' said Quinn.

Donald Metcalfe lurched forward. 'It isn't right,' he repeated.

'Do you know something about what has happened here?' asked Quinn.

'Where's Sir Aidan?' demanded Metcalfe, in obvious distress.

'We don't know. Someone has taken him. If you know anything about what has happened, please tell me.'

But all Metcalfe would say was: 'It isn't right.'

'Yes, I agree. It isn't right. I understand that you're upset. I can only apologize. I assure you, we're doing everything we can to find Sir Aidan's body.'

'No. You don't understand. His ring. It was on his right hand. It isn't right.'

Quinn narrowed his eyes and looked at the accompanist closely. He remembered that Metcalfe had once said he never lied, and yet a detail from Metcalfe's earlier statement nagged at him. 'Mr Metcalfe, you once told me that you didn't know Roderick Masters' address, and yet I think you did. It was written on a sheet of music that you had certainly seen – the composition that Masters had submitted to Sir Aidan. I do not think it is the kind of detail that would have escaped your notice.'

'No,' said Metcalfe firmly. 'You asked me where you might find him. That was a question I couldn't possibly know the answer to. You might find him anywhere. You then asked me if I had ever been to his house. I have never been to his house. You then asked me if he had told me where he lived. He had not told me where he lived.'

'But you knew his address!' cried Quinn, his exasperation getting the better of him. 'Did you not realize that that was what I wanted from you?'

'You didn't ask me for his address.'

'No, I didn't. You're right. That was my mistake.' Quinn turned to Macadam. 'Back to the car.'

'What was all that about?' demanded Leversedge, hurrying to keep up with Quinn.

'I'll tell you on the way.'

'On the way to where, sir?' asked Macadam.

'*Hampstead!*' Quinn could not keep a note of impatience from his voice, as if the question was too obvious to need asking.

FORTY-SIX

The door was opened by the butler, Callaghan. His face was unusually grey, the only colour coming from the broken capillaries on his nose. His expression was strained, nauseous even, his eyes staring in alarm. And yet it was almost as if he was expecting them. 'Thank heavens you're here,' he cried as he let them in. 'The doctor is with Lady Emma now.'

Quinn exchanged a quizzical glance with his two officers. 'Doctor?'

'Lady Emma collapsed. Understandably. The shock was too much for her.'

'Ah. She has been informed then?'

'Informed? Of course she has been informed! She was here when Miss Greene came back from the Heath.'

'I'm sorry. I don't understand. What has Miss Greene got to do with this?'

'Miss Greene was there when it happened.'

'When what happened?' Quinn had the uncomfortable sensation that they were talking at cross purposes.

'When Master John was taken!'

'What do you mean, taken?'

'Kidnapped! Young Master John has been kidnapped! I had assumed that's why you're here. We tried to get hold of Inspector Pool but he had been called away on urgent business, or so they told us. What could be more urgent than this?' Callaghan shook his head incredulously, before adding, 'They sent a *constable* instead!' He gave the word a disparaging emphasis, as if he considered this an unforgivable lapse of protocol. 'He's with Miss Greene now, taking a statement.'

Quinn nodded tersely, accepting the invitation to join them that was implied in Callaghan's statement.

Hattie Greene was in the drawing room. Her face was pale and drawn and streaked with tears. She looked up with two huge red eyes as Quinn and the others came in.

Quinn acknowledged the constable's presence with a brief nod that was also a dismissal. 'What happened?' he demanded of the nanny.

Pale lids trembled down to veil her raw, glistening eyes. It was a relief to have that anguish hidden from them, if only for a moment. A huge sob shook itself out from her, wracking her suddenly frail body in an uncontrollable shudder.

But when she opened her eyes, she seemed to have found the composure she needed to speak. 'I had taken John to Hampstead Heath. He was very excited about his impending trip to Scotland Yard this morning.' She flashed Quinn a look of rebuke, as if this was somehow all his fault. 'He was rather playing up, I'm afraid. Being beastly to his sister. As you can imagine, Lady Emma's nerves were somewhat frayed, what with everything that has happened, so I thought it best to take him out of the house. I hoped he might burn off some energy. Thought it might calm him down. Or at least get him out of his mother's hair.' She had held herself together well until now, but suddenly the reality of what had happened must have hit her afresh. Her face crumpled and a high, keening wail came out of her mouth.

The policemen stood over her, helpless in the face of her over-whelming emotion. All they could do was wait for the anguish to work its way through her.

Eventually, she was able to dab her eyes with a tightly clenched hanky. She drew herself up on the sofa with an involuntary groan. Her eyes flitted about the room, as if it was the first time she had taken in her surroundings. It seemed to appal her to find herself in such elegant surroundings at this moment. 'This is all my fault!' Her voice was small and tremulous. Even so, it brooked no argument.

None was offered. No mercy, either.

'You went to the Heath,' prompted Quinn. 'Just you and John?'

She nodded, *yes.*

'And what? What happened?'

'As soon as we got there, he ran away from me.' She gave an anguished grimace. 'He can be quite a handful, you know.'

'Has he done that before?'

'Oh, he always does it. I don't try to keep up with him. There's no point. He always comes back.'

'But this time it was different?'

She closed her eyes and nodded tensely. 'He ran off shouting *poop-poop!*'

'Poop-poop?'

'His head has been full of Mr Toad these last few days. Especially since you said that you wanted him to go to Scotland Yard to look at pictures. He was convinced that you were going to arrest Mr Toad. Oh, I don't know how seriously he believed it, but that was what he said. Anyhow, he came running back to me . . .'

'Yes?'

'And he said that he had seen Mr Toad. That Mr Toad was there on the Heath and had been waving to him.' Miss Greene began to sob. 'I thought it was just make-believe! I didn't think he really had!'

'But he had seen someone?'

'Yes! Oh, God forgive me!'

'What happened then?'

'He said he was going to warn Mr Toad that the police were looking for him. And he ran off again.'

'Go on.'

'And then I lost sight of him.' She squeezed her eyes tightly shut, as if replaying the moment when John Fonthill disappeared from her view. Perhaps she hoped that when she opened her eyes again, he would reappear. 'At first, I didn't think anything of it. We often play hide and seek. It's always John who hides. We have our set hiding places. I always know where to find him. I looked in every one of them. But he wasn't there. I began to get worried. Frightened. I called out his name. He didn't come. Didn't answer. And then I saw . . .'

'What?'

'In the distance. A man. Holding a boy's hand. Leading him away towards the exit. I shouted and ran after them. I screamed for people to help me. John looked back. And waved. I ran. I ran, as fast as I could. But when I got out on to East Heath Road, there was no sign of them.'

'This man who took him. Did you see his face?'

She shook her head with her eyes closed.

'Did you form an impression of how tall he was? His build? What was he wearing?'

'I don't think he was tall. Not tall. Quite stout. He had a cap on, I think. The kind of cap men wear when they are driving.'

'A chauffeur's cap?'

'No, more like a flat cap.'

'Like Mr Toad,' said Macadam.

Hattie Greene's mouth rippled with an involuntary spasm and she gave a weak little nod.

'One more thing, Miss Greene.' Quinn did not allow himself any pity as he looked down at the nanny. He knew that she was at her weakest now, frightened, vulnerable, and no doubt feeling guilty over what had happened to the boy in her charge. Which was precisely why he needed to press her mercilessly. 'Your friend, Private Delaware. We contacted his regiment. He has been on leave since Friday.'

'No. That's not true.' The confusion in her eyes seemed genuine. 'Jack would have told me.'

'Did you meet him? Did you talk about Sir Aidan?'

'No! I haven't seen Jack! I swear.'

She began to cry. Quinn did not believe that any woman could feign the ugly, uncontrollable sobs that took her over.

Quinn did not like to ring the bell for a servant. Instead he opened the drawing-room door and called out. 'Hello. I say . . . Mr Callaghan?'

Callaghan appeared hurriedly, his face flushed with anger. 'Keep your voice down, will you?' he hissed. 'The doctor has given her ladyship a sedative.'

Quinn did not like the sound of that. 'What on earth for? We need to speak to her.'

'That won't be possible.'

'Where is she? Unless you want to be arrested for obstructing the police, you'll take me to her. Now.'

Callaghan shook his head unhappily but led Quinn upstairs all the same. Quinn had Leversedge and Macadam wait for him in the hallway. Three heavily booted detectives in her bedroom was unlikely to induce Lady Fonthill to cooperate. Even one was pushing it.

She lay barefoot but fully clothed on top of a large four-poster bed, her chestnut hair fanned out around her head. Her eyes were closed, but she did not seem to be asleep, rather cast under a spell, like a princess in a fairy tale. There seemed to be no weight to her, as if she might float away at any moment.

Her mouth was slightly open, in a downturned curve. Now and then it seemed to twitch, as if she was crying out in a dream.

At that moment, all her privilege and inherited wealth was stripped from her. The luxuriousness of her surroundings meant nothing. None of this would help her in what she was facing now.

Beside the bed, the doctor was packing his things away in his bag.

'Can you rouse her?' demanded Quinn.

'Good heavens, no!'

'But I need to ask her some questions. Her son's life may depend on it.'

'You can try, but I doubt you'll get any sense out of her.'

Quinn leant over the woman on the bed. 'Lady Fonthill. Emma. It's DCI Quinn.'

There was no sign of a response. Not even the pattern of her breathing changed.

Quinn turned to the doctor. 'Can she hear me?'

'I should think so. Whether or not she will be able to respond is another matter.'

Quinn felt a sudden surge of rage at the doctor's infuriatingly calm demeanour. 'Why did you do this?'

'What?'

'Sedate her.'

'Because she was hysterical.'

'So what? Her son's been kidnapped. It's natural that she would be hysterical. Did it not occur to you that the police would want to speak to her? Or that she herself might want to stay conscious? She is his mother.'

'My only consideration was the wellbeing of my patient. I deemed sedation necessary on medical grounds.'

'And she let you do it?'

'She was in no state to refuse.'

Quinn shook his head in frustration. 'She's run away. Away from us. Away from John. She's abandoned her son.'

There was a stirring from the bed. Lady Fonthill's mouth juddered in a spasm of distress. A murmur that could have been 'no' trembled in her throat.

Quinn bent over her again. 'Lady Fonthill. Is there anything you want to tell me? Anything that you have kept from me, that you now wish to share, now that John's life depends on it?'

A quick, darting movement showed beneath her eyelids. In the next moment, they flickered open. Her whole head quaked under a tremendous effort to lift it. 'Find. *Him!*'

Quinn wondered at the less than gentle – almost venomous – force with which she expelled that last word. But perhaps it was simply the strain of rousing herself from the bonds of oblivion.

But before he could challenge her about it, her eyes closed again, and her head sank back into the pillow.

'Well, that was a waste of time,' said Leversedge, after Quinn had relayed the details of his interview with Lady Fonthill. 'What now?'

It was a good question. Quinn ran his hand down over his face as he thought through his next move. 'DS Macadam, what can you tell us about Sir Aidan's clubs?'

With a flash of temper, Leversedge demanded, 'What the devil have his clubs got to do with anything?'

Quinn tried to keep his voice calm as he explained, 'We don't yet know what links Sir Aidan Fonthill to the man who has taken his son. That is because we don't yet know enough about Sir Aidan Fonthill. We need to find more answers. We need to look more deeply into his life. There is something in his life, some huge aspect of it, that is so far unknown to us. We will not discover it from his wife, not now, not in her current state. There have been inklings of this secret life revealed by some of those we have spoken to already. Charles Cavendish hinted at Sir Aidan's need for money, for example. And we know a mysterious stranger came to the house.'

'Mr Toad,' put in Macadam. 'You know my views on that, sir.'

'Yes. And the only person who saw him other than Sir Aidan was John Fonthill.'

'That's why he was taken,' observed Leversedge. 'Because he could identify the man.'

'It's a possibility,' was all that Quinn would concede.

Macadam rounded on Leversedge. 'Your old governor, Coddington. He was thick as thieves with Tiggie Benson.'

'What of it?'

'If I'm right, that's who Mr Toad is.'

'*If.*'

'Anyone would think you didn't want to find the boy.'

'I just don't want us to waste time on any more wild goose chases. What if it's not Tiggie Benson? We don't have a positive ID. All we have, in fact, is your wild guesswork. Besides, if Benson has taken the boy, he's unlikely to be holding him at any of his known haunts. Benson may be many things, but he's not stupid.'

It was time for Quinn to intervene. 'That's why we keep digging. That's why we keep talking to people who knew Sir Aidan. It's the only thing we can do. Those clubs, Macadam.'

'Sir Aidan Fonthill is listed in Debrett's as having membership to three clubs. White's. The Athenaeum. And Pootle's.'

Quinn was aware of experiencing a slight sense of relief. He had half-expected Fonthill's clubs to include The Panther Club, an esoteric establishment which had figured in an earlier investigation; he found he had no desire to return there.

'Mr Callaghan?' The butler had been standing discreetly to one side as the three detectives conferred in the hallway. He now answered Quinn with a solemn bow. 'To which of those were you in the habit of forwarding Sir Aidan's mail during his absences from the house? Think carefully before you answer. A boy's life may depend on it.'

But Callaghan did not hesitate. 'Pootle's.'

It was as good a place as any to start.

FORTY-SEVEN

D S Inchball hammered on the door of the house in Tufnell Park. He always preferred to knock, even when there was a bell. It made more of an impression, he always thought.

The door was opened by a middle-aged woman, whose face was illuminated with a fragile happiness.

'Is Jack Delaware here?'

'Yes, he is!' the woman cried excitedly. 'We didn't expect him back but his leave came through and he's going to be here for Christmas! Can you believe it!' It was only now that she seemed to take in the warrant card that Inchball was holding up. The happiness vanished from her expression, which grew suddenly anxious.

'DS Inchball of the Special Crimes Department, Scotland Yard. May I come in?'

The young man sipped the tea that his mother had made. Out of uniform, he didn't look like much of a soldier. He was slight and pale. His eyes – well, some might call them sensitive, no doubt. But to Inchball they had a weak, shifty look about them.

'I say, what's this about?'

'Where were you from about half past twelve onwards on the afternoon of Saturday, the nineteenth of December?'

'Last Saturday?'

'That's right.'

Delaware paused a moment before answering, rather shame-facedly, Inchball couldn't help thinking, 'I was having lunch with a friend.'

'This friend of yours, he'll be able to vouch for you, will he?'

'It's not a he, it's a she.'

'You saw Hattie!' Delaware's mother cried out excitedly. Her expression darkened as she thought about what he had said. 'But wait a minute, it wasn't Saturday, surely? You only came home yesterday.'

Delaware avoided looking at his mother. 'It wasn't Hattie.'

'What do you mean? Who was it then?'

'Look, what *is* this about?' Delaware repeated, shifting uneasily on the settee.

'It's about whether you have an alibi for murder or not.'

'Murder?'

There was a shriek from Delaware's mother.

Delaware's face was suddenly drained of colour. He looked as if he was about to be sick. 'It wasn't Hattie. Hattie doesn't even know I'm home. I was . . . with someone else. Another girl.'

'Oh, Jack!' His mother's disappointment was almost sharper than if he had been found to be a murderer.

'Don't look at me like that, Mother! After all, it's not like we're engaged, Hattie and I.'

Inchball was not impressed with Delaware's defence of his behaviour. He took against him on Hattie's behalf, although he had never met her. 'Who were you with?' he barked sternly.

'Yes, who is she?' echoed Delaware's mother, even more sternly.

Inchball decided he might as well sit back and let her lead the interrogation. He had a feeling that she would be more successful at extracting the truth from her son.

'Just someone. A friend. I spent the last few days with her.'

'Did. You. *Sleep.* With. Her?' Mrs Delaware's disgust was loaded into each carefully enunciated word.

Delaware threw up his hands hopelessly. 'What kind of a question is that?'

'Well, did you?'

'She's the kind of girl who . . . well, who likes company. Male company.'

'She's a *prostitute!*'

'Mother! For goodness' sake. It's not like that. *She's* not like that. You make it sound so . . . sordid.'

'But what about Hattie?'

'You don't understand. Hattie will always be very special to me. But I needed something . . . something that I couldn't go to Hattie for.'

Mrs Delaware closed her eyes and shook her head in denial, her mouth pinched tightly shut.

Jack pressed on: 'I'm shipping out on the thirtieth. To Belgium.'

'You didn't tell me.'

'I didn't want it hanging over us. Well, the thing is, you see . . . I just wanted a bit of fun. Before . . . well, you never know what might happen out there. This might be my last Christmas.'

'No! Don't say that!' cried his mother.

'I didn't want to pressure Hattie into anything. And I wanted the idea of her to stay pure and good.'

'While you were off doing something dirty and wicked!'

'Look, it just happened . . . I didn't plan it, I swear. Things just got out of hand and I suppose I went along with it.'

'This friend,' said Inchball at last. 'She have a name?'

'Vera.'

'Last name.'

'I don't know her last name. But if you go to the Dog and Duck in Soho and ask for Vera . . . she's a barmaid there.' He turned to his mother. 'Not a prostitute.'

Inchball closed his notebook and stood up. Then he remembered the tea and picked up his cup to gulp down the last few mouthfuls.

FORTY-EIGHT

Pootle's was housed in a Palladian mansion on St James's Street. Although it was just around the corner from the Panther Club, it was a far cry from the only other gentlemen's club Quinn had ever stepped inside.

He felt the difference in the two clubs immediately. For one thing, Pootle's did not have a secret entrance, nor was there a caged panther in the lobby. Quinn suspected that particular eccentricity had been dispensed with by now, after the unfortunate incident that had occurred when Bertie, the animal in question, had escaped from her cage earlier in the year. (The panther in the Panther Club was always female, and always called Bertie.) A brief glance around confirmed another difference: the members here did not conceal their identities behind celluloid masks.

Perhaps his experience in the Panther Club had given him a distorted view of private members' clubs, but he found that his distaste for such establishments ran deep. Even if things appeared more transparent here, he nevertheless disliked the air of quiet privilege that he was obliged to breathe. The hushed reverence of the club's servants grated on his nerves.

In a bastion of exclusivity, Quinn's natural sympathy was always with the excluded. This was a place where strings were pulled, some of them no doubt to trip up men like him. For there was that sense that the club's rules superseded the laws of the outside world. He did not need to ask to know that members looked out for one another. If his foray into the Panther Club had taught him anything it was that villainy was not solely the preserve of the lower orders, although when it was practised by the upper classes it was more properly called vice. And that when push came to shove, even gentlemen were not above closing ranks.

As if to confirm the thought, he counted several former prime ministers among the distinguished members looking down on him from gilded frames. Their expressions were suitably forbidding.

Do not dare to storm the citadel! they seemed to say.

The ageing club official behind the reception desk gave every impression of having stepped down from one of the portraits. He was merely the servant of the diplomats, cabinet ministers and mandarins who made up the club's memberships. But some part of their authority had clearly devolved to him. He stood as their proxy, indeed their gatekeeper, which gave him a level of discretion that amounted to power. He bore it modestly, but there was no doubt that it was there. The tilt of his head was guarded rather than imperious. He radiated a suave charm that would not have been out of place on a head waiter or high court judge. But something was withheld.

He greeted Quinn with a measured smile, as if it was dispensed by means of a precision-engineered mechanism.

There was not a hair out of place on his head, or a speck on his night-black swallow tailcoat.

Quinn held out his warrant card. 'Detective Chief Inspector Quinn of the Special Crimes Department. These men are also police officers. We are investigating the murder of one of your members.'

The man gave no indication of being shocked by any of this. Instead, his lips pursed regretfully, as if he were disappointed that any one of the members should show such a lapse in taste as to get themselves murdered. 'I presume you are referring to Sir Aidan Fonthill?'

'Have you had any other members murdered?'

'Fortunately not.'

'I understand that he stayed here at the club from time to time.'

A minuscule frown suggested that the major-domo didn't know what that had to do with anything.

'We are anxious to speak to as many of Sir Aidan's associates as we can. We would appreciate your cooperation in identifying those members who had any connection with him. His friends, of course. But anyone who might have spoken to him.'

'But that would require me to give you a list of our entire membership! Anyone here might have spoken to him. Pootle's is a very sociable club.'

'I will need that, yes. And a list of club employees. It would help us if you could mark with an asterisk those who come into contact with members.'

'An asterisk?'

'It doesn't have to be an asterisk. You could underline them. I thought an asterisk would be easier.'

'That will take time.'

'Of course. To speed things along, perhaps you could supply me now with the names of people who were particularly close to Sir Aidan.'

The man's expression changed. The *something* that had been withheld before was brought out for all to see. It was the snarl of a mother fox preparing to defend her kits. 'You must understand, Chief Inspector' – he was of course fastidious in remembering Quinn's rank, when most people unconsciously demoted him to inspector – 'our members have a right to expect a certain discretion from those of us who are privileged to serve them.'

'You are refusing to cooperate?'

'It is not a question of *refusing*. We do not *spy* on our gentlemen. With whom they associate is their business, not ours. So even if I wished to supply you with this information, I cannot. It is simply the case that neither I, nor any of the staff here, ever *see* – and we certainly do not *remember*! – anything that goes on between individual members. So, as to who is a particular friend with whom, I am afraid we are not qualified to say. In addition, I must point out that what you are asking me to do is engage in tittle-tattle.'

'I am asking you to help me save the life of a young boy. Sir Aidan's son was abducted this morning.'

What calculation took place behind the man's calm gaze Quinn could only guess at. He suspected it was something to do with the greater good; it usually was in these circumstances. His primary duty was to protect the reputation of the club, and the membership as a whole. From time to time, that might entail sacrificing one of its members.

To save the body, one sometimes has to cut off a limb.

He leant forward confidentially across the counter. 'There is one gentleman . . .'

Quinn nodded for him to go on.

When it came to it, the name slipped out more easily than the three detectives might have expected. And with it came more than they could have hoped.

Quinn's pencil flew across the page of his notebook as he tried to keep up with the man's disclosures.

'Thank you, you have been very helpful,' said Quinn as he pocketed the information. 'In the light of what you have told us, I do not think it will be necessary to supply those lists.'

The major-domo closed his eyes to give a minute bow of appreciation. A moment later, his mask of guarded composure was back in place.

FORTY-NINE

Quinn left it to Macadam to hammer on the door to the apartment in the New Cavendish Street mansion block. 'Police! Open up!' Macadam did his best to create an intimidating racket, but he was no Inchball, as Quinn reflected with a tinge of regret.

The concierge had let them in and was there beside them ready with a spare key should it be necessary.

The element of surprise was on their side. In addition, it was still early enough in the day to catch a man like Simon Symington napping. His reputed habits were not generally conducive to early rising. That said, his livelihood depended to some extent on his ability to maintain at least the appearance of respectability. And so, he would be eager to cut short the scandalous commotion outside his door.

Quinn's calculations turned out to be correct. The lock was turned from within, the door opened and a tall, thin man in silk pyjamas and dressing gown appeared. Simon Symington rubbed a hand through his already tousled hair and stood blinking on his threshold. 'I say, what the devil is going on?' He took in the three detectives with an untroubled sneer, reserving a look of wounded rebuke for the concierge.

That worthy individual defended himself with an imploring whine: 'These gentlemen are *policemen*, Dr Symington.' As if to say, *what do you expect me to do if you will be bringing policemen here?*

Quinn held up his warrant card to confirm the concierge's statement. 'DCI Quinn, Special Crimes Department.'

'*Special* crimes?' Symington gave an effete giggle. 'Oh, well, in that case, I suppose you'd better come in.'

Symington let the detectives in, gleefully closing the door on the disloyal concierge. He showed them into a sitting room that was tastefully furnished but layered with the debris of a disordered life. Unwashed crockery, discarded clothes, upturned bottles and broken glasses littered the floor and even the furniture. An ashtray had been kicked over, scattering ash and cigarette butts all over the carpet. Symington showed no sign of embarrassment, nor made any effort to tidy up. The air was thick with the fug of the previous night's indulgences.

'Now what's this all about?'

'The concierge called you *Dr* Symington?' began Quinn.

'A misunderstanding on his part. My friends call me "doc", you see. Old Barker got the wrong end of the stick, I suppose. It's just a nickname.'

'Why do they call you that?'

'I don't know. I suppose because I . . . am . . .' Inspiration came to him. 'Always a tonic when they see me.' He giggled appreciatively at his own wit.

'But you're not actually a doctor? And never have been?'

'No.'

'And you never thought to put Mr Barker straight?'

'What is this about?' Symington forced out an incredulous laugh. 'I told you, it's just a nickname. I have never claimed to be a doctor.'

'We have a witness – a very reliable witness – who is quite prepared to go on record to testify that you are regularly to be found dealing cocaine at a certain gentlemen's club.'

'What of it? It's not against the law.'

'You are not aware of the 1908 Pharmacy Act then, which classifies cocaine as a poison which may only be sold by a registered pharmacist? You are not a registered pharmacist, I think?'

Symington was on the verge of answering but thought better of it.

'Perhaps if we were to have a look around now . . .?'

Macadam and Leversedge tensed at Quinn's side, like bulldogs straining at the leash.

'Well, to do that, you would need a warrant, I believe.'

'Actually, no,' corrected Quinn. 'As I said, we are from the Special Crimes Department. Given the nature of the crimes we were established to investigate, the warrant I have already shown you gives us the right to conduct a search wherever we deem necessary.'

Symington shrugged as if this was of no concern to him, although he was unable to suppress a deep, agitated sniff. The chaos evident in the room seemed to reflect a disorder in Symington's mind. He began to twitch and fidget, as if the cravings that ruled his life were beginning to make themselves felt. The thought of losing the means to satisfy them was no doubt a cause of deep anxiety.

It was time for Quinn to play his hand. 'There's a way to make this all go away, Mr Symington.'

Symington's face opened up with desperate hope.

'Did you ever deal cocaine to Sir Aidan Fonthill?'

'Fonthill?' Symington seemed genuinely surprised. He thought for a moment before shaking his head decisively. 'No. I – he may have dabbled once or twice. I sometimes give my friends little gifts. Samples, you might say.'

'In the hope that they will become addicted, no doubt.'

Symington did not deny it. 'It never took with Fonthill.'

As soon as the major-domo at Pootle's had told Quinn of Fonthill's association with an alleged drug dealer, he had entertained the theory that Fonthill's need for money stemmed from an addiction. Symington's emphatic denial put paid to that idea.

'No, powder was not Fonthill's vice, more's the pity.'

'He did have one, however?'

'Who doesn't?' Symington's gaze as it took in Quinn was like a chill shadow passing across him. 'Even policemen have vices. Don't try and deny it. I have experience in these matters, remember.'

'What was Sir Aidan's?'

'Nothing too vile. Quite innocent, in fact. He liked to gamble.'

'Did he ever get into debt over his gambling?'

'He did, yes.'

'Recently?'

Symington drew a hand over his face. He was becoming increasingly agitated. '*I* don't know!' His voice was suddenly petulant. 'Recently? I suppose so. It must have been. *I* can still remember it.' He gave a high-pitched giggle.

'You were there?'

'Yes, we were all there. Me, Lucas, Fonthill. Soapy was there too, I seem to remember. And some other fellow. Porter, Potter or something. He was there as someone's guest, I think.'

'Where was this? At Pootle's?'

'The party started at Pootle's. And then we went on somewhere.'

'Where?'

'I don't know. It was dark. It took an age to get there. It was a filthy rotten room in a filthy rotten house. Belonged to a filthy rotten man.'

'What man?'

Symington gave a high nervous laugh. '*The* man.'

'The man Fonthill owed money?'

'I've said too much as it is.'

'How much was the debt?'

'Oh, come on! Who do you think I am? Datas, the Memory Man? Do you think I care enough about Aidan bloody Fonthill to remember every detail of his sorry life?'

'We need you to remember as much as you can, Mr Symington. Otherwise we may be forced to take action on that other matter after all.'

'Other matter?' Symington frowned and then remembered the threat to search his apartment. He screwed his face up, wincing in concentration. There was an element of performance to it, especially when his face brightened as the memory seemingly came back to him. 'I remember now, it was a lot. Fonthill was in a funk about it. He begged us all to chip in. The chap he owed . . . let's just say, he's not the sort you want to get on the wrong side of.'

'Who was it? Who was the man?'

'Don't remember his name.'

'Can you describe him?'

'No.' The answer came quickly, without any attempt at recollection. Symington was almost certainly lying. He was also growing increasingly restless.

'Whose idea was it to go there?'

'Listen, all these questions . . . questions . . . questions . . . they're frying my damned brain, you buggering bastard.'

'You watch your language!' warned Macadam.

'Perhaps you would like a moment to refresh yourself in the privacy of your bedroom. We'll wait here for you.'

Symington pointed a finger at Quinn. 'I like you. You're a good man. Very understanding.'

As Symington slouched off, Quinn gestured for Macadam to follow. 'Get him with the gear in his hands. Don't let him take any. Just grab him with it and bring him back here.'

Alone with Leversedge, Quinn felt the other detective's critical gaze on him but did not turn to meet it. 'Do you have something to say, Inspector Leversedge?'

'I hope you know what you're doing, guv, that's all.'

'Really? Wouldn't it suit you better if I didn't?'

'I don't know what you mean.' But Leversedge's answer had been a beat too slow in coming.

Shouts of protest erupted in the other room. Macadam marched a sullen-looking Symington back in. He held up a green leather pouch, tied with a draw string. 'Unless I'm very much mistaken, this is cocaine.'

Symington wriggled beneath Macadam's hand on his shoulder. 'I thought you said I could refresh myself? I thought you were a decent chap.' He gave a recriminatory pout.

'I'm saving you from yourself. Sergeant Macadam, I think you know what to do with that junk.'

Macadam started to move but was detained by Symington's howl. 'No-o-o-o! Have you any idea what that's worth? Listen, listen, listen . . . I know what you policemen are like. I know what you're after. Can't we come to some arrangement? Let's say, three per cent. Each.' To Quinn, he added confidentially, 'Four per cent for you, as you're the boss.'

'Are you trying to bribe us?'

Symington appeared on the verge of tears. His bottom lip stuck out like a petulant toddler's. 'I don't know what you want of me.'

'Who was it? The man Fonthill was in debt to?'

But Symington closed his eyes tightly and shook his head. Then a huge sob exploded from him and he began weeping in earnest.

'You do know him, don't you? You know him very well. Is he your supplier? He's the kind of chap who can get hold of large quantities of cocaine quite easily, I imagine.'

Symington's flinch was all the confirmation Quinn needed.

'Was it you who introduced Sir Aidan and the others to him?'

'You don't understand. He'll kill me.'

'I won't let him hurt you.' Even as Quinn said them, he knew they were empty words, given what he had in mind. Even so, that didn't stop him adding, 'I promise.'

Symington sniffed loudly.

'Let me make this easy for you. If you help us, you can have that.' Quinn nodded at the pouch in Macadam's hand. 'We'll even let you stay in business. If you don't help us, you're going to jail.' Quinn waited for this to sink in. Then took a gamble that he hoped would tip Symington over the edge. 'And we'll let it be known that you were the one who fingered Tiggie Benson.'

'You know! You already know!'

So Macadam had been right. Quinn saw the beam of satisfaction on his sergeant's face. The mysterious Mr Toad was none other than Tiggie Benson.

'Yes. And we can easily put it about that we found out from you. I dare say Tiggie Benson has friends on the inside. One or two of them probably owe him a favour. None of them will look too favourably on a snitch.'

'Why do you need me if you already know?'

'That will become clear in the car.'

'In the car?'

'Yes. You're going to take us to Tiggie Benson. I have no doubt you know perfectly well where to find him.'

The terror that showed in Symington's eyes was not feigned.

But Quinn let out a deep sigh and nodded to Macadam, who reluctantly handed the leather pouch back to the desperate addict. Symington's face went into a reflexive spasm, as a series of loud, involuntary sniffs anticipated the imminent relief of his cravings.

FIFTY

Symington was squeezed in the back of the Model T, between Quinn and Leversedge. He was seated bolt upright, staring straight ahead, his right knee jerking up and down compulsively. The junkie had calmed down a little since Quinn had allowed him access to his bag of powder. That is to say, his terror of Benson had abated, to be replaced by a belief in his own invulnerability, which Quinn had exploited. An electric energy pulsed in him, which was as likely to burn him up as power him forward.

He appeared to be capable of anything, except understanding the situation he was in.

As usual, Macadam was driving too fast, taking too many risks, and leaning on the horn too much. But Quinn could hardly blame him.

As they hurtled along the streets of the East End, Quinn was aware of a growing sense of déjà vu. It was not so surprising. He had often sat in the back of this car, to be driven at speed towards the denouement of an investigation by DS Macadam. But the presentiment sharpened into something precise and irrefutable. He identified it as a sense of impending doom.

'What makes you think the boy will be there?' said Leversedge, speaking across Symington. His tone was interested rather than challenging. There might even have been a hint of respect in it. As always with Leversedge, it was hard to tell for sure.

Quinn turned to face his questioner. 'We now have a positive link between Sir Aidan and Tiggie Benson. Fonthill owed Benson money. Perhaps when he heard about Fonthill's death, Benson considered the debt still outstanding and decided to take John Fonthill in lieu of the money.'

'Good God! For what purpose?'

Quinn looked into Leversedge's eyes, as if the answer to that question lay there. 'Who can say?'

'Do you think Benson killed Sir Aidan?'

Quinn chose to evade the question. 'At the moment, my priority lies in recovering John Fonthill alive.'

Beside him, Symington continued to jiggle his right leg frantically. Quinn felt it bumping against his own. He reached out his left
hand and clamped it down tightly on the offending limb. Under the
pressure of Quinn's hand the leg stayed still, but the rest of
Symington's body began to quake. His face gradually turned bright
red as he clamped his jaw shut. A moment later, he threw back his
head, his mouth gaped open and an animal howl filled the car.

Macadam pulled up outside Shadwell Police Station at Leversedge's
suggestion. 'We can't go in without back-up,' he had argued.

To Quinn's mind, Leversedge was showing himself to be too
much of a stickler for procedure, perhaps because he had a reputation for playing fast and loose with such niceties during the earlier
part of his career. He didn't want Leversedge crashing in with a
troop of big-booted bobbies, ruining everything. 'Remember, DI
Leversedge. Softly softly.'

Leversedge nodded impatiently as he got out of the car. 'You'll
wait for me here?'

'No,' replied Quinn bluntly. 'We don't have time.'

Leversedge hesitated with the open door in his hand. He glanced
at the quivering wreck of a man next to Quinn. 'This is insane.'

Quinn did not disagree.

'What if . . .?' But there were so many ways of ending that
sentence that Leversedge left it at that, merely shaking his head in
despair.

Macadam gunned the engine. Leversedge gave a grim nod and
threw the door away from him.

The Model T lurched away.

Symington took them to an unmade street of rundown, terraced
houses.

'You're sure this is the place?' said Quinn, taking in the broken
windows and missing roof tiles of some of the houses in the street.
The feeling of déjà vu had intensified. So too, his dread.

A large, ostentatious car with gleaming gold paintwork was parked
up in front of one of the houses, which had its curtains drawn. The
car actually looked like two models that had been welded together,
or a motor car joined to a horse-drawn carriage with facing seats.
The front was a boxy compartment with open sides and a hard
canopy, while the rear, which stuck out like a beetle's behind, had

a folding hood for touring. Whatever the effect, it was at odds with the air of poverty that prevailed in the street.

'You see that car?' said Symington, sniffing frantically, as if it was the only way he had of keeping his panic inside him. 'Who do you think that belongs to?'

'Benson?'

Symington nodded energetically.

Macadam turned round in the front seat. 'I say, sir. You know where we are, don't you? It was night when we last came here. But there was a full moon, I seem to remember. And I'd recognize the place anywhere.'

A chill passed through Quinn as he remembered the details of the earlier case. It was the smell from the buckets of blood in the cellar that came back to him most vividly, so strong in his nostrils that he almost believed the street was flooded with blood. 'It's the same house.'

'I'm afraid so, sir.'

Quinn nodded. His earlier feeling of impending doom made sense now. 'How many men will there be in there?' he demanded of Symington.

Symington shrugged. 'Varies.'

'Between what and what?'

'Hard to say.'

Macadam chipped in. 'That's a 1912 Praga Grand. It will seat two in the front and four comfortably in the back – five or six at a squeeze. That's a maximum of eight, with the possibility of a couple of extra men on the running boards. That could mean we're looking at as many as ten. Possibly even more, if others came here by other means. On the other hand, it may just be one, if the driver is here on his own.'

'Thank you, Macadam,' said Quinn drily. 'That was very helpful.'

'Do you think we should wait for Leversedge and the locals?'

Quinn sighed. 'The longer we wait, the more chance there is of something happening to the boy.' He turned to Symington, whose sniffling was nonstop now. 'As long as you stick to the plan, everything will be fine. You remember what we discussed?'

But Symington stared at him with vacant eyes.

Quinn ran through the details one more time. 'You want to talk to him about a deal. A big deal. A very big deal. There's a man you want him to meet. A man from out of town by the name of . . .'

'Quinn!' cried Symington excitedly, pleased with himself for remembering something.

'No. Not Quinn. You don't use my name. Any name but mine. Let's say . . .' But strangely, Quinn found it impossible to think of a suitable name. Until it suddenly came to him. 'Moon. Mr Moon. Mr Moon from out of town. Mr Moon is very wealthy. Mr Moon has society connections. Mr Moon can shift a lot of product. You tell him he really should meet Mr Moon. Mr Moon could be very good for business.'

'Who's Mr Moon?'

'*I'm* Mr Moon. I'll be here in the car waiting.' Quinn glanced out at the rubble-strewn street. A gang of ragged children, malnourished and filthy, ran about, screaming for all they were worth as they played out their angry, unfathomable game. Quinn noticed that they kept their distance from the golden touring car. No doubt they knew who the owner was. Perhaps they were keeping an eye on it for Benson. They could even be watching the street. In which case, they'd almost certainly raise the alarm the moment the local police turned up. They may have had outlying detachments in the adjoining streets who would pass the word along.

There was no time to waste.

'Off you go then, Mr Symington.'

But Symington was shaking his head in a big, side-to-side pivot of refusal. 'He's not going to buy it! He'll never believe it! You don't know him. He can see right through you. He's got these big, bulging eyes that see right through you!'

'Remember what we talked about. Remember why you're doing this. This is your chance, Symington. This is your chance to be rid of Benson. You hate Benson, remember. Benson is a giant toad who squats on you, holding you back, squeezing the life out of you. With Benson out of the way, you'll be free. You'll be Mr Big. Cock of the walk. You'll take over his business. Deal directly with his suppliers. All his men will come over to you. You don't need Benson.'

Symington's violent head shaking had transformed into equally violent nodding at Quinn's vision of a grandiose future. 'Yes. Yes. Yes. I just . . . need . . . some more . . . snow.'

Quinn nodded to Macadam, who had turned round in his seat to watch. Macadam handed over the leather bag. The two policemen averted their eyes as Symington indulged his weakness.

A moment later, they were watching Symington stride across the

street with a drug-charged swagger. The street children broke off
from their game to watch him in silence. Symington reached the
front door of one of the houses. They saw his body twitch with
the force of a massive sniff, then he raised his hand to rap a knuckle
against the flaking paintwork.

Quinn counted twenty tense seconds. Symington knocked again.
The door opened; Quinn did not see by whom. Symington was
admitted. The door closed with an ominous shudder behind him.

'What do you want me to do, sir?' asked Macadam.

Quinn watched the children, whose game had become suddenly
subdued at the action on the street. They watched him too, with
large, unblinking eyes. 'Neutralize *them*.'

'*Neutralize* them?'

'Yes. Ten to one they are in Benson's pocket. I don't want them
tipping him off when Leversedge arrives with back-up.' As an
afterthought, he added, 'Also, I don't want them getting caught in
any crossfire.'

A deep frown rippled across Macadam's brow at the mention of
crossfire. 'How do you suggest I *neutralize* them?' It seemed he
was still struggling with Quinn's choice of word.

'You'll think of something, DS Macadam. You always do.' Quinn
took out his warrant card and handed it to his sergeant. 'By the way,
you'd better have this. In case they make me turn out my pockets.'

Macadam shook his head unhappily but took the warrant card.
'I really wish we'd waited for Leversedge.'

The door to the house opened and Symington stepped out. He
raised his hand and waved for Quinn to come inside.

'Too late for that now.'

Quinn knew immediately that the situation was more dangerous
than he needed it to be, and was in fact already out of his control.

He identified Tiggie Benson from his bulbous eyes. Some kind
of thyroid condition, he speculated. Either that or internalized rage
forcing his eyes out. Benson certainly appeared angry. He was pacing
the room – a dingy parlour at the back of the house – with the
quick, jerky steps of a short-legged man. He repeatedly punched
the fist of one hand into the palm of the other. There were two other
men there. Big brutes with clippered haircuts, sharp suits and
confused expressions. Physically, they dwarfed Benson, but there
was no doubt who had the power in that room.

There might be others in other rooms, of course. If John Fonthill *was* being held there, Benson may have stationed men to guard him.

What complicated things was the presence of two women. Quinn was not prepared for that. They were dressed flashily, literally – the sparkle of diamonds flickered about them. Fur stoles were draped over their shoulders as they shuddered away their distaste for their surroundings. No doubt they knew the grisly history of the place. They were pale, cold-eyed, pretty things, seated side by side on a tatty chaise longue, one filing the other's nails. They barely glanced up from the task when Quinn came in. But still, they had enough time to take in all they needed to. He revised his opinion of one of them, the subservient one engaged in grooming the other. He had been unfair to her, he now thought, lumping her together with her companion. He now saw that she had a softer face, which hinted at some chink of humanity that he might be able to exploit. It was possible that her fixed, empty expression came from fear. Equally, it could be narcotically induced.

Benson broke off from pacing the room to look Quinn up and down thoroughly. 'Who the fuck are you?'

'My name is Moon.'

'Man in the moon?'

'No. Mr Moon.'

'Mr Moon? What are you, Mr Moon?'

'What am I? Did my friend not—?'

'Your friend? This your friend, 'ere?'

'Yes.'

'Tut-tut. You're not very good friends, are you? I don't think you know each other very well at all. You say your name is Moon. Mr Moon. That's what you said, ain't it?'

'Yes.'

'Well, your friend 'ere, he says your name is Quinn.'

Quinn did not miss a beat, kept his tone even and unflustered. 'Yes.'

'Yes? What do you mean, fucking yes? Is you Quinn or is you Moon?'

'I do sometimes go by the name Quinn. I find it useful in my line of business to have a number of aliases I can call upon.'

'Now what line of business would that be?'

'It's one that sometimes places me on the wrong side of the law. And so, I am obliged to take precautions. I am sure you understand.'

'No. In fact, I haven't got a fucking clue what you're talking about.'

Quinn pressed on. 'I have other names too. Thompson, Mendez, Pettifer, Dunston . . . So, yes, now that I think of it, it's quite possible that Symington knows me as Quinn. I sometimes forget what name I've given to whom.'

'I'll just call you Cunt then, shall I?'

Quinn winced in the aftershock of Benson's rage.

'Or maybe Copper.'

Symington began to shake uncontrollably. At the same time, he let out a strange, stifled snorting noise that resolved itself into high-pitched laughter. It was certainly an annoying sound. Tiggie Benson screwed up his face in a pained wince before screaming in Symington's face: '*Shut up!*'

But the overstimulated junkie couldn't stop.

'I said shut the fuck up!'

It went on for what seemed like an eternity. Symington giggling horribly. Benson screaming at him to *Shut up!*

Giggling.

Screaming.

Giggling.

Screaming.

Giggling.

Until Tiggie Benson pulled a revolver from inside his jacket and held it up towards Symington. When even the threat of a gun did not stem the laughter, Benson did the only thing he could. He fired into Symington's mouth at point-blank range. The crack of the report was startling. As was the deafened silence that rushed in to fill the vacuum in its aftermath. Symington slumped to the floor, writhing like a hooked fish. There was still some noise coming from him that might – still – have been laughter, but it was very changed from the giggling he had just been producing. It was more of a gurgling. It suggested something rent and ragged and flapping and flooded. It went on for longer than any of the men standing over it would have thought possible. In many ways, it was a far more jarring noise than the one Benson had attempted to silence.

It was only now that one of the women screamed and ran from the room. The delayed reaction could be put down to shock. Quinn was not surprised to see that it was the woman whose more sympathetic face he had noted. She dropped the nail file as she fled. Her companion tilted her head upwards in an expression of icy disdain that seemed to have been provoked by the dropped nail file as much as anything. A small, tight, vicious smile played around the corners of her mouth.

'Right,' said Benson, when the noise in Symington's throat finally died down. 'I can hear myself think now.'

'I'm glad you did that,' said Quinn.

'What?'

'We don't need him.'

'You know what, Mr Moon? I don't give a fuck what you think.' Benson's gun hand hung limply by his side, his energy spent by the violence he had just unleashed, for the moment at least. His other hand trembled as he held it up to pinch his forehead in thought.

The look of confusion that Quinn had detected in the two henchmen deepened. They were out of their depth, that much was clear. And it was their boss who had taken them there.

The only person who seemed to be enjoying herself was the woman on the chaise longue. Quinn could not be sure, because he was not looking at her directly, but he had the sense that she licked her lips.

In these situations, if it was possible to think in terms of 'these situations' in what was essentially a unique moment in the world's history, Quinn had often noticed that time simultaneously moved both quickly and slowly. Perhaps there had not been an eternity of giggling and screaming before Benson had shot Symington. It had just felt that way. Perhaps there had not been a delay between the gunshot and the sympathetic girl running from the room. It had just felt that way.

And perhaps the interval between each beat of his heart was not really a lifetime. It only felt that way.

How many of these lifetimes passed before the shrieking began, he could not say. And how long after that was it before the door to the parlour crashed open and DI Leversedge burst in, holding the once sympathetic but now terrified girl in front of him in a one-armed stranglehold, the barrel of his Weber service revolver pressing against her temple.

'Drop it, Tiggie,' said Leversedge quietly, his voice almost intimate. The calmness of his demeanour impressed Quinn. He felt the relief flood through him.

Benson's expression went through a series of complex mutations as he calculated his options. It settled on a look that came as close to tender as he was capable of. A look which the ice-eyed girl on the chaise longue noted with displeasure.

For it was clear that while she was his floozy, his good-time girl, the little soft-eyed one shielding the copper from bullets was the girl he loved.

Benson's gun clattered to the floor.

A moment later the room was filled with uniforms.

FIFTY-ONE

'Where are they, Benson?'

'They?' It was Leversedge who was confused by Quinn's use of the plural.

Quinn flashed his DI a holding glance. Although he owed him his life, Quinn did not feel he owed him an explanation quite yet. There would be time enough for that soon.

'Upstairs. They're both upstairs.' Now in handcuffs, Tiggie Benson drew himself up as tall as he could. Although he had been bettered, he did not appear defeated. In fact, a new hopefulness seemed to have entered him. His eyes were fixed on the girl who had provoked his capitulation.

'Is the boy unharmed?'

'I was never gonna 'urt 'im.' Benson looked imploringly at the girl, begging her to believe him.

'Any of your men up there?'

Benson shook his head.

Despite the reassurance, Quinn drew his revolver.

The stairs were narrow and steep. Every step he took set off a creak. He heard Leversedge's tread behind him, and his urgent questions. 'What did he mean when he said *both*? Who else is here? Guv?'

The door was locked from the outside; fortunately the key was in the lock.

There was a wrought-iron bed with a stained mattress on it. A boy of about five or six in green velvet knickerbockers and jacket lay curled up and shivering. His arms were bound at the wrists, his legs at the ankles. There was a gag over his mouth. He looked up at Quinn with eyes enlarged by fear.

Slumped on the floor against one wall was a man, also bound and gagged. He had a loose fringe of sandy hair flopping down over his eyes. His face was shadowed with stubble and his clothes were streaked with rust-coloured stains. He too looked up, though his expression was more wary than the boy's.

'It's all right. We're the police,' announced Quinn. 'You're safe now, John.' Then he added, with a quick bow to the man huddled on the floor, 'Sir Aidan.'

Despite Leversedge's impatience, the explanations would have to wait until the captives were untied and John Fonthill was held in his sobbing father's embrace.

'How did you know he wasn't dead?'

Quinn regarded his DI with a vague frown, as if trying to place him. He blinked, which seemed to cause his memory to return. 'I knew something wasn't right from the very beginning. The crime scene was simply not consistent with Lady Emma's presentation of what happened.'

'Please.' Sir Aidan broke off from kissing the top of his son's head repeatedly, compulsively, uncontrollably, as if he were instead drinking in a quenching draught. 'Please leave my wife out of this. She is not to blame for any of it. It's all my fault.'

Quinn cocked his head as he considered Fonthill's request. 'I think we should get young John back to his mother and continue this conversation with Sir Aidan at Hampstead police station.'

And so Leversedge was forced to wait a little longer for the answers to the many questions he had.

They found Sergeant Macadam outside sitting cross-legged on the ground, with a loose semicircle of grubby children in front of him. The little ones sat quietly, hanging intently on his every word. Macadam caught his governor's eye and did his best to wind it up. 'And that is the story of how the elephant got his trunk.'

But as he made a move to get up, the children cried out, 'Another one! Another one!'

It was only by handing over a whole quarter pound bag of gobstoppers that he was able to extricate himself.

'Stories, Macadam?' said Quinn.

'Children love stories, sir. They also love magic. Therefore, I thought I would start with a few sleight of hand tricks. I find there is nothing can capture a boy's attention as a sixpence pulled from his ear. When I had exhausted my stock of magic, I'm afraid I rather shamelessly plundered the imagination of Rudyard Kipling.'

'You are a constant wonder to me. I am sorry to tear you away from your friends, but I need you to drive us to Hampstead. We have a couple of extra passengers. Leversedge can sit in the front with you. We can fit John and Sir Aidan in the back, I'm sure.'

'Sir Aidan?'

Quinn closed his eyes to discourage further questions. The nod of confirmation that he gave was minimal.

'It was the position of the body that first alerted me. It was obvious that it had been *placed* there. If you imagine the force that would have been required to drive that implement into the ear, it would not have left the victim sitting upright. My suspicion was confirmed by the appearance of a polished swathe across the front of the piano, as if it had been wiped clean there. That was the action of the victim's hair – or should I say wig – rubbing against the surface as the body collapsed.' Quinn turned to Leversedge who was sitting next to him in the Hampstead interview room. Sir Aidan was on the other side of a plain table. 'You will remember, I found a red hair in the hinge of the piano lid, where the head landed, with some force, we may speculate. That suggested to me that the wig had originally been worn by the victim, not the killer. The appearance of the blood on the victim's body was odd too. There was not as much blood on the victim's clothes as you might have expected. None on the outside of the shirt collar, for example, only on the inside.'

'I noticed that!' cried Leversedge.

Quinn frowned at the interruption. 'That suggested to me that the clothes had been changed after death. At some point, Sir Aidan, you decided to change clothes with the man you had murdered. And don his disguise too. Whose idea was that? Your wife's?'

'Emma had nothing to do with it, I tell you. She wasn't even there when I killed him.'

'But she came in soon after, did she not? We will have to talk to her, you understand.'

Fonthill flinched as if he had been slapped across the face.

'Was it she who noticed the passing similarity between you and the dead man, once the false hair and whiskers fell off? That was why there was blood on the beard found in Willoughby's pocket, by the way,' Quinn explained in an aside to Leversedge. 'Not because the victim's blood had sprayed in the murderer's face, as I once speculated. But because the victim was wearing the false beard at the moment he was killed. It also explains the neat edge to the bloodstain on the victim's face. That was where the false beard covered his skin.' Turning back to face Fonthill, Quinn added, 'It must have been a disgusting object to have against your face. That was why you discarded it in the churchyard, I suppose, which was where my officer tracked you down.'

'I didn't kill the policeman. You must believe me, I didn't even have a gun. And I am no marksman. I'm a musician.'

It was a fair point. 'No. That was Benson, wasn't it? We have his gun now. We haven't had the report from the medical examiner concerning DS Willoughby yet, but I imagine he will find the bullet, or if he doesn't, I'll have Inspector Pool's men comb the church. Once we have it, we will be able to check it against Benson's gun. I have no doubt it will confirm your story.'

Fonthill gave a weary nod, as if it pained him to show his appreciation. 'He held me at gunpoint and made me call out to the policeman.'

'And so, had you gone to the church to meet Benson?'

'Yes. He had come to the house earlier in the week. I owed him money.'

'The gambling debt?'

Fonthill nodded. 'He had been hounding me for it. I didn't have it, of course. And I couldn't go to Emma this time. So he proposed an alternative arrangement.'

'Which was?'

'He wanted me to provide him with information on my friends. What valuables they had in their houses and when they would be away. I refused, obviously.'

'What happened?'

Fonthill closed his eyes with a shudder. 'He told me if I didn't agree . . .' Fonthill swallowed hard but couldn't go on.

'He threatened to take John?'

'He threatened *both* the children. He gave me a day to think about it. Told me to meet him in the church on Saturday with some

information he could use. I wasn't going to go. But after what
happened, I thought perhaps he could help me.'

'Help you? How?'

'Well, he's a criminal, isn't he? He would know how to stay out
of the way of the police. Emma had promised to get money to me
and so I told Benson he could have that. But he lost his temper.
Told me he had waited long enough. Promises were no good to
him, he said. That was when the policeman came in.'

'And he shot Willoughby.'

'I had to go with him after that. He said the police would have
me down for it. If ever I was caught, I'd be hanged as a double
murderer. And a cop murderer to boot. He said there was nothing
the police hated more than a cop murderer. That was why he did
it, I think. To tie me to him.'

'But who was the man you killed?' cried Leversedge wildly, no
longer able to contain his frustration.

'That was the blind piano tuner,' said Quinn.

'Yes,' said Sir Aidan.

'Very well! It was the blind piano tuner!' The impressive calm
that Leversedge had shown when disarming Tiggie Benson had
deserted him entirely. 'But why did you kill him?'

'He wasn't really blind, of course,' began Sir Aidan, somewhat
pointlessly. 'Or a piano tuner.'

'I think we knew that.'

'Who was he, Sir Aidan? A German agent?'

'I suppose you could call him that, though traitor would be the
more accurate word. His name was Peters. He was there. That night.
At that house. I'd never met him before then. I wasn't even sure
what his name was, until he came to see me on the day of the
rehearsal. It was strange, at the time . . . a friend of mine, I say
friend, but really, I think I hate him. Well, you see, the thing was,
Lucas thought it was amusing to keep getting us muddled up, as if
we were identical, which we weren't, of course. But as you say,
there was a superficial resemblance. We were both clean-shaven,
with sandy hair, and I suppose our features were similar. I couldn't
see it myself. Emma did, though, straight away.'

Leversedge groaned. 'No, I'm sorry. I am still confused. You will
have to go back to the beginning.'

'The beginning? What was the beginning, I wonder? The beginning for me? Or the beginning for him? For me, I suppose it was

twenty or so years ago in Baden-Baden. I got into a spot of difficulty on the tables. I was there as a guest of Baron von Reventlow. We were not at war with Germany at the time, of course. Baron von Reventlow was one of the most civilized and intelligent men I have ever met. And possibly, I see now, one of the most evil. I ended the evening owing the house more than a thousand marks. An amount I could never hope to pay. Von Reventlow had of course loaned me the money, so really it was to him that my debt was owed. And do you know what he said? He said, "Think nothing of it, my dear boy! We had fun, didn't we!" And then he slapped me on the back and laughed. I was in a daze. Stunned. "You are such a talented young man," he said. "It is my pleasure to do this for you. It would be a crime if the world were to be deprived of your talent because of this youthful foolishness." I thanked him profusely and said – it was I who said it, you see – that is what was so clever . . . I offered myself voluntarily. I said, "If there is ever anything I can do for you, please do not hesitate to ask." He bowed solemnly and thanked me. "You are a man of honour," he said. And he made a little speech about honour, about how hard it is to find honour in the world today. "When honour is lost," he said, "all is lost." And he put his hand on my chest, and he said, "Here. It will always reside here, I know. For when a man of honour gives his word, he can never go back on it."'

'"*Ehre verloren, alles verloren*,"' said Quinn.

'Yes.'

'The music box.'

'When I received that, I knew he was calling in the debt. The next day Peters turned up at the rehearsal in disguise . . .'

'The blind piano tuner?'

'Yes. He told me that Baron von Reventlow sent his regards. That sent a chill right through me. It was a shock, even though I had received the music box warning me that something was about to happen. I had no idea that the baron and Peters knew one another. But the baron knows many people and I dare say he has a hold over them all. Anyhow, it was then that Peters told me what was expected of me, how I was to repay my debt.'

'You were to assassinate Winston Churchill?'

'No. My role was simply to facilitate the crime. I was to arrange for the assassin – Peters – to get close enough to Churchill so that he could . . .' Fonthill winced at the memory. 'He had a stiletto. His intention was to stab Churchill with it.'

'A stiletto in the shape of a tuning fork?'

'That's correct.'

'The very weapon with which you killed Peters?'

Fonthill gave a deep sigh and his shoulders quaked. 'He thought it was funny. This loathsome object which he had made himself. He was fooling around with it. Pretending it was a real tuning fork. He held it to his ear, as if to listen to the note it produced. There was no note, of course.'

'That explains the blood on his right hand. He was holding it when you . . .'

'Something came over me. Rage, I suppose. I was under a lot of stress. And the man was so infuriatingly flippant. I just rammed it in.'

'You stopped him. He was the assassin and you stopped him.'

'Yes, I suppose I did.'

'In which case, you prevented England's enemies from killing the First Lord of the Admiralty. That makes you a hero, not a criminal. Why did you then attempt to conceal what you had done?'

Fonthill looked down at the table and refused to answer.

'That was Lady Fonthill's idea, wasn't it? She saw the resemblance between you and the dead man. Not knowing the reason for the crime perhaps, or simply thinking that you had gone mad, she panicked and suggested that you change clothes with him. That way she would at least save your children from having a murderer for a father. She then helped you to arrange the body at the piano. Am I right? Was it Lady Fonthill who put the ring on the wrong finger? We have Donald Metcalfe to thank for pointing out that detail. "It's not right!" he insisted. He knew that you wear your ring on the left hand. But the ring was on the victim's right. Was that because the victim's left hand had blood on it? And Lady Fonthill could not bear to touch it?'

Fonthill's small, flinching shrug suggested Quinn was on the right lines.

'And then, of course, there was the painting which she destroyed. Augustus John's portrait of the two of you. She couldn't risk one of us policemen seeing it.'

Fonthill groaned. 'She needn't have bothered with that. It didn't look the slightest bit like me.'

'You were in shock. Unable to think for yourself, you went along with her plan. You were used to Emma sorting out your problems for you, after all. And she offered you money to go away, I suppose. One last cheque for you to cash. She wanted you out of her life. She wanted you out of the children's lives. This was a way to get rid of you.'

'No. It wasn't . . . like that.' Fonthill's face flushed with colour. 'You don't know Baron von Reventlow. If he thought I had gone back on my word, if he thought I had failed as a man of honour, he would have hunted me down and killed me. That is to say, he would have sent another one of his agents to do his work. I would be looking over my shoulder for the rest of my life. I could not be sure that he would not have gone after the children. This way, with me dead, with my death reported in all the papers, I would be safe, and so would my family.'

'But your children would never know their father?'

'Perhaps it would be better that way. Or perhaps one day, when we are no longer at war with Germany, I could come out of hiding and make my confession to the authorities.'

'How were you going to live? When Lady Fonthill's money ran out?'

'I don't know. I hadn't thought that far ahead, I suppose.'

Quinn paused for a moment to take in everything Fonthill had told him before asking, 'And this Peters, what do you know about him?'

'He had reasons of his own to hate Winnie. I think in some ways he was an accidental traitor. His soul was . . . twisted. He had lost all perspective. It was not so much that he wished to harm his country, rather that he was hellbent on destroying Churchill.'

'But why? Do you know?'

'They were at Sandhurst together, apparently. I heard a strange rumour. Peters was a promising young cadet. Physically courageous to the point of reckless. A great horseman too. Well, it seems that Winnie, for some reason best known to himself, decided to spread a vile rumour about Peters. He accused him of sodomy with one of his fellow cadets. According to the rumour, Peters insisted that it was a lie, and that in fact it was Churchill who was indulging in these practices. The whole thing was hushed up. Except that Peters was forced out, in disgrace, of course. His career, and his life, was ruined. He went abroad. To Germany. Where it seems he was befriended by Baron von Reventlow.'

The room was silent for several minutes before Fonthill asked, 'What will happen to me now?'

CODA

The Hampstead Voices' Christmas Concert in aid of Belgian refugees went ahead as planned on Christmas Eve, with Sir Aidan Fonthill, recently raised from the dead, at the podium. Every seat in the Great Hall of University College School was taken. The gallery was packed, and extra seats had been crammed in at the rear of the hall, as well as along the sides and in the aisle. A total of two hundred and ninety pounds and six shillings was raised for a cause that was universally agreed to be worthy.

Among those attending, in addition to the distinguished guest of honour and his black tie-clad security detail, were DCI Quinn, DI Leversedge and DS Macadam of the Special Crimes Department. Inchball was also there, proudly wearing the uniform of a sergeant in the Military Police. He had orders to report to army headquarters in Colchester on Boxing Day. To supplement the SCD's now depleted manpower, following Inchball's departure and the death of DC Willoughby, Sir Edward Henry had transferred over to Quinn a new recruit from his own staff. A person whose loss Sir Edward felt deeply, but whose ambition he could not in all conscience stand in the way of. He was confident that she would prove a valuable addition to DCI Quinn's team. For the new recruit was none other than Lettice Latterly, who was also at the concert, seated next to Silas Quinn.

Despite his feelings for Miss Latterly, or perhaps because of them, Quinn had initially objected to the appointment. The SCD, he argued, was no place for a woman. Besides which, she was not a trained police officer.

But Sir Edward would have none of it. These were special times. The force, as well as the country, was losing men to the war. Women were stepping forward to fill the vacancies. They were taking on all manner of tasks that had previously been considered unsuitable for the so-called weaker sex, from driving buses to manufacturing armaments. And proving themselves more than capable. There was no reason Sir Edward could see that a woman, provided she had the aptitude, which he did not doubt Miss Latterly did, should not become a police detective. What training she needed, he felt sure that DCI Quinn, DI Leversedge and DS Macadam could between them provide on the job.

And so, despite his misgivings, Quinn had acquiesced. When he saw the beam of pride on Miss Latterly's face the day she reported for duty, he had to admit he was happy to have done so. Perhaps it would not be so bad to have her working alongside him. And he knew from his own experience that she was a resourceful and courageous individual.

Also in attendance at the concert was Special Constable Elgar, whose contribution had proved vital in cracking one aspect of the case. He was the only police officer there to have a piece of his composition included in the programme.

As far as the case was concerned, the case of Sir Aidan Fonthill's 'murder', Quinn had submitted his report to Kell, who had passed it on to Churchill.

On the strength of that report, it had been decided that no action should be taken against Sir Aidan and Lady Fonthill. In fact, Churchill recommended his old schoolfriend for the George Cross. This conferred on Sir Aidan a degree of bravery that he had not been aware of possessing at the time of the incident, but which he was now determined to live up to. If he was still afraid of reprisal from the agents of Baron von Reventlow, he did his best not to show it. Indeed, he appeared to be more anxious that the choir was under-rehearsed.

In general, a certain discretion concerning the affair was deemed expedient. The extreme danger that the First Lord of the Admiralty had been in, and how close the country had come to disaster, could not be allowed to get out. And so that aspect of the affair was kept out of the papers, the official story being that Sir Aidan had been acting in self-defence. The necessary paperwork was produced to make the thing go away, from a judicial point of view. The absence of a body doubtless facilitated that, perhaps even necessitated it. No one was terribly inclined to enquire too closely into the circumstances of Peters' death. In general, he was thought to be a bad lot and the feeling seemed to be that he was best forgotten about.

As for the missing body, that was Tiggie Benson's doing, all on his own initiative as a way of increasing his hold over Fonthill. He had directed his men to steal it and subsequently dump it in the Thames. He had no idea who the dead man was, or why Fonthill might have wanted to kill him. In Tiggie's world, a man did not need much of a reason to kill another man. The way Benson saw it, if Peters' body disappeared, there would be no chance of the police ever finding out that Fonthill was still alive. That would place Fonthill even more in his debt, so he would be obliged to overcome his scruples and provide the information Benson wanted. The information itself no longer mattered to Benson and was of dubious value anyhow. 'It's the principle of the thing!' he had protested to Quinn, his exasperation clear. Fonthill owed him money which he couldn't pay, so Benson had proposed an alternative arrangement, 'To my considerable detriment, I'll have you know.' In his view, that made it all the more unreasonable that Sir Aidan refused to play ball.

But the theft of the body had failed to produce the desired effect. Fonthill, who had been Benson's prisoner since they had met in the church, sank into a traumatized depression and was incapable of doing anything. That proved too much for Benson. 'What can I say? I got angry.' It was then that he decided to snatch Fonthill's son, 'To teach that stuck-up fucker a lesson,' as he put it.

The scenes from the Nutcracker Suite were a particular hit with the audience. Quinn could not take his eyes off the sylph-like Ekaterina Volkova. And it was only when la Volkova was not dancing that he noticed Miss Latterly was equally enrapt with her partner, Andrei Kuznetsov.

'So graceful!' she gasped, as she joined in the enthusiastic applause.

'Leversedge has met them,' said Quinn. 'Perhaps he will introduce you after the concert.'

'Would you?' cried Miss Latterly.

But Leversedge was strangely unforthcoming.

Quinn had gained a new respect for his DI since the incident at Tiggie Benson's house. There was no getting round it – Leversedge had saved his life, and had demonstrated considerable initiative, not to mention courage, in the process: he had gained admission to the house next door, gone through to the rear garden, climbed over the tumble-down fence and entered Benson's house through the back door, which was unlocked. He had then opened the front door to let in the local boys. All this had been executed with great stealth and speed. He had even kept his head when the woman ran out of the parlour screaming.

Perhaps, thought Quinn, *it was time to trust Leversedge, after all.*

It was against the advice of Lieutenant-Colonel Kell that Churchill had insisted on going ahead with his appearance at the concert. He saw it as a way of expressing his gratitude to Sir Aidan. The minister had argued that the threat to his life was over, now that the would-be assassin had been killed. Perhaps so. But Quinn suspected that he was not the only one there who experienced a degree of apprehension. Once, he caught Commander Irons' eye, there as one of Churchill's discreet bodyguards. The MO5 (g) man looked unusually tense.

But it was not just apprehension that Quinn was feeling. He felt oddly out of sorts. Frustrated, even. Which was irrational, given that the case had been concluded to everyone's satisfaction. He had even managed to solve it without killing anyone. Symington was not entirely out of the woods, but he was somehow still alive, for now at least. If he did pull through, it was likely that he would spend the rest of his days in a wheelchair, paralysed from the neck down. And he would always have difficulty speaking and eating. But it was not as if Quinn had been the one to pull the trigger that blew away his mouth.

Perhaps that was the problem. Had he now become so used to discharging his firearm in the course of an investigation that if he was deprived of the opportunity, it left him with this strange feeling of dissatisfaction?

Quinn stood, along with everyone else, for the carols that the audience was invited to join in. But he did not sing, except occasionally to move his lips and murmur a tuneless fragment of one chorus or another. He saw, out of the corner of his eye, Miss Latterly's sly smile at his efforts, and could not help smiling back.

As they took their seats after a spirited rendition of 'Deck the Halls', Quinn looked down at the programme and saw that they had come to the final piece in the main part of the concert. (It amused him that an encore was listed, obliging the audience to call for it, whether they wanted to or not.)

It was now time for Elgar's song, 'A Christmas Greeting'.

There was a moment of quiet as the audience settled and the soloists took their positions, Émile Boland wielding his violin as if it was an extension of his own body and Dame Elsie Tatton moving with dignified serenity. Fonthill made an upward gesture to the choir and half the women got to their feet, including Lady Fonthill. Quinn was surprised to see that Anna Seddon was among them too, but not Ursula Cavendish. She did not appear to be among the women who remained seated either.

Whatever Lady Emma felt about her husband's resurrection, her look gave nothing away. For now, she was focused entirely on the performance to come.

Nods were exchanged between Boland and Fonthill. Fonthill lifted his baton and something wondrous suddenly existed, a sound produced by the tiny instrument in Boland's hands, playing in close harmony with one of the violinists from the orchestra.

But just as Dame Elsie drew breath in preparation for her first note, the performance was disrupted by a cry from the audience. A young man had leapt to his feet and was shouting. It was hard to make out exactly what he was shouting, but Quinn thought he made out the word 'imperialistic' and perhaps also 'rubbish'. Quinn's right hand instinctively flew inside his ulster, to touch the handle of his Weber service revolver. As it did so, he felt a surge of elation. But he was prevented from drawing his weapon by Leversedge's restraining grip around his wrist. 'No, guv. Not here. Not now. I'll deal with it.'

The secret service chaps had formed a barrier around Churchill, leaving it to Leversedge to approach the shouting man. Leversedge showed the same coolness under pressure that had been evident in Limehouse. He merely had a quiet word with the protester and encouraged him to leave. Quinn noticed a look pass between Leversedge and Commander Irons that he did not like. Something was undoubtedly communicated between them, and he could not shake off the impression that it had to do with him.

Inchball cut short Quinn's reflections by snarling, 'It's that bloody Masters!' He sprang to his feet and pointed at Roderick Masters as he was escorted out. 'I warned you!'

A look of terror came over Masters and he practically ran from the hall.

Naturally, the disturbance unsettled the audience and the choir. Sir Aidan appeared ashen-faced and shaken. He seemed to forget where he was. His mouth gaped in shock.

Lady Emma Fonthill stepped forward from her place in the front row of the choir and made her way through the orchestra to her husband's podium. She placed a hand on his arm and whispered something into his ear. Her look was not tender, exactly; it was firm, but not devoid of sympathy. Fonthill nodded as he took in her words and seemed to recover.

He tapped the podium with his baton and the music began again. This time, Dame Elsie was allowed to begin singing.

Quinn closed his eyes and thought of the time, a few days ago, when the moon had appeared in the morning. It was such a fragile thing, barely there, and yet huge and wondrous.

He felt something touch his hand and opened his eyes to see Lettice Latterly's hand on his. He took hold of it and turned to look at her. She was facing straight ahead, towards the music, smiling. At the same time, she blinked, and a tear ran down her cheek.

ACKNOWLEDGEMENTS

This novel could not have been written without the help of my wife, Rachel Yarham. She sings in an excellent choir, which, it goes without saying, is nothing like the entirely fictional choir featured in this novel. She very helpfully checked the musical parts of the story for glaring errors. If any remain, it's my fault for not listening. More importantly, she gave me the idea for the murder method. I could say it's a little bit worrying, but then I'm the one who's written all the crime novels.

I'd also like to thank my agent, Christopher Sinclair-Stevenson, and the team at Severn House, in particular my editors, Kate Lyall Grant and Sara Porter. Thanks also to Piers Tilbury for another great Silas Quinn cover design.